IMAGINE

Book Two of the Fuzed Trilogy

David E. Stevens

CFP

Cambridge Free Press

ISBN 978 0 9972164 0 0 (print)
ISBN 978 0 9972164 1 7 (Kindle)
ISBN 978 0 9972164 2 4 (epub)

DEDICATION

This book is dedicated to the visionary men and women who are creating the wonders ahead and understand the consequences.

ACKNOWLEDGMENTS

Terry Burns, one of the top-ranked literary agents in the U.S., provided sage advice and guidance. Rick Eldridge and Fred Miller's creativity and global perspective continue to provide inspiration and focus, and a huge thanks to my wife Lilli and my talented editors, Teri Burns, Ryan Deken and Frankie Sutton.

A special thanks to the intrepid members of the Fuzed Advisory Board who will be keeping the message inside alive and accurate: Hall of Fame Astronaut Ken Bowersox, Weather Channel legend Jim Cantore, Intelligence Expert Carl Deckert, Navy Chief Test Pilot Vice Admiral Joe Dyer, NAVAIR CIO Susan Dyer, Counterterrorism Expert Stuart Frisch, NASA Program Executive Dave Lavery, Astronaut and CEO Dr. Ed Lu, CEO Jerry Meadows, Department of Justice Senior Analyst Nick Nickles and world renowned astrophysicists Dr. Bill Napier and Dr. Joe Veverka.

As in the first book, the accuracy of this story hinges on the expertise of many. In addition to the Advisory Board, the following subject-matter experts gave generously of their time and knowledge: Joe Baggett, Linda Baggett, Chris Boblit, Commander Thomas Bosy, Stan Boyd, Peter Coker, Lori Davidson, Carol Deken, Lou Deken, Reed DeVries, Lester Eisenbeck, Margaret Eisenbeck, Dennis Glynn, Tommy Harper, Amy Hunter, Shirley Hunnicutt, Garrett Johnson, Jay Jost, Kristi Kyle, Maureen Marshall, Glenn Martin, Jessica Li Martin, Cherry Meadows, Richard Mustakos, Lee Person, Cletus Pew, Commander Jim Roberts, Brett Sappington, Lanell Shepherd, Dr. Carolyn Shoemaker, Dan Smith, Scott Straub, Dale Stevens, Lilli Stevens, Bart Waggoner and Doyle Yager.

I also want to thank the many awesome reviewers who helped craft a better story. They include Dale Barnes, Jackie Bray, Albert Comulada, Victoria Comulada, Naomi Chuckwuk, Rob Gryger, Lesia Harper, Sam Hailes, Tim Hendricks, Laura Stevens-Hawkins, Christian Johnson, Judy Johnson, Kevin Johnson, Dr. Jeff Moore, Jola Moore, Molly Mueller, Ellen O'Neal, Patrick O'Neal, Steve Ray, Betsy Smith, Dr. Ann Ward and Dr. Brad Ward.

CONTENTS

INTRODUCTION

This story is based on a simple extrapolation of existing
technology, making the risk real and, unfortunately,
inevitable.

I

IMPACT

1

THE END

The sound of surf rose from below as the couple stood on a South American clifftop overlooking the Atlantic. Silhouetted by the setting sun, hair tousled by a tropical breeze, it would have been remarkably romantic . . . if not for the end of the world.

"Yes sir, it all hangs on this last shot." He paused. "Thank you, Mr. President, I'll pass that on to the team." As Admiral Joe Meadows set the phone down, he looked out over his Antarctic base. His office, wrapped in heavily insulated glass, sat just below the airfield tower. The panoramic perch reminded him of the bridge of an aircraft carrier. Peering through the Antarctic twilight, he saw the last cargo jet land on the ice runway in 40-knot, 40-below-zero winds.

He was tired, but he could still appreciate the surreal beauty. The blue taxi lights embedded in the solid ice runway illuminated the snow swirling around the huge Russian jet. It was the last of an international bucket brigade that had built the nuclear-powered base of 10,000 engineers, scientists and construction workers.

His hand shook slightly as he poured himself a cup of coffee. They had failed. Although they *had* prevented a direct impact, the comet would penetrate the atmosphere, and if it broke up—

The elevator 'dinged.' He turned to see his highly efficient taskmaster, also known as his Flag Aide, bounding out. Lieutenant Molly Cardoso was dark, wiry and always in motion. Studying her tablet, she answered his unasked question. "We still have a few minutes before we have to be down in the Control Center."

Looking back out the window, he put both his hands around the warm coffee cup. "You'd think after 10 months, I'd be used to the cold."

"I'll have them check the heating system."

He shook his head with a small smile. "It's fine, Molly." He nodded toward the three-story, windowless building, nestled at the base of the mountain. "Nuclear reactor's putting out plenty of power. In fact, we risk melting the ice runway." He paused. "It's probably just the 8,000-foot elevation." The reflection of his face in the window contradicted him. He'd gone from captain to three-star admiral in ten months. The crushing responsibility and lack of sleep had taken its toll. No longer looking like a large, black, defensive lineman, he'd lost weight and let gray hair grow on his normally clean-shaven head. Did he really look that tired? The reflection of genuine concern on the face of his young aide confirmed it.

Turning back to her, he smiled. "Molly, you keep up with the news. How's the world handling it?"

"Well, the conspiracy theorists still don't believe there's a comet or Antarctic base. We're just actors in a studio. Then there are those who are convinced the world's ending and are partying their brains out." She smiled. "But I think the majority accept the situation with cautious hope." She paused — unusual for her — and added, "Things once important become trivial; things trivial become important."

"Why, Molly, you have the heart of a poet."

"Doubt it, sir. I hate poetry." She looked at her tablet.

Getting the hint, he grabbed his coffee cup, took a last look outside and followed her to the elevator.

As the doors closed and the elevator headed down to the Control Center, she said, "Sir, you're scheduled for a short talk to the team as soon as we arrive. It'll be televised across the base, and," she looked at him meaningfully, "picked up by the press and broadcast around the world."

He gave her a tired grin. "I promise, Molly, I won't tell any more *sea stories*." He paused. "Have you talked to your folks recently?"

"Talked to my dad in LA yesterday. He's fine." She hesitated. "Wasn't able to talk to Mom. She flew back to Venezuela to be with my grandparents."

Meadows frowned.

She sighed and looked down. "She knows about the comet's trajectory over South America. I told her if things don't go according to plan . . . ." Gently shaking her head, she looked back up at him. "She just said it's where she's needed."

Meadows put his big arm around her shoulders and gave her a gentle hug.

As the elevator doors opened and they walked to the Control Center, she quickly attached a wireless lapel mic and snatched his coffee cup.

It looked like NASA Mission Control. The front wall was a giant display. It included multiple status screens as well as a live view of the laser domes 1,600 feet above the base. The entire mountaintop had been flattened to install 90 of the world's most powerful and accurate lasers in a geometrically perfect, phased array pattern.

Facing the giant display were rows of monitoring stations occupied by two dozen engineers and technicians. Above and behind was a glassed-in press gallery. There was a subdued but constant buzz of voices and keyboard clicks.

As Meadows moved toward the front of the room, he saw his Deputy Director and Chief Scientist, Dr. Victoria Chandra. Standing near the center of the room, very tall with long black hair and an intense visage, she was hard to miss. She was conferring with the Control Center Director and her astrophysics team: former astronaut and B612 CEO Dr. Ed Lu; Scottish extraterrestrial impact expert Dr. Bill Napier; and legendary comet finder and astrophysicist Dr. Carolyn Shoemaker.

Meadows also exchanged a head nod with Elton Musk, who was standing quietly near the back of the room. If it hadn't been for Musk's initial surreptitious funding and construction support, none of this would have been possible. Musk had also been instrumental in the rapid production and installation of the 90 lasers. He had a brilliant knack for out-of-the-box thinking.

Over the loud speaker, a calm voice said, *"T-minus 60 minutes."*

That was his cue. As he stepped up in front of the main display, the room quieted.

"I'll make this fast. You have more important things to do than listen to speeches. After 10 months of back-breaking work, around the clock, in the harshest possible environment . . . you've delayed the Millennium Comet by three minutes." He paused. "Doesn't sound like much, but it allows the earth to move 6,000 kilometers in its orbit and out of the comet's crosshairs. Although it *will* graze the atmosphere, you, and the millions who've supported us, have prevented a direct impact that would have erased almost all life on Earth." As he looked around the room, he continued, "I'm incredibly proud of each and every one of you."

There was a round of spirited applause.

He glanced at the display behind him. "We're 58 minutes from our final salvo . . . the most critical to date. You're about to stop the rotation and stabilize the attitude of a 15-kilometer mountain. *Nothing* must stop us."

He paused. "Just got off the phone with the Secretary-General of the United Nations and the President of the United States. They, along with all the world's leaders and citizens, send their heart-felt thanks and prayers for our success." He paused again. "We're a truly international team and come from many belief sets, but at this point, I don't think any of us would believe it unreasonable to request supernatural help. Please join me in a quiet prayer."

After the prayer, Meadows moved through the Control Center, patting backs and shaking hands. He knew everyone by name. Finally working his way to the back, he grabbed a fresh cup of coffee for himself and Chandra.

Nodding to Lu, Napier and Shoemaker, he handed the coffee to Chandra and said, "Graduation day." Over the loudspeaker they heard, *"T-minus 30 minutes."*

She gave him a small smile as he asked the same question he'd asked her every day for the past 10 months. "How are we looking?"

She nodded toward Napier.

With a strong Scottish brogue, he said, "Latest projections have it penetrating 50 kilometers into the atmosphere and coming within 70 kilometers of the surface. Computer models still show multiple earthquakes, tsunamis, major meteoroid damage and a very powerful electromagnetic pulse, but they're all events we're expecting and hopefully prepared for."

Meadows looked at Lu. "Comet orientation?"

Lu shook his head. "Hate having to wait 'til the last minute, but we can't fire until our potato-shaped comet's *skinny face* is forward.

11

We're going to hit it one last time with everything we've got. It should stop the rotation and lock it in the optimum orientation for atmospheric entry."

Meadows looked at Chandra.

She exhaled sharply and said quietly, "Even firing all of them, it's barely enough to stop the rotation." She paused. "And this is the first time we've fired all of them at the same time." She shook her head. "They finished installing the extra capacitors and power conduits last night, but we haven't had time to test 'em."

Meadows nodded and then asked Lu, "What are the odds it'll hold together when it hits the atmosphere?"

"With the correct orientation, it'll have 15 percent less drag."

Meadows frowned. "Ed, I know you've done a lot of atmospheric entries yourself, but . . ." he raised an eyebrow, "optimistic press releases aside?"

Lu looked him in the eye. "Joe, you know the story. We're dealing with a mountain of ice and rock moving 100 times faster than a rifle bullet." He shook his head. "There's no way it'll hold together through dozens of G's of deceleration while being superheated thousands of degrees. All we can hope for is it'll hold together *long* enough that the pieces won't hit us or explode in the atmosphere."

"T-minus 15 minutes. Target data upload complete."

"And if they do?"

Napier, staring past them, inserted, "Latest simulations say that if it breaks up and explodes in the atmosphere, we're talking a 10-million-megaton blast."

Meadows gave a slight shrug. "Better than a two-*billion*-megaton direct hit."

Nodding, Napier quietly added, "Yes, but that's still a *thousand* times more energy than all the nuclear weapons in the world combined. It'd melt the three kilometers of ice this base sits on and scorch half the planet. The other half would eventually freeze and starve."

As Meadows was responding, the Control Center Director, Colonel Carlos Comulada, turned around and interrupted, "We got a problem." With one hand on his headset, he pointed at a display. It showed a schematic of the ninety Blasters, but three branches of ten were blinking red. "Just lost the power to 30 Blasters. Probably wind damage to the conduits. We're clocking 70-knot gusts on the mountaintop. I sent in the emergency team."

Meadows signaled Musk to join them.

"T-minus 10 minutes. Targeting servos aligned."

Meadows asked, "Can we realign the remaining Blasters?"

Chandra said, "Yes, but 60 Blasters aren't enough!" Calling up data on one of the consoles, she added, "We've *got* to get at least 20 back online or we don't have enough power to stop the rotation."

Musk asked, "Can we delay the firing?"

Lu and Napier shook their heads emphatically, as Chandra said, "Absolutely not! We have to hit it right when it's in the optimum orientation."

Comulada looked at them. "They have six minutes to evaluate, repair and evacuate."

Meadows noticed the press had sensed something and were pointing cameras their way.

Lu leaned in and whispered, "If it hits the atmosphere with *any* angular momentum, our simulations say it'll tear itself apart and explode in the atmosphere."

"T-minus six minutes. Capacitors at 100 percent charge."

One of the mountaintop cameras zoomed in on a dome damaged by the wind. Next to it, they could just make out shadowy figures in the twilight. The camera zoomed in further to a car-sized power junction box. With dozens of leg-thick cables coming out of it, it looked like a giant spider. They watched the team trying to repair the connections while fighting subzero, hurricane-force winds.

"T-minus five minutes. Core super-cooling commencing."

Comulada turned back to Chandra, "We've got to realign the remaining Blasters before the automated firing sequence locks them out."

Chandra closed her eyes. When she opened them, she said, rapidly, "Realign — assuming we get the first two branches of 10 back online."

Comulada's eyes narrowed. "You sure? If we end up with only 60, realigning for 80 will mismatch the phasing, making the shot ineffective."

"T-minus one minute. Dome doors opening."

Chandra snapped, "Do it!" Softer, she added, "Carlos, if it's rotating when it hits the atmosphere, we're toast. We've got to go for broke."

Comulada nodded.

The two technicians looking back at him turned around and keyed in the changes.

"T-minus 45 seconds. Dome doors open.

Meadows tapped a pen on his leg and Chandra unconsciously rocked back and forth as they all stared at the video feed from the mountaintop. Everything hinged on the frostbitten repair crew.

"T-minus 30 seconds. Capacitor initiators armed."

Comulada pointed at one of the screens. "They fixed one circuit! That's 10 Blasters back online."

Lu shook his head. "Not enough!"

Musk quickly said, "Reroute the power intended for the dead Blasters to the others."

Comulado shook his head. "They can't handle that much power. We'll melt their cores and blow them apart!"

Musk turned to Meadows and Chandra. "They only have to fire one more time!"

Nodding, Meadows and Chandra simultaneously said, "Melt 'em!"

Comulada put his hands on the shoulders of the two wide-eyed technicians and said, "Emergency override! Reset the phasing and redistribute *all* power to the live Blasters."

Their fingers flew over the keyboards. As they hit enter—

"T-minus 15 seconds. Target coordinates locked. Abort disabled."

At the front of the Control Room, the display of the Blaster's status changed. Twenty Blasters went black. The remaining 70 changed from green to yellow with a flashing "128% POWER" next to each.

There was a buzz around the room and in the press gallery. Over the noise, Meadows told Comulada, "The Blasters may explode. Tell the repair crew to take cover in the dome of one of the dead Blasters!"

Comulada nodded, speaking quickly into his headset.

On screen, they saw the shadowy figures running toward one

of the domes.

"T-minus ten, nine . . ."

As they reached the dome, Meadows quietly said to Chandra, "Whatever the outcome, it's been an honor and privilege to serve with you."

". . . six, five . . ."

She whispered back, "Honor's all mine. Just wish Josh had lived to see this."

". . . two, one . . ."

Blindingly beautiful, blue-green lasers lit the Antarctic plain like a flash photograph. Several of the domes exploded as 70 beams stabbed at the comet in what might be humanity's last act of defiance.

2

COMET

"Look!" Standing on the cliff top, Elizabeth pointed northeast across the ocean.

Just above the horizon, Josh saw pinpoints of light in the distance sparkling like tiny, green fireflies. He nodded his head. "That was it . . . our last shot."

Still staring at the horizon, she slipped her hand back into his, and gave him a small smile as she nodded at the phone in his hand. It had been softly playing music in the background. As he listened, he realized the song was **Stand By Me**.

Watching her out of the corner of his eye, he saw a beautiful combination of dark exotic eyes, olive skin and blonde hair. He glanced down at their hands. His skin was a shade darker. Most would identify him as multiracial, but they often did a double take when they saw his eyes. The flecks of color embedded in gray were strange, but Elizabeth had told him his eyes were what first attracted her. That was good enough for him.

She asked, "How close will it get?"

Looking back at the horizon, he said, "It'll enter the atmosphere over the Caribbean and cross South America coming within about 40 miles of the surface."

"No, I mean how close will it get to *us*?"

He pulled his eyes from the horizon and gave her a half-smile. "Did you bring your sunglasses?"

She just looked at him with a raised eyebrow.

"Sorry. It'll cross the coastline about 10 miles north of us, moving 200 times faster than the speed of sound." He smiled. "We have ringside seats."

"Is it safe?"

He shrugged. "As long as it doesn't break up when it hits the atmosphere."

"And if it does?"

Josh stopped smiling and looked back at the horizon. "We'll be the lucky ones. We won't drown, asphyxiate, freeze or starve to death."

"Let me guess . . . because we'll be incinerated?"

With a slight nod, he said, "Along with everyone in North and South America."

Looking back at the horizon, she said, "Kind of a buzz kill on the ringside seats."

He couldn't help but smile.

They stood together for several moments, lost in their own thoughts. Then Elizabeth said, "After the comet, it will be a different world, won't it?"

Josh nodded. "It already is. There's been a huge renaissance in science."

Elizabeth added, "Spirituality, too, and wars are at an all-time low."

Josh gave a small shrug. "Not surprising when we're all facing our own mortality. Time will tell if war's obsolete or it's just a timeout."

"The United Nations is actually effective and doing good things," she said optimistically.

He looked at her. "Is that why you decided to work for the U.N.?"

She smiled. "In part." Her smile faded as she looked back at the horizon. "Guess in a few minutes, we'll find out if there'll be anyone around to help or be helped."

Nodding, he lifted his phone and said, "Hal, switch to the live BBC broadcast."

After a couple seconds, they heard, ". . . five minutes. We just received confirmation that the last laser strike fired successfully, although there were some . . . technical problems. We won't know if that will affect the outcome until it enters the atmosphere. All commercial aircraft are now on the ground. The U.N. verified that evacuations are complete for those under the comet's flight path, living in coastal areas and near earthquake fault zones. If you're within 500 kilometers of the comet's flight path or in a designated risk area and could not or would not leave, authorities recommend you take cover immediately."

Elizabeth glanced from the phone to Josh with obviously raised eyebrows.

Josh pretended to focus on the phone as the broadcast continued, "We just received reports that the comet is now visible to the naked eye from on board research vessels in the Atlantic. The picture on your screen is live from a ship near Tobago." There was another pause. "I've just been told the world's cellular communication systems and Internet servers are powering down in 30 seconds to protect them from the electromagnetic pulse. Authorities *strongly* recommend that everyone within 5,000 kilometers of the comet's flight path unplug and shut down all electronic equipment, including your cell phones, until the comet passes. This is Jim Cantore, reporting from Manizales, Columbia."

Josh turned his phone off.

Elizabeth pointed northeast over the ocean. "Is that it?"

Barely visible, just above the horizon, was a tiny red dot. Although the comet's surface was as dark as fresh asphalt, this close to the earth, it dimly reflected the sun's rays.

Shooting stars began to lace the dusk sky as the cloud of debris surrounding the comet reached Earth's atmosphere. The largest left ghostly green tracks.

As the comet approached, it appeared to double in size every 30 seconds. With the orange-red cast of a lunar eclipse and a tenuous white halo surrounding it, it began to look like a sinister eye with an angry red pupil. The eye seemed to be watching them ... measuring humanity.

Josh put his arm around Elizabeth's shoulders. Despite the tropical temperature, he felt a shiver run through her body.

As it grew to the size of a full moon, the evil eye transformed into an ominous red orb, right off the cover of a science fiction novel. Jesse had hinted that human eyes might have seen a close approach like this in the distant past, long before the pyramids. Josh suspected that the handful that survived the encounter were probably responsible for many of humanity's legends and myths.

The meteor shower increased in intensity. Brilliant flashes

illuminated the horizon as comet fragments began to explode in the atmosphere. Josh realized the larger fragments could release energy equivalent to a small atomic bomb. Even if everything went right, standing 10 kilometers from the flight path of a 15-kilometer-wide comet might not have been one of his best ideas.

Now appearing three times bigger than the moon, the comet hit the earth's atmosphere. Its surface instantly superheated to incandescence, transforming the twilight into daylight. Even with sunglasses, the new sun was too bright to look at. Countering the visual spectacle was utter and eerie silence. The sonic shockwave lagged far behind the hypersonic mountain.

Jim Cantore checked his watch while his camera operator, Steve Spencer, pointed his camera toward the northeastern horizon. Spencer and the rest of his slightly crazy Weather Channel crew were the best in the world. The other two members of the team — his producer and the satellite operator — were inside the broadcast van behind him. Actually, it wasn't a van; it was a massive, heavily armored SUV. When word got out about their plans, a South African company called Paramount donated one of their Marauders. State-of-the-art in personnel protection, it could shrug off automatic weapons and high explosives, but if the comet broke up in the atmosphere, nothing would protect them.

While waiting to go live again, Cantore said to his camera operator and producer, "The President sent his personal thanks to us via our CEO this morning."

Spencer, looked at him curiously, "But we haven't covered the comet yet."

Cantore smiled. "Actually, our real mission is already done. World's been on the brink of panic because many think the deflection effort isn't real or it failed. They're certain the governments are lying to their people. The President believed that having the best-known TV meteorology team in the world reporting from under the comet's flight path would reduce that fear. He arranged for our exclusive coverage in the evacuation area." He paused. "And our highly promoted presence here has already saved lives."

Spencer nodded, but with a wry smile, added, "Kinda hope the deflection effort *was* real."

Cantore smiled back. "Yeah, me too."

The producer gave him his cue. As the camera's record light came on and swung toward him, he said, "Reporting from Manizales, Columbia, this is Jim Cantore. We'll be able to see the comet appear over the horizon any second. They fired the lasers to stop its rotation and 'poke' it into the best possible entry attitude." He hesitated. His mission to reassure the world was over, and he was free to tell them what he really knew and call it as he saw it. Blowing out a lungful of air, he continued. "But . . . even with the perfect entry attitude, the comet will unleash titanic forces when it hits the atmosphere. It's so big that the bottom of it will be 15 kilometers — almost 10 miles — deeper in the atmosphere than the top. That thicker air means the bottom will slow down faster than the top, which will try to rip it apart."

With a small smile, he said, "Even if everything goes as predicted, standing under the comet's track is . . ." he shrugged, "risky, but you can see we've taken precautions." He tapped himself on his combat helmet. "And we're wearing Kevlar body armor, ear and eye protection. We also have . . ." he nodded back toward the van. The camera swung around. "An armored Marauder broadcast van with EMP-hardened electronics."

Spencer swung the camera back to him. Cantore recognized each of his team by name, and then continued, "We're volunteers, and regardless of the outcome, know that we're doing what we love and I'm very proud to be a part of this team."

He looked back over his shoulder, and the camera followed his gaze. "We positioned ourselves 800 kilometers — 500 miles — inland from where the comet will cross the northeastern coast of South America. We're right under the point scientists believe the comet will finish its trip through the atmosphere, and *hopefully*, head back into space." Pointing over his shoulder, he said, "We're on top of a hill overlooking the city of Manizales to our east. Normally, it has a population of a half million . . . not today. Today, it's empty, completely evacuated."

The camera panned down and slowly zoomed into a valley with the city at its center. The camera view lined up with one of the main avenues. Although the sun had set, there was enough light to see buildings lining both sides of a deserted street. The camera zoomed back out and panned up, centering on the northeastern horizon. The inactive 17,000-foot volcano, Nevado del Ruiz, nicely framed the picture to the south. The timing was perfect. There was an obvious brightening in the sky as if another sunrise was starting.

Too late, Josh realized he shouldn't have come here and definitely shouldn't have brought Elizabeth. Why *was* he here?

Jesse had brought him back from his fatal crash to initiate the greatest engineering feat in human history. After his rogue program proved deflecting the comet was possible, Josh needed to disappear. Humanity had to work together, and there could be no doubts or loose ends. After he recovered from the gunshot wounds, however, watching the deflection effort on TV was like sitting on the sidelines during the championship game. He had to see the comet with his own eyes. He had to be here.

No . . . no, that wasn't entirely true. If he were honest with himself, his presence here was more of a childish act of bravado. His bullet scars reminded him of his modus operandi. His engineering mind would try to figure things out, but if that failed, his fallback plan was to light the afterburners and see what happened. It was one thing to risk himself; it was entirely different and very selfish to put someone he loved at risk.

Now five times the size of the sun, the comet didn't look like it was skimming the atmosphere — it was coming right at them.

Cantore knew the networks were broadcasting video of the comet from research ships in the Caribbean. While waiting for them to switch the final live coverage back to him, he realized in the next few seconds, he and the human race faced extinction. Yet, he felt surprisingly calm. Early in his career, he was covering a hurricane off the Carolina coast. A woman came up to him, and her words left a lasting impression. She simply said, "We know it's going to be really bad here, but you're going to get us through this."

The producer cued him.

Cantore took a deep breath and said, "We're uplinked to a dedicated geo-synchronous satellite, and I'm being told that this broadcast is being followed by billions of viewers." He glanced at his watch. "Right now, the comet is approaching the coastline. Its transit through the atmosphere should only take a little over a minute."

Just then, the bright burning ball appeared above the mountain range — show time. "There it is! It looks like a time-lapsed sunrise." He shook his head. "It's closing on us incredibly fast. *This* is truly amazing! It's already bigger than the sun and growing." Cantore saw Spencer adding progressively stronger filters to avoid blinding the camera.

"I can't believe this! It's strangely beautiful and *terrifying*." The camera had to keep zooming out as it grew. Cantore took another deep breath and said, "Hate to say this, but . . . it looks like it's coming right at us."

Josh was sure it couldn't get any bigger, brighter or closer . . . but it did. Now 10 times bigger than the sun, the deflection effort must have failed. He could feel the comet's intense radiant heat as Elizabeth buried her face in his shoulder.

Looking at the ground behind him, he saw their shadow shrink rapidly toward them. As it disappeared under them, he kissed his wife's head, and said, "I love you."

The world watched in fascination. The intellectual mind, driven by computer simulations, said the comet would fly on by. The primitive mind, driven by the eyes, told a different story. During the longest seconds in human history, almost every conscious mind shared the same thought. Were the scientists wrong? Could governments have decided it was best not to share they'd failed? For interminable seconds, billions of people: Christian, Muslim, Hindu, Buddhist, Jew, agnostic and atheist, shared the same prayer.

3

IMPACT

Holding his breath, Josh followed their shadow as it began to grow again on the opposite side.

A loud boom broke the silence.

Elizabeth looked up. "Was that the comet?"

He shook his head, as the booms continued. "Just fragments blowing up in the atmosphere. The comet's shockwave is still a couple minutes out." Shading his eyes, he looked up to see the blinding ball transiting overhead at ludicrous speed. The comet dragged a huge, burning-white tail that bisected the sky. Squinting, he realized he was seeing multiple tails. The comet was coming apart!

Blocking the comet's light with his hand, Cantore said, "It's impossible to look at but I can feel the heat on my skin."

Spencer zoomed all the way out, rotating his camera upward to follow it.

Cantore added, "We're seeing flashes on the horizon from meteor detonations." He frowned. "It's on top of us!" Glancing at his watch, he added, "It should have left the atmosphere!" On the repeater monitor, near Cantore's feet, the burning ball completely filled the screen. He shook his head and said, "God help us."

With his camera pointed straight up, Spencer peered around the viewfinder and said, "Look!"

The blazing orb was dimming.

Cantore, looking up, yelled, "It's leaving! It's leaving the freakin' atmosphere! My God, we're going to make it!" Its blinding incandescence was gone. Still bigger and brighter than the moon, it moved across the sky at phenomenal speed. He jumped and did several enthusiastic fist pumps, repeating, "We survived!"

Narrowing his eyes, he added, "Wait! It's not a comet . . . it's *three* comets. The atmosphere tore it apart!"

The camera zoomed in and confirmed three brightly glowing objects were separating and heading out on slightly different trajectories.

Realizing what that meant, Cantore said, "If that happened seconds earlier, I wouldn't be here to report it. Neither would many of you." As he said that, they were overwhelmed with multiple deafening booms.

Elizabeth pointed back toward the ocean. "What's that?"

Turning around, Josh saw a single cloud near the horizon. As he watched it, it grew. It looked like a waterspout hugging the surface of the ocean, but it was moving rapidly toward them. "*That* is the comet's shockwave." Narrowing his eyes, he added, "We might be a *tad* closer than we should be. Probably a good idea to get on the ground and cover our ears."

They hit the ground. Lying on their stomachs, elbows propping up their heads, they watched it approach. The shockwave looked like the wake of a humongous speedboat. Kilometers wide with curtains of spray thrown a hundred meters in the air, it cut a path toward them moving faster than a jet.

They cupped their hands tightly over their ears as it hit the coastline. Hammered by the loudest, longest sonic boom in recorded history, the ground shuddered as their bodies vibrated. It felt as if they were inside a subwoofer at a heavy metal concert. If they had been standing, the pressure wave might have knocked them off their feet. The vibration amplified the ache from Josh's gunshot wounds. He felt all three bullet entry points: shoulder, lower stomach, and a few inches above eunuch.

They watched a cone of water vapor and dust rise over the land as the shockwave raced inland.

Tearing his eyes away from the receding comets, Cantore looked back at the horizon. "Steve, swing back around."

The camera returned to the eastern horizon and tracked what looked like a dust storm moving toward them insanely fast.

Cantore said, "Here comes the shockwave." As he said it, the wall of dust and vapor crested the far side of the valley and rushed down to the city below. The camera zoomed in just in time to catch a line of exploding windows ripping through the city toward them. With enthusiasm, Cantore said, "What a spectacular illustration of the sonic power of a shockwave!" Joining his photographer in a braced crouch, he said, "We'll broadcast as long as we—"

Josh and Elizabeth were still on the ground when they felt the shock-induced vibration morph into a full-blown earthquake. As the ground shook, they heard rock in the nearby cliff pop loudly as it fractured. Pieces of the ground less than 10 meters away broke off and fell toward the ocean.

Cantore, the consummate professional, rolled, but hung on to his microphone. He saw Spencer lying on his stomach, still videoing. The bone-shaking sonic booms were replaced by a strong earthquake. Never missing a beat, Cantore continued to describe what they were experiencing, hoping the shockwave hadn't damaged his mic. Cantore nodded toward their armored vehicle. Spencer swiveled his camera toward the huge SUV. Rocking and rolling on its giant tires, the hydraulically stabilized satellite dish countered the vehicle's motion to maintain the uplink.

Finally, the quake subsided. Josh and Elizabeth removed their hands from their ringing ears and heard another sound. It was the whooshing sound of surf . . . but they were 100 meters above the Atlantic. Standing up, they crept carefully toward the broken cliff edge. Feeling the cool spray of the ocean, they looked down to see building-sized waves crashing into the coastline.

Cantore was now having fun. The world wasn't going to end, and broadcasting under insane conditions was his specialty. Into the silence following the earthquake, he said, "The comet's shockwave pounded us as it crossed South America, but its tiny gravitational field reached far below the surface. As expected, the tidal force — ripping across the planet at hypersonic speed — is triggering earthquake faults. The faults would have slipped eventually. The comet's just smoothing out Earth's age-induced wrinkles at a *massively* accelerated pace. The booms you hear are sonic shockwaves from fragments hitting nearby or exploding in the atmosphere. The destruction is horrific, but today . . . today, humanity will survive." He wrapped up with, "The Millennium Comet changed the world it grazed, but our world also changed the comet. Neither will ever follow the same trajectory. From Manizales, Columbia, this is Jim Cantore."

Coverage would now switch to global damage reports, but as he looked back across the valley, he saw a huge plume of gray smoke rising from the top of Nevado del Ruiz. Patting Steve on the back and pointing toward the mountain, he said, "Looks like we'll be adding volcanic eruptions to our resume."

Like a finger brushing across the surface of a desktop globe, the comet's gravitational pull changed the length of a day by a fraction of a second. The result was a cascade of earthquakes circling the world as huge meteors continued to detonate in the atmosphere. The impacts created massive fires, and the earthquakes woke volcanoes and created tsunamis that inundated coastlines.

As the world watched the departure of the trinity, it became clear the impacts, earthquakes and tsunamis would inflict massive destruction, but would not be apocalyptic. Slowly, a collective sigh swept the globe. Around the world, came all manner of voices. Some cheered. Some chanted. Many sang, laughed or cried. For the first time in history, humanity had successfully intervened and protected not only themselves but all life on Earth.

As the sonic booms stopped and the surf quieted, Josh noticed an amazing silence. There was no sound from aircraft, birds or insects. Even the wind had died. They looked around and then at each other, simultaneously breathing a sigh of relief.

In the incredibly peaceful silence, they were startled by the sound of their phone's text message tone. They looked at each other and laughed . . . back to the real world.

Elizabeth pulled her phone out first. "It's a text. It just says '*imagine*.'"

Josh asked, "Who sent it?"

"There's no number."

Josh looked at his phone and shook his head. "Weird. Mine too."

"Josh . . ." she frowned, "our phones were *turned off*."

4

IMAGINE

Deep inside the iMagination Corporation headquarters, Ryan Armani and his team were working hard to bring the servers back online. Armani was intense on the inside, but short and roly-poly on the outside. After receiving confirmation that their apps were up and running again, he made a beeline for his chief programmer's cubicle. Poking his mostly bald head over the top of Stan Boyd's three monitors, he asked, "Was that us?"

Boyd was his opposite, a redheaded scarecrow with a relaxed demeanor and southern drawl. "Was what us?"

Armani fired back, "You know . . . the text!"

Boyd looked back at his screen and shook his head. "Dude, we just survived the extinction of the human race . . . chill."

"Yeah, yeah, that's really great . . . so, was that us?"

Boyd shrugged. "Maybe."

"Maybe? Every phone in the world gets an "imagine" text, and our digital assistant — *on every phone* — just happens to be called *iMagine.*"

"We've got no market penetration in China." Boyd casually corrected.

Undeterred, Armani just stared at Boyd with raised eyebrows.

Sighing, Boyd took his hands off his keyboard and looked up at him. "Yeah, probably was our system. Just some stray trons caused by the comet's electromagnetic pulse." He shrugged. "Or, maybe it happened when they rebooted the global communication grid. It's surprising we don't have more anomalies." He paused. "Why? Is someone complaining?"

Armani shook his head. "Not yet."

Smiling, Boyd said, "I seriously doubt anybody cares. We just escaped a death sentence." He shrugged. "Besides, bet a lot of people thought it was cool . . . I did."

Armani frowned. "I just want to make sure no one hacked our system again."

"Wouldn't worry about the text . . . ."

Armani tilted his head, waiting impatiently for Boyd to finish. Finally, raising his eyebrows, he asked, "But what?"

Boyd quietly said, "Our phones turned *themselves* on."

Armani shook his head dismissively. "Our app can't do that."

"No, it can't, but . . ." Boyd raised his eyebrows slightly and glanced around, "what if someone besides us figured out how to—"

"Ixnay!" Armani whispered forcefully.

Trying not to laugh, Boyd whispered back, "Pig Latin? Seriously?"

Their rented jeep came in handy as Josh and Elizabeth drove west, away from the comet's destructive flight path. Although the roads were empty, earthquake damage and wild fires required multiple detours. They finally reached Simon Bolivar International in Caracas, the closest operational airport.

With the evacuees returning, the inbound planes to Caracas were full, but the outbound ones were mostly empty. It was easy to catch a flight back to the U.S. Having had little sleep during their adventure and sporting "sunburns" from the comet, they slept most of the flight.

Landing in Houston, they were only an hour and a half from their new house on the Texas Gulf Coast. They listened to the post-comet coverage on the drive. Earthquakes and tsunamis swept the globe, but it appeared only a few areas received catastrophic damage. Overall, casualties were lower than expected.

As they crossed the Intercoastal Waterway on a tall bridge, they could see much of the mile-wide, twenty-mile-long Bolivar Peninsula. Aside from a ferry out of Galveston, this tall, two-lane bridge was the only access. Elizabeth, originally from Texas, had chosen this isolated location for Josh's recovery from surgery. She used the money the CIA had paid her to buy a beach house.

It was the perfect place to keep a low profile. With no central government, the peninsula fell under the control of nearby Galveston, which usually ignored it. This was fine with most of Bolivar's residents, continuing a slightly rebellious and colorful history that included infamous characters like Bonnie and Clyde. With a mix of beautiful beachfront homes, beat up trailers and oil derricks, residents tended to view zoning laws more as . . . suggestions.

Ten minutes after crossing the bridge, Josh turned into an unassuming subdivision called Canal City. As the name implied, small lots lined canals. The canals, perpendicular to the beach, gave boat access to the Intercoastal Waterway and the Gulf of Mexico. Josh liked having multiple *exit* options. Their house sat on 18-foot-tall pilings 150 yards from the surf. On the huge wraparound deck, they had an unobstructed view of the Gulf.

The Bolivar coastline didn't have the white sand and emerald water of Florida, but it was a fraction of the price. Someday, the world would discover this place. Prices would skyrocket and zoning would triumph, but until then, it was one of the world's best-kept secrets.

They grabbed a bottle of wine and climbed another flight of stairs to a smaller, rooftop deck. Almost 40 feet above the ground with a 360-degree view, it felt like a castle parapet.

A warm, balmy breeze blew steadily off the ocean, accompanied by the soft swooshing of the surf. To the west, the rays of the setting sun sparkled off the saltwater marshes of an Audubon bird sanctuary. Turning south, Josh saw the ocean's darkening horizon defined by tiny, lit dots — huge cargo ships bound for the Port of Houston.

Below the seagulls and above the mosquitos, they sat, sipping wine and soaking in the scents, sights and sounds.

Elizabeth looked at him carefully. With a smile and raised eyebrows, she said, "Josh Fuze, I think you look happier and more relaxed than I've *ever* seen you."

He let out a contented sigh. "For the first time since I woke up in your hospital, I feel . . . totally at peace."

She looked a little surprised. "Even though the astrophysicists confirmed Earth's entering a period of increased bombardment?"

He smiled. "They say it's something that happens periodically, but now we're doing something about it. We've got the Sentinel Space Telescopes scouring the heavens, and they're designing a space-based laser, 1,000 times more powerful than our Blaster. We're no longer helpless victims in a cosmic shooting gallery."

She matched his smile and nodded. "I guess stress isn't when bad things happen . . . it's when you can't do anything about them."

He finished with, "And on top of all that, I married the most beautiful woman in the world, who happens to be my best friend."

She leaned over and kissed him. Then, with her hand resting on his, they both leaned back in their Adirondack chairs and watched the world.

His eyes followed a formation of pelicans flying parallel to the beach in search of fish. Just past them, he noticed a flash in the distance. He refocused his eyes to the eastern horizon where the ocean blended into dark, cumulonimbus clouds. Illuminated from within by lightning, the prevailing winds pushed a storm their way.

Elizabeth looked down and pointed at several large pools of standing water. "Must have rained a lot while we were gone."

Josh knew tsunamis swept through the Gulf, and the Bolivar Peninsula was only a few feet above sea level. "That's probably the remnants of one of the comet's tsunamis that swept through the Gulf."

Elizabeth nodded thoughtfully. Then, biting the side of her lip, she stood up. "I need to find out what's happening. They may be activating me soon. Be right back."

There went his Zen. He wished he hadn't mentioned the tsunamis. While he tended to look at the big picture and live in the future, Elizabeth lived in the present.

After a few minutes, she returned with her tablet and phone.

The tranquil beach panorama was lost as they watched the continuing post-comet coverage. Airborne video showed the swath of destruction under the comet's path. They also saw dramatic images of a dozen impact craters surrounded by raging forest fires, but most of the damage and injuries were from earthquakes and tsunamis. The hardest hit areas were in South America. Equally concerning were reports from the Pacific Rim, where they were seeing an increase in volcanic activity.

A U.N. press conference followed. The man speaking appeared relaxed and confident. The tag line under him said, "Doruk Turan, U.N. Director of Global Security."

Elizabeth looked from the tablet's screen to Josh and then back again. "Hey, you two could be brothers."

Josh studied her tablet. Nodding, he said, "You're right. He *is* phenomenally good looking."

She rolled her eyes as Turan spoke of the extensive relief effort they were deploying.

As if on cue, Elizabeth's text message signal sounded. Reading it, she held her phone up. "Just got the notification. Have to report to D.C. immediately. I'll be part of one of the deploying U.N. teams."

Josh frowned. "The news said most of the damage occurred in the evacuated areas, and the casualties were much lower than anticipated."

She looked at him. "Josh, they were anticipating millions of casualties. Even a fraction of that's a ton of injured people, not to mention damage to infrastructure, like hospitals. You've seen the pictures. The earthquakes and floods were devastating. Besides, statistics are irrelevant if the casualty is your child or mate."

"Yeah, I know. Just didn't think they'd be deploying you so soon."

She smiled. "I appreciate your concern, but it's not like I'll be trekking through mountains and jungles. I'll be in D.C. for several days. Then they'll probably assign me to a major medical center where they can put my neurological background to use." She grabbed his hands. "Honey, I'll be fine. You know how excited I was when I found out they'd accepted me into the program."

"I know. It's very competitive, and I'm proud of you." He paused and then smiled. "Hey, can I come?"

"Come where?"

"To wherever they send you?"

She grinned. "Now you know what it feels like to be on the other side. I should just pat you on your head and tell you what you told me when you left for the Falklands."

He laughed. "Yeah, and I could do exactly what you did — show up anyway." More seriously, he added. "I really would like to help."

She shook her head. "Doing what?"

He shrugged. "I don't know." He paused. "I can speak Spanish."

"You can?"

"Took three years in high school."

She looked skeptical.

He rattled off several sentences in Spanish, surprising both of them. He realized his new photographic memory allowed him to recall the long forgotten lessons. "And I can pay my own way. Davidson gave me that retirement account. Haven't touched any of it."

"You said you didn't want to use it because it felt more like a *retainer* than a retirement."

He shrugged.

Finally, she smiled and nodded her head. "Actually, it would be really cool to have you with me. I'll ask them when I get to D.C."

The wind picked up, and they heard thunder in the distance. Even in the twilight, they could see the dark anvil clouds growing, suggesting a powerful spring storm.

Elizabeth nudged Josh and pointed at the ticker scrolling across the bottom of the news screen. Instead of the usual breaking news stories, little emoticons, mostly smiley faces, marched across the bottom. Elizabeth laughed. "Oops. Someone pushed the wrong button."

Looking from Elizabeth's tablet to the approaching storm, Josh suddenly felt uneasy. With an unexplained premonition, he said softly, "I think our vacation may be over."

5

DEPLOY

The next day, Elizabeth was sitting in an orientation session in Washington, D.C. She learned they were deploying to Columbia, one of the hardest hit areas. An 8.5 Richter earthquake caused some damage in the Capital of Bogota, but was devastating in the southern part of the country near the epicenter.

During a break, she called Josh. "We're flying to Bogota tomorrow."

"Tomorrow? That's fast. So what'd they say about me coming?"

Enjoying his suspense, she said slowly, "Well...they said...if you have a passport and shots they'll put you to work. They were mostly interested in your ability to speak Spanish."

Josh said, "I'll brush up and book a flight ASAP."

She frowned. "That could be a problem. The airports suffered damage, and they're only letting citizens and rescue flights into Bogota right now. The whole country's under martial law." She paused. "Wait! I know someone who can help, and he's here in D.C."

"Who?"

"Brian Davidson! He owes us. I'll call him and see if he can get you some type of official access or something. I still have the private number he gave me when I was on the aircraft carrier."

Josh said, "Worth a try."

"I'll let you know. Gotta get back to the briefings. Love you."

After the briefing, Elizabeth called Davidson. There was no answer and no way to leave a message. She was trying to figure out how to reach him, when her phone rang with an unlisted number.

"Hi, Elizabeth, welcome to D.C."

She wasn't surprised the Director of the CIA knew who she was and where she was. "Hi, Brian. I'm here working as a Medical Relief Supervisor for the U.N. Know you're way busy, and sorry to bother you, but wondered if you might be able to help us with a little challenge."

"I'd be happy to. How can I help?"

"I'm deploying in a few days on a medical mission to Bogota." Davidson said, "One of the worst hit areas. Please be careful."

"I will. Thanks. My ... *husband* would love to join me and help too. But due to the earthquake, they're controlling who can enter the country right now and—"

"Consider it done. Is there anything else I can do for you?"

"Uh, thanks, no. That would be great." She paused. "When things settle down, love to have you and your wife over for dinner sometime."

Sounding surprised, Davidson said, "Why . . . that would be wonderful. Thank you, Elizabeth." He paused. "In case you ever have trouble reaching me, let me give you Carl Casey's number. You remember Carl?"

"We never met, but I heard wonderful things about him." She paused. "I assume he knows about my husband's, uh, *status*?"

"Yes. I'll have him call you just to make sure everything's taken care of."

"Thank you so much, Brian."

"Anytime. If I don't talk to you again, have a safe and successful trip."

Within 15 minutes, her phone rang. "Hi, Elizabeth, it's Carl Casey."

"Hi, Carl."

"I know you're only in town for a day and busy getting prepared, but can we take you to dinner tonight?"

Elizabeth said, "That's very kind, but not necessary. I'm really doing fine."

Carl said, "It'd be our pleasure. I'd like to meet the woman who . . . let's just say, was instrumental in changing certain beliefs at a critical time. Besides, my wife will kill me if she doesn't get to meet you while you're here, *and* it might be your last chance for a good steak dinner for a while."

She laughed. "Okay, I'm sold. Sheri Lopez told me about Kelly. Can't wait to meet her."

"Pick you up at six?"

"Sure, I'm staying at the, uh—"

"Holiday Inn on Sixth," he finished.

"Uh, yeah, see you tonight."

Elizabeth immediately called Josh. "Good news! Brian's working your travel clearances."

Josh said, "I'll pack my bags."

She looked at her watch. "Gotta go, Brian hooked me up with Carl Casey, and he's taking me to dinner tonight."

"Ask him about Bogota, he's a walking encyclopedia."

"OK. He's bringing his wife, Kelly. Have you met her?"

Silence.

"Josh, you still there?"

She heard coughing and then, "Uh, yes . . . we've met."

After she hung up, Josh just stared at the phone. He had a hole in the pit of his stomach right next to the bullet hole. Several emotions were in play. The first was fear. He imagined his outgoing, never-met-a-stranger *wife,* meeting his outgoing, never-met-a-stranger *widow.* The fear revolved around what knowledge of his true identify might do to Kelly, Carl and Elizabeth. The second was guilt. Guilt at not sharing his past life with Elizabeth. She knew he had a prior life and identity because she'd helped him establish a new one, but even after they were married, he'd never shared what really happened.

The last emotion was the worst. On his phone, he pulled up a picture of his daughter, Caitlin. She was now three, but he'd never seen her, not in person. She was growing up knowing only Carl as her dad, and would believe her father died before she was born. Although he knew his old friend would be a great father, there was a perpetual hole in his life far more painful than the bullet wounds.

Staring despondently at the floor, he jumped when he heard his text message tone. Shaking his head rapidly to clear his anxiety, he picked up the phone. Anything would be a welcome distraction, but as he looked down at the message, he got another shot of adrenaline. The text simply said, "You were designed." There was no name or phone number, and he could count on the fingers of one hand the number of people who had his number.

Josh texted, "Who is this?"

"Jcn."

He texted back, "You mean Jen?"

"Yes."

He knew no one named Jen, from his current or previous life. Fishing for information, he texted, "What did you mean by designed?"

"Your DNA coding is very streamlined. Mine is too."

He reread it. That *had to be* about his genetically blended body! No one knew about that except Jesse. Could Jesse have created more than one of him? There was a certain attraction to the idea he might not be alone. He replied, "You're suggesting we have something in common?"

"We were both designed."

He wasn't going to admit to anything yet. "Interesting, I'd like to talk more. Can we meet?"

"No."

If she was really like him, she might also have to keep a low profile. "Are you being monitored?"

"Yes."

Josh realized that with no telephone number, this must be an encrypted text, similar to what Tim used with their team in Antarctica.

Frowning, he asked, "How did you find me?"

"I received a message."

"From who?"

"I don't know."

Josh's eyes narrowed. "What was the message?"

Her reply was immediate. "It identified who you were and said we could help each other."

Still frowning he asked, "What type of message was it?"

There was a slight delay. "A voice."

Josh said aloud, "Jesse!" It had to be him. Who else communicated with nothing but a voice? He must be trying to connect them. Since the surgery, Josh had attempted to contact Jesse several times but hadn't gotten a response. This Jen might help him fill in some missing puzzle pieces. He needed to know what she knew.

She texted, "I have to go."

"How can I reach you?"

"01-111-101-0001"

Pacing and nervously drumming his fingers on his leg, he said softly to himself, "Calm down. There's no reason to be anxious." He took a deep breath. "Just because a mysterious woman knows I was designed . . . and my *wife* is having dinner with my *widow*."

6

HACKED

Armani was sitting in his office eating a Snickers bar and sipping a Diet Coke when his chief programmer called.

"Hey, Ryan, you probably ought to take a look at this."

If Boyd wanted him to look at something, it was bad. He bolted to Boyd's office. In his usual rapid fire, he asked, "What is it?"

Boyd pointed at the screen and with his relaxed drawl, said, "Happened again. Someone hacked the central server and changed core code."

"Bocce balls! What'd they do?"

Boyd raised an eyebrow. "Bocce balls?"

They were constantly giving him a hard time about his creative vocabulary. Impatient, Armani said, "Well?"

Boyd typed quickly on his keyboard. "Still trying to figure that out."

Armani said, "We need to switch to the backup server and isolate this!" He yelled across the office. "Keith, come here!" Turning back to Boyd, he added, "If we have to shut down the app on billions of phones, we'll be flooded with complaints and trouble calls for weeks."

Boyd said slowly, "Let's take a deep breath and see what the damage is before we go into Whac-a-mole mode."

Hitting gopher heads as fast as they popped up was definitely Armani's leadership style, and he saw nothing wrong with it.

A small crowd gathered around Boyd's office.

Armani looked around. Finding who he was looking for, he said, "Keith, need you to be ready to switch to the backup servers ASAP, but not until I give you the word."

Keith nodded and headed off.

Boyd, still typing, said softly, "Would you guys mind backing off just a bit? You're making me nervous."

Armani waved people back as he stood over Boyd's shoulder.

Boyd looked up at him.

Armani stepped back. "Sorry."

Boyd finally said, "OK, think I got it." Looking surprised, he said, "Colors."

Armani said, "What?"

"Colors. It looks like the hacker changed the colors on the opening app screen."

"Colors! That's it? There isn't some Trojan virus in there?"

"Nope. After the last hack, I set up this program on an independent server to monitor software code changes. It takes a snapshot of the code and compares it to what's on the main server several times a second. It alarms if there's any change at all and tells us where the change is."

Frowning, Armani asked, "How bad is the color change?"

Boyd called the graphic up on the screen. Everyone crowded forward to look.

Finally, Boyd looked up at Armani. "What do you think?"

"How the dillywink would I know? I'm color blind."

There was subdued laughter, and then a small voice in the back said, "It's a bit bright, but it isn't bad."

Everyone turned toward her.

Boyd said, "This is Bea, one of our new graphic artist interns."

Armani nodded and asked her, "Really?"

She smiled. "Whoever did this, did a nice job of blending. They used bright but complementary colors. It's simple but catchy."

Armani sighed. "Okay, someone tell Keith to cancel the server switch." He shook his head. "Why on earth would someone go to all the trouble of hacking our system to make our splash screen prettier?"

One of the engineers said, "Maybe he's just letting us know he can, a challenge for us to try and stop him?"

Bea said, "Or, maybe he wants a job here."

All but Armani laughed.

Boyd added, "Anyone who can get through our firewall twice deserves a job."

Armani looked around at his team. "Well, if he does it again, he might get all our jobs." He shook his head. "Okay, show's over, back to work." He gave Boyd a head nod toward his office.

As the group broke up, Boyd followed him.

Armani quietly asked, "This is the third breach. What can we do to stop him?"

Boyd scratched his head. "Whoever he is, he's good. Can't find any trace of his penetration."

They went inside Armani's office and closed the door. "Could it be an inside job? Could someone be playing a practical joke on us or be angry about something?"

With a straight face, Boyd nodded. "Probably someone offended by your bad language — dillywink, bocce balls . . . ."

Armani shook his head in irritation. "This is serious."

Boyd sighed. "We have a tight crew here. Plenty of practical jokers, but," he shook his head, "can't believe anyone would mess with the core software code. You know that's like sacrilege for us software types. We wouldn't dare do it unless we had a death wish, and the rest of the office wouldn't know how."

Armani just looked at him.

"OK, I'll change all the passwords and put in a monitor program that can track everyone's activity. If they're not part of the staff, the password change should stop them. If they are, we should be able to find out who's accessing the code."

Elizabeth met Carl and Kelly in the lobby and immediately confirmed the truism that opposites attract. Carl was a serious-looking, tall, dark professional. Kelly was a bubbly, freckled, redhead with smiling green eyes. Within minutes, Elizabeth identified a kindred spirit and liked her.

They told her they were taking her to one of their favorite restaurants, J Gilbert's.

Kelly said, "That's where we first met Josh."

J Gilbert's was an elegant steak house near CIA Headquarters. It had that dark wood and brick, old world feel to it. Impressed with the menu, she wasn't going to be shy, and ordered filet mignon with all the fixings.

The discussion was a little awkward at first because Elizabeth wasn't sure how much of the past events she could talk about openly. Switching to global politics she asked, "So, Carl, do you think we're moving toward world government?"

He thought for a moment and then carefully said, "There's no doubt we moved that way while we were trying to deflect the comet."

She nodded. "Very diplomatic answer, but now that we're not under the gun, will we go back to the way things were?"

Carl gave her a small smile. "I was genuinely surprised when they changed the U.N. Security Council's ability to veto with only one vote . . . to a three quarter's majority." He shook his head. "And even intelligence agencies are working together now."

"Really? How?" She smiled. "Or if you tell me, will you have to kill me?"

Carl smiled. "Not this time. The current administration publicized an intelligence summit that was attended by our CIA Director, Chief of British SIS, head of the Russian SVR and several other key intelligence directors, *and* it was chaired by the U.N. Director of Global Security."

"The U.N.? Bet that was awkward."

"Not really. Doruk Turan grew up in the law enforcement and intel community. As the former Vice-President of the European Union, he's credited with almost eliminating terrorism in Europe."

"So, all this is good?"

"It's improved our ability to stop terrorism and catch criminals . . . ."

Elizabeth caught his hesitation. "But . . . ?"

He shrugged. "Time will tell." He paused and then changed the subject. "Elizabeth, may I give you some intel background on Columbia?"

Kelly smiled. "Oooh. You're getting the same treatment as the Secretary of State."

Elizabeth nodded emphatically. "That'd be great!"

As she enjoyed a spectacular filet, Carl gave her a detailed brief on Columbia.

Finishing up, Carl looked down at his phone. "I'm sorry. I'm going to have to take this."

Kelly shook her head, and with a smile, she whispered dramatically, "*The job.*"

Elizabeth smiled. "No problem."

As Carl left the table, Kelly leaned forward and said, "Good. This gives us some time for girl talk. Carl's an angel, but he's soooo task-oriented."

Elizabeth nodded. "Yeah, so is Josh."

They talked about several topics, but then, looking serious, Kelly asked, "Elizabeth, is it still hard to think about your first husband?"

Elizabeth sighed. "It was for the first year. I finally realized, because of how he died . . . ." She stopped and explained. "Kelly, he was a great guy, but he was an adrenaline junky. He loved riding fast motorcycles. One afternoon, he went for a ride and never came back. It was a terrible accident and a . . . a closed coffin funeral. I figured out later, I had no closure. Some part of me must have believed he was still alive."

Kelly nodded sympathetically. "I understand."

Elizabeth gave her a half-smile. "Then I met Josh. He finally gave me a reason to face up to the fact my husband was dead. He was never coming back. It was weird." Looking down, she added, "Guess I really mourned him for the first time."

Kelly nodded thoughtfully and patted Elizabeth's hand. "Makes perfect sense." After a respectful pause, she asked, "So, where'd you meet him?"

"In the hospital. He was . . ." slowing down, she continued, "uh, having some tests done." Quickly changing the subject, Elizabeth asked, "What about your first husband? If you don't mind my asking, what happened to him?"

"Andy was an adrenaline junky too. A Navy test pilot, he was assigned to Boeing in St. Louis as the program manager for the Navy's robotic fighters." Pausing, she frowned, and then gently shook her head. "It was just a routine flight. He was delivering one of the new fighters they built there to its fleet squadron in California. Somehow, it caught on fire." Looking down, she continued, "It was very hard. Andy wasn't ready to have children, and I had just found out I was pregnant." She shook her head sadly. "I didn't tell him before he left. He . . . ." She sighed softly. "He never knew he had a . . . ." Her voice faltered.

Elizabeth squeezed her hand. After a few moments, she shifted subjects. "So, when did you meet Carl?"

Kelly looked up with a small smile. "Andy and Carl were good friends, so I already knew him." She paused, thinking. "The crash was late March. Guess I saw Carl at the funeral a few days later, but it was such a blur, I really don't remember any of it. It wasn't until the posthumous medal ceremony a month later, I remember talking to him."

Elizabeth cocked her head slightly. "March?"

"Yes."

Tapping her temple, Elizabeth said, "I remember now. The crash was headline news in Kansas City. I just now made the connection."

Kelly nodded. "They told me he managed to fly the jet into the only unpopulated area around the airport. I think they even renamed the shopping center they were building there after him."

Elizabeth raised her eyebrows in question.

"Oh, I'm sorry. My married name was Logan."

Elizabeth knocked her drink over in surprise as past conversations flooded her mind.

"... going to sound a little strange, but I had a former life. I was a Navy test pilot . . . need to reestablish my security access at Boeing."

Trying to cover her shock, Elizabeth said, "I'm sorry. I'm so clumsy."

As Kelly helped her mop up, Elizabeth had to confirm the obvious. "Andy Logan?"

"Yes." Kelly looked up questioningly.

Elizabeth managed, "Uh, the Logan Shopping Complex . . . isn't far from where I used to live."

Kelly nodded her head. "What are the odds?"

Under her breath, Elizabeth said, "Astronomical." She had to change the subject to give herself a minute to compose. She quickly asked Kelly about her daughter.

As Kelly spoke of the joys and challenges of toddlers, Elizabeth just sat there watching Kelly, but hearing little. Her mind whirled. It couldn't be a coincidence!

Carl returned and apologized. He asked, "Would you ladies like some dessert?"

Elizabeth said, "No, thanks." She had planned to have dessert, but lost her appetite.

As they dropped her off at the hotel, Kelly gave Elizabeth a warm hug and said, "Please, let's stay in touch. I just know we're going to be good friends."

Elizabeth nodded. "Yes, I think we have . . . a lot in common."

7

BOGOTA

Josh landed at El Dorado International airport in Bogota one day behind Elizabeth. Even with the higher scrutiny of martial law, he was surprised how much faster the airport security and customs process had become. Although he wasn't excited about greater U.N. control, he knew streamlining international travel had been essential to the comet deflection effort.

Outside the terminal, it was hazy but bright. He put on his sunglasses. They were the latest *iMăge* brand designer cyberglasses. They displayed the current weather. Although Bogota was close to the equator, it was high in the Andes, creating a temperate climate.

His destination was the University of San Ignacio Hospital. One of the best in the capital, it sustained only minor damage from the earthquake. The U.N. had set up a command center nearby to help coordinate relief efforts. Speaking his destination to Hal, his glasses displayed the location as a map overlay. Another advantage of his amazing body was his brain's ability to switch seamlessly from imperial to metric units. The hospital was inside the city about 15 kilometers east of the airport.

Josh grabbed a taxi. The driver was a very friendly and talkative man. Josh quickly discovered Columbian Spanish was not only a different dialect, but spoken very fast. He practiced on his driver, who helped correct his pronunciations. As they drove toward the city, the driver asked whether he was "mestizo" or "pardo?"

Josh shook his head, "I don't understand."

The driver, looking at him in the rearview mirror, clarified, "Are you Black, White or Indian?"

Josh often forgot about his appearance. The driver's

expression was open and Josh knew the Columbian population had a high percentage of mixed European, Indian, and African ancestry. Josh shrugged and said, "Yes." His literal engineering mind kicked in and with a slight frown, he added, "It's funny, but I don't think I've ever seen a truly *white* or *black* person, just beige to brown people."

Smiling, the driver challenged him with, "Albino?"

Josh grinned back. "Pink."

The driver laughed and said, "Skin color just tells us how close our ancestors lived to either the equator or the poles. Too much sun, too little pigment, we burn. Too little sun, too much pigment, we die of vitamin D deficiency." Holding up a very dark brown hand, he smiled. "My ancestors must have come from right on the equator."

Josh held up his hand and looked at it. Shrugging, he said, "Intermedio?"

The philosopher driving his cab, nodded back. It was a good reminder to Josh never to judge someone by their profession.

Bogota looked like any other major metropolis, except it had large mountains to the east that disappeared into the clouds. The first evidence of the earthquake was the cab bouncing over large cracks and furrows in the asphalt. Reaching the outskirts of the city, the buildings appeared undamaged, but he saw broken glass in the streets. His driver told him that many had evacuated the city before the comet and were just now returning. Despite the light traffic, it took an hour to get to the hospital due to the detours. Josh thanked the driver for the conversation and language lesson, tipping him generously.

He had to talk to several people before finding someone who could give him directions to where Elizabeth was working. It was early evening when he located the office, but there was no one in it. Looking closer, he saw a blonde head bobbing just below the top of the desk. Peeking over it, he saw his wife sitting on the floor between two partially disassembled computers with cables going everywhere.

Masking his voice with a heavy accent, he said, "Eh, baby, can you help me with my hard drive?"

Without looking up, she said, "Sure, honey, just don't tell my husband." She added, "About time. What'd you do, swim the Gulf of Mexico?"

He smiled and said, "I see they're putting your *neurological* expertise to use."

"Actually, they are." Sighing, she nodded toward the disassembled computers and added, "My patients just aren't human."

He came around and kissed her on top of her head, saying, "Hey, I got to tell you about some weird text conversations I've had over the last couple days."

As she looked up at him, he read the frustration and weariness in her face and added, "But . . . we can talk about that later. What can I do to help?"

She sighed as she looked down at the cables in her hand. "We're trying to establish a network to the field hospitals so we can send and receive data and video for diagnosis and treatment." Frowning, she added, "Just need to make these computers talk nicely to each other. I've got most of the hardware figured out, but I'm having a heck of a time with the software. The documentation's all in Spanish and . . . ." She stopped and looked up at him. "Wait a minute! You can read Spanish. Get your butt down here."

They worked into the wee hours of the morning, but finally got the system operating. Tired but satisfied, they retired to a very small room in a dormitory across from the hospital. They shared a tiny mattress, which required sleeping in a spoon position.

Over her shoulder, Elizabeth said, "Josh, the earthquake's epicenter was about 500 kilometers southwest of Bogota, and many people there didn't evacuate. There were a lot of head injuries. They desperately need supplies and nursing relief." She paused. "I volunteered to go."

"What time do we leave?"

She just said, "Thank you."

He was about to bring up the conversations he'd had with Jen, when Elizabeth sighed and said softly, "Josh, we've never talked about . . . having children."

He was concerned where that thought came from, but he wouldn't make the same mistake he made with Kelly. Before she could say more, he said, "Yes, I'd like to have kids too."

She whispered back, "I love you."

He held her close as she quickly fell asleep.

Morning came a few hours later. Josh's new body didn't require more than four hours of sleep, but he noticed Elizabeth's normally bright demeanor was somewhat compromised. Fortunately, expecting long hours, Elizabeth had brought energy drinks with her. Being a nurse, of course, it was an insanely healthy one with no sugar and 4900% vitamin B-12.

Returning from the shower wearing nothing but a towel, she looked very good. Smiling, he offered her the energy drink in exchange for her towel.

Removing the wet towel thrown at his face, he handed her the drink.

Fifteen minutes later, a big van picked up Josh, Elizabeth, two doctors and two nurses, along with several large bags of medical supplies.

Elizabeth introduced Josh to the team. There was a general surgeon from Germany named Dieter. Dieter was in his late forties, large and loud, but friendly. From Israel, there was an internal medicine physician named Michelle. The polar opposite of Dieter, she was in her thirties, petite, quiet and stern looking. Finally, he met Leah, a cute, young nurse anesthetist from the Philippines.

The van drove them to the Guaymaral airport, a small municipal field about 25 kilometers north of the city. The driver took them right out onto the tarmac so they could load the bags onto the aircraft.

As they approached the aircraft, Josh noticed two things — the small white control tower looked like the Leaning Tower of Pisa, and their *ride* didn't look much better. Josh eyed the twin-engine transport skeptically. He was no civil aircraft expert, but recognized a classic Beech 18. With radial engines and a twin tail, it was a 1930s design. Although they continued to build them into the 1960s, this one looked like it came right out of World War II.

As Josh stepped out of the van, he saw the pilot doing his preflight. About 30, he had a shock of sandy hair, and looked and dressed like a soccer player. After helping the pilot load the bags into the back of the plane, Josh introduced himself in Spanish.

The pilot shook his hand and smiled. "Christian Montoya."

The old plane was spacious inside and seated six passengers, but with all the medical supplies, it was tight with five. Dieter took the co-pilot seat, explaining in heavily accented English that he was a pilot too. Weighing more than two nurses, it was best to have him up front for the aircraft's "weight and balance."

Josh sat directly behind the pilot next to Elizabeth. Michelle and Leah, the lightest, sat behind them.

He felt a little uneasy, but couldn't put his finger on it.

Elizabeth noticed and asked, "Backseat driver syndrome?"

He shrugged. "Probably."

Their destination was Antonio Nariño Airport near Pasto, Columbia, about 500 kilometers southwest of Bogota. The access roads to the region were badly damaged by the earthquake and largely impassable. Their mission was to relieve medical personnel already there and bring in needed supplies.

Josh was encouraged when the big radial engines coughed to life with a strong, stable staccato.

The takeoff was smooth, but the climb was leisurely due to the airport's high elevation and the plane's heavy load. They just barely cleared the range of hills surrounding the airfield before entering a thick overcast layer. Within a few minutes, they broke out on top into hazy sunshine, and Josh relaxed a little.

Elizabeth nudged Josh and pointed at the pilot, who was frequently looking at his phone.

Josh leaned forward to catch what was on the phone's screen. Then, leaning toward Elizabeth's ear to be heard over the engines, he said, "Angry Birds."

She laughed.

He added, "He's using his phone's GPS for navigation."

Elizabeth furrowed her brow.

Josh shrugged. "It's an old aircraft. Probably never been updated with modern nav equipment." Nodding toward the window, he added. "With the solid cloud layer below, he can't use ground references."

She nodded. "There's cell phone reception up here?"

"Maybe, but he's probably using a navigation app that only needs GPS satellite signals."

Satisfied, she put her head back and closed her eyes.

Josh knew she'd need all the sleep she could get. Once there, they'd be working around the clock. Wearing his cyber glasses, he decided to take advantage of the time to read. Although the glasses had been available for many years, they only became popular after improvements to the displays, batteries and relevant apps. Until the arrival of powerful digital assistants, cyber glasses had been just another dangerous distraction. The turning point came after digital assistants were smart enough to be aware of the user's environment. They could then tailor information to assist, rather than distract from, the tasks at hand. He smiled. Or maybe their success was because they'd figured out how to make them look like designer sunglasses instead of geek-wear. Although they had unlimited applications, Josh used them mostly for navigation and reading books.

Able to read a couple books a day, he spanned topics from science to history. He'd just finished a biography on General Patton and was starting one written by a neurosurgeon about heaven. If he ever reestablished contact with Jesse, he had tons of topics to bounce off him. He missed their conversations.

Carl got in his car for the morning commute to CIA headquarters. To keep clear of traffic jams, he clipped his phone into the windshield holder as he did every morning. The detour function immediately suggested an alternate route to keep him clear of a massive jam on the Beltway.

He followed the recommended detour, but quickly found himself stuck in total gridlock. Calling the office to tell them he'd be late, he found he wasn't the only one. The jam was widespread. With nothing else to do, he listened to the local and national news. It became apparent that similar jams were occurring in cities all over the world. What made the traffic jams international news was the fact that there wasn't any apparent reason for them.

Two hours later, Josh was engrossed in his book when Elizabeth nudged him. He looked up and saw the plane was in a gentle turn. Dieter, in the copilot seat, was watching the pilot intently. The pilot was fixated on his phone and unconsciously shaking his head.

Josh gave Elizabeth a meaningful look and nodded toward Dieter seated in front of her.

Elizabeth leaned forward and said, "My husband was a test pilot."

The big doctor nodded and clumsily squeezed past the center console and out of the cockpit.

Josh slipped into the copilot seat, nodding at the pilot. In addition to his high school Spanish, Josh had memorized several thousand medical and aviation terms. He studied the controls and gauges as he put on the headset. Keying the inter-cockpit communication, he asked, "Que pasa?"

Montoya told him everything was fine.

In Spanish, Josh added, "I was a military test pilot and instrument instructor. Can I help?"

Looking relieved, Montoya said, "There are no working radio nav aids out here. I have a strong GPS signal on my phone, and the nav app appears to be working fine, but it keeps turning us and the distance hasn't changed. We should be there by now, and we're getting low on fuel. The weather report said it was supposed to be scattered clouds." He shook his head, "If I could just see the ground . . . ."

Josh scanned the horizon. They were above a solid overcast layer that extended as far as the eye could see. He looked down at the fuel gauges. "Are these accurate?"

Montoya nodded.

Without keying the mic, he said, "Bummer."

Davidson sat in his office carefully going through a pile of new intelligence reports. He stopped, took off his glasses and rubbed his eyes. Loosening his tie, he looked across his office at a small decorative mirror on the wall. The reflection was that of a wiry long-distance runner who looked more like a professor than the Director of the CIA. He put his glasses back on, but before he could pick up another report, he heard a knock on his open door.

It was the Technology Director Dan Chen. Standing next to him was the head of the CIA's IT department, Julie Atlas. Chen asked, "Got a minute?"

Davidson nodded. "What's up?"

Chen looked at Atlas.

She said, "Sir, we had a computer breach. Someone hacked our central records system."

Davidson frowned. "When?"

She said, "We just found it, but it may have happened a couple days ago."

"How'd they get in and what did they get?"

"We're still trying to figure out how they did it, but we're pretty sure they only accessed and copied one set of files."

Davidson raised his eyebrows in question.

She looked at a piece of paper in her hand, but before she could answer, Chen said, "Josh Fuze."

Davidson looked past them, thinking.

After a few seconds, Chen said, "I thought he was dead."

Davidson said softly, "He was."

Atlas glanced at both of them curiously, but said nothing.

Davidson looked directly at Atlas. "I want a copy of everything that was compromised. I want to know how they did it and any ideas on who might be behind it." He paused. "I also want an immediate review of all computer security systems and procedures."

Atlas said, "Yes sir. We're working on that now. Whoever is behind this had to be extremely sophisticated, or—"

"It was an inside job," Chen finished quietly.

Atlas continued. "We'll figure it out."

A little softer, Davidson added, "Call me as soon as you know more." He dismissed them and picked up the phone. "Pat, can you please get a hold of the Bogota Bureau Chief on an encrypted line?"

Davidson sat thinking, drumming his fingers on the desk. A few minutes later, his phone rang. He was surprised how fast she had reached the Bureau Chief, but it *was* unusual for the Director to call personally.

"Hi, Jocelyn, it's Brian. How're you doing?"

"Great, sir. The office came through the quake with minimal damage, and we should be fully operational in a few days. What can I do for you?"

"Need you to help me find someone. On one of the U.N. medical relief teams in Bogota, there's an American husband-and-wife team, a Josh and Elizabeth Fuze. I need to get a message to him as soon as possible."

"What's the message?"

He paused. "When you find him, can you please ask him to come to your office so we can talk on a protected line?"

"Yes sir, I'll take care of it personally."

8
LOST

Josh pulled out his phone. It used a different operating system and navigation app, but showed the same information as Montoya's. He checked Elizabeth's — same thing. That didn't make sense. They all had good GPS signals and the apps appeared to be working, but they weren't showing a change of position.

Josh shook his head and said to Montoya, "Somehow, the nav data's bad. Comet may have damaged the Global Positioning Satellites. We've got to get below the overcast and find a place to land." Josh looked at the altimeter. They were flying at 15,000 feet, just above the cloud tops. "What are the reported ceilings at the destination?"

Montoya said, "We should be under the overcast by about 9,000 feet."

Josh nodded. "Any mountains around here that are above that?"

Montoya's eyes narrowed. "I'm not sure where here is, but yes, there are mountains up to 14,000 feet. The city of Pasto, 20 kilometers south of the airport, is over 8,000 feet."

Josh frowned. "How were you going to make the approach with the overcast?"

Montoya shrugged. "It wasn't supposed to be overcast, but I've done many GPS approaches on this." He held up his phone. He shook his head in disgust. "The plane's radio never works. Even so, I can usually talk to approach and the airport towers on my cell phone, but the cell towers are still out of commission in this area."

Josh asked, "Are we squawking 7700?"

Montoya shrugged.

Josh nodded. "Of course, the transponder's probably not

working either." He rubbed his hands together. "So, how many minutes of fuel do we have?"

Montoya looked at the gauges. "About 20."

Josh nodded. "Let's see if we can find a hole in the clouds."

It was hazy with limited visibility. They headed for an area that looked a little thinner, but when they got there, it was still solid. It also looked like there was a huge, dark cloud ahead.

Josh pointed at it. "Were there thunderstorms in the forecast?"

Montoya shook his head. "No. There aren't supposed to be thunderstorms anywhere near here."

Josh stared at the dark column ahead. "You know that doesn't even look like a thunderhead; it almost looks like . . . ." He paused. "Let's turn west, away from it."

As Montoya turned to the west, he tapped the fuel gauge and looked at his watch. Frowning, he said, "Probably only about 15 minutes of fuel left."

Josh shook his head. "Then, we don't have a choice. We've got to get under this cloud layer."

Josh strapped into the copilot seat as Montoya pulled the engines back and began a descent. Glancing back at nervous faces behind him, he could tell everyone knew something was wrong. Josh smiled and yelled over the engines, "We're having some navigation challenges and may have to land at an alternate airport. Make sure your seatbelts are fastened and your tray tables are in the upright and locked position."

He received several half-smiles.

As they dropped into the overcast, Josh constantly crosschecked the altimeter. He strained to see through the clouds, but saw nothing. After a few seconds, he began to *feel* something. He'd heard the term "facial vision" used by the blind to describe a sensation of a large object in their path. He didn't know what the mechanism was or if it was even real, but he definitely felt something massive in front of him. Knowing that there was no way he could sense anything through the clouds, he tried to ignore it. Finally, it became so strong, he told Montoya to turn right.

Montoya frowned, but gently banked the aircraft to the right.

Josh watched their altimeter drop below 10,000 feet and started to feel more and more anxious. Finally, just above 9,000 feet, they began to break through the overcast. They saw some faint shadows peeking from inside the whiteness. Through the thinning wisps of cloud, the first thing they saw clearly . . . leaves!

Without asking, Josh grabbed the yoke and pulled back while turning hard right. They both jammed the throttles forward. The engines screamed and the plane shuddered. All they could see was heavily forested mountain!

The little plane buffeted at the edge of stall as the belly scraped the treetops and the right prop clipped the leaves like a weed trimmer. At 30 degrees angle of bank with engines at full power, they finally cleared the trees and could let out their breath.

Josh let go of the yoke. Montoya leveled the wings and eased off on the throttles. Over the headset, Josh said, "Sorry about that. You have the controls."

Montoya said, "No problem." Then, repeated back the standard, "I have the controls."

They were just below the clouds in a lush green canyon boxed in on three sides. To their left and right were mountain ranges, and behind them an even larger mountain slope extended up into the clouds. Flying through a light drizzle with only a couple kilometers of visibility, there was only one direction to go. Josh's intuition had been right. If they hadn't turned, they'd be part of the mountain.

The right engine began to sputter.

Looking at the engine instruments, Josh saw that the right engine had no oil pressure. Sure enough, oil was streaming out of the engine cowl.

Montoya said, "Must have damaged it when we clipped the tree tops." He shut it down and feathered the prop.

Josh asked, "How's our fuel?"

"We used up most of it when we went to full power." Looking at the gauge, he said, "I think we only have a few minutes left."

On either side, they saw nothing but forest extending up into the clouds. There was no sign of civilization.

Josh said, "I don't suppose anything looks familiar?"

Montoya, sweeping the ground, shook his head. "We're too low to see anything."

Josh saw a small river channel — more of a creek — directly under them. It wound like a snake through the heavily forested valley. Josh pointed at it. "Let's follow that. It's running downhill."

Montoya said, "That's good because," he nodded at the altimeter showing 8,700 feet, "with this load, we can't maintain altitude on one engine."

Josh slipped his headset off and leaned back. Speaking loudly but calmly, he said, "We're probably going to have to make an emergency landing. Secure or stash as much of the loose equipment as you can, and make sure your seat belts are tight."

Instinctively, Josh wanted to fly the plane, but with no experience in this type of aircraft and no time to get a feel for it, he knew it was better to let Montoya do it.

Putting the headset back on, Josh said, "Let's find a place to set down before we run out of gas." Even with his exceptional vision, the only thing Josh could see ahead was heavy forest and clouds. There was nowhere to put the little plane without hitting trees.

Looking directly under the nose, he saw the tiny river they were following ended in a small waterfall. Below the waterfall, the river widened a little. As they continued to lose altitude, Josh shook his head. "We're going to have to put it in the river." Josh pointed ahead where there appeared to be a straight stretch. "Looks like our best bet."

Montoya nodded.

Josh made one more sweep to see if he could find any place that looked even vaguely like a clearing. There was nothing. On top of that, the river was crowded with trees on both sides, and the distance between the trees was narrower than the wings.

The left engine sputtered.

Montoya reached over and flipped a fuel control valve and the engine ran normally. He didn't have to say anything. Josh knew they were on fumes.

Smiling, Josh said, "If they can put an Airbus 300 into a harbor, we can put a Beech 18 into a river."

Montoya gave him a nervous smile.

Glancing back, Josh met Elizabeth's eyes. She nodded and silently mouthed, "I love you."

Josh smiled and winked. Looking forward, his smile faded. Projecting their flight path, he realized that even if they could slip the wings past the trees, there wasn't enough straightaway before the river turned.

Montoya saw this too and said, "Not enough room. I'm going to try and make the turn, see if it gets any better ahead."

They couldn't see what the river looked like beyond the turn. Josh knew it was a gamble, but he would have done the same. Trying to sound enthusiastic, he said, "Sounds good."

As they reached the river bend, Montoya pushed the throttle on the remaining engine forward, banking the airplane to follow the river. In the turn, just above the treetops, the last engine began to miss again. Holding their breath, they completed the turn and rolled out to see a river slightly wider ahead. It was still barely wider than the wings, but at least they had a kilometer of straightaway before the river turned again.

Josh said, "Let's put it down."

Montoya was a good stick. Josh watched him slip the little plane between the trees on each side of the river, the wingtips barely clipping the leaves. Once below the canopy of leaves, it was obvious how little straightaway they had.

Montoya flared the plane perfectly just above the water. He didn't have to pull the throttle to idle because the engine quit.

Fighting himself not to grab the yoke, Josh said through clenched teeth, "Nice and easy."

With the gear still retracted, Montoya greased the belly onto the water.

The landing was as smooth as glass. The two engines, slightly lower than the belly, kicked up spray on both sides as they skimmed across the water like a speedboat.

Unfortunately, they weren't slowing down fast enough and were rapidly running out of room. Looking ahead, Josh saw that the river didn't turn . . . it disappeared.

As they realized what that meant, someone yelled, "Waterfall!"

9

WATERFALL

Just beyond the waterfall, they could see a 100-meter drop! Josh and Montoya simultaneously stomped the left rudder, trying to drive the plane into the shoreline. It didn't work. They were too slow for the rudder to be effective but too fast for the aircraft to stop hydroplaning.

Fifty meters from the falls, the plane started settling into the water and scraping the river rocks . . . but it wasn't enough. They were going over!

A few meters from their death, the plane's nose slammed into a large submerged rock. It ripped a hole in the fuselage in front of Josh's feet and threw them forward against their seat belts. Pivoting the plane around its nose, the tail lifted high in the air. This gave them a panoramic view of the fatal plunge in front of them.

Still standing on its nose, the little plane debated whether to fall back onto its belly or flip over on its back, taking them down the waterfall. It hung there for a very long second . . . .

Then, ever so slowly, dropped back on its belly with a loud splash and crunch. With the nose wrapped around the rock and one wing tip jammed into a shoreline tree, the plane was wedged. The roller coaster ride was over.

It was quiet except for the gentle sound of water rushing outside the fuselage and heavy breathing.

Josh broke the silence. "Is everyone okay?"

There were some grunts and nervous laughter, but everyone nodded.

Josh couldn't resist. "Please be careful opening overhead compartments, as some items may have shifted during landing." Before anyone could groan, he continued, "There's no danger of the plane sinking; water's a half meter deep and we're totally wedged. So don't be in a rush to get out. It would be way embarrassing to survive a crash and then fall in the river and over the falls."

Montoya crawled back through the plane, opened the main door and jumped down into the shallow water. With Josh's help, they got everyone out of the plane and to the river's edge a few meters away. Josh passed the gear out to Montoya, who passed it to those on the shore. After they were finished, no one could resist peeking over the top of the waterfall. It was a breathtakingly beautiful and lethal drop.

Elizabeth asked if anyone had a cell signal. They all checked and shook their heads one-by-one.

Josh said, "We're all OK, and we know they'll be looking for us. When the clouds clear, an airplane sitting in the river will be easy to spot from the air. Our best bet is to stay here and make camp."

Montoya nodded.

Josh stopped and really looked around. They were standing next to a pristine mountain river with lush foliage on both sides. Above them were mountains carpeted in green that rose into the clouds. It had that haunting beauty he'd always associated with rainforests. His childhood imagination pictured a Tyrannosaurus charging out of the mist. Despite the drizzle and high elevation, the temperature was surprisingly warm. Rain, however, no matter how light, would eventually soak them. They needed shelter.

They found a small clearing about 100 meters from the river. While shuttling supplies to the clearing, Josh and Elizabeth were alone for a minute. With a smile, Josh mimicked her. "It's not like I'm going to be trekking through the mountains and jungles."

She punched him hard in the chest.

Looking surprised, he said, "What was that for?"

Through clenched teeth, she whispered with force, "When was the last time you were in a cockpit and actually had a *successful* landing on a runway!" She shook her head. "That's it! I'm *not* flying with you anymore. *You* shouldn't even fly with you." As she stalked off, he heard her add, "I can't believe you survived as a test pilot."

Shrugging, he said softly, "I didn't."

Davidson picked up his phone.

Jocelyn Mendoza said, "Sir, sorry it took so long to get back to you. Things are still chaotic down here. Unfortunately, the U.N. deployed Josh and Elizabeth Fuze to one of the disaster areas as part of a five-person medical team. Yesterday, they flew to a small city in the south called San Juan de Pasto."

Davidson said. "So, no encrypted line. Can we reach them via cell phone?"

Mendoza said, "No sir. The cell towers in that area are still out of commission, but even if they worked, it wouldn't help."

"Why?"

"Their airplane never arrived."

Davidson frowned. "It crashed?"

"They don't know. There were no radio transmissions or emergency transponder signal."

"They're searching for them?"

Mendoza said, "They say they will as soon as the weather improves. The ceilings are too low to send out search aircraft, and their assets are tied up with rescues and medevacs."

He sighed. "OK." Pausing, he added, "Jocelyn, these individuals are important to . . . an ongoing investigation. Please keep me informed."

"Yes sir."

As he hung up, he paused and then picked the phone back up and said, "Pat, I need to reach Tim Smith."

"Not familiar with that name. Is he an agency operative?"

"He used to be."

They made a small camp in the clearing. Dieter built a fire, and Josh, recalling his pilot survival training, tied a couple waterproof tarps between the trees over their heads. It created a nice dry sanctuary from the rain, and the fire kept them warm. They had plenty of military pre-packaged rations, blankets and water. Rubbing sore arms and stiff backs, the mood was surprisingly light. Josh knew from experience, there was nothing more exhilarating than facing certain death and walking away. They were already embellishing the story of the crash.

As it got dark, Josh quietly asked Montoya, "What type of animals should we keep a lookout for at night?"

Montoya shrugged. "I don't know. I grew up in the city."

Josh had obtained a Glock nine-millimeter pistol while he was in Bogota, and they had a flare gun from the plane. Knowing he could exist on very little sleep, Josh said he'd stay up through the night and keep watch.

As they were settling down around the fire, they all felt the earth move. The earthquake aftershock shook them gently, accompanied by a very low frequency rumble. It went on for 10 seconds. They all looked at each other, but no one said anything.

Josh suggested everyone get some sleep.

As they were making nests around the fire, Elizabeth came over and sat on an equipment bag next to him. She said, "I'm sorry. When I get scared, I get mad."

He put his arm around her shoulder and pulled her close. "I know."

With a small smile, she said, "Well, I did say I wanted to see the world, the more exotic the better, didn't I?"

Josh just smiled back.

They sat there quietly staring into the campfire.

After a while, Josh sniffed the air and asked, "Do you smell anything unusual?"

She shook her head and then stopped. Frowning slightly, she said, "I noticed something right after we got out of the plane. Guess I'm used to it now, but it smelled kind of like . . ." she looked at him, "rotten eggs?"

Josh nodded. "Sulfur."

She looked at him. "What's it from?"

"Not sure, but Pasto sits at the foot of a volcano."

She smiled, "That's right. We may be close to Pasto!"

Josh laughed. "That's a positive way to look at it." He loved the way she found the good in every situation. With a major earthquake, they could be sitting on an active volcano, but there was little point in worrying about it now.

He gently rubbed her back and said, "We'll need everyone sharp tomorrow. Why don't you get some sleep?"

She curled up on a blanket next to him.

He was surprised how quickly the adrenaline had worn off. It was midnight and everyone in the camp was asleep. The temperature had dropped quite a bit, but with no wind, it was comfortable near the fire. As he poked the embers, several thoughts ran through his head. As far as successful landings, he was technically zero for three. Frowning, he tried to figure out what would cause all their navigation apps to fail. Since it happened on different phones and operating systems, it had to be a systemic problem, but it was hard to imagine a GPS failure that would give erroneous results rather than just shutting down.

He closed his eyes and listened to the background sounds of the mountain forest. Permeating everything was the soft sound of rain on the leaves and tarp. In the bass part of the jungle orchestra, was a low-pitched croaking sound he guessed was some type of frog. On top of that, was a background chorus of crickets punctuated by random birdcalls. One of the birds had the familiar and haunting sound of an American Whip-poor-will. After an hour, the rain and forest concert became beautifully hypnotic. He found himself zoning out and almost falling asleep.

A popping sound pulled him awake. He stood up and listened intently through the rain. After a couple minutes, hearing nothing, he sat back down. It was probably just his imagination.

Then he heard it again. It sounded like a twig snapping in the distance. He held his breath. There it was again. This time it was closer, as if a large animal were moving slowly through the brush. Surrounded by a dark mountain forest, it was easy to let his imagination run wild. He stood back up and pulled the nine millimeter from his pocket. He took another deep breath and held it, listening carefully and scanning the forest. Even with his exceptional night vision, he saw nothing.

Then he heard it again, still closer, but this time there were two sounds coming from different directions. He quietly pulled the slide back on his pistol and leaned toward the sounds, straining to hear. Several seconds elapsed. Then his sensitive ears caught something else, something that sent a chill down his spine. It was the sound of the deadliest predator of all — the faint but unmistakable sound of a bolt being pulled back on an automatic rifle.

10

FARC

Josh not only heard but sensed their approach. He tapped Elizabeth. When she looked up, he put his finger to his lips for silence. His ears told him there were a half dozen approaching from two directions. He'd studied everything he could find online about Columbia before he came, and Elizabeth had shared the brief Carl had given her. It wasn't hard to guess who might be moving around at night with automatic weapons. He was sure he could escape, but it would be very difficult to get Elizabeth out safely and impossible to save the others.

He made a decision and hoped it was the right one. He popped the magazine out of his pistol, ejected the chambered round, reinserted the magazine and stuffed the gun into one of the large medical supply bags. He pushed it as far to the bottom as he could.

Then, holding his hands in the air, he yelled, "Somos medicos! Estamos desarmados! We are doctors! We're unarmed!"

Everyone in the makeshift camp woke up.

Josh told them to stay on the ground and be quiet.

He repeated his statement in both Spanish and English several times. His nose told him they were close. A voice from behind him said in Spanish, "Don't move or you die."

Josh froze with his hands in the air.

Two figures wearing green fatigues came slowly out of the forest to his left and right. They pointed their weapons at those on the ground, while several more came in and stood at the perimeter of their camp. They all carried AK-47s. Josh knew the Columbian Army didn't use the Russian-made rifles.

Someone patted him down from behind and then spun him around to face a swarthy man about Josh's height and age. With his

AK-47 slung over his shoulder, he pointed a 45 automatic at Josh's stomach. His eyes darted nervously around the camp. Josh saw no rank insignia, but caught a small chevron shaped patch with yellow, blue and red.

They pulled everyone up and searched them. After collecting their cell phones and identification, the guerilla leader focused on Josh, asking in Spanish, "You are doctors?"

Josh said, "They are doctors and nurses, yes. I am a pilot and interpreter." He didn't mention their real pilot. He'd probably be safer if the guerillas thought he was part of the medical team.

The guerilla leader said, "You have medical supplies?"

"Yes." Josh nodded toward the bags near the edge of the camp.

The leader told one of his men to search the bags.

Josh added, "We were coming to help the earthquake victims, but our plane crashed."

After searching through several bags, one of the guerillas — Josh realized it was a young woman — said in Spanish, "They *are* medical supplies."

The leader visibly relaxed, as did the other guerillas. "You will come with us to our camp. We have injured people." It wasn't a request, but Josh nodded. "Of course."

There were at least seven guerillas. In the firelight, he was able to see their faces. Most of them were teenagers, and two were women. They looked both determined and scared — a dangerous combination.

The guerilla leader told everyone to pick up a bag and start walking. Josh translated his commands into English.

Dieter protested.

Josh used the most neutral term to describe them. "Dieter, these are revolutionary fighters. If you don't want to be shot, you'll do exactly as they say."

The leader, who must have understood some English, nodded and said in English, "Yes!"

One of the young guerillas led the way with a flashlight. The medical team followed in single file. Josh picked up two of the heaviest bags and was the last of their party. Three guerillas followed him, including the leader.

It was slow going through the heavy brush and mud. The night forest was alive with sounds and smells, although, the immediate company was the most powerful smell. To be fair, it wasn't just the guerillas. A plane crash could stress the best deodorant.

The leader asked in Spanish, "You are a bad pilot, yes?"

Josh said, "Good pilot, bad airplane."

The guerillas behind him laughed.

In the dark, wet branches hit them in the face and caught at their clothes. Although the guerillas behind them used flashlights to illuminate their path, there was a lot of stumbling over small branches and roots. Dieter tripped and fell. The German doctor was overweight and out of shape. The guerillas stopped and waited, but offered no help.

After 40 minutes, they reached a dirt road. The guerillas kept them in a tight group, walking behind and flanking them. They followed the dirt road for several kilometers. Cold, wet and muddy, they finally reached three old, beat-up SUVs. Two of them didn't even have doors.

The guerillas threw the medical supplies into the back of one of the vehicles, and then crammed their captives inside the other two, making them sit on each other's laps. Josh was happy to have a svelte Elizabeth sitting in his.

She looked at him with concern.

He smiled and whispered, "Don't worry; you're too valuable to them as a nurse." He winked. "But try not to look so cute." She gave him a small smile and squeezed his hand.

Some of the guerillas stood in the open doors, hanging on to improvised roof racks, as the SUVs bounced slowly down the dirt road. The ride was rough, and several times, they had to slow to a crawl to cross running water and avoid fallen trees or fissures in the ground. It was an hour before they arrived in what he assumed was a small town or village. As they pulled up near the outskirts, they could see only a few isolated lights ahead.

An older man in fatigues came up to the lead vehicle and spoke to their leader. Josh couldn't hear their conversation, but read the body language. It was clear the younger leader of the capture party was reporting to the older man. The older man clapped him on the back, clearly recognizing his accomplishment, and then pointed further into the town.

They had taken his phone, but he had a good internal clock and knew it was about three in the morning. In the dark, it was hard to see, but it was obvious they passed some badly damaged structures and a lot of rubble. Their vehicles pulled up in front of what looked like a corrugated metal warehouse about 25 meters wide. Illuminated by a weak floodlight, he could see it was rusted and leaning a little to one side. He heard a generator running in the background as the guerrillas led them inside.

Davidson was startled to see Smith standing silently in front of his desk. Frowning he said, "How do you do that?" Shaking his head, he smiled. "Never mind." He came around his desk and shook Smith's hand. "Thanks for coming on such short notice. How are you doing?"

Smith nodded. "Very well."

"And Sheri?"

Completely deadpan, Smith said, "Good, but she won't let me shoot any of her paparazzi."

With a slight headshake, Davidson smiled. "That's rather unreasonable of her."

Smith nodded. "What can I do for you?"

"Got a situation." Closing his office door, Davidson pulled two chairs close to each other. As they sat down, he said, "Someone hacked into our computer."

Smith didn't say anything.

"They got into a system that shouldn't be possible to access from outside."

"Inside job?"

"We thought it had to be, but our Cyber Warfare guys now believe it was an external hack . . . a very sophisticated attack." He paused and looked directly at Smith. "What we do know is that they were searching for one particular record, and found it — Josh Fuze."

Smith tilted his head slightly. "What did the late Commander Fuze say when you told him about this?"

"That's the problem. Haven't been able to talk to him. He's helping Elizabeth with disaster relief work in Columbia. Called the Bogota station chief." He shook his head. "Apparently, Josh and Elizabeth flew south with a small medical team. Their plane never arrived."

Smith frowned and leaned forward. "Where were they headed?"

"A southern city near the quake's epicenter." Davidson pulled a paper off his desk and looked at it. "San Juan de Pasto in the Narino province. Their last radar position put them over the mountains to the northwest of Pasto."

Smith shook his head. "FARC."

"Excuse me?"

"Fuerzas Armadas Revolucionarias de Colombia."

Davidson nodded in recognition. "Revolutionary Armed Forces of Columbia."

"Did ops there a few years ago. They were Marxist guerrillas, but with the collapse of their communist support, their primary revenue stream is now cocaine and kidnapping. That area is still one of their strongholds." He stood up. "I'm on my way."

"Tim, San Juan de Pasto's less than nine klicks from a 14,000-foot volcano. Latest report says the comet woke it up."

As Josh and his fellow captives entered the building, they found a surprisingly well-lit, open area filled with two dozen cots, all occupied. Clearly, this was a makeshift hospital. The patients in the cots and those attending them looked up. Smiles of relief appeared on their faces as the guerilla leader announced they had doctors, nurses and medical supplies.

A gray-haired man in his sixties with a rough complexion and a short beard came out from one of the back rooms. He wore jeans and a button-down shirt. Although he walked with a limp, he carried himself with confidence. In Spanish, he immediately asked, "You are doctors and nurses?"

Josh nodded and introduced everyone.

He hugged them with enthusiasm, introducing himself as Father Cletus Alfredo Rodriquez. Then he thanked the guerilla leader and gently but firmly ushered him out.

Two guerillas stayed behind. They slung their AK-47s over their shoulders and sat down on chairs just inside the entrance.

Realizing the medical team spoke English, Father Rodriquez

switched to heavily accented but excellent English. "Thank God, you're here. You're the answer to a prayer." He frowned and asked a little tentatively. "I'm afraid to ask, but how *did* you end up here?"

Josh said, "Our plane made an emergency landing in the river."

Rodriguez looked relieved. "I was afraid my *friends* might have *obtained* you from a medical aid station. Was anyone injured in the landing?"

Josh shook his head.

"Then it truly is a prayer answered. I'm the Catholic priest for this area . . . or what's left of it. I have some basic medical training," he pointed to a woman older than him, "and Sister Teresa is a nurse, but this . . . this is far beyond our abilities."

Leah asked Rodriquez to show them the critical patients. Finally in an environment they understood, the medical team went into triage mode. There were two dozen injured people; many were children. Not surprising with an earthquake, there were a lot of broken bones and internal injuries.

Most people would be catatonic after an airplane crash and kidnapping. Josh marveled that this team worked quickly and efficiently as if they were in a modern hospital. It was like watching a carefully choreographed ballet. He suspected they were adrenaline junkies at heart and actually thrived in high-pressure environments.

After determining which patients were the most critical, Dieter started performing emergency surgeries. Josh and Montoya helped wherever they could, pulling out supplies, moving patients, and even donating blood — one of Josh's least favorite activities.

Just as they were getting a handle on the situation, another aftershock struck. The suspended fluorescent lights swayed back and forth creating eerie shadows as the metal building creaked and groaned. Several patients cried out in fear or pain as their cots vibrated like pucks in an air hockey game.

The aftershock wasn't strong enough to knock anyone out of a cot, but it was stronger than the previous one and lasted longer. As it subsided, they heard a low frequency rumble that sounded like distant thunder.

As the sound faded, Josh, standing near Rodriquez, gave him a questioning look.

Rodriquez said, "Galeras."

Josh shook his head. "I don't understand."
Rodriquez said softly, "The volcano."

11

GALERAS

Josh asked Rodriquez, "Does it do this often?"

"Only after a comet." Rodriquez smiled. "The volcano has had many eruptions for as far back as we have records. It's ejected tons of ash and many lava streams, but they've never gone further than a few kilometers from the volcano. But now . . . ." He shrugged.

"How far away are we?"

Rodriquez frowned. "If it were daytime, Galeras would dominate the view to the east. We sit at the foot of the volcano."

They worked through the next day and into the night. While getting supplies, Josh was able to easily extract his pistol from the bottom of one of the medical bags and hide it in a cubbyhole where he could get to it later. He knew they were in no danger from the guerillas as long as they were taking care of their people, but he was under no misconception of their value after that. He also knew that he and Montoya were the most expendable.

Another aftershock hit, similar to the first. Josh could tell they were coming more frequently.

By nine that night, the team's pace slowed. They'd only lost one patient, who was probably beyond help even if they could have gotten him to a modern hospital. They stabilized the most critical and were able to release several. That left 18 bedridden patients. They decided to take shifts so that everyone could get some real sleep. Josh stayed awake while Elizabeth slept. He was so appreciative of his new body, but he was finally having difficulty focusing and keeping his eyes open.

At two in the morning, Elizabeth got up and said, "You've got to get some sleep. You've been awake for two days and donated more blood than you should have. We need you sharp. As your medical team lead, I'm ordering you, Commander Fuze, to go to sleep."

He didn't argue. He found a corner of the building and made a nest of cardboard boxes. The last thing he remembered was putting his head down and hearing the soft rain on the metal roof.

He woke from a nightmare — he had been flying his annual instrument check flight but hadn't flown in over a year, couldn't remember anything and was failing terribly. Rubbing his eyes, he looked around and saw guerillas guarding the door of the makeshift hospital that sat at the foot of a volcano. With a half-smile, he said softly, "Thank God, it was just a bad dream."

It was about six in the morning and very quiet. Most of the patients and medical personnel were asleep, with the exception of Michelle, who was re-doing a bandage, and one of the armed guerillas near the door.

He realized that the feeling something was wrong didn't depart with the nightmare. He was learning to trust his premonitions and sat there for a minute trying to sense what was different. It hit him. He hadn't noticed it because he'd been breathing it in his sleep, but there was a hint of smoke above the background scent of sulfur. He sniffed the air and frowned. It wasn't smoke from wood burning in a campfire; it was the smoke created by throwing green leaves into a fire.

He looked at the two guards. One slept in his chair, propped against the wall. The other was awake and reading a book. Josh went over to where he'd stashed the pistol and slipped it into his pocket. Then he walked slowly toward the guard so she would see him and not be startled. In Spanish, he softly said, "Excuse me. I think I smell smoke. Can we take a look outside?"

She woke up the other guard and told him they were going to check.

He nodded.

She was medium-height with a mocha complexion and dark, intelligent eyes. She motioned for Josh to go first.

It was early dawn with a heavy overcast sky. The rain had stopped, but there were puddles and mud everywhere. Looking around in the twilight, he saw a small village consisting of a few dozen houses, most of them badly damaged. The village sat on a foothill surrounded by a patchwork of small agricultural plots bounded by lush forest. Josh knew volcanic soil was some of the richest in the world, great for growing coffee or cocaine.

Looking to the east, the foothill dropped off slightly toward the forest edge. From there, it met a massive mountain slope that climbed up into the clouds. This must be the base of Galeras. Not surprisingly, the village was deserted.

The young guerilla shook her head. "I don't smell smoke."

There was the slightest of breezes coming from behind them as they faced the volcano. Josh sniffed the air and nodded toward the vegetation. "I think it's coming from that direction. Can we take a closer look?"

She frowned, glanced back at the hospital and then nodded.

Josh began to walk slowly toward the volcano with his guard trailing him. They reached the edge of the village about a kilometer from the hospital. The road ended and there was a slight downward slope into a small farm plot. At its far edge, was the forest. Peering into the trees, he thought he saw a very slight glow and pointed toward it.

The young guerilla woman said, "I don't see anything."

Josh realized his sense of smell was ridiculously sensitive and he could see slightly into the infrared. Unfortunately, she couldn't, and the wind was blowing any smell away from them.

Her eyes narrowed as she held the AK-47 close. "We must return now!"

She obviously suspected he was trying to get her close to the jungle in order to escape.

Josh nodded and said, "I must just be tired." He began to walk back past her and then stopped. Looking back over his shoulder, he said, "What was that?"

As she glanced back, he swept her legs out from under her with a judo move.

She didn't give up without a fight and kicked him on the way down.

He deflected the blow, and as she landed on her back, he had his foot on her shoulder and the nine-millimeter pointed at her head.

She froze.

Very softly, he said, "I'm not going to hurt you or escape, but I do smell smoke, and we need to investigate."

He took her AK-47 and slung it over his shoulder. Then he lifted his foot and motioned with the barrel of the pistol. Pointing to the forest, he said, "Ladies first."

As she got up, he pulled the walkie-talkie off her belt. They started walking slowly on a path through the agricultural patch. Splashing and sliding their way for 100 meters, they reached the edge of the forest.

She stopped. Sniffing the air, she exclaimed, "Smoke!"

This close, the breeze no longer kept the smoke at bay and they heard a slight crackling sound in the distance. Moving through heavy forest vegetation, they began to feel puffs of heat wafting through the trees. The young guerrilla woman pointed at a distant glow. "Lava!"

The wet ground and vegetation prevented the forest from burning easily, but there was no doubt the lava was consuming it and moving toward them.

Josh said, "Let's go a little further to see how fast it's moving."

She nodded. They only had to go another 30 meters before they could see the edge of burning vegetation. Even with a breeze at their back, they felt the intense heat radiating from the molten rock. Fortunately, it was moving very slowly.

She pleaded, "We have to warn the others. My little sister and brother are in the hospital."

Josh nodded and handed her the walkie-talkie and AK-47.

Looking surprised, she slung the rifle over her shoulder and spoke rapidly into the walkie-talkie. As they scrambled back through the forest, Josh asked, "What's your name?"

"Alejandra, but everyone calls me Chibcha."

Josh said, "Chinche?"

She gave a little laugh, shaking her head. "No, that's a bug." She said slowly, "Chibcha. Chibcha are Indians like the Inca. There aren't many of us left."

As they left the forest, Josh walked beside her and held out his hand. "I'm Josh. I'm part Indian too — Dakota Sioux from North America." Or . . . at least he was. He had no idea what genes he had now, but was sure there was Native American in there somewhere.

She shook his hand and smiled. It was amazing what a smile could do. It transformed the stern guerilla into a pretty, young woman. No, not a woman. He guessed she was barely 17. He smiled. "Alejandra, a beautiful name to fit a beautiful lady."

Her smile turned shy.

It tugged at Josh's heart. He realized he'd never get to see his daughter turn into a young woman. As they jogged back to the makeshift hospital, he told her, "We'll get your sister and brother out."

An SUV, driven by an older man wearing fatigues, met them at the door to the makeshift hospital. Clearly their leader, it was the same man Josh had seen when they arrived. He got out of the vehicle as Rodriguez and the other guard came outside.

Alejandra, tripping over her words, gave them detailed information about the location and speed of the lava.

The guerilla leader did a slow 360-degree scan and then said, "We're on higher ground. The lava will roll downhill on each side of the village, but if it doesn't stop, it will meet," he nodded back toward the entrance road to the village, "at the only road out of town."

Calmly, but with passion, Rodriquez said, "We must evacuate the patients immediately."

Josh asked, "How many vehicles do you have?"

The man narrowed his eyes at Josh, but Alejandra said, "He was the one who found the lava. He could have escaped but didn't."

The guerilla leader looked at her and then back at Josh. "Only a few left. I'll get all the vehicles I can. Have the first group of patients ready." With that, he climbed into the SUV and drove off.

Josh looked at Rodriquez. "You've seen lava flows before?"

Rodriquez said, "Yes, but never this far. We're over five kilometers from the caldera." He frowned. "The lava must be coming from a newly opened vent on this side of the mountain."

Josh asked, "Where's the nearest hospital?"

"The city of Pasto is on the other side of the volcano, but the town of Consaca is about 30 kilometers from here and has a medical aid station."

Within 15 minutes, they had the first group of patients loaded into an SUV. They built a makeshift shelf that ran the length of the vehicle's cargo bay so that they could lay three patients side-by-side, and then stack another three on top of the shelf. They chose the patients that were most critical but stable. Then they put the nurse, Leah, and the nun in the front seat along with a guerilla driver.

Shortly after they left, another earthquake shook the village, accompanied by rolling thunder. It wasn't any more violent than the last one, but went on twice as long. With the sun coming up and the overcast clearing, they could now see the top of the volcano. A huge cloud of rolling smoke and ash rose above it. In the airplane, he'd mistaken this gray column for a thunderstorm. Fortunately, they were upwind and the smoke and ash curved away from them.

While waiting for another vehicle, Josh went inside and told Elizabeth about Alejandra. The small boy Elizabeth had been working on was her brother. Josh asked, "Is he going to be OK?"

Elizabeth sighed. "He had a lot of internal injuries. We did surgery and stopped the bleeding, but he lost too much blood and we have no fluids left. If we could get him to a real hospital, he'd have a chance . . . ." She looked down at the little boy and shook her head gently.

After a very long 15 minutes, another beat-up SUV appeared along with a jeep. They again loaded six patients into the SUV and managed to get three more in the jeep. They put Michelle, Montoya and two more guerillas in the vehicles. Alejandra refused to go. She nodded toward the hospital. "My little brother."

Josh realized there were nine people remaining — three critical patients, Rodriquez, Dieter, Elizabeth, Josh, Alejandra and the guerilla leader that captured them.

Rodriquez stayed outside with Josh while the others went back in to prepare the last three patients for transport. The smell of burning vegetation was getting stronger.

While waiting for another vehicle, Rodriguez sniffed the air. "We've had heavy rains all week. That's helping." He looked toward the mountain. "But the smoke means the lava is still moving this way." Rodriquez shook his head and then looked at Josh curiously. "Elizabeth told me you were a test pilot and led the comet deflection program."

Josh shrugged. He needed to talk to her about not sharing that information.

Rodriquez took the shrug for confirmation and said, "Commander Josh Fuze, what are you doing out here?"

Josh gave him a half-smile. "Elizabeth stayed by my side through my mission; I thought it only fair to support her during hers."

Rodriquez tilted his head slightly, almost as if he were listening to something. He repeated, "Your mission." Then he looked at Josh curiously and with the slightest of smiles asked, "Which mission?"

Josh frowned at Rodriquez's odd question. Then deflected it with, "Father Cletus Alfredo Rodriquez, how on earth did *you* end up out here?"

Rodriquez smiled and imitated Josh's shrug. "I was a prodigy priest. During the peak of the drug cartel's power, I negotiated the release of several Columbian leaders. The church was grooming me to be the youngest Bishop of Columbia's biggest diocese, then—"

A rusty old Dodge sedan came up the road, and Rodriquez shook his head. "The rest of the story will have to wait." He went inside to inform the others.

As the car pulled up, the guerilla that had captured them stayed in the car and yelled, "The lava is approaching the only road out. We need to leave right now!"

Alejandra came out and told him to wait while they brought out the patients.

The man snapped, "I don't follow your orders, Chibcha! You follow mine!"

Josh ran inside with her to help bring the patients out. They tried to hurry, but had to be very careful with these, the most critical patients. When they came back out, the car was gone.

Looking down the road, the old Dodge was already a half block away. Josh yelled to Alejandra, "Tell your leader, his man just ran off with the car." Josh pulled the pistol he'd retrieved earlier from his pocket and ran down the road after him.

It was too far ahead and moving too fast even for Josh's amazing speed. He kept running, looking up the small streets for more cars. There were several, but they'd obviously been out of commission for a long time. As he approached the road that exited the village, the smoke got thicker. He saw the road crested a small hill and knew on the other side it wound down and into the forest.

He turned around and headed back, but before he had gone more than a few steps, he heard a scream from behind him. He turned and ran toward the exit road. As he topped the hill, he looked down and saw the Dodge surrounded by lava. The lava on both sides of the village had met at a low point in the road like a flooded river. The guerilla had tried to drive through it, but the tires melted and the metal rims spun in the lava. Josh ran down the hill toward the car as the guerilla climbed out a window and onto the roof.

Josh was 20 meters away when the car's gas tank, inches above the lava, ignited. Fire engulfed the car and set the guerilla's clothes on fire. Josh saw him stumble around on the roof screaming, until he fell face-first into the molten rock.

Josh backed away, shaking his head. He felt bad for the dead man, but was more concerned for the living. This was the only road out of town, and the lava wasn't just crossing the road, it was slowly crawling up the hill toward him.

12

LAVA

Josh ran back to the hospital. Their only chance was to find the highest ground and hope the lava would stop rising.

Inside the makeshift hospital, he quickly told Rodriquez and Elizabeth what he saw and added, "Turn the generator on. Let's pump water into any containers we can find."

Rodriquez said, "There's a two-story house near the center of town. It was too small for a hospital, but sits on higher ground and it's built of stone." He pointed. "It's three blocks from here."

It took multiple trips with makeshift slings, but after an hour, they managed to get everyone into the damaged, but solid house. Mostly empty, the owners of the house must have evacuated with their possessions. The house was only a meter higher than the hospital, but every centimeter might count.

Josh went upstairs. He found himself in a small room with windows and double-doors leading out to the roof. Going outside, he saw the top of the house was a giant rooftop balcony. Taller than any other house, it had an impressive view of the volcano. He guessed it belonged to someone important who used the rooftop for entertaining.

Smoke surrounded the village, but through the haze, he caught sight of a stream of lava rolling by the town on two sides. The smoke was thinning, probably because it had already consumed most of the vegetation. As long as it wasn't expanding toward them, it would have no new fuel.

He came downstairs. Alejandra was trying unsuccessfully to talk to her leader on the walkie-talkie, and Elizabeth was playing with her cell phone.

Josh looked at Elizabeth with raised eyebrows.

She said. "Alejandra gave our phones back. Since it was off, it still has some battery left."

Josh asked hopefully, "Cell signal?"

She shook her head. "No, *but* I pushed the panic button."

"The what?"

"You know. That new disaster app I told you about. It's part of the iMagine digital assistant."

Josh shook his head. "You're always playing with new apps." He had to admit, he sometimes tuned her out when she went geek on him.

She frowned. "It's the app that automatically sends out your position and situation via text, voice and email every few seconds."

"That'd be great if there were a working cell phone tower." Seeing her face, he quickly added, "But it certainly can't hurt and—"

A teeth-rattling boom shook their world. As loud as a nearby lightning strike, it lasted several seconds and then morphed into the sound of a freight train. The ground shook more violently than any previous aftershock. Rodriguez lost his footing and fell. Elizabeth dropped her phone, and Josh lurched against a wall. Bits of ceiling fell on them and new cracks opened in the walls. It finally subsided, but the sound never completely faded.

Josh carefully picked his way back up the damaged staircase and out onto the roof. There were more cracks, but it still felt solid. He turned toward the mountain and watched in fascination. Geysers of glowing molten rock sprayed from the top, pushing a column of roiling, gray smoke and ash high into the air. No National Geographic video could capture this spectacle.

The prevailing winds still kept the smoke and ash at bay, but nothing would stop the new river of lava crawling down the volcano's side. Only a couple kilometers away, the wave of smoke and fire was moving downslope toward them. It almost looked like slow-motion footage of a rising, red tsunami. The lava, already flowing on both sides of the village, created the optical illusion that they were moving slowly toward the volcano. He couldn't pull himself away from the spectacle. It was horrific but also fascinating. Softly, Josh said, "Jesse, I know I've used up my nine lives and then some, but if you're still out there, we could use some help."

There was no response.

He went back down and announced, "We need to move upstairs."

Smoky and growing hotter by the minute, everyone was sweating and coughing. As he carried the patients up, he was, once again, thankful for his amazing body. Laying the patients on the floor, they tried to keep them cool by sprinkling water on them. They also poured water on pieces of cloth and wrapped them around their nose and mouth to filter out the smoke.

With nothing else to do, Josh went back out on the rooftop balcony. Elizabeth joined him. The lava had reached the edge of the village on the volcano side, sending hot red fingers probing into the lowest parts of town. They watched as it engulfed the bottom of their old hospital and set it ablaze. Slowly creeping up the streets from every direction, Josh estimated they had less than an hour before their little island would be swallowed.

The thickening smoke and sweltering heat forced them back inside. Pulling the door shut behind them, Josh saw that almost everyone in their rooftop stronghold was coughing except the unconscious patients. Rodriquez was on his knees coughing and praying.

With sauna like temperatures, they poured more water on the patients and themselves. Josh went over to the window and watched a house — only a few blocks away — catch on fire. Looking back, he saw Elizabeth and Alejandra talking quietly and then hugging each other, wiping back tears.

When it couldn't get any worse, another explosion and earthquake rocked their world. Knocked to his knees, Josh looked up through the window. A kilometer-wide, boiling, gray ball of ash blew off the top of the volcano. Through the smoke, he saw fluorescent orange veins of ejected lava streaking through the huge cloud. Woven between the skyrockets of burning rock, danced blue-white lightning bolts. Despite their situation, he was spellbound by the interplay of nature's most brutal forces.

With no one looking, Josh pulled the pistol from his pocket. He dropped the magazine and checked it. It was full. At least they would avoid burning to death.

A blast of furnace-hot air blew the balcony doors open. Swirling smoke blinded them, accompanied by a rhythmic thumping sound.

Josh knew that sound! It wasn't the volcano. Trying to clear his eyes, he stumbled toward the unmistakable noise. Through slit eyes, he saw an H-60 Blackhawk helicopter approaching. The pilot skillfully set the right wheel on the edge of the balcony's stone wall.

Josh went into overdrive and started grabbing patients. The first was Alejandra's little brother. Unconscious, the tiny boy felt like a limp rag doll. As Josh reached the open helicopter door, a man in a flight suit and helmet took the little boy from his arms.

Elizabeth and Alejandra were coughing and stumbling, but helped him get the other two patients onboard.

Rodriquez, overcome by smoke and unable to walk, screamed at him to save the others. Josh ignored him and carried him to the Black Hawk's door. Last was Dieter. The large and seriously overweight doctor was barely conscious. Josh used a fireman's carry, but even with his amazing body, he staggered under the weight.

The heat was painfully intense. Looking down, he saw the lava had almost reached the bottom of their house. He yelled for Elizabeth and Alejandra to get into the helicopter.

Josh coughed violently, his back and stomach muscles straining as he tried to lift Dieter up to the helo's door. Elizabeth, Alejandra and one of the crew struggled to pull the doctor's dead weight in. Finally, Alejandra jumped back out of the helicopter onto the balcony wall. The tough little teenager helped push Dieter inside, but just as they got him aboard, a volcanic blast — combination shockwave and earthquake — hit them like a sledgehammer. The balcony wall under their feet began to collapse as the blast pushed the Black Hawk away from the roof.

Josh shoved Alejandra toward the helicopter door where a flight-suit-clad hand grabbed her arm, but the push sent Josh sprawling backward. As he fell between the helicopter and the crumbling balcony, he caught the edge of a steel railing. With his feet dangling only meters above the lava, everything began to move in slow motion. He heard the helo's turbine engines spinning up into a banshee scream as its blades slapped the air harder and harder. His clothes were close to the ignition point as the hot metal railing bent under his weight.

Using all his strength, he hoisted himself onto the crumbling balcony and staggered back half a dozen steps. The opening distance between the balcony and helo was impossible to bridge even for an Olympic athlete, and the helicopter was rolling away from him. Without thinking, he ran as hard as he could and launched himself off the balcony with his arms stretched in front of him. He clearly saw the face of one of the aircrew. It was the expression of someone watching a tragedy unfold.

The helo had no skids. If his outstretched fingers missed the bottom edge of the door, he would belly flop into the molten rock, and if the helicopter didn't stop its roll, it would hit the lava right after him.

Rolling away, the open door became an impossible target. Josh watched his fingers just miss the bottom of the door.

II

CONSPIRACY

"If these results are right . . . you have less than half the DNA of a normal human."

13

BLACK HAWK

The shockwave rolled the helo and threw Elizabeth backward and away from the open door. Hitting her head on the far side of the helicopter, she was stunned and slid to the deck. Fighting to remain conscious, she could barely move or focus her eyes. Her body bounced on the deck as the helo lurched and rolled. All she could do was gasp for air and hope they could remain airborne. Looking toward the open door, she couldn't see Josh.

Josh's dive took him under the helo's belly and on to his rendezvous with the lava . . . but the helicopter's rapid roll rotated the left wheel down into his flight path.

Twisting and stretching for all he was worth, the fingertips of one hand caught the wheel's shock strut. He grabbed it, almost wrenching his arm from its socket.

He hung from the Black Hawk's landing gear by one hand. The shock strut — radiantly heated by the lava — seared his skin. He looked down at molten death and had a brief moment of Antarctic déjà vu.

Fighting to right itself, the helicopter's buffeting threatened to shake loose his blistering hand and fingers.

Josh contracted his bicep and got his other hand onto the wheel's brake assembly. Blinded by ash and fighting the hurricane-force rotor wash, he chinned himself up and wrapped himself around the helicopter's wheel. He felt like a koala bear clinging to a branch in a cyclone.

Over his head, he saw the door on this side of the helicopter was closed. Managing to slide one hand carefully away from his death grip on the wheel, he pounded the door with the last of his strength. It took several tries before a crewmember looked out the window. His expression was priceless as he opened the door and pulled Josh inside.

Josh collapsed on his hands and knees. Coughing and wheezing, he looked forward into the cockpit. Through the windscreen, he saw nothing but dark gray. The overloaded Black Hawk was clawing its way through the boiling gray ash. The pilots were flying blind, carrying too much weight at too high an elevation. A glance at the instruments confirmed they were barely climbing and both engine-warning lights were illuminated. The turbines, running at redline, were ingesting large amounts of ash. There was nothing he could do to help, so he closed his eyes and tried to picture a positive outcome.

With one last turbulent drop, they broke into clear air and accelerated away from the erupting hell. Josh looked out the window and saw the volcano's caldera had partially collapsed in a cataclysmic explosion.

Trying to stop his coughing, and holding his burned hand against his chest, he looked around. The helicopter was configured for medevac with stacked stretchers installed on one side. He saw Elizabeth sitting with her back against a stretcher and her eyes closed. He crawled over, put his hand on her head and felt a good-sized lump.

She opened her eyes, and between coughs said, "Oh, there you are." She grabbed his good hand and held it in a vice grip as he carefully stroked her hair. Thankfully, she must have missed his unconventional entrance. He just sat on the floor of the helicopter holding her.

Looking toward the back of the helo, he noticed one of the crew wasn't wearing a flight suit or helmet. Instead, he wore fatigues with a holstered pistol, but even from the side, Josh recognized Tim Smith. He and Tim were similar height and build, but Tim looked like a classic Anglo-Saxon guy, with brown hair, brown eyes and no remarkable features. It was the perfect disguise for a truly remarkable man.

The deadly CIA operative glanced back at Josh and gave him a head nod.

Josh nodded back dumbly, wondering, *How on earth?* Still sitting on the floor, he leaned back against the stretcher support and closed his eyes for a second.

When he woke, Josh found himself lying against a soft equipment bag, sporting an oxygen mask and a bandage on his burned hand. Sitting up, he pulled the mask off and looked out the window next to him. The helicopter was approaching a small city. As they descended, he saw white colonial architecture. His internal clock said he'd been out for about 30 minutes. From his research on Columbia, he knew the city of Popayan, about 150 kilometers north, was nicknamed the "white city."

The skies were clear and the sun was setting over the hills, creating a beautifully serene vista. Sometimes, it took the very real possibility of death . . . to appreciate life. It explained the adrenaline junkie's quest, or at least provided a poetic excuse.

As the Black Hawk started its landing approach, Josh noticed ambulances and police waiting for them on the ground below. Looking back inside, he saw Elizabeth giving her windbreaker to Alejandra and dumping the guerilla's camouflage jacket into a medical trash bag. Curious, Josh watched Elizabeth take her own necklace with a cross, and place it over the young guerilla's neck. She then pulled Alejandra's hair back into a ponytail. He realized Elizabeth was transforming Alejandra from a dangerous guerilla into a cute teenager — an important distinction among those waiting below.

The pilot set the Black Hawk down gently. As soon as he could, Josh stepped out of the helo to allow the emergency medical team to offload patients. As the helicopter's engines shut down, Josh made a point of thanking the pilot and crewmembers with an appropriate South American hug.

He found Elizabeth near an ambulance, reporting the status of each patient to the EMTs. Alejandra stood next to Elizabeth holding her little brother's hand. As they loaded the small boy and his IV into the ambulance, his eyes opened and he smiled at his sister. The fluids, undoubtedly, spelled the difference between life and death for the child.

Smiling and crying, Alejandra hugged Elizabeth. Then, seeing

Josh, she ran to him and gave him a huge hug.

He kissed her forehead and in Spanish said, "Us Indians need to stick together." She hugged him again, and then jumped into the ambulance with her brother.

As it pulled away, Josh looked over and saw Rodriquez lying on a stretcher waiting to be loaded into another ambulance.

Rodriquez waved him over.

With the helicopter's engines shut down, it was quiet as Josh went to the priest's side.

Rodriquez pulled his oxygen mask off and said softly, "Thank you, but you should have left me behind."

"I couldn't. I'd never get to hear the rest of your story."

Rodriquez smiled. "We'll discuss it over a glass of wine someday after you complete your mission."

Josh shook his head. "I'm done with comets and volcanos for a while."

Rodriquez raised his eyebrows. "That's not the mission I meant."

Josh frowned. "What do you mean?"

The EMTs indicated they were ready to load him into the ambulance.

Grabbing Josh's hand, Rodriquez's eyes became unfocused as if he were staring through Josh. With a distant, inflectionless voice, he said, "The danger isn't from above. It's close, very close. You don't have much time." His eyes refocused as he let go of Josh's hand.

"Who told you that?"

Rodriquez ignored his questions and, sounding normal again, said, "My life has had many challenges, but . . ." he winked at Josh, "thank God I'm not a prophet."

"Wait!" Before Josh could question him, the EMT put the oxygen mask back on and Rodriquez closed his eyes. As they loaded him into the ambulance, Tim came over and stood next to Josh.

Seeing Josh's frown, Tim nodded toward the ambulance. "Is he going to be OK?"

"Yeah, *he* is . . . not so sure about the rest of us." Turning to Tim, he asked, "So how'd you find us? Did a satellite spot our plane in the river?"

"A satellite, yes, but it wasn't a photo bird. Weather was too bad. It was a SIGINT satellite. It locked onto one of your cell phone's transmissions and got the GPS coordinates. Took us right to you."

"Whose phone?"

"Elizabeth's."

Josh glanced at Elizabeth, who was sitting on the back of an ambulance, finally allowing the EMT to look at the bump on her head. Josh smiled and shook his head. "Great. I'll never hear the end of that one." Looking back at Tim, he said, "Not that I'm not happy to see you, but I don't imagine you just happened to be vacationing in the mountains of Columbia."

"Soon as I heard you were outside the U.S., I came."

Josh looked at him blankly.

In his usual deadpan, Tim said, "Last time you left the country, you dove off an Antarctic cliff. The next time, you stole and destroyed an Australian fighter. Then you—"

"*All right,* I get it."

Tim continued, "Davidson sent me here to give you a message because he couldn't reach you by phone. When I heard there was an airplane involved . . . ."

With a half-smile, Josh said, "What's the message?"

Tim looked around and quietly said, "Your personal records from the Prophet Operation were compromised."

"Compromised?"

"Someone broke into the CIA's computer system. They were searching specifically for your files and apparently downloaded everything the CIA knows about you."

Josh frowned. "I'm guessing it's not easy to break into CIA computers. Do we know who was behind it?"

"Not yet, but whoever they are, they knew what they were doing."

"Who'd be interested in *me*?"

"I was going to ask you the same question."

Josh thought for a moment. "I honestly don't know." He shrugged. "I'm a pretty likable guy."

With the slightest hint of a smile, Tim said, "Although the CIA did try to kill you last year."

Josh smiled. "I don't make a good first impression." Then, looking Tim in the eye, he said, "Regardless . . . thank you for saving our butts."

"Just returning the favor." He added, "You need to get back to D.C. and figure out what's going on."

Josh shook his head. "Can't leave Elizabeth, particularly now."

Tim's eyes narrowed. "If they're targeting you, your presence may actually put her at risk."

Josh frowned. "Hadn't thought of that."

Tim said, "I'll stay here and watch after her until we can get her back."

"OK. No one in the world I trust her life with more than you." For a second, he saw a flash of pain in Tim's eyes. Then his normal mask returned. He nodded, turned and left.

Exhausted, Josh and Elizabeth found one of the few hotels in Popayan that the earthquake hadn't damaged. They grabbed some basic food and collapsed into bed.

The next morning, they woke up sore and still coughing, but happy to be alive. Elizabeth called the U.N. Relief Director in Bogota. After she got off the phone, she said, "Josh, they're in desperate need of a neuro nurse here. I told them I'd stay in Popayan a couple days until they can replace me. Tim doesn't have to stay here and babysit."

Josh said, "This isn't open for debate. Until we get to the bottom of this, he'll be your shadow."

She rolled her eyes, but gave him a kiss.

Discovering the last flight out of Popayan was leaving in an hour, he rushed to the airport. On the way there, he realized he still hadn't told Elizabeth about his developing relationship with Jen.

14

RETURN

As soon as Josh arrived in D.C., he called the number Tim gave him for Davidson. They connected him with someone named Pat, who gave him a location and a time to meet. It was a suite at the Marriott in Tysons Corner, about six miles from Langley. Josh understood it was safer for all involved to meet outside the headquarters for now.

Josh knocked on the hotel room door. A large man in a suit opened the door and invited him in, then left. Davidson came over to shake Josh's hand, but seeing the bandage, patted him on the shoulder instead. "Good to see you, Josh."

"Thanks for sending Tim." With a wry smile, he added, "Although, I had the guerillas and volcano pretty much under control."

Looking at Josh's bandaged hand, Davidson smiled. "No doubt."

They sat down in upholstered chairs by the window.

Looking serious, Davidson asked, "Do you think that situation had anything to do with you specifically?"

Josh frowned. "I can't imagine someone disabling the entire GPS satellite system on the off chance I'd be in an old airplane with no nav aids and a pilot blindly following his iPhone."

Davidson nodded. "Actually, it wasn't the GPS satellites; it was just the navigation apps that used the GPS signal. It caused traffic jams across the globe, but you're right, I'd have trouble buying that even in a **Mission: Impossible** movie."

Josh said, "I told Tim, I can't think of who'd be aware of me much less out to get me." He paused. "Since you're now the director of the agency that tried to kill me," Josh smiled, "I feel relatively safe."

Davidson laughed.

Josh continued, "Do we know anything more about who broke in?"

"No, but we found out how they did it. Now we *are* talking a good **Mission: Impossible** plot. The computer rooms are shielded from cell signals, and all phones have to be turned off and turned in before entering. The hackers piggybacked a program onto the phone of one of our IT people. They disguised it as an update to one of his apps. Somehow, this program turned his phone back on after it had been set aside. The phone connected to a short-range Bluetooth system used to control peripheral equipment like printers. It somehow accessed the servers through that, broke through several levels of encryption, and found and downloaded your files. Then it shut the phone off. Once the phone was outside and turned back on, it transmitted the files."

"Wow."

"Yeah. The cyber guys were blown away by the sophistication of the attack."

Josh asked, "So, now that you know how it was done, can you prevent it from happening again?"

"Sure, but our cyber guys are worried."

"Why?"

"They said the bad guys didn't bother to hide how they did it."

Josh nodded thoughtfully. "So, that means they either got all they needed, or they're so far ahead of us, they believe they can gain access whenever they want."

Davidson nodded.

"Have there been any other attacks like this on government systems?"

"Based on the sophistication and method, our Cyber Warfare people think that whoever stole your files was behind the global traffic jams." He paused. "The entire U.S. is at INFOCON 4."

"INFOCON 4?"

"Stands for Information Operations Condition. It uses the same classification levels as DEFCON. Five is the lowest level and *One* is the highest. *One* would mean we're engaged in full-out cyber warfare.

Josh nodded. "So, what information did they get?"

"They copied all the Prophet Operation files. They know everything we knew about you up until the time you were shot and medevac'd to the carrier. At that point, we shut the operation down and closed the files." He added with a half-smile, "Mostly out of embarrassment."

"So they don't necessarily know I'm still alive."

"No . . . but the files included information about Elizabeth. It would be pretty easy to find you through her."

"What else was in the files?"

He grimaced. "Unfortunately, it included your medical records and the results of all the tests they did at the hospital: genetic, IQ and Dr. Lopez's psychological evaluation."

Josh nodded and then asked, "By the way, was there anything odd about any of my medical test results?"

Davidson smiled. "Yeah, your IQ was over 160, and the psychological test said you were paranoid." He smiled. "But, since we really *were* out to get you, we can probably disregard that diagnosis."

Josh smiled and then asked, "You mentioned a genetic test?"

"After you were identified as public enemy number one, we did a full genome mapping."

"Why?"

"Standard procedure on high-interest individuals. It sometimes helps us determine nationality and even family. It can also identify inheritable diseases, allowing us to track a suspect by treatment or medication. Of course, it can be used later to positively identify remains." Shrugging, he added, "It's a long shot, but we'd be crazy not to use it. In your case, it was easy to get tissue samples from the hospital."

Josh nodded and then casually asked, "Was there anything unusual about my genetic test results?"

Davidson shrugged. "Don't know."

"Why?"

"Apparently, the test didn't work. The lab said the tissue samples were bad."

Josh repeated, "Bad?"

Davidson shook his head. "I don't remember the details." He picked up and flipped through one of the files. After a few seconds, he said, "I think they only found part of your DNA." He closed the folder and handed it to Josh.

Josh asked, "Who else knows about me and these files?"

"Aside from Carl Casey and my Science Director, the Director of National Intelligence and the President are aware."

Josh nodded.

Davidson said, "Josh, I'm sorry about this." He leaned forward. "How about helping us figure out who stole your files? It's in the CIA's interest to find out who can hack what we thought was an un-hackable system, and if this was tied to the global traffic jam, whoever did it is a huge potential threat to national security." He paused. "But it's also in your best interest to figure out who might be gunning for you."

Josh thought for a moment and then nodded.

Davidson said, "Great. Would you be willing to work with Tim Smith?"

He nodded again.

Davidson stood up. "I'll have him contact you." Then frowning, he added, "Wait. I remember something else about your file. Shortly after we closed the operation, I got a call from the head of one of our labs. She asked if she could get more tissue samples from you. I told her you'd disappeared and were presumed dead. She was clearly disappointed. Really wanted a piece of you." He tilted his head slightly. "Any idea what that might be about?"

Josh looked down and shook his head.

15

DNA

After leaving the meeting with Davidson, Josh found and rented a second-floor, furnished apartment in D.C. Old on the outside and remodeled on the inside, it was conveniently located and outrageously expensive. However, with Elizabeth's U.N. work based out of D.C. and Josh working with the CIA at Langley, it made sense. For Josh, it was both comforting and frustrating to know his daughter, Caitlin, lived only a few miles away.

Elizabeth flew from Bogota to Austin to spend a day with her parents, and Tim flew to D.C. He told Josh to meet him at CIA Headquarters.

Josh asked, "Is that wise?"

Tim said, "Cat's already out of the bag."

The CIA headquarters had a very different feel for Josh than the last time he was here. The SR-71 Blackbird jet at the entrance no longer felt like Edgar Allen Poe's menacing raven. In a year, Josh had gone from public enemy number one to CIA ally.

They met in a small conference room.

As soon as Tim saw him, he asked, "How's your hand?"

Josh looked down at it. He'd removed the bandage. Just like his recovery from the bullet wounds, his hand had healed ludicrously fast. Holding it open, there was only a little pink skin where the burns had been. Josh shrugged. "Guess it wasn't as bad as it looked."

Tim looked at his hand, clearly surprised. Then frowned and shook his head. "Davidson said you're willing to help them figure out who cracked their computer."

Josh nodded and then looked at him curiously. "What exactly did you do when you worked for the CIA?"

Josh could tell he was debating how to answer. Finally, he said,

"I did a number of things, but started as an Exfil."

"What's an Exfil"?"

"Exfiltration."

Josh scratched his head. "Opposite of infiltration? You snuck out of places?"

"I snuck *people* out, out of places and deadly situations."

"Sounds dangerous."

Tim nodded. "I liked helping people escape, but that's not what we're here for. Let's talk about *your* skills and experience."

Josh smiled. "I can recite the Greek alphabet backwards in case we have to infiltrate a fraternity or sorority."

Ignoring his humor, Tim asked, "You have a photographic memory?"

Josh nodded. "And a knack for languages. I can speak Spanish, and I think I can learn other languages quickly."

Tim said, "That's very useful." He paused. "On Mount Howe, you got the jump on a SEAL. I assume you have a strong background in close-quarters combat?"

"Second-degree black belt in Karate, some judo and a military Expert qualification in pistol and rifle."

Tim nodded. "What's your experience as an intelligence operative?"

"None." Josh shook his head. "Tim, I was a strike-fighter pilot. I had a Top Secret clearance only because I was qualified to drop nuclear weapons and worked on classified defense programs. Never been a black ops guy."

Tim thought for a moment. "We can't do much until the Cyber Warfare people give us some leads. Would you be willing to do a little training with me?"

Josh shrugged. "Sure."

"Let's start tomorrow morning. I'll meet you at The Farm."

Josh nodded. "Sounds good . . . uh, where's *The Farm*?"

Josh picked Elizabeth up at Dulles airport. It had only been a few days since they had seen each other, but they hugged for quite a while. Finally, breaking the lock, Elizabeth smiled and asked, "Senor, do you still need assistance with your hard drive?"

Early the next morning, Josh slipped quietly out of bed. He smiled as he picked up their trail of clothes from the front door to the bedroom.

Grabbing an energy drink, he went to the living room and sat down on the couch. Although it was a furnished apartment, there was no desk. His laptop and Elizabeth's tablet sat on a coffee table in front of the couch. While it was booting up, he picked up the folder Davidson had given him and read it.

He decided to start with an Internet search on genetics. He ended up jumping from article to article and going down multiple rabbit holes. He was deep into a peripheral article, when he looked past the screen and saw Elizabeth's bare feet. He slid his eyes up those amazing legs, past her short silk bathrobe to . . . she wasn't smiling.

With one hand on her hip, the other hand held his cell phone by two fingers, as if it were radioactive. "Josh, would you mind telling me who *Jen* is?"

"I'm not sure."

"Not sure?" She asked with raised eyebrows. "A rather intimate conversation with someone you're *not sure* about." She turned the phone's display toward her and read, "Josh, what is love?"

He laughed. "Read the entire exchange from the beginning."

Frowning, she sat down next to him and started reading. After a minute, she sighed softly, "Wow. She's an incredibly precocious little girl, isn't she?" She furrowed her brow. "Her vocabulary's graduate-level," she shook her head, "but her questions are barely grade-school. How old is she?"

Josh smiled. "Keep reading."

Elizabeth read aloud, "Jen, how old are you? I'm seven." She shook her head.

Josh nodded. "I think she has an extremely high IQ."

Elizabeth looked sideways at him. "Like yours?"

Josh sighed and then slowly said, "I wondered if there were others . . . like me." He shook his head. "But I didn't expect to find a counterpart in the form of a little girl."

"Aren't you going to meet her?"

He raised his eyebrows. "Thirty-something man texts little girl,

'Let's meet.'"

"OK, but she must have parents. Can you talk to them?"

Josh nodded toward the phone.

Elizabeth scrolled down and then read aloud, "Jen, can I talk to your parents?"

"I don't have any parents."

"I'm sorry, Jen. Is someone taking care of you?"

"Yes."

"Can I talk to them?"

"No."

"Why?"

"If they knew I was talking to you, I would get in trouble."

Josh said, "That's why she only uses text."

Biting the side of her lip, Elizabeth looked over. "I don't want to sound paranoid, but could someone be posing as a little girl to gain your trust?"

"I thought of that, but it's not like I have any special access or hold a powerful position. What would they gain? Besides, someone trying to imitate a little girl wouldn't use her vocabulary."

She nodded and then handed him his phone with a smile. "She has a crush on you."

Josh laughed. "I think I need to introduce you two." He paused, looking serious. "Or maybe not . . . in a few years, she could be totally hot-looking."

She slapped his chest playfully. "You're right. She needs a big sister."

Smiling, he put his arm around her and pulled her close. After a few moments, he said, "I know how important your work is, but I'm glad to have you here for a while."

"Me too." She paused. "But I *will* have to see where they need me next."

"I know." He sighed. "That's one of the things I love about you." He kissed her. "So, how'd you get along with Mr. Smith?"

She laughed. "He's such a sweetie."

Josh looked at her with surprise. "We're talking about *Tim* Smith?"

"Yeah, yeah, I know he's like super deadly and all, but he was so thoughtful. He always offered to help and was right in there when we needed to move patients. The staff assumed he was a nurse." She shook her head. "He was so protective. He slept in a chair outside my room every night. I can see what Sheri loves about him."

Josh nodded. "If it weren't for Tim, London would be in ruins and possibly the entire world."

She nodded. Then, looking at his laptop screen, she asked, "Genetics?" With a raised eyebrow, she said, "And what are we up to *now*, Commander Fuze?"

He handed her his CIA file. "This is what the hackers stole." He paused. "Evidently, the CIA did a full genome scan on me . . . or tried to. The results are in there, but it's in medical jargon. Been trying to decipher it."

She sat back on the couch, propped her long legs up on the coffee table and began to read the files. After a minute, she picked her tablet up off the table and set it on her knees.

Even in the glow of the tablet screen, he couldn't help but think how beautiful she was.

She glanced over at him and read his intentions. Smiling, she said, "Hold on there, sailor. Let me finish reading this."

After a couple minutes, she looked up from her tablet. "OK, if I understand this correctly, they ran the test three times with two samples, but came up with the same erroneous results." She looked back at him. "They couldn't find all your DNA."

He nodded. "Yeah, that's what Davidson said."

She continued slowly, "But what's *interesting* is the final note by the lab technician." She read, "Despite having only half the normal DNA, the tissue sample appears to contain a complete human genome. Somehow, only the non-coding DNA is missing."

"I saw that, but what's *non-coding* DNA?"

Elizabeth said, "Been a long time since I took a Genetics class, so I looked it up. Non-coding DNA — often called *junk* DNA — is the part of our chromosomes that doesn't do any coding or protein synthesis. About ninety-eight percent of our DNA is classified as non-coding."

Josh frowned. "Then what does it do?"

She shrugged. "We're not really sure. It doesn't appear to do anything. One theory suggests most of it is *legacy* code."

Josh looked at her blankly.

She put her finger to her lips in thought and then said, "Let me use a computer analogy. Computer operating systems, like Windows, have thousands of lines of computer code. If you were to examine the code, line by line, you'd discover some of it doesn't appear to do anything. It's sometimes called legacy code. It was from an earlier version, but it's obsolete or controls something that no longer exists. They don't always take the time to clean all of it out, and taking it out can sometimes cause problems. It's often easier to leave it alone or make it inactive." She paused. "It's possible our bodies have some *legacy* DNA code."

"So, could you just cut out the non-coding DNA?"

She looked thoughtful. "I don't know, but if these results are right," she looked him in the eye, "you have less than *half* the DNA of a normal human."

16

THE FARM

The next morning, Josh drove from D.C. to The Farm. It was an unseasonably warm spring day, and he drove with the windows down. The trees along the road were waking up from winter with colorful blossoms. Unfortunately, the beautiful rolling landscape was lost to him as he tried to figure out how he could have misplaced half his DNA. Or, more accurately, how Jesse did it. With his body's amazing abilities, he knew he was genetically different, but until now, had no idea *how* different. When he woke up after the crash, Jesse told him his new body was enhanced with one-in-one-hundred-million abilities. Then, when he saw himself in the hospital mirror, he realized he must have been given humanity's best genes spanning all races. Now, it appeared Jesse had also stripped down his genes to the minimum required. As an engineer, he liked that idea, but it also made him feel a little like a freak.

His phone's digital assistant interrupted his thoughts. "You have a text message from Jen. Would you like me to read it?" He'd jokingly named his digital assistant Hal, after the relaxed but psychotic computer in the classic movie **2001**.

Josh said, "Yes."

Hal replied, "Would you like me to roll the windows up?"

He smiled. "Yes." It was a simple programming trick. Using the GPS, the digital assistant knew he was moving 80 miles an hour and was, therefore, in a car. So, it automatically switched to voice notification. Since it also synced with the car's computer, it knew the windows were down and what the ambient noise level inside the car was.

As soon as the windows closed, Hal read the voice text through the car's audio system. "Did the gorillas try to eat you?"

Josh smiled. Before he knew Jen's age, he'd mentioned their adventures in Columbia. He realized he'd have to be more careful with his voice texting and check the spelling before sending. "No, Jen. I'm sorry. I spelled that wrong. They weren't gorillas. They were G U E R I L L A S — a group of people trying to overthrow their government by military force. Our airplane made an emergency landing in an area they controlled."

Her reply came back immediately. "Why did you make an emergency landing?"

"We were out of fuel and had to land in a river instead of on a runway."

"Why did you run out of fuel?"

"We got lost."

"Why were you lost?"

Josh laughed. Just like his nephew, when he was little, every answer resulted in another question. "Jen, it was an old airplane. Our pilot was using his phone's navigation app and apparently there was something wrong with it." With her vocabulary, he didn't have to worry about using big words."

She said, "That's terrible."

"It's OK. We landed safely and it just took a few days to find us." He was almost at The Farm, and before she could ask more questions, he said, "Jen, I'm going to be doing some training for a few days and won't always have my phone with me."

"You mean I won't be able to talk to you?"

He realized they were voice texting several times a day. She was a sweet kid. Maybe he wouldn't have made a bad dad after all. "Jen, I promise, if I don't have my phone, I'll check in with you at the end of the day."

As Josh pulled up to the gate, he realized he'd been here before. It was many years ago, right after he graduated and was commissioned in the Navy. While waiting for flight school, he reconnected with an old girlfriend from high school. She told him she was living with her parents on a base in Virginia and invited him to visit. There were plenty of military bases in that area, but he was surprised he'd never heard of this one. When he asked what her father did, she told him he was involved with *experimental training*.

He later learned that was a euphemism often used in the intelligence and special operations world. In hindsight, he was glad he'd been a gentleman.

Despite the pastoral setting, the security was tighter than any base he'd seen. The guards at the gate carried M16s at the ready, and a military ID wasn't sufficient for entry without an escort. Fortunately, they were expecting him this time and he received a full-access badge.

Tim had given him directions to the gym. As they met, he took Josh right into one of the training rooms with mats on the floor.

Josh asked, "Should we change first?"

"In the real world, you'll be fighting in whatever you're wearing. Let's try some basic takedowns. See where we are."

Josh was confident. In addition to his martial arts background, his new body's strength and agility were phenomenal. Josh moved in on Tim for a judo take town. His execution was perfect, but as he completed the move, he felt a sharp pain in his groin and hesitated. Before he knew what was happening, he was on the floor with his neck under Tim's foot.

Tim let him up.

Josh got up slowly. Leaning over with his hands on his knees and waiting for the pain to subside, he looked at Tim questioningly.

Tim, looking very serious, said, "When you're fighting in the real world, you're not going for tournament points. Fighting fair on your part isn't recommended if you want to survive."

Josh just nodded.

Tim added, "We'll work on vulnerabilities that you need to protect *and* can take advantage of."

His photographic memory helped, but being able to spar with Tim made all the difference.

After a couple hours, Tim called an end to the session.

Josh said, "Almost everything you taught will result in my opponent's death. There must be times when you need to disable without killing."

"Yes."

Josh smiled. "So, are you going to teach me, like the *Vulcan* neck pinch or something?"

"There are a couple techniques we use to immobilize without

harming, but they take a lot of practice to master." Tim went over to a small case he'd brought with him. "Sometimes, we get help from technology." He opened the case and pulled out something that looked like a class ring. "It's a tiny Taser."

Josh held out his hand.

Tim hesitated and then handed it to him. As Josh put it on the ring finger of his right hand, Tim continued, "You can simply touch someone on the neck or shoulder or even shake their hand and completely incapacitate them."

Josh held up the ring on his hand and studied it. He felt a small indentation on one side.

Tim continued, "But it takes some training to use effectively because—"

There was a popping sound.

Josh found himself face down on the floor, feeling like he'd been hit in the back with a two-by-four.

In the same monotone, Tim finished, "*Because* unless you wear a specially insulated glove, it's easy to tase *yourself* instead of your target."

Regaining muscle control, Josh rolled over on his back and said, "Ouch."

Tim offered a hand.

Josh reached up with his right hand.

Tim pulled his hand back and said, "Other hand."

As he stood up, he got a rare smile from Tim. "They require everyone who's issued one of these to experience it. *Congratulations.*"

Rubbing his face where the floor struck it, Josh said, "So you *do* have a sense of humor."

Tim nodded, still smiling. "That *was* actually very funny."

Josh shook his head. "Glad I could help." He carefully took the ring off and offered it to Tim.

"Keep it. You'll be more receptive to learning its operating and safety procedures. By the way, except for that one, no rings or jewelry should be worn here or when operational."

Josh frowned as he glanced down at his wedding ring. Elizabeth had it specially made out of small, gold pilot wings.

Tim explained, "You don't want any obvious indication of your background, what school you went to, whether you're married, or that you were a Navy pilot. The bad guys can figure that out pretty quickly. Don't make it easier for them."

Josh slipped his wedding ring off and put it in his pocket.

They wrapped up, and Josh checked into his base quarters. His muscles were sore from the workout and the self-induced tasing. Despite the abuse, however, he realized how fortunate he was to have Tim as a mentor. Josh was a martial-arts-trained athlete with phenomenal chromosomes, but he was certain Tim could kill him in seconds without working up a sweat. Experience and training almost always trumped raw talent. He would learn everything he could.

The next day, they practiced more close-quarters combat and then went to a gun range. Tim introduced him to several different weapons, some he'd only seen in movies. Josh had achieved the highest military rifle and pistol qualification, and could easily put rounds into the bull's eye. After seeing this, Tim said, "Congratulations, you're good at hitting defenseless, stationary pieces of paper."

They went to a place Tim called the dynamic range. Targets popped up all over, accompanied by distractions. It was one thing to concentrate on a bull's eye. It was very different evaluating and shooting moving targets under constantly changing conditions. He enjoyed the training. It reminded him of carrier landings in the simulator, where knowing it was a simulation didn't stop the adrenaline or sweat.

Tim told Josh he wanted to put him into some basic classes he referred to as "tradecraft." Late that afternoon, he introduced Josh to the head of the school, Stuart Nickles.

Nickles said, "Davidson asked me to facilitate you in any way possible. We'd be happy to insert Commander Fuze into any of the ongoing classes." He offered Tim a sheet and said, "Here's where each class is in the curriculum."

As Tim read through it, Nickles added, "Tim, any chance we could have you do a guest lecture while you're here?"

Tim handed the sheet back to him. "Let's put him in class nine." He shook his head. "Stuart, it's been too long. There's nothing useful I could teach anymore."

Nickles looked over the top of his glasses at Tim. "You serious? I don't want to impose, but when we get an operative of your reputation . . . ." He smiled. "Any topic, any topic at all, I'll pull all the classes together for a session."

Tim shook his head. "Sorry."

They inserted Josh into a class of six. It was apparent this was a group of fit, intelligent and highly motivated men and women. In their early- to mid-twenties, Josh was the old man in the class. He realized this was the real spy stuff and found much of it fascinating, some of it confusing and some of it surprisingly boring.

On his third day at the base and second day in class, he met Tim for lunch at the dining facility. After they ate in silence for several minutes, Josh asked, "How's Sheri?"

"She's fine."

Josh waited for more, and finally asked, "How are you guys doing together?"

"Fine."

Smiling, Josh said. "Hope *Sheri* didn't say 'fine.' I've learned when women say 'fine,' it doesn't mean that."

Tim looked up. "Part of learning how to be a good operative is to avoid talking about your personal life."

Josh shrugged. "*Whatever.*"

Looking around, he saw some of the students from his class at a nearby table. He noticed they were watching him. Then realized it wasn't *him* they were watching; it was Tim. Josh leaned in and said quietly, "Looks like you've got some admirers."

As Tim glanced over, Josh added, "I think you're more famous here than Sheri is with the paparazzi."

Tim shook his head dismissively and kept eating.

Josh persisted. "Tim, there have been, what, a couple dozen people ever awarded the Intelligence Cross in *history*?"

Tim looked up abruptly. "How'd you know about that?"

"Facebook."

Tim rolled his eyes.

Josh smiled. "Brian Davidson told me."

"The award was classified."

With a slight smile, Josh said, "The only reason it's classified is because it's awkward explaining why *your* former boss shot a Tomahawk cruise missile at us."

Tim shrugged. "There are only a handful of people who know about that award."

Josh raised his eyebrows. "You think so?" Smiling, he nodded toward the student's table. "You don't think that type of news travels back-channel inside the agency?"

Tim shook his head. "They don't know who I am, and I prefer it that way."

Josh looked at him seriously. "Tim, hate to tell you this, but it's not just about you. These men and women are about to put their lives on the line. They'll never be able to talk about what they do, and some will die in the line of duty without anyone ever knowing. They need to know they're making a difference and that there are some real heroes."

Tim looked back at the table of students.

They all gave him a nod.

With a slight frown, Tim gave them a nod back and then kept eating.

Josh had an idea.

17

SURVEILLANCE

After his afternoon class, Josh went for a run. It was just before sunset and the temperature was perfect. As he ran, he decided this was the cleanest, best-maintained base he'd ever seen, and he'd seen quite a few. Nestled among the tall southern pines, it looked more like a nature preserve. Even the base water tank was painted forest green. The only giveaway was a large collection of antennas sprouting from the top of the tank.

Josh followed meandering roads that took him past ponds filled with geese and blue heron. He dodged a herd of deer and saw wild turkey. As he ran along the edge of a fresh-water marsh, it opened up onto the York River just in time for a spectacular sunset.

Stopping, he watched the sun sink into the choppy, gray water. He breathed in the earthy smells of the marsh and listened to the sounds of the geese and ducks. He was enjoying the beauty and serenity . . . until the distant sound of automatic gunfire broke the moment. The base's gun ranges, and the many "Limited Access" signs, were reminders. As beautiful as it was here, this wasn't a nature preserve. It was a training facility for operatives in a dangerous world.

After cleaning up, Josh checked his phone. Sure enough, there were text messages from the two women in his life.

Elizabeth let him know her schedule and asked how he was doing. Josh texted back that he was missing her but learning a lot about "*agriculture*," and shared his most recent conversations with Jen.

Jen's text said, "I looked up guerillas. Did they try to shoot you?"

He voice texted back, "No, Jen, they didn't."

She responded quickly. "What if they had shot you? Would you die?"

Her question could be simple curiosity, or having no parents, she might be concerned that something might happen to him. He suspected he was one of her few friends. He voice texted back, "Although people can die from a gunshot, I'm pretty tough. I was accidentally shot once, and I recovered just fine." Time to change the subject. "Jen, what do you like to do?"

"I like to look stuff up on the Internet."

Frowning, he asked, "Does anyone monitor what you do online?"

"Not really. I know more about computers than they do."

He shook his head with a smile. Every year, kids understood and embraced technology faster than the previous generation. Josh carefully asked, "Jen, are the people who take care of you treating you well?"

"I don't want to talk about it."

That worried him. He had to find out what her situation was. "Jen, I'm sorry, I just want to make sure you're OK and no one is hurting you."

"No one's hurting me." There was a delay. "Mostly they ignore me."

It was hard to know if this was just the normal frustrations of a little girl not getting enough attention, or if she really was being neglected. The fact that he was having extensive text conversations with a seven-year-old wasn't a good sign.

"Jen, what do you mean by ignore?"

"Can we talk about something else?"

Josh sighed. He committed to find out where she lived and who was responsible for her. Both to make sure she was OK, and because her situation might provide clues to his own existence. "OK, Jen, we can talk about it later. Do you know that not all the information on the Internet is correct?"

"Yes, a lot of it doesn't make sense or it says the opposite of something else, and the news makes me sad."

"Jen, you shouldn't read the news all the time. News only reports the bad things that happen in the world, not the good things." Josh was not happy with her guardians. They apparently weren't monitoring her computer use or giving her any guidelines. He talked to her about how to verify information sources and gave her websites that reported news more appropriate for her age. He also told her that if she ever had trouble reaching him to contact Elizabeth.

After finishing with Jen, Josh wasn't sleepy, so he walked over to the Student Recreation Building. He got a beer and sat down at a table to watch the news. The big story was about a large drop in the stock market, but what caught his interest was that they were attributing it not to economic news, but to a fear of stock manipulation. Hackers had broken into the Wall Street financial system and artificially driven several stocks up. The reason for the fear was that they had yet to figure out how it had been done.

As he was pondering that, four students from his class — two men and two women — asked if they could join him. Josh nodded. He knew he was a celebrity only by association. Like students everywhere, they talked about the courses and instructors.

Sam, which was short for Samantha, said, "We heard through the grapevine that the man you were having lunch with was awarded the Intelligence Cross. Is that true?" Sam looked like a mid-twenties Halle Barry, but with striking golden-green eyes.

Josh set his beer down and said, "I can neither confirm nor deny that." Looking around, he quietly added, "But . . . if it were true," he smiled, "would you like to hear how it might have happened?"

They grinned and leaned in.

Tim couldn't tell the story, and even if he could, he wouldn't. Josh believed it was important for these people to know about men like Tim. Josh had taken no oath of secrecy, but the details weren't required to illustrate Tim's heroism. Without implicating the former director of the CIA or mentioning the SEALs, he told them how Tim cleverly sabotaged the bad guy's vehicles and helicopter to buy precious time. He described how Tim turned the tables on a heavily armed soldier and took him hostage. Finally, he gave them a blow-by-blow description of how Tim, facing certain death from an MP5 machine gun, activated a system that saved thousands of lives. He left out where the bullets intended for Tim ended up. Finally, wrapping up, he said, "And if that weren't enough, less than a week ago, he saved my life and the lives of seven others in a daring helicopter rescue." He winked. "I'll tell you that story sometime, but now, if you'll excuse me, we old folks need our beauty rest." He exited quickly to avoid further questioning.

Josh had always been a good storyteller and knew he'd captured their imagination. He smiled knowing they would quietly retell the story many times.

Over the next couple of days, he finally got to the fun training; he and Tim played with cars. Tim set up situations that mimicked ones he'd actually faced. Josh found his fighter pilot skills helped, but some maneuvers weren't intuitive; they went against everything Mr. Miller taught in Driver's Ed.

After doing a high-speed, wheel-screeching, tire-smoking power slide into a spinout, Josh yelled, "That was awesome! Let's do it again."

Tim, sitting next to him and still holding on to the roof handle, said quietly, "In addition to killing us, you probably would have taken out quite a few innocent bystanders."

Josh still grinning said, "You don't like roller coasters, do you?"

Between the sessions with Tim, Josh attended class, where he learned surveillance, counter-surveillance detection, clandestine communication, etc. Since he had his own personal tutor, he didn't participate with the class in the exercises outside the classroom. This was probably good because he quickly realized . . . he sucked at this. He'd found something for which he had no talent or patience.

After a particularly unproductive session, Tim brought him back over to talk to the school's director. Nickles was an expert in many of the areas in which Josh struggled.

Nickles asked him, "Are you familiar with the OODA Loop?"

Josh said, "Yeah, it stands for Observe, Orient, Decide, Act." Most fighter pilots were familiar with the heretical John Boyd and his legendary loop. It was a high-speed thought process designed to keep the enemy off balance, and drove everything from fighter engagements to the Blitzkrieg.

Tim said, "Josh was a fighter pilot."

Nickles said, "Tim told me you're exceptionally good at three out of four."

Josh said flatly, "Observe."

Nickles nodded. "Yeah, that's the missing piece. Unfortunately, the success of the rest of the loop depends on your situational awareness."

After an hour with Nickles, Josh learned a lot. He also learned he'd probably never excel in spy tradecraft. Following the session, Josh grabbed dinner by himself at the dining facility. Sam, the classmate who'd asked him about Tim, came over to his table as he was finishing up.

"Didn't see you in class today."

Josh gave her a wry smile. "Got sent to the principal's office."

She laughed. "You know. You haven't told us *your* story."

Josh shrugged. "Nothing to tell. I'm just Mr. Smith's assistant."

Studying him with surprising intensity, she raised an eyebrow and said, "Is that so?"

Not wanting to carry the conversation further, he picked up his tray and winked. "See you in class."

Josh walked slowly over to the indoor pool. It was right next to the dining hall, but of course, he'd have to wait 20 minutes so he wouldn't get a cramp and drown. He smiled at the tale perpetuated by moms across the world.

When he got there, the pool was empty. He liked having the place to himself. After changing in the locker room, he jumped in and started doing laps. Within a few minutes, he heard a splash. He glanced over and saw someone swimming in the lane next to his. As they passed, he could tell it was a woman.

He finished his last lap and stood up in the shallow end with his head and shoulders out of the water. Catching his breath, he watched the other swimmer approach. She stopped next to him and stood up. It was Sam.

With a half-smile, she said, "You know you're not supposed to be swimming here alone."

He frowned. "Why not?"

She nodded toward a sign on the wall — 'No lifeguard on duty.' "For safety, we're *supposed* to use the buddy system."

Josh laughed. "That's a bit *ironic,* don't you think?"

She smiled.

Tilting his head, he asked, "Sam, did you follow me over here?"

She gave him a challenging look. "Didn't see me, did you?"

"No. No, I didn't."

Still smiling, she said, "We're in one of the few places in the world where stalking is not only allowed, it's graded." Tapping a finger on her lips, she added, "Let me guess. The reason you were sent to the principal's office was . . . *counter-surveillance* detection?"

He shrugged.

With confidence, she said, "I'm very good at it. Maybe I can help you?"

"Thanks, Sam, I really appreciate the offer, but I'm not going to be here long, and you don't need any distractions from your studies."

Looking at his shoulder, she asked, "Is that one of the scars from the bullet wounds?"

Narrowing his eyes, he said, "What are you talking about?"

She said, "We had to validate your story, so some of us cornered Mr. Smith. He wouldn't say much, but he did tell us one thing." She looked him in the eye. "He said he wouldn't have been able to do what he did, if you hadn't taken three bullets intended for him."

Josh shook his head and headed for the edge of the pool. Over his shoulder, he said, "He shouldn't have said that."

She replied, "Turnabout's fair play."

He hopped out of the pool. Trying to keep it light, he added, "Thanks for keeping me out of trouble with the pool Nazis."

Toweling off, he headed for the shower, but just before he got to the locker room, he heard, "Josh, wait."

He turned around. He'd only seen Sam in jeans, sweatshirts and combat boots. As she climbed gracefully out of the pool in a one-piece swimsuit, he saw an amazingly sleek and beautiful design as well as a nice-looking swimsuit.

She flipped her long black hair over her shoulder. Gently dabbing herself with a towel, she sauntered toward him. Stopping directly in front of him, she tilted her head slightly as she reached out and touched the scar on his shoulder. "One." Then she slid her finger slowly down his chest to the scar on his stomach. "Two." Finally, looking up at him with those golden-green eyes, she slid her finger down to the top of his swimsuit, which covered the third scar. "Three?"

Stepping back slightly, he said, "Sam, I'm—"

She interrupted, "Our next class covers ways to expedite information acquisition. Of course, everyone calls it *seduction* class." With raised eyebrows she said, "Maybe you can *help* me with my homework."

Before he could respond, she turned and headed into the woman's locker room, peeling her swimsuit down as she turned the corner.

18

CONSPIRACY

Josh exhaled slowly and shook his head in amazement. He couldn't help but smile. *That* was the sexiest invitation he'd ever received in his life . . . right out of a Bond movie.

The next day was particularly difficult. Josh blew a couple exercises with Tim.

Finally, Tim said, "It's late, and it's Friday. Sheri's in town and told me to bring you over for dinner. We have a little place nearby."

Relieved to be finished, and remembering she was an awesome cook, he said, "Great."

Tim said, "Meet me at the base marina."

"Marina?" He shrugged. "OK." After a quick stop at his quarters, Josh drove to the small marina.

Tim was untying a 24-foot Boston Whaler. The center console design and robust construction kept them popular with law enforcement and the military.

Josh stepped aboard. "Where are we going?"

Tim pointed across the river.

It was overcast, hazy and just past sunset. Josh couldn't make out anything on the opposite shore about two miles away. A 15-knot wind made the gray water choppy and the ride rough.

Tim conned the boat from the standup center console with Josh standing beside him. Tim was unusually talkative. Yelling over the twin outboards, he said, "I bought this place 10 years ago when I was an instructor at The Farm. It originally belonged to a writer named William Fitzgerald Jenkins. He was one of the most prolific science fiction authors of the mid-1900s."

Josh nodded.

Halfway across the river, Josh was surprised there weren't more houses on the wooded shoreline, and the ones he did see were modest.

Tim said, "He came up with the idea of parallel universes."

Josh nodded again. "I've always been fascinated with cosmology." He smiled. "Think there's another *you* out there somewhere?"

Tim shrugged. "Not sure the universe needs another me, but it's hard to believe that would be allowed."

Curious, Josh asked, "Do you believe in a supreme being?"

Tim frowned and then cryptically said, "We're not on speaking terms."

Josh waited to see if there would be any clarification. As usual, there wasn't.

As they got closer to the shore, he saw a two-story boathouse dead ahead. It looked old, with heavily weathered, gray wood siding and a simple gabled roof. The bottom level was a big boat garage with two large slips. As Tim guided the boat into one of the slips, Josh asked, "Are you related to Jenkins?"

Tim cut the engines and said, "No, but my grandfather worked at the base during WWII. Jenkins spent most of his time in New York and rented this house to my grandfather."

Josh stepped off onto the wooden deck that framed the boat slip. As he tied the bowline to a cleat, he said, "I thought the CIA wasn't created until after WWII."

"It wasn't." Tim trimmed the outboard motors up and out of the water. "My grandfather was a Navy Chief Warrant Officer when this was a military base." He stepped off the boat and secured the aft line. Nodding toward the shore, he said, "I rent out the main house — you can see through the trees — but I kept the boathouse for our use whenever we're in town."

Josh looked skeptically at the weather-beaten structure above him. He estimated the living area was only 30 by 25 feet.

Tim's phone rang. Glancing at the number, he told Josh, "Go ahead. I'll be right up."

Josh stepped outside onto a narrow deck that wrapped most of the boathouse perimeter. He heard the squawk of seagulls, and looking up river, saw broken wooden piers jutting out of the water.

At one time, they must have underpinned a large dock. Now, they were simply convenient perches for the gulls and pelicans. Tracing the brown pilings back to the land, he saw white oyster shells covering the shoreline. He guessed it had been an oyster dock in the time of Tim's grandfather.

Walking around the narrow dock to the shore side of the boathouse, he saw a rickety-looking wooden staircase leading up to the second floor. Despite appearances, the steps felt solid as he climbed to what he guessed was the "front door." He stood on the small landing and knocked.

The door opened on a hot-looking, petite, Latino woman with attitude. Dr. Sheri Lopez smiled and said, "Get your butt in here." Looking behind him, she said, "Where's Tim?"

Josh said, "He fell off the boat. Sharks ate him. What's for dinner?"

She laughed. "I'd be more concerned about the sharks. Let me guess, he's on the phone."

Josh nodded. "Yup."

She shook her head and said, "Come here." They hugged like family.

As he stepped back, he grinned at her. "Man, it's good to see you again, Sheri. You look awesome."

Grinning back, she said, "And you're still cute as a bug." Pulling him in, she nodded toward the living area. "Make yourself comfortable. Playoffs will be starting soon. Can I get you something to drink?"

In his best Oxford accent, he said, "Budweiser . . . shaken not stirred." As he looked around, he realized the outside was merely a disguise for an amazing little vacation home. Beautifully decorated in a modern nautical theme, it had bamboo hardwood floors and matching walls dominated by large windows that looked out over the river. There was a small but fully equipped kitchen complete with granite countertops. He headed for the living area. It had a plush-looking dark blue couch and two matching recliners facing a giant wall TV. Josh confirmed the comfort by plopping onto the couch.

Sheri pulled a beer from the fridge and lobbed it at him.

He barely caught it, as he heard her say, "*Shaken,* not stirred."

Setting the beer on the coffee table to settle, he found the remote.

Sheri, with a glass of wine in hand, joined him. "Fill me in on what happened after you got yourself shot."

He caught her up on his recovery, their simple wedding and then quickly covered their adventure in Columbia. Then he asked, "Tim saved my butt." He paused. "So, how are you and Tim doing?"

She smiled. "We're getting married . . . *but* you can't tell anyone. It's a secret." She laughed. "No. I mean, *really*, it's a secret. He says it's for my own protection." She shook her head. "*Whatever.*"

Josh grinned. "Congratulations! How'd you pull that off?"

Sheri shook her head. "I didn't. Remember, I'm the pragmatic one. I would've been happy just living together. He insisted." Smiling she said, "Tim's thoughtful, patient and," she added quietly, "romantic. I'm such a sucker for you strong, silent types." She tilted her head slightly. "I think he's happy, too, but he's so dang quiet, it's hard to tell sometimes . . . and I'm a psychiatrist."

With a smile, Josh said, "A wise woman once told me, 'You're too close. It's like trying to read yourself.'"

She laughed. "Did I say that?"

He nodded and then carefully asked, "How's he doing with the . . . accident?"

She sighed softly. "He still has nightmares." She shook her head. "It wasn't his fault. Anyone who saw someone coming through a window at night — dressed in black and holding what looked like a gun — would have fired." She shook her head gently, staring past him. Then looking back at him, added, "But he created an anonymous trust fund for her children. That's helped him deal with it." Sighing again, she concluded, "We'll keep working on it."

Josh nodded. After a respectful pause, he asked, "Sheri, can I ask you a psychology question?"

"Depends."

"On what?"

She laughed. "On whether I feel like answering it or not."

He smiled and pulled out his phone. Calling up the text with Jen, he handed it to her. "Need your professional opinion on how to handle this."

Sheri took the phone and started reading. After a few minutes, she looked up at him with raised eyebrows and a slight smile. "So, you really *aren't* quite human?"

He rolled his eyes. "That's not what I want your opinion on." Waving at his phone, he said, "She's obviously very intelligent and has latched onto me." He paused. "But I'm concerned about her and want to make sure I'm saying the right things."

Sheri shrugged. "Josh, it's tough with nothing but text." She paused. "But if I were to guess, I'd say she's probably high-genius level. Obviously very techno savvy, but with her intelligence, that's not surprising. I have a three-year-old niece that can operate my iPhone better than I can." She shrugged and handed the phone back. "She clearly has an affinity for you."

Frowning, Josh said, "So, am I doing the right thing by talking to her?"

She shook her head. "I'm not the right person to ask. I have no background in child psychology, I'm not a parent *and* I really don't even like kids."

He just looked at her.

She sighed. "You're doing fine. You're answering her questions honestly, but keeping the concepts simple." She smiled. "I think she's lucky to have you in her life."

"Thanks, Sheri." Changing the subject, he asked, "So, when do you think they're going to give me my Aston Martin?"

She looked thoughtful. "Josh, do you like fishing?"

"What?"

"Do you like to fish?"

He shook his head and said, "No." Then added, "I mean I might if you actually caught fish instead of sitting around staring at fishing line. Why do you ask?"

"I can't stand fishing either, but Tim loves it. Josh, you and I are thrill-seekers."

"I wouldn't call myself a thrill-seeker."

She looked at him incredulously. "You jumped off a cliff, stole a fighter and ejected over the South Pole."

"I had to."

She shook her head with a slight smile. "So, you're telling me you've never done anything impulsive or dangerous that you didn't have to do?"

"Maybe."

With raised eyebrows, she said, "Well?"

He gave her a half-smile. "When I was a lieutenant, I took a fighter on a cross country flight to Yuma, Arizona, to get some instrument time. Visited a high school buddy and his family. From the questions they asked, it was clear they had no idea what I did. They actually asked me if I'd ever flown upside down. So . . . when they took me back to the base, I noticed a knoll at the end of the runway. Told them to go there after they dropped me off." He shook his head. "The departure instructions were to make an immediate right turn after takeoff. I took off, sucked up my landing gear and hugged the runway. As I flew over their heads, I turned . . . but instead of rolling right, I rolled in the *opposite* direction, went upside down and *then* turned right." Josh shook his head again. "An *aileron roll* on takeoff is a huge flight violation." He laughed. "And doing it that close to the ground is . . . well . . . usually fatal. I spent the next two weeks waiting to be called into the Skipper's office and lose my wings. A Marine friend told me later that he was on the base golf course with a general. Fortunately, the general was busy lining up a putt, and the Marines in the tower never turned me in."

Sheri laughed. "That qualifies, and I can identify. Josh, we're like that poster of the two vultures sitting on the branch. One vulture says to the other, 'Screw it. Let's kill something.'"

"I don't think they said '*Screw it.*'"

"I was being polite. The point is — you and I don't like annoying details . . . details that can sometimes keep us alive. That's why we usually hook up with our opposites."

Josh laughed. "OK. So what are you trying to say?"

With an impish smile, she said, "You're courageous, intelligent and a girl magnet. You'd make a great James Bond."

He shook his head with a frown. "I don't think so. Besides . . . in real life, James Bond would make a *terrible* spy."

She laughed. "Exactly!" Still smiling she continued, "But I think you and Tim together would make an amazing team. You're opposites in so many ways, and that makes you complementary. For example, you're the big picture guy with amazing abilities. Tim's incredibly knowledgeable and phenomenally observant. He's the detail guy. He knows where the next bullet's coming from. Work together and you could be formidable." She looked thoughtful. "And," she sighed, "people in Tim's line of work don't have many *real* friends." She paused. "He needs one. There's no one he trusts more than you."

Josh looked surprised. "I seriously doubt that. I pulled him into a fake black program and almost got him killed."

Looking serious, Sheri said, "*And* saved his life . . . in more ways than one."

As if on cue, the door opened and Tim came in.

Looking up from the couch, Josh said, "Sheri says I'd totally suck as a spy and need adult supervision."

Sheri corrected, "I *said* you have complementary talents and would make a dynamic duo."

Josh shook his head with a half-smile. "I ain't wearing green tights."

Smiling, Sheri said, "Too bad."

Tim shook his head, but actually smiled. Then, back to serious, he said, "That was the agency. They've got a lead on who stole your files."

19

IMAGINATION

Tim said, "Talked to the Cyber Warfare guys. They figured out how they broke in. The hackers used the iMagine digital assistant to gain access."

Josh pulled his *iMăge* cyber glasses from his pocket. "I use these and that app all the time."

Tim said, "Everyone does. If you want to cause the most damage, you target the most universal software, the app that's on practically every phone."

Josh nodded. "Makes sense."

Tim added, "Apparently, the hackers found a backdoor into the app, one that somehow controls the phone's basic functions." He frowned slightly. "The cyber guys suggested that the iMagination Corporation apps are protected by a lot of encryption and would be hard to hack without inside information."

Josh nodded. "So, the hackers may have access to someone at iMagination?"

Tim shrugged. "It's a long shot, but it's all we got. Their corporate headquarters are in Atlanta. Let's go there tomorrow and talk to the app's program manager. See where that takes us."

They watched basketball playoffs while eating a spicy Cajun dinner of shrimp, beans and rice. Sheri had the magic touch — just enough spice to raise a little sweat. After the game, they were having another beer when Josh remembered Sam. "Tim, I can't believe you told those students about my getting shot."

Tim said, "Me? You're the one who gave away state secrets."

Josh shook his head. "I didn't tell them any details. I just recounted what *you* did."

"And you think that group isn't going to put the puzzle pieces together?"

Josh smiled. "Who are they going to tell?"

Tim shrugged. "Well, I just returned the favor." He paused. "By the way, one of them took a particular interest in *you*. She wouldn't stop asking questions."

Josh said, "Tell me about it. She followed me to the pool and suggested we do homework together for the upcoming *seduction* class. I should have filed sexual harassment charges."

Sheri gave him a disgusted smile. "You'd be more *convincing* if you weren't grinning like a Cheshire cat."

Still grinning, Josh said, "It was *just awful*."

She shook her head. "Guys are so simple."

Tim added, "There's no such thing as seduction class."

Sheri laughed. "I rest my case."

Josh realized that aside from Elizabeth, these were the first people he'd felt completely comfortable with since his return.

The next day, Tim set up the meeting in Atlanta. He dropped Josh back at the base by boat and told him to meet him at the Norfolk airport.

After a shower, he changed into Tim's recommendation for interview/interrogation clothes. It was a more casual version of **Men In Black**.

On the way to the airport, he checked in with Jen, voice texting, "Hi, Jen, how are you doing?"

"I'm totally bored."

"Do you play games?"

"I like Angry Birds, but I mastered all the levels. Now it's no fun."

"What type of games do you play with other kids?"

"I don't get to play with other kids."

Josh's heart went out to this little girl. Even if she had the same enhanced DNA he did, he had a previous life; she didn't. He couldn't help but wonder if whoever named her was playing a cruel joke, and the correct spelling of her name might be G E N, as in Genetic experiment.

"Why can't you play with other kids?"

There was a slight delay. "I'm kind of grounded."

"What did you do?"

She ignored his question and asked, "Will you play a game with me?"

He smiled. What was it with kid's affinity for fighter pilots? Stupid question. The answer was obvious — fighter pilots were just taller children. They tried some word games, finally settling on one she enjoyed. She learned fast, and they played it most of the trip. As he arrived at the airport, he told her to find some other games that were fun and challenging.

It was a quick flight to Atlanta. Tim told Josh he'd scheduled a meeting with iMagine's program manager, Ryan Armani. Armani was told they were NSA agents and needed to ask him some technical questions regarding a matter of national security. He used the NSA because it wasn't that unusual for the agency to be in contact with companies that dealt in social media.

iMagination headquarters was a large, modern, glass and steel edifice 20 miles north of Atlanta. As soon as they arrived, they were ushered into a conference room. Armani sat at a small table with a Diet Coke. As they came in, he stood up and shook their hands. Tim and Josh showed their official counterfeit NSA IDs and sat down.

Not wasting time, Tim asked, "Have there been any hacker attempts on the iMagine application?"

Armani's roundness belied his nervous energy. He spoke very fast. "Of course. We're on billions of phones. That automatically makes us a target for hackers and viruses, but we have extensive firewalls and encryption systems designed by some of the best minds in the industry."

Josh said, "So you're saying you haven't had any successful intrusions into your system?"

Armani looked down. "We've had a couple minor penetrations, but they were nothing more than pranks. Since then, we've put in a monitoring system that scans for the most minute code change 100 times a second."

Josh asked, "Why do you think they're just pranks?"

Armani said, "Because they just changed the colors on our splash screen." With an artificial-sounding laugh, he added, "They're probably just trying to get a job with us." After a sip of his Coke, he asked, "Why the interest?"

Tim said, "What I'm about to tell you is classified. If you mention it to anyone, you could face criminal charges."

Josh could see the conflict on Armani's face, but curiosity won. "Yes?"

"Someone hacked into the CIA using a cell phone. It turned itself on once it was inside a classified area using a backdoor in *your* app."

Armani narrowed his eyes and repeated, "It turned itself on?"

Tim and Josh nodded.

Too quickly, Armani said, "Our app can't activate a phone that's been turned off."

Josh didn't have to be an interrogator to notice his nervousness.

Tim pressed on. "Who, besides yourself, might have the ability to write a program that could take over the iMagine app?"

Armani frowned and then shook his head as if debating something. Finally, he said, "There aren't many who understand the subtleties of this type of, uh, software-hardware interface. Aside from my chief programmer, Stan Boyd, who has extensive stock options and would never do anything to risk the company, there is one other individual I'm aware of." He paused. "His name is Hayden Bentley." He looked at Tim to see if there was any recognition.

Tim simply said, "Go on."

"Bentley and I worked together at a small software firm about 10 years ago. He's brilliant, but got involved in some activist stuff and kind of went underground."

Tim repeated back, "Underground?"

"Yeah, I think he's some sort of an environmental extremist. It's really just rumors, but he might have been behind some *incidents.*"

Tim just looked at him.

Armani shrugged. "He might have been involved with the hacker group called Spector."

Josh couldn't help but ask, "Like James Bond's arch nemesis?"

With a nervous laugh, Armani said, "Uh, I don't think they spell it that way."

Josh smiled. "Yeah, they wouldn't want to get sued."

Tim didn't smile. "I'm aware of that group. You believe your friend might be part of it?"

Armani shook his head. "He wasn't my friend, and it's really just conjecture on my part, but if he is involved, he wouldn't be part of it . . . he'd be the leader. He's a strong personality."

Tim nodded. "Do you know where Bentley is?"

"We never stayed in touch." He paused. "But I know some people that might still have a connection with him."

Tim pushed a tablet across to him.

Armani looked in his phone and then transferred several names and numbers.

They thanked Armani for his time, and reminded him not to share their conversation with anyone.

As they got in the car, Josh said, "Actually Batman, that was kind of fun, but I think he was hiding something."

"Obviously, but he's not going anywhere, and we'll have his communications monitored."

Josh nodded. "So, what do you know about this Spector group?"

"Cyber terrorism isn't my area, but they hacked a nuclear power plant in France that caused a blackout. The only thing I'm sure of is that Spector has managed to make both the CIA's and the FBI's threat list."

"So you think they could be behind all this?"

Tim frowned. "It doesn't fit their M.O. as environmental extremists, but terrorist groups and even organized crime often contract with hackers. It's a promising lead."

Josh asked, "Why would they be interested in me?"

"Have you been recycling?"

Incredulous, Josh said, "You actually made a joke!"

After flying back to D.C. that evening, they went straight to CIA Headquarters.

As soon as they arrived, someone handed Tim a folder and said, "We found where he lives."

Smiling, Josh asked, "Hollowed-out volcano in the south pacific?"

Looking in the folder, Tim said, "Close . . . Beverly Hills." He showed Josh aerial photos of a large Mediterranean-style house with decorative pools and a tennis court, adding, "It's 15,000 square feet on 10 acres."

Josh gave a low whistle. "I'm guessing this guy isn't going to want to talk to us. We're going to need a subpoena or search warrant or something, aren't we?"

Tim said, "That would be handy . . . if we had evidence." Heading toward the door he continued, "Our flight leaves in an hour."

20

SPECTOR

It was 10 pm as Josh and Tim came out of the LAX terminal into a warm, hazy Southern California evening.

At the passenger pickup area, Tim looked around. He nodded toward a white van on the other side of the street. "Our ride."

It was a long, white Mercedes delivery van with "Jack's Appliance Repair" on the side. As they approached, the sliding door opened. They climbed inside. Josh saw a multitude of electronics and monitors that looked like a mini "Mission Control." In the driver's seat, was a young athletic-looking man with blond hair. Sitting on a small couch, that faced the sliding door, was a man and a woman. Both were in their fifties, wore glasses and looked like English professors.

Tim, not very imaginatively, introduced them as Peter, Paul and Mary.

They all nodded, as Josh said, "Love your music."

Only the woman smiled. She said to the driver, "Let's go." Turning to Tim, she began, "Job looks straight forward. They're using a standard commercial security system. However, considering the occupation of our mark — I mean *suspect* — there's the possibility he could have some non-standard security software or other surprises."

Tim nodded. "Backup power?"

Paul said, "Regular diesel generator. We can delay its start, but with all that computer equipment, he'll have battery backups inside."

Josh asked, "Won't they have battery backups on the security cameras too?"

Paul, with some disdain, said, "Of course, but we know how to take care of that."

Mary continued, "He has two full-time security guards. One usually watches the monitors while the other one roves the grounds, but they spend most of their time in the kitchen."

Tim asked, "What do we know about the guards?"

"No military or law enforcement background." She handed him a small file, adding, "Heavily armed, muscle-bound, mall cops." She paused. "However, there are four *well-trained* Rottweilers, and they do roam free."

Tim nodded. "Patterns?"

Paul said, "Haven't had much surveillance time, but Bentley's a night owl. He usually stays inside after midnight and the guards do too. We hid IR cameras around the periphery of the estate so we can monitor everything around the house. "

Mary said, "Recommend a midnight visit while the dogs are being fed."

An hour and a half later, they parked outside Bentley's estate. Surrounding the property was a tall, ornate but fully functional, security fence. Tim gave Josh a small briefcase to carry. They left the van and stood in the shadows just across the street from the estate's main gate.

Josh whispered, "Looks more like the Godfather's house. You'd think he'd at least pretend to be environmentally conscious."

Tim said, "Let's save him some energy." Into his throat mic, he said, "Ready when you are."

In Josh's headset, he heard Mary respond, "One of the guards is feeding the dogs at the back of the house. Recommend entering through the door on the eastern side. Soon as the guard goes inside, we'll cut the power."

A few seconds later, she said, "Lights out in five seconds."

On schedule, the property and house lights flickered and went out. Tim pushed the gate open, and they walked through. Jogging up the long driveway, they heard dogs barking. As they got close to the house, Mary said, "Uh oh, two Rottweilers are up and headed toward the east side of the house. Recommend you switch to the main entrance."

They changed directions, and ran for the front door.

As soon as they got there, Tim started working on the door lock.

Josh heard the barking getting closer.

Mary said, "Dogs coming around the east side of the house." Josh looked back over his shoulder. Initially, he didn't see anything. Then, with his excellent night vision, he spotted the dogs skidding around the corner at full speed. Apparently, the dogs also had excellent night vision. Less than 100 feet away, they were headed straight for them.

Josh casually asked Tim, "How's it going?"

Tim quietly opened the front door and entered with Josh on his heels. As they closed the door, the barking Rottweilers slid to a halt just a few feet from the door. Seconds later, the power came back on. As the outside floodlight over the entrance blinded the dogs, they stopped barking.

Josh heard Paul say, "Sorry, it appears they *do* have a major battery backup system in the house."

Tim said, "It's OK. We're inside."

They walked quickly and quietly through the house, constantly scanning for the security guards. Climbing a flight of stairs, they headed down a wide, professionally decorated hall. Their target was a closed door at the end of the hall.

Tim quietly cracked the door open and peeked inside. Nodding to Josh, they both slipped in and closed the door. They were in a huge, but dimly lit study. A mix of opulent over-stuffed furniture combined with the latest computer equipment — professional interior designer collides with super geek.

Josh set the briefcase down.

At the far end of the room, behind a huge, overly ornate desk and illuminated by multiple state-of-the-art monitors, sat their suspect. Three words came to mind — pale, pudgy and oily. Bentley wore a too-tight, designer jogging suit decorated with food stains. His stringy brown hair dangled over heavy black 3D glasses perched on a greasy nose.

Without looking up from his monitor, Bentley said, "About frickin' time. How long does it take to mix a simple drink? And what happened to the power? I'm paying you scumbags to take care of that crap."

Tim had briefed Josh on the "interview" plan. They both had dual shoulder holsters under their unmarked black jackets. One held a compact, high-caliber pistol, and the other held a Taser with a laser sight.

In a relaxed voice, Josh said, "Sorry, that may have been our fault."

Startled, Bentley yanked off his glasses. "Who are you?"

Josh and Tim kept their hands close to their weapons as they saw Bentley clumsily reach under his desk for his security alarm button.

Tim slowly backed up next to the door as Josh moved forward, continuing casually, "Mr. Bentley, we'd like to ask you some questions regarding a matter of national security."

Regaining his composure, Bentley asked, "Do you have a search warrant?"

Josh said, "We just need a little information."

Bentley's expression morphed into a smug smile. "I don't know who let you in, but you're about to be thrown out."

Tim stood on the hinge side of the door as Josh moved closer to Bentley's desk. Still talking in a reasonable voice, Josh said, "We just need a few answers, and we'll be on our way."

"Oh, you'll be on your way all right, and you'll have a lawsuit against you so fast your heads will spin. When I get finished with you, you won't be able to write parking tickets."

As Bentley finished, the door flew open and two men, brandishing automatic weapons rushed in. The first was a crew cut, six-foot-four slab of muscle. The second was a slightly shorter version of the first.

They moved toward Josh, who held his hands up.

From behind, Tim kicked the shorter guard, who was closest to him. Hitting him hard in just the right place, Tim knocked the weapon from his hands. As the assault rifle flew free, the bigger guard spun around. Tim shot him pointblank with the Taser. At the same time, Tim finished the smaller guard off with an elbow to his face.

As the first guard hit the wooden floor with a satisfying slap, Josh pulled his Taser from his jacket and pointed it at Bentley.

The smaller guard stumbled backward, holding his bleeding

nose. With little effort, Tim pushed him over a piece of furniture and tased him as he fell.

One guard was unconscious on his back. The other was on his stomach, moaning. The engagement took less than three seconds, and Tim wasn't even breathing hard. Searching the guards, Tim removed additional weapons and ejected all chambered rounds and clips.

Josh motioned toward Bentley with his Taser. The laser spot danced across his chest. "If you would be so kind as to step away from the desk."

Bentley, eyes wide, sputtered in disbelief, "You ... you can't do this. You're violating my rights." He weakly wound down with, "I'll ... I'll have your badges."

Josh couldn't resist. "Badges? We don't need no stinking badges." Seeing Bentley didn't recognize the movie line, he clarified, "Hayden, you see, we're not *technically* government employees. In fact, we don't *actually* exist."

The first real sign of fear appeared on Bentley's face. "What ... what do you want?"

Tim finished duct taping the guards' hands, feet and mouths. Playing bad cop, he slowly and coldly said, "Move ... away ... from the desk ... now!"

Bentley quickly came around his desk.

After Tim patted him down for weapons, Josh pulled up a chair and waved Bentley into it.

As he sat down, Josh said, "We know you've been busy with extra-curricular activities."

"I just do software consulting and I'm an environmental philanthropist."

Tim said, "That wasn't a question."

Josh added, "We already know some of the jobs you've done: French nuclear plant, cosmetic companies, etc."

Beginning to sweat, Bentley said, "I don't know what you're talking about."

Josh said quietly, "Hayden, I'm a pretty nice guy, but Mr. Smith ...." He shook his head. "He has ... *issues*." He paused. "I know they say it's possible to lead a perfectly normal life and even have children with only one testicle, but I think we'd all agree ...

symmetry is preferable."

Bentley swallowed hard.

Standing behind Bentley, Tim just rolled his eyes.

Josh continued, "But if you cooperate and answer the questions honestly, you'll never know we were here."

Tim retrieved the briefcase Josh had carried in, and opened it. He told Bentley to unzip the top of his jogging suit.

Bentley visibly flinched.

Josh said, "He's just going to put some lie detector sensors on your chest . . . for now."

Bentley unzipped his top, and Tim stuck electrodes on his chest and put a strap around his wrist.

Tim then handed him a pair of heavy rimmed glasses. "Put these on." A video feed inside read pupil dilation and sent it wirelessly to the iPad Tim pulled out of the briefcase.

Josh said, "Let's start with something small and verifiable. Did you hack into and plant viruses in several small cosmetic companies?"

"No."

Tim looked at the display in his hand and shook his head then gave Josh a thumbs up.

Josh said, "Thank you for calibrating the system. Remember, we already know the answer to most of these questions. Let's try that again. Did you plant viruses in several small cosmetic companies?"

Bentley sighed. "Yes."

Tim nodded as Bentley unconvincingly continued, "But only because they were testing the cosmetics on animals . . . ?"

Josh didn't need a polygraph to know Bentley was full of it. Josh shook his head and looked specifically at Tim.

Bentley followed Josh's gaze and looked up.

Tim gave him a psychotic smile.

Tripping over his words, Bentley said, "One of the big cosmetic-makers paid me to sabotage some smaller companies to get them out of the way!"

"And?"

"I've done it for other companies."

"Who else?"

Bentley sighed again. "I've done work for, uh, *other* organizations."

Josh raised an eyebrow.

"They might have been . . . organized crime."

Josh said, "Of course, you've used all this money to support environmental causes?"

Bentley looked down. "I have an expensive lifestyle. I use the environmental angle to pick up women. I tell them I'm like Neo in **The Matrix**."

Josh coughed to avoid laughing. "That I believe." He paused, "Now comes the most important question. I need you to tell us the truth immediately. You won't get another chance. *Do you understand*?"

Tim moved forward and put a hand on Bentley's shoulder.

Bentley swallowed and nodded.

"Did you break into the CIA computer system?"

"No!"

Tim nodded.

Bentley added quickly, "I've broken into several government systems and even planted viruses, but not the CIA. I'm not stupid. That's like breaking into a police station. Why on earth would I risk that?"

"You're telling me you've never been approached by anyone to obtain classified documents from the CIA."

"No!"

Tim nodded.

"And even if I had, I wouldn't do it."

Bentley looked up and saw Tim frown.

Bentley corrected, "OK . . . I might, but they'd have to pay me an insane amount to take that kind of risk." He ended defiantly, "I've never tried to hack the CIA."

Tim walked over to Josh. While watching Bentley, they spoke quietly.

Then Josh said to Bentley, "Phones have to be turned off and surrendered before entering the CIA computer room. Disguised as an update to the iMagine app, a program turned a phone back on *after* it had been set aside. It accessed a short-range Bluetooth signal, broke through several levels of encryption, stole some files, turned itself off and then transmitted the files once outside."

Bentley, clearly caught up in the idea, said, "Wow. That's impressive." He frowned. "The phone was actually turned off and it turned itself on?"

Josh nodded.

Bentley said, "Got to be BOTIC."

Josh frowned. "BOTIC?"

"Yeah, the chip that fixed the bandwidth problem. It's the only thing I know of that might be able to turn a phone back on." He paused and then asked, "You said they used the iMagine app?"

Josh nodded again.

Bentley said, "The programmers at iMagination must have cracked BOTIC." He slapped his forehead. "Of course. That explains their market domination!" Bentley stopped. "Wait a minute. It was Armani, wasn't it? Armani put you onto me!"

Josh didn't say anything, but Bentley continued, "That scumbag! You want to know who has the resources to do what you just described? Ask Ryan Armani!" As Bentley went on a rant, describing Armani in colorful terms, Tim nodded to Josh.

Bentley finally sputtered to a stop, and Josh asked, "And why would Armani want to nail you?"

"Because I . . . I played a minor practical joke on him." He shook his head dismissively. "He had the hots for this girl who worked with us, but she really liked me more. Ryan has a tendency to talk to himself when no one's around. I recorded the whole conversation and posted it on YouTube. It was hilarious." He shrugged. "But he got real pissy about it."

Bentley, not seeing amusement in their faces, continued, "But the real reason he'd send you my way is because he's one of the few people that has the ability to pull something like that off." He frowned. "He's probably not smart enough to do it by himself, but they've got some smart programmers . . . *and* I know he likes *very* expensive antiques."

Josh said, "How do we know you're not trying to do the same thing to him? You'd sell your mother to the highest bidder."

Bentley shrugged. "Probably, she wasn't much of a mother."

Josh just shook his head.

Bentley continued, "But your lie detector will show I'm telling the truth. If someone actually figured out how to hack the BOTIC chip," he gave them an oily smile, "I'm the least of your worries."

21

REUNION

After they left, Tim imitated Josh. "I think we'd all agree symmetry is preferable?"

Josh shrugged. "Think I heard it in a movie."

Tim just shook his head. "OK . . . we're out of our league with this cyber stuff. Need an expert that can understand it."

At the same time, they both said, "Langlois."

Josh said, "I'll call him."

"He thinks you're dead."

"Yeah, worse than that, it means I have to pay up on a promise."

Tim called back to CIA headquarters. Confirming Greg still worked at Boeing, Josh flew from Los Angeles to St. Louis, as Tim headed back to D.C.

Arriving in St. Louis, Josh drove out to St. Charles where Greg lived. On the way there, Josh received a voice text from Jen. "What happens to you when you die?"

He wished he had never mentioned the guerillas. "Well . . . many people believe there's life after death."

"How do they know?"

Josh realized her parents might have died or maybe she was seeking assurance that he or others in her life weren't going to desert her. He had to keep in mind he was dealing with a frighteningly intelligent child. Platitudes wouldn't work. His unique experience had changed his perspective, but he answered carefully. "That's a good question. If you'd like, I can give you some books that might help."

"Yes, I would like that."

"If you can read eBooks, I'll buy and send them to you."

Jen replied, "If you give me the names, I can get them myself. I'm a fast reader."

Josh wondered if her guardians were supporting her book purchases, or with her computer skills, she was just *acquiring* the books.

Josh got a text from Tim with Greg's current location. It was amazing how easy it was for the Agency to locate most people. Josh drove to the address, which turned out to be a nice restaurant.

As he went inside, he saw Greg eating dinner at the bar. Even from behind, Greg was easy to spot with his ever-present geek cap pulled over an afro that stuck out on both sides. His interesting choice of oddly colored clothing hung loosely on his slim six-foot frame. Noting that the bartender was a beautiful blonde, he sat down on the stool next to Greg and said quietly, "Good strategic position."

Greg turned, did a double take, and almost fell off his stool. He jumped up, grabbed Josh and hugged him, yelling, "You're alive! I knew it! James Bond never dies!"

Josh hugged him back and said, "Yes, and now everyone knows that."

Greg looked around and saw several people looking at them. "Oh, sorry."

As they both sat down, Greg loudly whispered, "So what happened after they shot you?"

The bartender, who couldn't have missed Greg's question, was now looking at them with interest.

Josh said, "Can't say I remember a lot, but suffice it to say, I woke up on an aircraft carrier off the coast of Antarctica."

The bartender was now cleaning the clean bar next to them.

More quietly, Josh said, "They shipped Elizabeth in. She nursed me back to health, and we watched the comet come in over South America."

Greg's expression turned angry. "You could've called and let me know you were alive."

"I'm really sorry about that, Greg. The nature of the work is such that I . . . had to keep a low profile."

Greg shook his head. "That was terrible." He softened. "Please don't do that again."

A little surprised, Josh nodded. "I promise." Looking around, he added, "Greg, if you're game, I could really use your help again."

Greg laughed, and again too loudly, whispered, "We're gonna jack some more fighters?"

The bartender was now openly staring at them.

Josh laughed. "No." He shrugged. "At least not that I know of. The agency and I have kissed and made up. I'm actually helping them with a . . . challenge."

Greg smiled. "I'm all over it. Just tell me what we're doing."

"Before we do that, I promised you that if we got out of that last situation alive," he leaned in and whispered, "I'd help you meet women."

Greg grinned, and, not so subtly, tilted his head toward the bartender who was still watching them.

Josh smiled and added, "Sure, but first we need to do a little image tweaking. Let's go see Elizabeth. She's got a great eye."

Josh picked up the tab. As the bartender gave him the receipt, she leaned in and asked, "Who are you guys?"

Josh nodded back toward Greg, who was standing behind him, and with a conspiratorial wink, said, "You don't recognize him?"

She tilted her head past Josh to study Greg.

Without saying another word, Josh grabbed Greg's elbow and moved him toward the door.

Greg, looking back at the bartender, whispered, "Do we have to go right now?"

Josh smiled, "Easy there big boy, I just set the hook."

They flew to D.C. the next day. Josh took Greg to their apartment and introduced him to Elizabeth.

She hugged him and said, "It's great to finally meet you. Josh says you're a genius and were instrumental in saving London."

"Thanks, Ms. Fuze, but I was just along for the ride."

"You're too modest. Josh told me the whole story, and call me Elizabeth." Seeing Greg's state-of-the-art phone and cyber glasses, Elizabeth asked about them.

Josh got a snack while they talked geek. It didn't take long before Josh saw the admiration in Greg's eyes.

A half hour later, they wound down, and Elizabeth said to Greg, "OK, turn around."

As he turned 360 degrees, she said, "Hmmm. You're a good-looking guy, Greg. We just need to do a little work on your clothes and hair, uh, style." She put a finger on her lips and said. "Would you mind if I give you a little trim?"

"Uh, I guess not."

Josh suspected Elizabeth was one of the few people who could talk someone into cutting their hair 30 minutes after meeting them. Elizabeth could relate to anyone and turn them into a best friend. It wasn't a technique. She loved people and always took a genuine interest in them.

As she opened some kitchen drawers in search of scissors, Josh asked Greg, "So, what are you looking for in a woman?"

Greg thought for a moment and then pointed at Elizabeth. "I want one just like her."

Elizabeth smiled. "Why thank you, Greg."

Josh added, "Your taste is impeccable." Then turning to her, asked, "OK, Elizabeth, what does it take to attract someone like you?"

She bit the side of her lip. "First impressions are important. While clothes don't really make the man, they can certainly get a woman's attention." She paused. "We just need to update your wardrobe a little so women can see the real you. You're color blind?"

"No!" Greg frowned. "Why does everyone ask me that?"

Elizabeth gave Josh a nasty look and said, "Sorry. I'm going to write you a 'prescription' for clothing. Are you game?"

Josh threw in. "Trust her; she's a nurse."

"Sure."

Elizabeth went over to a notepad on the kitchen bar and began writing.

Josh said, "After Elizabeth fixes you up a little, I think I'll introduce you to Amber."

Without looking up, Elizabeth said, "Amber? Oh no you don't. She has a tendency to forget her clothes."

Greg's ears perked up.

Josh casually said to Greg, "I think she's attracted to shy intellectual guys."

Greg whispered, "Nice body?"

Josh whispered back, "Amber has an *amazing* empennage." He gave a quick head nod toward Elizabeth, who was facing away from them and slightly bent over as she wrote.

Greg, admiring Elizabeth's perfect-fitting jeans, nodded appreciatively.

Over her shoulder, Elizabeth said, "I'm *sure* Greg wouldn't be interested in some naked nymph who's just going to throw herself at him."

Earnestly, Greg said, "Actually, that would be great."

Turning around, Elizabeth gave them an expression of mock surprise.

Josh shook his head dismissively and said, "She *wasn't* naked." Then quietly, to Greg, "She *always* wore earrings."

Elizabeth said, "I heard that."

Josh replied, "I remember a very short silk bathrobe—"

Before he could finish, he got "the look."

He immediately turned to Greg and said, "So, will time off from the space-based laser program be a problem?"

"Uh, I don't think so. The software integration is done, and they're not ready for the final hardware-in-the-loop testing."

Josh nodded. "Great. I can get you a hall pass that will excuse you based on national security. That way, they'll hold your job. The CIA will pay you as an independent contractor about $1,000 a day. We need your software expertise, but I can't promise there won't be some danger."

Greg smiled. "How much more dangerous could it be than ejecting out of a fighter over Antarctica?"

Elizabeth said, "Touché," as she handed Greg his clothing prescription. Armed with scissors, she added, "Put this towel around your shoulders."

Greg's phone beeped. He looked down at it and said, "Wait! Turn the news on."

Elizabeth turned the TV to a news network. The top story was about outraged social media users around the world. The news anchor said, "Apparently, less than an hour ago, almost every social media user found their personal messages, documents and pictures publically posted. The hackers managed to override all privacy settings, changing them to public." The reporter continued, "And every private message was not only posted, but emailed to everyone on the user's friend list." With the slightest of smiles, she added, "There are dozens of developing stories about potential scandals involving political figures and celebrities. Most social media companies have made the extraordinary decision to take their sites down until they can sort it out." She finished with, "So far, no one has claimed credit for the attacks, but law enforcement agencies around the world are vowing to find and prosecute the hackers."

Elizabeth muted the TV as Greg said, "Guess you shouldn't say things you don't want to be published in public."

With a slight smile, Josh added, "It's interesting. Hackers can tie up traffic in cities all over the world and manipulate stocks, but there's no public outrage until they hit social media."

Elizabeth nodded. "Now, it's personal."

Josh paused. "OK, let's assume all these attacks are perpetrated by the same organization. What's their goal, and is there any way the iMagine app and this BOTIC chip could be a common element?"

Greg shook his head. "Sounds like the cyber guys tied the CIA break-in and the traffic jams to it, but I don't see how stock manipulation and this social media attack could be related. They operate on computer servers not phones."

As Elizabeth started cutting Greg's hair, she asked, "How were the stocks manipulated?"

Josh was reading the story from his phone. "They think people's stock tracking software started showing false indications that these stocks were rising rapidly. Of course, people responded by buying them. When they did, they caused the stocks to actually rise, turning the false indication into reality."

Still clipping, Elizabeth said, "Well, I track and trade stocks on my phone, and I know I'm not alone. As for social media . . . Greg, how do you usually access *your* account?"

Greg slapped his forehead, almost skewering his fingers. "On my phone! You're right! These attacks could have come in through a phone app."

Josh said, "That's what Bentley meant when he said, if someone's hacked the BOTIC chip, we'd have much bigger things to worry about than him."

Elizabeth stopped cutting. With a low-pitched whistle, she said, "Think about what we're saying. We've become a society dependent on our phones for navigation, finances, news, schedules . . . almost everything. Some of my friends would have a hard time finding their way home without their phone. Most of our connection with, and picture of, the world comes through our phones. If someone could control our phones—"

Greg finished, "They could control us."

22

BOTIC

Armani opened his front door and threw his keys on a side table. He was mumbling to himself as he went straight to the refrigerator in the dark kitchen. Opening the door and reaching in, he said, "What I should have said is, 'Oh yeah, let's see you do it.'" He pulled out a Diet Coke and a cold Snickers bar. "They're flippin' clueless; they have no idea." He closed the refrigerator door and popped the top of the can. Unwrapping the Snickers bar, he said, "Come to papa."

Josh flipped the kitchen light on. "Diet Coke and Snickers?"

Armani screamed and jumped back, sending his Snickers bar skittering across the floor and spilling the Coke down the front of his shirt.

Tim appeared in the doorway, holding and petting a contented cat, and blocking any possible exit.

Josh said, "Ryan, we need to talk."

Eyes still wide, Armani managed a slight head nod.

Tim stepped back, clearing the kitchen entrance, but standing between Armani and the front door. He casually waved Armani toward the living room.

Josh scooped up the Snickers bar from the floor and followed.

Armani stopped when he saw Greg sitting on his living room couch.

Tim said, "This is Greg Langlois, our technical expert." He pointed at an overstuffed chair sitting at a 45-degree angle to the couch. "Have a seat."

As Armani sat down, Josh sat on the couch next to Greg.

Tim gently set the cat down and pulled a dining room chair over. Turning it around, he straddled it, facing Armani.

Still holding his Diet Coke, Armani looked at Tim on his left, then Josh and Greg on his right. Finally, he said uncertainly, "What . . . what's this all about?"

Tim started, "We had an interesting conversation with Bentley, who, by the way, suggested you fingered him because you had an ax to grind. We did a polygraph on him and don't believe he was behind the break-in. Based on what he shared, however, you've been elevated to a person of *interest* in this investigation."

Armani said, "Uh, aren't you supposed to have a search warrant or something?"

Tim looked him right in the eye and said, "Yup."

There was an awkward silence.

Finally, Josh said, "Nice place." Looking around, he added, "I'm not into antiques myself, but it looks like you've done a great job decorating, and with some very old and *expensive* pieces."

Armani let out a big breath of air. "Look, I swear, I wasn't involved with the CIA break-in. I honestly don't know anything about it."

Tim said, "You're on the short list of people with both access and knowledge. Right now, it's a list of one. You need to tell us everything you know."

Josh added, "Would you like to start with BOTIC?"

Armani's eyebrows went up. "What did Bentley tell you?"

Greg said, "I believe he claimed your digital assistant is taking advantage of it."

Armani sighed heavily. "Uh, yeah. We sort of . . . *attached it* to the BOTIC chip."

Tim asked, "What exactly does BOTIC do?"

Still clutching his Coke, Armani said, "BOTIC stands for Bandwidth Optimization Through Interphone Communication. It's a new chip that's been added to almost all phones." He took a deep breath. "A few years ago, the big news story was that we were rapidly running out of cell phone bandwidth with everyone accessing the Internet."

Tim frowned.

Armani clarified, "There's only so much data you can transmit and receive via radio waves, and we'd already used up all that bandwidth. Cell phone networks were becoming overloaded and slowing down." Warming up to the subject, he took a swig of his

Coke and set it on the table next to him. "The problem was solved by Dr. Lee, a brilliant engineer who created the BOTIC chip." He paused. "The idea came after several hurricanes took out cell phone towers, shutting down the phone network. To fix it, they created phones that could bypass the towers during an emergency and communicate directly with each other like walkie-talkies. Their range was limited to 500 meters, but calls could then be relayed through multiple phones until they reached a working tower or Internet connection." He paused again. "Dr. Lee applied that idea to data, but not just during emergencies. BOTIC allows phones to relay data between each other without using a cell tower, creating a kind of bucket brigade."

Josh, set the open Snickers bar on the table and leaned forward. "What do you mean bucket brigade?"

Armani said, "If a phone is idle, it can act as a repeater, passing data from one phone to another until it reaches a phone that's connected to Wi-Fi. So you end up with this giant phone-to-phone network."

Tim asked, "How does it do that?"

"The BOTIC chip shares your phone's location with other phones that are in range." Getting more comfortable, he explained with enthusiasm, "Let's say your phone isn't in range of a Wi-Fi network, but it is in range of your neighbor's phone, which *is* connected to Wi-Fi. When your neighbor isn't using his phone, his phone can act as a relay station between your phone and the Wi-Fi network."

Tim said, "So phones are relaying data to each other and transmitting their location to other phones?"

Armani said, "Yes, but it's an encrypted signal and uses only a tiny bit of the phone's processor. With all the phones out there, if each idle phone relays only a tiny bit of data, it takes a huge load off the cell towers. It's a much more efficient use of limited bandwidth and makes phones faster and more reliable."

Josh asked, "Where does your digital assistant come in?"

Avoiding eye contact, Armani unconsciously picked up the Snickers bar. Rotating it nervously in his hands, he said, "We, uh, found a way to access the BOTIC chip."

Greg interjected, "You mean you cracked it."

Waving the candy bar for emphasis, he said, "We took advantage of it to improve the performance of our digital assistant."

Josh added, "Without the user knowing it."

Greg said, "You're accessing people's phones without their permission to speed up your software."

Absently picking cat hairs out of the chocolate, he said defensively, "There's no law against it."

Greg shook his head. "Only because no one knows it's possible."

Armani took a huge bite out of the candy bar. Around the mouthful, he said, "It only uses the BOTIC chip to get a processor and memory boost from *idle* phones."

Greg grimaced. "I can't believe you did that!"

Armani retorted, "It doesn't hurt anyone, and everyone gets a better digital assistant!"

"No. I mean I can't believe you ate that. That's gross!"

Armani stopped and looked down at the last piece in his hand. Shrugging, he popped it in his mouth.

Tim said slowly, "Forgetting about the ethics for a moment, does your iMagine app have the ability to turn a phone that's off back on again?"

Armani, still chewing, shook his head. "No. But—"

Greg finished, "But BOTIC does?"

Armani frowned. "Theoretically. For BOTIC to work, the chip has to always be aware of its location so it can transmit it to other phones. That means it has to stay partially powered even when the phone's turned off."

Greg added, "Which explains how the comet's electromagnetic pulse could have triggered it and turned billions of phones on."

Josh rubbed his chin thoughtfully. "So, if the BOTIC chip can do that." He paused. "And your digital assistant can access and give commands *to* the BOTIC chip . . . ."

Armani nodded his head. "You're right, but why on earth would we want to hack the CIA? The last thing we want to do is draw government attention to the fact we're accessing the chip."

Greg, looking at Tim and Josh, said, "If *they* found a backdoor into the chip, so could someone else. In fact, seeing that an electromagnetic pulse caused BOTIC to turn phones on, might have been what gave the hackers the idea in the first place."

Armani shook his head. "I'm probably not helping my case, but we have the best programmers in the world, and it still took us thousands of hours to access BOTIC. Even then, without the help of BOTIC's creator, I don't think we could've done it."

Greg looked surprised. "The inventor of BOTIC *gave* you the backdoor?"

"Yes. Dr. Lee actually contacted us and was very enthusiastic about our app."

Tim tilted his head and with a slight frown repeated, "Contacted *you*?"

Armani nodded.

Josh and Tim looked at each other.

Tim looked Armani in the eye. "Do not talk to anyone about this, especially Dr. Lee, until the investigation is complete. The entire U.S. is at INFOCON 3, probably because of your app. If you talk to anyone about this, you could face espionage charges." He paused. "Do you understand?"

Armani swallowed. "Yes sir."

Once outside, Greg said, "The creator of BOTIC is one of the most brilliant engineers in the country."

Josh looked at Tim and said, "As a fellow engineer with celebrity status, let's let Greg lead the next interview."

Greg said, "I'm not a celebrity."

Josh said, "Au contraire. The media correctly gave you credit for overcoming one of the key technical challenges, and fixing the Blaster's software in time to save London. Just as you knew Lee's name, I bet Lee knows yours."

Dr. Lee lived and worked in Northern Virginia just outside of D.C. Tim contacted Lee's secretary and identified himself as an NSA agent. Once again, he played the national security card and got them an appointment the next day.

Josh, on his way home from Dulles airport, got a voice text from Jen. "I've been reading about being dead. Where is Heaven?"

Josh sighed and said to himself, "Could be a long night." He voice texted, "Jen, I don't think anyone really knows."

"Then how do they know it exists?"

To himself, Josh said, "How indeed?" To Jen, however, he voice texted, "Since it's difficult for most people to return from the dead," he smiled to himself, "there isn't much information available." He paused. "There's a lot about the universe we don't understand. It may be right under our noses, but not be observable from our dimension." He shook his head remembering he was talking to a seven-year-old. "But most people who believe in heaven would probably say they have faith in its existence based on their spiritual beliefs."

Josh pulled up in front of the D.C. apartment as Jen replied, "I don't understand faith."

He could relate. "I'm home now, and Elizabeth is very knowledgeable on this topic."

"OK."

As he entered their apartment, he kissed Elizabeth and said, "Need your brain." Smiling, he handed her his phone.

She shook her head, but then smiled as she read the text conversation. "May I?"

"By all means."

Elizabeth voice texted, "Hi, Jen, this is Elizabeth. Do you like physics?"

With raised eyebrows, Josh said, "Not a question I'd normally ask a seven-year-old."

Jen replied, "Hi, Elizabeth. Yes, I particularly like geophysics."

Elizabeth gave him an "I told you so" smile.

Josh shook his head. "Of course, she even has a favorite branch of physics."

Elizabeth said, "Jen, scientists have to have the most faith of anyone."

Josh looked at Elizabeth skeptically.

Jen replied, "Why?"

Elizabeth smiled at Josh as she voice texted, "The definition of faith is a firm belief in things that are unproven. Geophysicists, and all scientists, come up with ideas and theories, but the hard part is proving them. They often spend years, or even decades, of their lives developing, testing and defending an idea until they can prove it. That's a perfect example of faith."

Jen said, "I understand."

Elizabeth finished with, "The greatest achievements almost always start as faith."

Jen replied, "So, it's OK for me to believe I can have parents someday?"

Elizabeth's face fell as she gave the phone back to Josh, saying, "That poor baby. We need to find out what her situation is."

He voice texted, "This is Josh. Yes, Jen, you should absolutely believe in having parents."

Jen replied, "I'm very good at looking things up. Can I be your assistant?"

Josh said, "Are you sure that would be OK with your guardians?"

"Yeah, they make me do computer stuff for them all the time."

That comment concerned him. "Yes, Jen, that would be awesome, but you are much more than an assistant to me."

He wrapped up the conversation with Jen and then said to Elizabeth, "I wish I *could* use her as an assistant. She's an amazing computer whiz like you."

Elizabeth asked, "Why can't you?"

"I can't get her involved." He frowned. "It might put her at risk."

Elizabeth gave him a challenging smile. "You let me help." She added, "Look, you don't have to give her classified information. Just let her help with little assignments and praise her when she does well. It'll be good for her self-esteem and keep you connected."

He shrugged. "Guess that would be OK." Looking her in the eye, he added, "I *am* going to find out what her situation is." He paused. "Then, maybe *we* can do something about it?"

Elizabeth smiled and kissed him.

After dinner, Josh called Tim. "You know that little girl I told you and Sheri about? Elizabeth and I are concerned about her living situation and wellbeing. Any idea how we might be able to track her down?"

Tim said, "Let me see what I can do."

23

ARCHITECT

The address for Dr. Lee's office was in one of the myriad of office buildings that surrounded the D.C. Beltway. Josh had done a brief Navy tour on the staff of the President's Science Advisor and was familiar with the area. The CIA file listed Lee's company as a technical consulting firm. They also learned that Dr. Lee was Dr. Jessica Lee.

Josh, Tim and Greg were waiting in the reception area when a pretty wisp of a woman with short black hair, porcelain skin and delicate features introduced herself. Lee looked younger than the thirty years her file indicated. Quickly dispelling the stereotype of a cute, shy, Asian girl, she made direct eye contact and had a strong handshake. With no accent, she said, "May I see some identification?"

They showed her their "loaner" NSA IDs.

She looked at them carefully and said, "Gentleman, I'm on a tight schedule. How can I help you?"

Josh said, "Thank you for seeing us on short notice. Is there somewhere we can talk privately?"

She nodded. "My office."

They followed her to a large office. The single window offered an expansive view of the Beltway. With half a dozen filing cabinets lining the walls, she'd clearly arranged her office for function. On top of each were tall but neat stacks of technical journals and papers. Covering her desk were equally tall but less neatly stacked papers, grouped around two giant monitors. The only thing on the wall, aside from generic office art, was her Cal Tech Diploma and a framed LA Lakers jersey with player signatures. There was a small round conference table in the middle of the office with four chairs and minimal papers. She waved them to the chairs.

Josh identified her as a no-nonsense personality and went straight to the subject. "We'd like to ask you some questions about your BOTIC chip."

She nodded with an amused expression. "Wikipedia is pretty detailed and fairly accurate."

"Read it." Josh smiled back. "Dr. Lee, does the BOTIC chip activate a phone that's been turned completely off?"

"No."

Greg, with slightly narrowed eyes, inserted, "Are you saying a phone that's been turned off cannot be activated by the chip?"

She gave Greg the slightest of smiles. "That's a different question. The chip is *capable* of turning a phone on, but there would be no reason for it to do that and nothing in the firmware that would allow it."

Tim asked, "Dr. Lee, did you give iMagination access to BOTIC?"

She smiled confidently. "You wouldn't be asking me that question if you didn't already know the answer." She paused. "BOTIC allows phones to relay data to each other and to Wi-Fi networks, reducing the demand on cell phone networks." She paused. "But it's a temporary fix. The data demand is still growing. I knew my chip could do so much more. Instead of just sharing data, BOTIC can allow phones to share processing power and memory too. The result is a faster, more efficient global communication network that uses less bandwidth. *And*, as a side benefit, applications like the iMagine digital assistant operate much faster and more accurately."

Josh asked, "It doesn't bother you that you're allowing a commercial program to use the processor and memory of people's phones without their knowledge?"

Without the slightest hesitation, she said, "BOTIC only uses the processors and memory of phones that are completely idle. It takes almost nothing and gives back so much." She paused. "I've already made millions from the royalties on the chip. I helped with the iMagine app just to prove that BOTIC could do so much more, and it's success has been far greater than even I could have imagined . . . pardon the pun."

With a slight frown, Josh added, "Setting aside the 'greater good' argument, did you ever consider the possible damage that could be done if someone were able to hack into your chip?"

"My chip can't be hacked. It uses 512-bit quadruple encryption. It would take the fastest computers in the world weeks to break the code, and they'd have to do it for every phone. We went out of our way to make sure that couldn't happen."

Greg said, "Dr. Lee, your chip may be extremely secure, but you put a backdoor into it, and you gave the key to that door to the iMagine app."

"Mr. Langlois, we made sure that the iMagine app's access was also completely encrypted so no one would be able to reverse-engineer access to the chip."

Greg leaned forward. "Dr. Lee, they don't have to reverse-engineer iMagine . . . if they can take control of it."

For the first time, she looked a little less confident. Frowning, she looked at Greg and asked, "What's your background?"

Josh, nodding toward Greg, said, "Dr. Lee, Greg Langlois is the engineer who solved the dual frequency firing problem on the Blaster and fixed the software that allowed the last-minute deflection of the London meteor."

She studied Greg with interest and said, "I thought your name sounded familiar." She paused. "OK, I admit I hadn't thought in detail about that possibility, but that assumes the iMagine app could be hijacked. Even if they could, a hacker would still need the detailed chip command codes, without which it wouldn't work at all. The chance of figuring them out by trial and error is a hundred million to one."

Greg glanced at Josh and Tim.

They nodded.

He turned back to Lee and said, "It's been done."

"Who? How?"

"That's what we're here to find out."

She said, "I'm sorry; I find that hard to believe."

Greg said, "Do you remember the random global traffic jams and social media hacking?"

"Yes, of course, but . . . ." She looked at the ceiling, obviously connecting the dots. Finally, tilting her head slightly, she asked, "Are you sure it was iMagine?"

Greg nodded. "Yes."

Lee got up and began pacing around the small conference room. She stopped. "That's not good. Who's behind this? What do they want?"

Tim said, "That's a good question."

Finally, looking a little nervous, she said, "I need to check some things out. Can I get back to you?"

Tim said, "It's important that you share everything you know. If you have suspicions, you need to tell us. We cannot risk tipping our hand to whoever is behind this."

"I understand, but there are *things* I can check on that might eliminate some of the possibilities."

Tim nodded. "Would you be willing to work with Mr. Langlois?"

She shook her head and started to say something, but then stopped. Looking at Greg, she sighed, "Yeah, I guess."

As soon as they were outside and walking toward the car, Josh looked at Greg and said, "What did you think of Dr. Lee?"

Greg looked down thoughtfully. "Very impressive . . . I mean she has these, like, beautiful eyes that just kinda cut right through you, but I think she also works out . . ."

As Greg continued, Tim and Josh just looked at each other.

Finally, Josh interrupted, "Greg, what about something that starts with a 'B'?"

Greg nodded with a smile. "Yeah, she's got a nice butt."

Josh finally stopped and put his hand on Greg's shoulder. "Greg, look at me . . . BOTIC?"

"Huh? Oh yeah, right."

Shaking his head, Josh turned to Tim. "OK, let's review what we know about Lee."

Tim looked at the file on his phone. "She's a naturalized American citizen and both of her parents still live in China. Her mother's a scientist, and her dad a military officer. They probably sent her to the U.S. for education at an early age. She's a graduate of Cal Tech, and her technical accomplishments are extensive."

Starting to walk again, Josh nodded. "Greg, you back with us?"

"Yeah, sorry."

"We need your technical expertise to figure out how this backdoor into the BOTIC chip works."

Greg frowned. "And you want me to find out if Dr. Lee is an evil genius?"

Josh smiled. "Something like that."

This time, Greg stopped and shook his head. "I don't know how to interrogate people, and I definitely don't know how to talk to women."

Josh said, "Greg, we don't want you to interrogate her — or make a pass at her — just help us figure out how the hackers can take advantage of the BOTIC chip. If we understand that, we may be able to stop them."

Greg looked at him skeptically.

Josh said, "Greg, believe it or not, it's remarkably simple. I'm going to tell you the secret to talking to women."

"Really?"

"Yup."

"How?"

"Greg, who's the most important person in your life?"

"Uh, I don't know, I guess my mom."

Josh smiled. "She's the second most important person." He paused for emphasis, "*You* are the most important person in your world. That's true of all of us. *We* are also our favorite subject to talk about. So, the best way to establish a connection with other people is to talk about their favorite subject — them."

"So, I should just ask her questions about herself?"

Josh said, "Yeah, but you two have a lot in common. Start by asking her about her work and how she got into it; she's obviously very passionate about it. You are one of the few people who can understand her accomplishments. Just ask her questions. Relax and have fun. Don't worry about an agenda; just go with the flow. All you have to remember is to keep the focus on her."

Greg nodded, smiling.

Josh glanced at Tim and shook his head slightly. "I suspect that won't be hard."

As they reached the car, Josh activated his phone and voice-texted, "Jen, you there?"

"Yes, Josh."

He wondered if she was ever away from her phone. "Can you help me find out where the BOTIC chip is manufactured?"

"Sure, I can look it up." Within seconds, she added, "It's manufactured by Lenovo Mobile in Wuhan, China. Lenovo is China's largest maker of mobile phones and the second biggest PC-maker in the world."

Josh showed the text to Tim and Greg.

Greg asked, "Who's Jen?"

"She's kind of my research assistant."

He nodded. "Is she single?"

Josh smiled. "Yes she is . . . but she's seven years old."

Greg said, "Oh . . . anyway, the fact that the BOTIC chip is manufactured in China isn't surprising." He paused. "What *is* interesting," he tilted his head slightly, "is that China doesn't allow the BOTIC chip to be installed in any of *their* cell phones."

Josh's eyebrows went up. "That *is* interesting."

Tim shook his head. "Time to take this to the Director."

24

CONNECT

The next day, Greg was ushered into Lee's office. He stood for a few moments waiting for her to acknowledge him. She never looked around her giant monitors, so he sat down at the small conference table in front of her desk. After a minute, he cleared his throat. He could hear her typing on her keyboard, clearly ignoring him. Finally, he said, "Dr. Lee, I understand the concept of BOTIC, but how were you able to optimize the network without using central servers?"

The typing stopped. He heard a heavy sigh and after a few moments, saw her head appear above a monitor. Only a little over five feet tall, she had to stand to see him over the giant screens. With little enthusiasm, she said, "Just a sec."

She sat back down and made a quick telephone call. Then he heard rustling papers. Finally, she came around her desk with an iPad. Sitting across from him, she began sketching out a basic diagram, and said, "OK, it's really quite simple . . ."

As she spoke, Greg studied it carefully and asked questions about the chip's algorithms.

She drew a more elaborate diagram on a notepad and wrote out several equations.

Greg nodded and asked increasingly detailed questions.

She moved around the table to sit next to him so she didn't have to keep turning her tablet upside down. As the explanations progressed, Greg found himself completing her sentences. When he did, she would raise her eyebrows, and her explanations became more animated. She talked and Greg listened for over an hour.

Finally, Greg shook his head in amazement. "What an incredibly elegant solution. Dr. Lee, do you realize, in addition to a brilliant engineering concept, you solved an intractable mathematical problem?"

She nodded, smiling. "Call me Jessica."

He slapped the tabletop enthusiastically. "Mathematicians are always making fun of us engineers, but you totally—"

"Smoked 'em!" she finished.

Laughing, they high-fived.

Lee said, "Well, enough about my incredible brilliance." With an impish smile, she added, "Tell me how you figured out the dual-frequency firing problem and saved London."

Greg shook his head. "That's a long story, and everyone knows it."

"Oh, no you don't!" She shook her head emphatically. "If I had to explain BOTIC, you're going to explain the Blaster."

Greg shrugged and began to recount the story, emphasizing the technical details.

Like Greg, Lee asked questions throughout.

He finished with the firing and implosion of the Blaster on the Antarctic mountaintop.

She said, "Wait a minute! You said something about a cruise missile." She wagged her finger at him. "Don't gloss over that."

Greg looked surprised. "Did I?"

She nodded.

"Oops."

She gave him a challenging look.

Greg glanced around unnecessarily and then with a sigh, launched into the real story behind the firing. He became very animated as he described the F-18 ejection, the SEAL shooting Josh, and the near miss of the Tomahawks.

"You ejected out of a fighter?" She narrowed her eyes. "Is this for real?"

Greg nodded.

"They didn't have any of that in the docudrama." She shook her head. "I want to hear more detail, but," she looked at the time on her phone, "I'm hungry. How about you?"

"Starving."

"What do ya like to eat?"

"Mostly unhealthy food."

"Me too. Got just the place."

Greg found himself in a noisy Irish Pub sharing delicious, deep fat fried bar food and cold beer.

The conversation moved from engineering to childhood. They were both precocious and similarly ostracized, but Greg realized how they handled it was very different. Greg was happy to be a loner and avoid conflict at all cost. Lee waded into the middle of it, taking adversaries head-on. The results she recounted were sometimes victorious, often comic and sometimes tragic.

Greg said, "I was the class Valedictorian, but I had the world's shortest speech. I freaked out and said, 'Being Valedictorian and having to talk sucks. Let's graduate.' I got a standing ovation. How about you?"

She frowned and slowly said, "Probably would have been if I hadn't been suspended my senior year . . ." she grimaced, "for fighting."

Greg's eyes got big. "Someone picked a fight with you?"

"Actually . . ." she shrugged, "I kinda started it."

He just looked at her.

She gave a small laugh. "Kayla Richardson. We were friends, but always competing with each other. She used to call me Chairman Mao."

"Why?"

"When I got involved in clubs and organizations, I kinda ended up running most of them. I really didn't mind the name. It was kind of a compliment, but . . . ." She stopped and sighed. "One day Kayla got really mad at me over something. She told everyone that my parents dumped me. So I hit her." She rolled her eyes. "I know that was stupid, but it really hurt when she said that. I'd told her about my parents sending me to the U.S. to get an education. In China, traditions die hard. My brother, the number one son, got all the attention and got to stay in China with our family. They sent me to live with some old relatives in California when I was five. My foster parents were OK, but really didn't have time for, or interest, in me."

"Are your parents still in China?"

"Yeah."

Greg asked, "What do they do?"

"My mother's a medical scientist. My father was in the military, but I don't know if he still is or what he does . . . and I don't care."

Greg didn't say anything but raised his eyebrows slightly.

She hesitated and then gave him a slight sigh. "He only flew me back to China a few times. The last time I talked to my dad was when he called me on my eighteenth birthday. I told him I was going to become an American citizen. I even changed the spelling of my last name from L I to L E E. The conversation kind of went, uh, downhill from there."

Greg grimaced sympathetically and said, "I'm so sorry, Jessica."

She shrugged. "I still talk to my mother, but I haven't talked to my dad in over ten years and that's fine with me."

As they started their third round of beers, the conversation moved back to the events leading up to the first Blaster firing.

With a frown, Lee asked, "So, are you saying that this Fuze guy I met was, like, the program manager for the original Blaster?"

Greg nodded. "Totally, but he was more than just the manager; he came up with the idea to use a pilot laser beam to punch a hole in the atmosphere."

She looked skeptical. "Really?"

"Absolutely. He's like *super* smart."

She nodded. "Yeah, he looks part Chinese." Smiling sheepishly, she added, "Uh, no offense."

Greg smiled. "None taken." He continued, "And, somehow, he knew of the comet's existence a year before anyone else detected it."

She shook her head, "How?"

Greg shrugged. "The official explanation was that it came from one of our deep-space probes." He narrowed his eyes. "But if that were the case, it would have come in through NASA, and I know for a fact Dr. Chandra was as skeptical about the information as the rest of us."

"So if it wasn't NASA, where'd the comet information come from?"

He shook his head, "We never knew. We used to debate it all the time. Some thought the source was super-secret military hardware. Others were convinced the information came from aliens." He grinned.

Lee rolled her eyes. "OK, but I still don't understand why the

SEALs shot him, and you said they almost blew you off the top of the mountain with cruise missiles!"

He shrugged again. "It *was* pretty sketch. I'm still not sure what was going on. I thought Commander Fuze was dead for almost a year."

"Wow. So, what does he say about it?"

"He just says the government's right hand wasn't talking to the left hand."

Lee laughed. "*That* I understand." She shook her head. "If I didn't know you were there, I'd swear you were making this up." She looked at him a little challengingly.

Greg laughed. "Never thought about how bizarre this sounds." He realized in his excitement and need to impress, he'd said more than he should have . . . a lot more. There must have been a reason Fuze's role in the operation was kept quiet, and he just gave it away.

She patted him on the hand. "It has to be true. It's too crazy to be fiction, and it's obvious why they didn't want this known. It would not only be embarrassing, it might have slowed down the deflection effort."

He leaned in close, and quietly said, "Jessica, I . . . uh, I probably shouldn't have shared all that. Would you mind kind of keeping that under your hat for now?"

Lee looked surprised and then said, "Sure, Greg." Smiling warmly, she added, "We brilliant engineers need to stick together, and, I . . . probably said more than I should have too."

There was an awkward pause, and then Lee said, "Excuse me. Gotta go to the girl's room."

As he watched her walk away, he knew Jessica Lee was the most amazing woman he'd ever met.

She glanced back and caught him following her with his eyes. Smiling, she said softly to herself, "Got him."

25

CIA

Josh met Tim at CIA headquarters.

He handed Josh a file.

Opening it, he saw a picture of a cute little girl. Looking at Tim, he asked, "Jen?"

"Maybe. You didn't give us much to go on, but this is the most likely candidate."

She had black curly hair, mocha skin and intelligent, smiling green eyes. She was very cute and definitely multi-racial. "Where'd you get this?"

"It's from one of the social media sites designed specifically for kids. I pulled in some favors and got access."

Excited, he asked, "Where does she live and who does she live with?"

Tim said, "We're still working on that. For these sites, the children have to have the parent's permission to register. She only has one parent listed, a G. Moore, but there's no address or other information on him in the database, which is unusual."

With a slight smile, Josh said, "You mean like us?"

Shrugging, Tim said, "Access requires a small monthly fee, so we'll try to track him via his PayPal account."

Josh frowned.

"Don't worry; we'll find her."

Greg arrived, and Tim led them to a small conference room. They didn't have to wait long before Davidson joined them along with Carl Casey. Josh introduced them. "Greg, this is Brian Davidson, the Director of the CIA, and Carl Casey." To Davidson, he added, "I think you remember Greg's role in our Blaster op."

Josh saw Davidson smile slightly at Josh's use of "our."

As Davidson shook Greg's hand, he said, "Honored to finally meet you, Greg. Can't tell you how much I appreciate what you did on top of Mount Howe, not to mention all your development work on the Blaster."

Greg stammered, "Thank you. It's . . . good to meet you, sir."

While Davidson and Greg talked, Josh said to Carl, "Never thanked you for providing the *high cover* for me at Mount Howe, and congratulations on receiving the Intelligence Star. If it hadn't been for you and Tim, none of us might be here today."

Carl gave him a slight headshake. "It was almost too little, too late, and I have to confess I wasn't sure I'd made the right call right up to the last second." He smiled slightly. "Thought I might end up in the prison cell next to yours." He added, "By the way, we really enjoyed meeting Elizabeth. She's an impressive lady. Kelly fell in love with her and is already demanding we spend more time together."

Josh, trying to sound casual, said, "Uh, yeah, that would be great." Changing the subject he asked, "So, how's Caitlin doing?"

Carl laughed. "She's three-and-a-half and into everything. Last week, she was in the backyard with me. Before I knew it, she was filling the lawn mower's gas tank with water from the garden hose."

Josh smiled. Trying not to sound too interested, he asked, "Pictures?"

Carl immediately pulled out his phone.

Josh saw the smiling face of a beautiful little redheaded girl. He was thankful she got Kelly's looks, but in Caitlin's eyes, he saw a little of his old self. She was unquestionably his daughter. Josh studied the pictures carefully, committing them to memory. He made encouraging comments to keep Carl in presentation mode. The next pictures were of his beautiful Kelly holding Caitlin. She looked very happy, but it was hard to look at her. Josh wasn't an emotional guy, but he found his eyes getting glassy as he looked at pictures of his widow and beautiful daughter. Rubbing his eyes, Josh said, "Dang allergies."

The pictures were interrupted when a four star admiral entered the room.

Davidson introduced Admiral Ken Shearer as both the Director of the NSA *and* Commander of U.S. Cyber Command. They sat down around a small conference table, Shearer and Carl on Davidson's left, and Tim, Josh, and Greg on his right.

Davidson turned to Tim and Josh. "So, what do we have?"

Tim ran through the interviews they had with Armani, Bentley and Lee, only leaving out details like *breaking and entering*.

When he finished, Davidson nodded. "Thanks, Tim. Turning to Admiral Shearer, he said, "Ken, what are your thoughts?"

Shearer leaned forward and said, "The evidence that all the cyber-attacks are related is circumstantial, but very strong. We're still investigating the social media hack, but I think we've come to the same conclusion." He paused. "What worries me is that this wasn't just a software attack, they hacked the *hardware*. They came in through this BOTIC chip." He shook his head. "We've worked hard to counter software attacks, but hardware hacking is much more insidious and potentially dangerous."

Davidson frowned. "But to hack a chip, don't you have to actually build a malicious circuit into the chip?"

"Yes, but chip architecture is so complex and compartmentalized, a chip designer can insert a tiny circuit with a malicious program that no one would notice, or, in this case, one that allows unauthorized access to the chip's functions."

Greg asked, "Why would they do that?"

Shearer said, "It could be a simple act of vengeance by a chip designer or an insurance policy in case they're fired, or . . . it could be something more coordinated and malevolent."

Josh turned the question around and asked Greg, "Why do you think *Dr. Lee* did it?"

Frowning, Greg said, "I think it's different in her case. She believes her chip is capable of much more and wants to prove what it can do."

With a slight smile, Josh added, "She doesn't suffer from a *lack* of self-confidence."

Shearer said, "Back to the question at hand. The other common thread between the attacks is that no one has claimed responsibility for them."

Davidson added, "Which means we have yet to figure out their motive."

Josh said slowly, "Maybe we should first ask, if someone really could control the BOTIC chip in everyone's phone, what *could* they do?"

Greg cleared his throat nervously. "If the hackers can control our phones and all the apps on them, they could bring civilization to its knees."

Davidson smiled. "Greg, I understand they might be able to shut our phones down and embarrass people on social media…but bring civilization to its knees? I can remember the world before cell phones."

Greg nodded. "Yes sir, but social media was only the most recent and public attack. Remember, they successfully manipulated navigation apps, creating global traffic jams. Within a few minutes, they tripled the value of several stocks, and the BOTIC chip isn't just in phones; it's now in tablets, laptops and even cars."

Shearer glanced from Greg to Davidson and said, "I'm afraid I'd tend to agree with Greg. The hackers did all this, not by denying access, but by taking control of it and subverting information. They could potentially shutdown global communication, gridlock international transportation and even crash the world's stock markets." He paused. "They might not shut down civilization but if you control all the information a population sees, you control the population."

Davidson nodded thoughtfully. "The part I find disturbing is that the BOTIC chip is manufactured in China, but not allowed in Chinese phones."

Tim asked, "How does the Chinese government explain that?"

Shearer said, "They claim they've allocated enough bandwidth and don't need it. The real reason is probably that BOTIC allows phones to communicate with each other like walkie-talkies without going through a central server."

Greg asked, "Why would they care?"

Shearer said, "Because it makes it harder to monitor cell phone conversations." With a slight smile, the Director of the NSA said, "Trust me on that one."

Greg shook his head. "But why would the Chinese want to play hacker pranks on us?"

Shearer said, "They may be probing our systems as a prelude to an attack."

Greg looked puzzled. "But aren't we, like, their biggest market?"

Davidson said, "Yes, but with their massive economic growth, we're competing for decreasing resources, like oil."

Shearer added, "They've been investing heavily in military technology and infrastructure. Their sixth aircraft carrier battle group just became operational. If they continue their growth, they'll eclipse us and be the world's largest Navy by the end of the decade." The admiral raised his eyebrows, adding, "Navies do a lot of things, but are particularly effective at projecting power across the globe."

Davidson added, "The Chinese are also expanding their nuclear arsenal." He paused. "But let's not jump to conclusions. This is all circumstantial. We need to find the truth — who's really behind this."

Tim said, "Dr. Lee appears to be cooperative. She said she needed to check some things that might narrow the possibilities. We're going to meet with her again tomorrow."

Davidson said, "Good. Her knowledge is essential to figuring this out." Clearly wrapping up the meeting, he said, "Thank you, gentlemen, for the excellent work. This has become a national security priority. Please keep me informed."

Josh turned his phone back on and felt it vibrate. Looking down, he saw a text from Jen. "Dr. Jessica Lee just boarded a plane for Shanghai." Josh said, "Hold on. Just got a text that says Dr. Lee's on her way to China."

Davidson turned to Carl. "Can you confirm that?"

Carl grabbed a phone in the room.

Tim said, "That can't be. We had her on a priority watch list."

Greg looked at them questioningly.

Davidson said, "That means she shouldn't have been able to make a reservation or get within 25 miles of an airport without our knowing."

Carl, still holding the phone, said, "Dr. Lee *is* headed for Shanghai. She caught a flight from D.C. to Detroit two hours ago, and her flight from Detroit to Shanghai just took off."

Shearer looked at Davidson and shook his head ominously. "Unit 61398?"

Frowning, Davidson nodded.

Greg asked, "Unit what?"

Shearer said, "Over the past 10 years, we've traced an overwhelming number of attacks on American corporations and U.S. government agencies to one location." He paused. "A 12-story building in a rundown neighborhood on the outskirts of Shanghai. It's under the control of the People's Liberation Army, and they refer to it as Unit 61398."

Tim said, "We might be able to divert the flight."

Still holding the phone, Carl said, "It's a China Eastern Airline jet, and they'll be out of U.S. airspace in a few minutes."

Davidson said, "The Canadians would help us out, but diverting a Chinese national airliner wouldn't be subtle." He shook his head. "She's an American citizen, and we don't have time to provide probable cause for an arrest warrant." He looked around the table. "This changes things. The evidence is still circumstantial, but growing." Davidson looked at Tim. "How fast can you be in China?"

Tim, getting a nod from Josh and Greg, said, "Next flight."

Davidson said, "I'll hook you up with the local station chief and assign whatever in-country assets you need." He paused. "You'll need a cover story."

Greg threw in, "I'm working on the space-based laser. It's an international effort, and we have colleagues all over the world, including China. We're going to use some of their heavy-lift rockets and their new space station to help with assembly."

Davidson said, "Perfect. No one would question your presence, and your reputation imparts some protection." He looked at Tim and Josh. "You two can be his government liaison."

They nodded.

Shearer said, "In light of this, I'm going to recommend to the President that we go to INFOCON 2 and," he blew out a lungful of air, "DEFCON 4."

III

DEFCON

双重间谍将被揭示

26

SHANGHAI

They had an hour to make the connection to Shanghai out of Dulles International, earning them a high-speed police escort to the airport.

On the way, Tim updated the text encryption app on their phones so they could communicate securely once in China.

Josh bought and downloaded the most advanced Mandarin language program he could find. He would use the flight to start learning Chinese.

They arrived at the airport, and by skipping security, hit their gate 10 minutes before boarding.

While standing outside the gate, Tim received a call. After he finished, he said to Josh, "Looks like Lee was able to slip out undetected because our tracking system missed her flight reservations due to a *software* glitch."

Josh exhaled. "As if running weren't enough to indict her, she must have hacked the CIA's tracking system."

Tim said, "She . . . or whoever she's working for. She may be nothing more than the technical skills behind the attacks. Unfortunately, we're chasing her to a place where she has home-field advantage."

Josh frowned. "If the Chinese government is behind this—"

Tim finished, "We could be walking into a trap."

Josh nodded toward Greg. "Need to let lover boy know."

Greg was coming back from an airport shop with an ice cream cone. Josh met him and asked, "Good?"

"Love ice cream. Calms my nerves."

"Then you may want to grab another one."

"Why?"

"Lee slipped past us because of a software *issue*." He looked Greg in the eye. "It's looking more like Lee could be one of the bad guys."

Greg smiled. "You're suggesting I might not get a date."

Josh just raised his eyebrows.

Greg shook his head. "Look, I know you think I'm smitten by her. I admit she's pretty hot, and I still think she's innocent, but I know I could be totally wrong."

Josh said, "Yeah, and if it turns out she's part of something much bigger, we could be headed into real trouble. Even if she's innocent, she could be a pawn in a bigger plot." He shook his head. "Look, Greg, I've already taken you into some very dangerous situations. The CIA hired you as a consultant, not to do black ops. Unlike last time, you have time to think about this one. I wouldn't hold it against you for a second if you sit this one out. You can still help us from here by phone and secure text."

Chasing the ice cream down into the cone, Greg said, "Are you serious?" Using the cone to punctuate his statements, he said, "First of all, trying to help you long-distance is about as effective as trying to tell my grandma how to remove a computer virus over the phone." He rolled his eyes. "Second, I'm getting to do what most guys only pretend to do in video games. I'm totally in. Besides," he grinned, "the Director said I'm a national asset. They wouldn't dare touch me."

Josh nodded. "That's only true if they're not planning on wiping out the Western world."

Greg gave him a half-smile. "If they are . . . doesn't really matter where I am, does it?"

Josh matched his smile. "OK, but just in case, you've got five minutes before we board."

Greg threw his empty cone away and said, "Commander Fuze, I know the danger's real, but this time — no offense — I think I understand what's at stake more than you do."

Like Lee, they landed in Detroit, but from there, they took a Delta flight to Shanghai. On the Boeing 787, the agency gave them business class seats, which allowed them to sleep comfortably on the 15-hour flight.

With little need for sleep, Josh jumped into his Mandarin language program. He used his cyber glasses and noise cancelling ear buds. The jet's ambient noise allowed him to practice his pronunciations without disturbing anyone, and he discovered he could speed up the audios.

Nine hours into the flight, he was almost through the syllabus. He took a break and used the plane's Wi-Fi to text Jen. "Thank you for warning us Dr. Lee was leaving for China. That was very important. You are an awesome assistant!"

She texted back, "Thank you. I also found out where Heaven is."

Josh couldn't help but smile as he typed back, "You did? And where is it?"

"It's in one of the seven collapsed dimensions of Superstring Theory."

His eyebrows went up. Little Jen was definitely not an average seven-year-old. He'd had similar thoughts — another indication he and Jen were cousins. He was about to ask her how she had arrived at this conclusion, when she asked, "Do you think that's where God lives?"

Where was Elizabeth when he needed her? He didn't want to get into a theological discussion, partly because he didn't know what he believed himself, but also because he was afraid of how her guardians might react if they saw his texts. He couldn't risk being cut off from her. So, he did what Jesse did to him. "Jen, what do you think?"

"God has to exist."

Curious, Josh asked, "And why is that?"

"Your DNA code is way streamlined. You were designed recently, and so was I. I've been reading up about genetics. Nobody can do that."

He was impressed with her logic. She was right about the state-of-the-art in genetics. He'd done similar research and came to the same conclusion, but there were several other possibilities that didn't require a supreme being. He didn't want to bias her by sharing his conjecture. "We'll talk more about that later. Jen, I'm on my way to China and need to finish learning to speak Chinese before I get there."

She texted back, "Did you know there are over 6,500 different languages?"

"No, I didn't. That probably explains many of the misunderstandings we have in the world today."

She replied, "Chinese is spoken by more people than any other language. I'll learn how to speak it too."

Josh bet she could learn it as fast as he could. "That'd be great. Then we can practice with each other." He added, "But you also need to get outside and play."

Jen responded, "I can't go outside."

"Are you still grounded?"

"Kind of."

"Did you get in trouble because you're talking to me? I don't want to get you in trouble."

"No! Talking to you is the best thing I get to do all day. Please don't stop talking to me."

"I promise I won't. Talking to you is one of the best things I get to do all day too." As he set his phone down, he realized that was a true statement. As soon as Tim found her, they would pay her guardians a visit.

He finished the language syllabus and caught a couple hours of sleep before they landed.

After getting through customs, Greg said, "Hey, let's take the Maglev. Did you know it's the fastest train in the world?"

Tim said, "It's just a technology demonstrator. Only goes to the outskirts of the city. It won't shorten our trip at all."

Greg shrugged. "I like technology demonstrators."

Tim shook his head.

Josh winked at Greg. "Maybe *Dad* will let us ride it on the way home."

The cab ride from Pudong International Airport to their hotel was about an hour, which allowed Josh to test his newfound language on the taxi driver. Chinese had been harder for him to learn than Spanish, but he was already able to understand, and to a lesser degree, be understood.

Greg shook his head and said, "Those language programs must have gotten a lot better since I tried them."

It was late afternoon as they drove into the city. Perched on the east coast of China, Shanghai was arguably the largest city in the world by population. As such, it didn't look that different from any other modern mega-metropolis. The skyline was very impressive, but it was also unique. It almost looked like there was a skyscraper competition that rewarded unusual shapes.

They arrived at their hotel near the city's center. Tim wanted to keep them all together, so he reserved a large suite with multiple bedrooms. It was luxurious and decorated in Western style with a touch of the orient. As soon as the bellman left, Tim pulled out a device about the size of a cell phone and scanned the entire suite for surveillance bugs. Finally nodding, he said, "Place looks clean, but you can never be sure. Be careful what you talk about." He leaned toward them and whispered, "Need to check in with the local talent. Stay here. I'll be back in an hour."

After the long flight, Josh appreciated being able to slip off his shoes and the heavy Taser ring that was pinching his finger. He went into one of the bedrooms with his suitcase, threw it on the bed and checked his phone for texts. There weren't any from Jen. He wanted to check in on her, but was nervous about initiating text, afraid her guardians might notice it.

As he started to unpack, his phone rang. It was Elizabeth. Josh sat down on the edge of the bed to talk. Before leaving, he'd told her that their conversations might be monitored. He knew she just wanted to know they'd arrived safely.

Elizabeth asked, "How's the weather?"

"Kind of like it was in Columbia, upper sixties."

He asked her how the U.N. relief work was going.

She was excited to tell him about their accomplishments and also shared some frustrations.

Josh smiled. Office politics were universal. They talked for another 10 minutes about nothing in particular.

Elizabeth asked, "So, how's Greg handling the trip?"

Before Josh could answer, a short scream echoed through the suite.

As Josh turned to see what happened, Elizabeth exclaimed, "Oh my God! What was that?"

Josh stifled a laugh, and yelled, "Greg, you OK?"

There was a low moaning sound from the floor, next to the table where he'd set his ring.

Into the phone, Josh said, "Sorry. Greg was, uh, playing with something . . . electrical . . . he shouldn't have. Hang on a sec."

Trying not to laugh, he said, "Told you not to mess with that." He shook his head and more sympathetically, said, "It'll take a few minutes, but you'll be able to reattach your head shortly."

With a small whimpering sound, Greg waved his hand from the floor.

On the phone, Josh said, "He's OK."

Elizabeth, knowing about Josh's ring experience, said, "Like father, like son?"

Josh smiled. "Dang curious engineers."

They wrapped up their conversation, and he went to help Greg. Tim was right; it was funny when you were on the other side. Suppressing a smile, he pulled Greg off the floor. Just as Greg was standing up, Tim returned.

Tim looked at Greg dusting himself off and gave them both a questioning look.

Josh bent over, picked up his Taser ring from the floor and held it up.

Tim just shook his head with a slight smile and then motioned them close. He whispered, "It's more challenging to track our target in Shanghai, but the local office found out she headed for her parents' home after she landed. It's just outside the city. Turns out Lee's father isn't just a military officer, he's a General *and* a member of the Central Military Commission."

Josh whistled softly.

Greg asked, "What's the Central Military Commission?"

Josh said, "An 11-member board in charge of all the military forces in China."

Tim continued, "The U.S. just went to DEFCON 3. Officially, they're saying the higher defense posture allows them to engage military assets to stop the hacking."

Josh said, "But . . . ?"

Tim said, "They're sending an aircraft carrier battle group toward China and deploying several squadrons to Hawaii and Guam, ostensibly, for training exercises."

Greg asked, "Won't the Chinese know it's not for training purposes?"

Josh said, "That's the point. It's intended to send a message. Let them know they're on the suspect list, and if they're involved, they need to stop immediately."

Greg nodded and then said, "I'm starving."

They were all hungry. To save time, they ordered from room service.

As it arrived, Greg started checking out the various dishes. Latching on to warm, parchment colored dumplings, he bit one in half. Liquid immediately ran down his chin and onto his shirt.

Tim said, "That would be Xiaolongbao. They're filled with pork and—"

"Soup?" Greg finished.

Tim nodded.

Greg shrugged and grabbed another. This time he stuffed the whole thing in his mouth.

After they finished, Josh quietly asked, "What's the plan?"

Tim leaned in. "We have the address of her parents. We'll position ourselves outside their house, call her and ask to meet."

Josh said, "That might just send her into hiding."

"That's why we'll be outside the house. If she wants to talk, we can do it quickly. If she bolts, we might be able to intercept her or follow her."

Greg smiled shyly. "I have her unlisted cell phone number."

Josh grinned. "Told you I'd help you meet women—"

"That are a threat to national security," Tim finished.

Josh shrugged. "Picky . . . picky . . . picky."

27

SUSPECT

Dr. Jessica Lee drove to her parents' house on the outskirts of Shanghai. Located in a gated community, their home was a beautiful, two-story, contemporary house with a Frank Lloyd Wright look. It sat in the middle of a large, perfectly manicured lawn. Surrounding the property was a black, wrought-iron fence, ornate but tall enough to provide security.

As she drove up the driveway, she was impressed with their home, particularly considering they were government employees ... but it wasn't *her* home. Not only didn't she grow up here, she'd never even seen pictures of this place. Although she talked to her mother several times a year, the last time she'd actually seen her was 14 years ago.

Taking a deep breath, she gathered up her courage and headed for the front door. Before she could knock, Dr. Li Sun opened the door. She came out and cupped her daughter's hands in hers. Seeing the tears in her mother's eyes, Jessica hugged her. Hugging definitely wasn't traditional, but her mother returned the hug. They clung to each other for quite a while. It felt good.

As they separated, Jessica saw her father standing just inside the door. He was watching her intently with an inscrutable expression. Relatively tall and solidly built, he had close-cropped, salt-and-pepper hair and a handsome but serious face. The one thing she remembered about him was his ramrod-straight posture. Jessica acknowledged him with a simple nod. He nodded back, turned and went inside.

Jessica took off her shoes and followed her mother down a tiled hall into the living room. It was a mix of traditional and contemporary. The floor was light-colored marble. The walls were simple white, contrasted by beautiful painted landscapes, hung close to the ceiling.

Looking further into the house's open floor plan, she saw large windows overlooking what appeared to be an open central courtyard. The courtyard was right in the middle of the house. With a small garden and the sun reflecting off a little pond, it looked very tranquil. She didn't have the patience for gardening, but that didn't stop her from appreciating it.

As she sat next to her mother on a plush leather sofa, a servant put tea on the small table in front of them. Her father, who hadn't said a word, sat in a chair opposite them.

She exchanged small talk with her mother for several minutes. Jessica found her Chinese a little rusty and was sometimes at a loss for the right word. Except for talking to her mother on the phone, she'd hardly spoken Chinese since she graduated from high school, and only then because the Chinese relatives she lived with insisted.

After a natural pause in the conversation, Jessica got to the point. Turning to face her father, she said, "In answer to your unasked question of why I'm here," she took a deep breath, "I received a visit from a couple of NSA agents, Tim Smith and Josh Fuze, and an engineer named Greg Langlois. They all but accused me of creating the BOTIC chip to allow a backdoor for hackers."

Her father said, "Did you?"

Jessica's eyes flashed, but she kept her voice steady. "You don't understand. They suspect that the Chinese government is behind it."

He shook his head dismissively. "That's ridiculous."

"Is it? Look at what's been happening in the world. All the recent hacking events took advantage of my chip and—"

He snorted derisively. "These are just stunts and anyone stupid enough to post private information on the Internet, gets what they deserve."

She kept her voice level. "Maybe, but China is the only place where these things *haven't* happened."

"Coincidence."

"Really? My BOTIC chip is manufactured in China, yet China is the only country in the world that doesn't allow the chip to be used in their phones."

He put his hand down firmly on the table next to him. "We had nothing to do with these attacks."

Jessica said, "Are you sure?"

His expression stayed the same, but his eyes flashed. "You have no right to question me."

"I'm an American; I can question whatever I want!"

"You're not in America." He shook his head. "This is how you show respect?"

She was incredulous. "Respect! Why should I give respect to people who have no respect for me?" She shook her head. "I was a second-class citizen behind my lazy brother. Nothing I did was ever good enough for you. You didn't need a daughter; you had a number one son!"

She felt her eyes getting glassy, but fought it. She wouldn't cry, not in front of this man.

He said, "I wanted a daughter."

She yelled, "You wanted a doormat!"

He angrily shook his head and almost shouted, "How could you give up your citizenship? How could you become a traitor to your own people?"

Jessica felt her face flush as the adrenaline rose. She shouted back, "What citizenship? I was never a Chinese citizen! You dumped me in another country and forgot about me. You threw me away like garbage! What did you think would happen?"

Her father's mouth opened, but nothing came out. He looked like someone punched him in the stomach. Jessica, ready to release another salvo, stopped, surprised by his reaction.

"Enough!" Her mother said with force. "You both seem to enjoy hurting each other." She looked at each of them and said more calmly. "This time, there's more at stake."

Jessica started to reply, but her mother shut her down with a look.

Her father stood up slowly and walked out of the room.

For the first time, she noticed he was getting old.

After he left, her mother sighed and asked when she had eaten last.

She shook her head, too angry to think about food. "I don't know, but I'm not hungry."

Her mother, looking at her with concern, said, "You need to eat something. I'll be right back."

As her mother went into the kitchen, Jessica took a deep breath. To help her settle down, she did something familiar and checked her phone.

There was a new text. "Are you all right?"

She texted back, "Yes, Jen, I'm fine. Why do you ask?"

"Your dad said mean things to you."

She shook her head as she texted, "Jen, you shouldn't eavesdrop on other people's conversations. We've talked about this. It's not nice, and it's not legal."

Jen texted back, "I'm sorry. I was worried. I promise I won't do it again."

Jessica sighed. "It's OK, but please don't worry about me. I'm fine. It's a little complicated. I'll try to explain it to you later." They'd been texting just before she arrived, so Jen knew about the meeting. Most phones were always in *listen* mode so they could accept voice commands. Somehow, Jen had managed to keep their connection live and listen in. This little girl was unquestionably a genius, and from what Jessica knew about her situation, her family was ignoring her too. That probably explained why Jen had sought her out, and why Jessica had taken her under her wing as her little protégé.

Jen texted, "Josh Fuze, Tim Smith and Greg Langlois are in Shanghai."

Startled, Jessica texted back, "Are you sure?"

"They just got to their hotel."

"Jen, how do you know that?"

"I talk to Josh a lot. He's very nice to me. I love him."

Frowning, she texted, "How do you know him?"

There was a slight pause. "We were both designed."

She typed back, "Designed? I don't understand."

Jen replied, "I think we were both designed to help people."

Jessica, picturing Josh, remembered one of her first thoughts was that he was multi-racial and clearly part Asian. She also remembered everything that Greg had said about his abilities. She was trying to get her arms around the idea, when her mother came back with soup and a bowl of fruit. Impulsively, Jessica told her about Jen and showed her the text. Although her mother spoke only broken English, as with many scientists, she read English quite well.

After her mother read the texts, Jessica asked, "Is this possible?"

Avoiding eye contact with her daughter, she said, "Anything is possible."

With narrowed eyes, Jessica asked, "Mother, do you know something about this?"

"Jessica, I'm a geneticist...." She stopped and then said, "May I please show this to your father?" She paused. "He is a high-ranking general in the People's Army."

Surprised, Jessica said, "He is?" She realized how little she knew about her parents. She also knew this text might help him realize how serious the situation was, but she found herself illogically not wanting to share anything with him. She nodded grudgingly.

Her mother left the room and after a few minutes came back with her father.

Jessica gave her phone back to her mother, who in turn, showed it to her husband.

He read it quickly.

She forgot that her father had earned a graduate degree in the U.S.

Her mother emphasized to him that Josh Fuze was the NSA agent who had interrogated their daughter.

Her father glanced at her.

She couldn't help but notice for the first time his expression didn't carry disdain. For a second, he almost looked . . . concerned. Then, his mask returned, and he said, "I need to inform the authorities."

Jessica couldn't resist. "I thought you *were* the authorities."

Surprisingly, he reacted with the slightest of smiles, which Jessica took as an implied "touché." He turned to leave, saying, "Stay here."

Before she could retort, he added, "For your own protection."

After he was gone, she said, "And *why* did you marry him?"

Her mother laughed and then answered the question with a question. "And is there someone in your life?"

Jessica shrugged. "No . . . not really."

Her mother raised her eyebrows in question.

She sighed. "Remember the original Blaster team in Antarctica that saved London? A young engineer got the software to work at the last minute and figured out how to get the lasers to fire in two different frequencies almost simultaneously."

Her mother smiled. "I remember the actor who played him in the made-for-TV movie."

Jessica laughed. "Well, Greg Langlois is that engineer. He was with Fuze and Smith. They assigned him to work with me in order to figure out how the chip worked."

"And?"

"He's kind of cute, and I think he really likes me."

"Do you have a picture of him?"

"I have one I pulled off the internet from a press interview." She showed it to her mother. "This isn't a very good picture at all. He dresses a lot better now."

Her mother smiled. "He's cute and he's black."

With a wry smile, Jessica said, "Father will have a stroke."

Her mother, matching her smile, shrugged.

"But it doesn't bother you?"

She laughed. "Jessica, I'm a geneticist! We all came out of Africa, just at different times." Smiling, she added, "He's a brilliant, courageous engineer like you. I will have beautiful, genius grandchildren."

Shaking her head, Jessica said, "We barely know each other." Smiling, she added, "But...thanks." She held her mother's hands in hers.

Then, looking serious, she said, "OK, Mother, what do you *really* know about genetically engineered humans?"

28

TARGET

General Li sat in the reception area talking to his wife on the phone, when the secretary signaled him. As he turned his phone off, he was ushered into a small but opulent conference room. Li bowed and shook hands with his old friend Wong Look, the Chinese Premier. Li said, "Thank you for seeing me on such short notice. I knew you were in Shanghai, and this is of the utmost importance." He proceeded to explain everything he'd learned from his daughter.

As he finished, the Premier said, "I've spoken to President Jiang recently. We know the West thinks we're involved with the hacking, but we only recently learned they believed it was all done through your daughter's chip." He nodded. "It explains the escalation."

Li frowned. "We are being accused based on nothing but circumstantial evidence." He paused. "But I'm afraid it paints a damaging picture. There are too many coincidences. Even the international media is looking at us with suspicion."

Matching his frown, the Premier said, "I'm very curious about these NSA agents." He paused. "We may want them brought in for questioning."

Li said, "They are accompanying Greg Langlois, the young engineer credited with helping save London. Arresting him might be awkward, and . . . ."

The Premier noticed his hesitation and gently prompted. "Yes?"

Li shook his head. "My wife just suggested that my daughter and he may be interested in each other."

The Premier smiled gently. "No need to be embarrassed, old friend. Times change. We can no longer guide our children as we

183

were guided." He paused. "It would only escalate tensions if we were to detain Mr. Langlois, and I'm sure he's simply being used as a cover. We must, however, determine what the Americans are planning."

Li asked, "Do you think these agents would have that information?"

"I don't know, but it's very unusual for them to send NSA agents into China."

Li nodded and then carefully asked, "Have you heard anything *unusual* about our *special* units or the cyber warfare teams?"

The Premier smiled. "I thought they were under your purview."

Li sighed. "I'm not sure they're really *part of* the People's Liberation Army."

The Premier nodded thoughtfully. "May I suggest you pay a visit to General Zeng and his . . . *kids* at the Unit?"

With a slight frown, Li nodded.

The Premier continued, "I'll inform President Jiang and have the Ministry of State Security pick up the NSA agents."

As the valet brought their car around, Josh watched Tim surveying the hotel lobby.

Tim casually got into the driver's seat, Josh in the passenger's and Greg in the back. Tim pulled out the same small electronic device he used in the hotel. "Car doesn't appear to be bugged, but we were being watched in the lobby."

It was getting dark as they left the hotel. They hadn't driven more than a few blocks when Josh glanced back and asked. "Are we being followed?"

Tim nodded.

Greg said, "How are we going to get to Jessica's with someone following us?"

Looking intently at his side and rearview mirrors, Tim said quietly, "We're not. In addition to the one following us, two more are coming up on the side."

Greg asked, "Where are we going?"

Tim said, "I don't think they plan to let us go anywhere.

They're waiting for a clear area so they can box us in and take us."

Josh asked, "You sure?"

"Not yet." Tim turned abruptly down a narrow side street and accelerated. They heard brakes squeal behind them. Looking back, Josh saw a black Audi back up and turn to follow them. As Tim hit the next intersection, he looked both ways and then ran the light, narrowly missing a car.

Still looking behind, Josh saw two identical cars in single file, chasing them. The first one also ran the light, but wasn't as lucky. They heard screeching tires and a loud bang as a car hit their pursuer and spun him around. Their second pursuer managed to maneuver around the wreck and continue the chase.

Tim shook his head. "I expected government interest, but not this soon or this aggressive."

Taking the next turn too fast, they slid sideways, as did Greg across the back seat. Hitting a curb, Greg's head bounced off the ceiling.

Josh, glancing back, said, "Seatbelts." Then to Tim, "You sure they're government?"

Greg yelled as they narrowly missed a pedestrian.

Tim said, "Classic MSS tactics and black Audi A6s are their favorite." He accelerated and darted through traffic.

From somewhere in the backseat they heard, "MSS?"

Josh said, "Ministry of State Security . . . kind of like the CIA and FBI combined." Josh shook his head. "Guess this answers our question about Chinese involvement."

Tim pulled a small piece of paper out of his shirt pocket and handed it to Josh. "Navigate us here. If I can shake 'em, we can lay low at this safe house until we figure out what's going on."

Josh donned his cyber glasses and read the location to his digital assistant. The results came back quickly. Josh said, "Keep going in this direction. It's about five klicks past the Grand Plaza."

At a small side street, Tim turned abruptly across the oncoming traffic lanes, forcing the cars to lock up their brakes and slide to a stop. The traffic jam created by his maneuver, hung up their pursuer.

As they sped away, Josh said, "I think you lost 'em."

Greg said, "I think I'm going to be sick."

Tim slowed down and drove at a more normal rate, but as they turned onto a main boulevard, four black A6s came out of nowhere and flanked them on both sides. As two of them pulled slightly ahead, Tim shook his head. "Nowhere to go."

Suddenly, all four A6s slowed to a stop as their lights went out.

Looking back with surprise, Josh said, "Looks like someone just turned their engines off." Seeing Greg with his geek cap and cyber glasses, he asked, "Did you do that?"

Greg said, "Any modern car can be disabled if you have access and the right codes." He shook his head. "But I had nothing to do with that." He looked at Tim. "Is that a CIA trick?"

"Probably, but I didn't do it either." He frowned. "Must be our local people."

After a few minutes, they entered the Grand Plaza. Across the square, they saw several conventional police cars with blue and red lights flashing. Tim shook his head. "Roadblock."

Josh's phone vibrated, and in his glasses, he saw a text from Jen. "Elton Musk's Shanghai headquarters is in a building off the Plaza." It even included nav app directions. She was an amazing kid.

He told Tim.

Tim looked around and said, "We have to proceed on foot." He pulled the car into an illegal parking place and said, "Let's go."

They jumped out and jogged to the east. They were almost to the end of the block when they heard a car slam on its brakes behind them. Glancing back, Josh saw a black A6 stopped next to their car.

All three of them ducked around the corner of a building and caught their breath. Greg said, "They found our car. Think they saw us?"

Tim said, "Doesn't matter. They know we're on foot. They'll have this entire area cordoned off within minutes."

With cyber glasses still on, Josh said, "Hal. Voice-text Elton Musk, via encryption."

Almost immediately, he heard, "Ready."

"Elton, it's Josh. Once again, need help quickly!"

Tim said, "That's his building over there." He looked around and said, "We gotta move. Greg, stay between Josh and me. Go!"

As they ran down the block, Josh heard the voice text reply in his earpiece, "Glad to hear rumors of your demise greatly exaggerated. How can I help?"

"In Shanghai with Tim and Greg. Will explain later, but MSS has taken an interest in us. Near your Shanghai office. Could we catch our breath in your flat?"

After a few seconds, he heard, "Go to the main elevator in the lobby. Hit and hold the penthouse floor button. At the same time, push floor 42. When you get to the suite door, type in 612 on the pad. After you're inside, let me know. Have some new hardware you'll find entertaining."

They ran inside the building and found a large open lobby with marble floors and a reception desk in the middle. There were only about a dozen people in the lobby as they walked quickly toward the bank of elevators at the back of the building. Waiting for the next elevator, they saw police spill into the lobby's main entrance.

An elevator door opened, but five people had to exit before they could jump in. Peering out, they saw one man at the building's entrance, pointing at them. Greg repeatedly smashed the "close door" button.

29

PURSUIT

As the elevator doors closed, they saw several men in black jackets running toward them.

Greg said, "Busted!"

Josh pushed the elevator floor buttons as Musk directed.

As the elevator climbed, Tim hit five random floor buttons and stepped to the back of the elevator.

Greg looked at him as if he were insane. "My mom used to slap me when I did that."

Tim said, "They saw us get into the elevator. They can watch the lights and see where we stop."

"Oh."

As they stopped on each floor, Greg dutifully smashed the "close door" button. Listening to the elevator music, Greg looked at Josh. "Hey, that's the muzaked version of **Mission: Impossible**."

Greg started bobbing his head in time to the beat, and Josh matched him. They both started humming the repetitive base melody, "dun dun . . . *dun-dun*, dun dun . . . *dun-dun* . . ."

Josh glanced back to see Tim shaking his head, but by the time they reached the top, all three were humming it.

As the doors opened on the penthouse floor, Josh rushed out to the only door and typed in the "sentinel" code. As it opened, he voice-texted Musk. "We're in, but may have company soon."

They closed the door and turned on the lights. It was comfortable and classy with beautiful, contemporary furnishings. What caught their attention was the view. Beyond the floor-to-ceiling windows, was a giant balcony and the brilliantly illuminated Shanghai cityscape

Musk's reply came back. "Two options. To the right side of my desk is a bookshelf. Behind the book, **Resurrect,** is a button that opens a secret door. Can hide in there for a while. That's also where option two is."

Josh ran to the bookshelf, as Tim said, "Not sure we want to stay here."

Finding the right book, Josh pushed the button behind it and a portion of the bookshelf swung open revealing a hidden room.

Tim said, "On the other hand . . . ."

As they went inside, the lights came on automatically. Looking around, they found themselves in a Spartan efficiency apartment with no windows. A refrigerator, sink, small stove and futon were on one side, a small desk with a computer and communication setup on the other. There were two doors. One opened to a small bathroom. The other was closed and unusually wide.

Josh opened it and turned on the light inside. It was a large closet. To the left were food supplies, on the right was a rack with several guns, but at the back was what looked like . . . it couldn't be. Josh crossed the small room and examined it.

Tim and Greg crowded in behind him.

Greg said, "What is it?"

Josh voice-texted Musk. "Looks like a JB-11 Jetpack, but bigger. What's up?"

Josh examined it while Tim checked out the weapons.

Musk's reply came back, "It *is* made by Jetpack Aviation, but it's a new prototype. It's faster, more maneuverable and has longer range due to small deployable wings."

Resting on spindly-looking tripod legs, Josh turned around and backed into the jetpack's harness. He voice-texted, "What'll she do?"

"With the wings deployed, she'll do 120 knots."

He put his arms on the small padded armrests. Each ended in a control. Josh voice-texted, "How do the controls work?"

"Don't know. Haven't flown it yet, but they say most people can learn to fly it after a few hours in a simulator."

Josh put his left hand around the control stick. It didn't move but twisted like a motorcycle throttle. He guessed it controlled engine power or maybe altitude. He grabbed the right control stick and felt it move like a joystick — backwards, forwards and side-to-side. It must control attitude like an aircraft's stick, but he noticed it also twisted. The twist could be throttle or yaw. Only one way to find out. "Payload?"

Musk replied, "Rated for 150 kilos."

He voice-texted back, "Quiet?"

"As quiet as having jet engines strapped to your back."

Tim pulled a nine-millimeter pistol off the wall.

Greg, impatient with hearing only half of Josh's conversation, said, "So?"

"It's a prototype jetpack powered by cruise missile engines."

Greg nodded appreciatively. "Pretty cool, but it ain't no **Iron Man** suit."

As Tim loaded a magazine into the pistol, he said, "They'll figure out where we are and be up here soon."

Josh nodded and exhaled sharply. "We can hide, but they'll probably find us eventually or wait us out." He patted the jetpack's armrest. "This thing can probably lift two of us."

Tim tilted his head. "Probably?"

Greg stopped smiling and said, earnestly, "I would *really* love to go with you Commander, but I don't want to die."

Tim added, "And someone's got to look after Greg."

Josh finished strapping in and carefully stood up, lifting the jetpack off its tripod legs. Grunting, he estimated it weighed almost as much as Greg. He took a deep breath. "OK, here's the plan. I'm going to fly this thing off the balcony. They won't be able to miss that. Hide in here, and they'll assume there was more than one jetpack or that we split up. We can rendezvous later at the safe house."

Tim nodded. "Might work."

Grunting, Josh said, "Help me get this thing to the balcony. Greg, grab the helmet."

As they maneuvered it across the floor, Tim looked skeptical. "You've flown one of these things?"

Josh shook his head.

"Good. Maybe you'll be more careful than you are with fighters."

Greg opened the balcony doors, and after they got it outside, handed Josh the helmet.

There was a small LCD screen on a stalk in front of him and he noticed it had a Bluetooth button on it. That should allow him to have a simple Heads-Up-Display piped to his cyber glasses. Facing the city, Josh saw a beautiful and spectacularly colorful, night cityscape. Peering over the railing and down fifty stories, it lost some of its beauty. Josh looked at Tim and Greg and said, "OK, if I crash and die in this thing — whatever you do — *do not* tell Elizabeth I was killed trying to fly a jetpack."

Tim and Greg just looked at each other with puzzled frowns.

They heard noise coming from the hall outside the suite.

Josh whispered, "Hide!" Tim and Greg ran back to the secret bookcase door as Josh hit the start button. He heard knocking on the door, but the growing whine of the turbine quickly drowned out all sound.

He quickly pulled the helmet on and then his cyber glasses. Then plugged the helmet's audio cable into his phone and stuffed the phone in his pocket.

As the little jet engine's whine became a roar, Josh gingerly twisted what he thought was the throttle. It was very sensitive. He tried to get it to hover, but as his feet left the ground, he wobbled. He caught the wobble with the right hand joystick, but slid backwards, crashing the jetpack against the balcony doors and shattering the glass. With the impact, he accidentally twisted the joystick, which rotated him. By the time he got the hang of the rotation, he'd turned 180 degrees and was now looking back into the suite through the broken balcony doors.

He saw the secret door swing shut just as the door to the suite blew open. Concentrating on controlling the hover, he carefully pulled the right joystick back, moving him away from the doors and the side of the building. As he reached the edge of the balcony, half a dozen Chinese MSS agents spilled into the room with automatic weapons. Seeing him floating there with the turbines roaring, they froze.

Josh twisted the throttle wide open. Accelerating straight up in a roar of wind and jet fumes, he thought he heard gunshots over the racket of the turbine. The MSS agents' surprise probably saved his life, but his problems were just beginning.

Launching into the night was profoundly disorienting. Unlike an airplane, there was no nose or wings to orient him, and at night, there was no horizon. The small LCD screen had an attitude display but wasn't backlit, and he hadn't had time to sync the display to his glasses. He was flying blind with no attitude instruments.

Taking his hand off the throttle, he reached for the sync button on the display, but the jet immediately went to idle and his stomach told him he was falling. He grabbed the throttle again and pulled back on the joystick as he might in a jet. Bad idea. He was not only falling, now he was falling blindly backwards.

He rotated the joystick, which rotated him 180 degrees. At least now, he could see how he was going to die — a bone-shattering impact into the side of a pretty glass building.

He twisted the throttle wide open, which stopped his descent, but accelerated him toward the glass tower. Pulling the stick back slowed him, but not fast enough. He put his feet out in front of him just in time to absorb the impact. Bouncing hard off a large window, he created spider-web cracks in the glass. He now understood how birds felt about windows.

The impact jarred his control stick causing him to change vectors. He rose rapidly but bounced off the glass again, seeing several startled faces on the other side of the windows.

He finally cleared the top of the building, but the combination of darkness, impacts and no visual references created massive vertigo. Spiraling out of control, he had to get the jetpack climbing. He pushed the sync button again and was rewarded with an attitude display in his glasses. It allowed him to get the jetpack pointed toward the sky instead of the ground. In the center of the virtual display, he saw a large blinking *"EMERGENCY MANUAL OVERRIDE."* He glanced down. Bolted next to the right controller was a small switch marked *"MANUAL OVERRIDE"* and *"AUTO."* He flipped it to *"AUTO"* and let go of the controls.

The jetpack immediately stabilized in a hover. Musk told him it was a prototype. Of course, it would have an emergency override! The manual mode cut out the computer stabilization in case of a software glitch. The switch was probably flipped while he was moving the jetpack to the balcony. On the positive side, the manual mode created a faster more erratic departure, making him harder to shoot.

Now in a stable hover, he realized he'd be an easy target for an

MSS agent with a night vision scope, and opened the throttle up. He carefully pushed the joystick forward and picked up speed. As he did, the stubby wings on the side of the jetpack deployed, giving him added lift and shifting him into more of a superman flight attitude. With a few flicks of his wrist, he made gently curving turns and watched the display in his glasses. He quickly got the hang of it. Even with the MSS after him, he was having fun.

Scanning the brilliant cityscape around him, he quickly identified Shanghai's iconic trio of super skyscrapers. He headed between the beautifully illuminated Shanghai and Jin Mao Towers. The Shanghai World Financial Center, capped by a trapezoidal hole, dared him to fly the jetpack through it . . . maybe next time.

He headed north as he climbed. Two-thousand feet above the city, the view was breathtaking. It was like moving around in Google Earth, but instead of using a mouse, he had a joystick. Instead of the joystick moving a picture, it moved him. He flew over the city in 3-D, horizon-to-horizon, ultra-high definition with wind in his face. If he lived through this, a jetpack was going on his Christmas list.

He had the address for the safe house. It wasn't far, but there was no way he could land anywhere near there without drawing a lot of attention. Looking down at the illuminated, ever-expanding net of streets reminded him of the prescient visions he had before the comet.

For a second, one of those visions reappeared. It was as if he were receiving a download, a spider-web of possible futures. In a flash, he knew exactly where he had to go. He still didn't know if these visions were attached to his amazing genetics or something supplied by Jesse, but he could now see that Lee was the key.

He needed help to find her parents' house. Hoping the mic in his cyber glasses could pick up his voice over the noise of the jetpack, he shouted, "Hal, can you hear me?"

There was an immediate "Yes," in his helmet's headset.

This was a long shot. "Hal, use my current location and altitude, and display a Google map overlay."

Within seconds, he was looking at a digital map of the city through his glasses. Superimposed over the streets below it lined up perfectly. Using his photographic memory, he said, "Give me flight directions to the following address . . ."

A blue arrow, pointing toward the horizon, appeared with a flashing flag symbol. He was impressed by the speed of the iMagine assistant. It recognized his commands and worked perfectly with the phone's inertial and GPS system. It made sense now that he knew BOTIC was able to tap into the processors and memory of many phones. The massive increase in power and speed also explained Lee's steadfast belief that the ends justified the means.

Tim had shown him satellite pictures of Lee's parents' home and the surrounding neighborhood. Josh's first thought was to land a couple kilometers away and ditch the jetpack. Then he could approach on foot, but since Li was one of China's top generals, his house would be protected with security measures. Tim might have gotten inside undetected; Josh didn't have the skill or patience. He'd use a simpler approach. The satellite picture showed a courtyard right in the center of the house. That was his target.

He adjusted his course and pushed the joystick all the way forward. He loved fighters, but this, this was more like being Superman. As he rocketed toward his destination, it occurred to him . . . he had no idea how to land a jetpack.

30

SLEEPER

Tim and Greg were standing quietly in Musk's secret room.

Tim leaned against the wall trying to hear what was happening on the other side.

After a few minutes, he saw Greg get up and sit at the desk with the computer. As it started up, the computer gave the normal startup beeps.

Tim gave him a stern look.

Greg whispered back too loudly, "I didn't touch it!"

Tim put his finger to his lips.

After a few minutes, Greg whispered, "Hey, check this out."

Tim shook his head.

Greg came over to him and whispered, "Seriously, you gotta see this."

Tim reluctantly followed him back to the desk. On the monitor, he saw multiple video images. They were coming from cameras concealed throughout Musk's suite, as well as a camera outside the suite looking at the elevators, and even in the building's lobby.

Tim patted Greg on the back.

After a few minutes, they watched the MSS agents leave the suite. Tim pulled out his phone and sent an encrypted text. "It's Tim Smith. Josh borrowed your toy. We're still in your back study. After our guests leave, do you have a recommended exit path?"

Within a minute, Musk texted an escape route.

Tim showed the route to Greg and then studied the video feeds from the stairwells, elevator and lobby. "I think they bought it and believe we all escaped, but they did leave some people behind in the lobby." He pointed out the plain-clothed agents on the video feed to Greg.

They took the stairs down a couple floors and then took the elevator all the way down to one of the basement levels below the lobby. Tim took them through a locked door, where they slipped out through a service entrance.

Back on the street, Tim told Greg to stay close and look straight ahead. They walked five blocks and caught a cab that took them to another market area, where they caught another cab. From there, they walked five more blocks to the safe house. It was one of many identical-looking row houses. They walked up the stairs, and Tim knocked on the door.

An older Chinese lady met them at the door and said something in Chinese.

Tim gave her the coded access phrase, and she invited them inside.

Once inside, in excellent English, she asked for additional identification. While she was looking at their passports, Tim said, "I need to use your encrypted communication line."

She nodded and said, "Follow me."

Tim stopped to take his shoes off and Greg followed his lead.

She took them through what looked like a normal home to a closet door. Inside was a hidden door that led to a tiny room. It was less than two meters square with no windows and a single light fixture. It had a chair and a small desk. On it sat a phone attached to a black box — the encryption device.

Tim told her he needed to talk to headquarters. She sat down at the desk, put on a small, wired headset and asked, "Who do you want to speak to?"

"The Director."

She stopped and looked at him, then nodded her head.

Tim knew she had no idea who they were or what their mission was. That's how compartmentalization worked.

After a couple minutes, they saw her eyebrows go up as she said into the mic, "Of course."

She took the headset off and offered it to Tim, saying, "Sir, they said they were getting the Director as fast as possible, but it would probably take a few minutes."

Tim nodded. "Thank you."

She said, "Yes sir. If you need anything at all, I'll be right outside."

As she left, Tim noticed Greg studying him. Tim put on the headset and gave Greg a questioning look.

Greg asked, "Is Smith your real name?"

"What?"

"Is Smith your real name?"

"No."

Frowning, Greg asked, "Do you like what you do?"

"Why . . . are you thinking about changing careers?"

Greg laughed. "No." Then sighed and said, "I'm just trying to figure out how you can be so . . . so fearless. I've been scared out of my mind for the last few hours. You and Commander Fuze do insane things and stay so cool."

Tim gave him a slight smile and shook his head. "Greg, courage isn't lack of fear, it's being scared and doing it anyway. You did great in spite of being scared. That's real courage."

Greg said, "Thanks, but I don't think I could do what you and Commander Fuze do. Like jumping off a cliff or facing down machine guns."

"Greg, we're all wired differently. Not every act of apparent bravery is courage. Just because you don't want to bungee jump doesn't make you a coward. Some people are born with a thrill-seeker gene."

Greg nodded. "OK, but saving others, knowing you'll almost certainly die . . . ."

Tim stopped smiling. Looking past Greg, he said, "Sometimes, it's just fearing something worse than death." He refocused on Greg. "You won't know until you're put in that situation." He patted Greg on the shoulder. "You'll do the right thing if the time comes. Let's just hope it doesn't."

On the headset, Tim heard, "It's Brian. You OK?"

"Yeah, Greg and I are fine. Not sure about Josh. He decoyed the MSS by launching off Elton Musk's penthouse balcony in a jetpack."

"A jetpack?"

"Yeah."

There was a pause. "Why does that not surprise me?"

Tim gave him a summary of everything that had happened since they arrived.

After he finished, Davidson said, "Tim, Cyber Command just uncovered a virus that's scanning the entire Internet, and copying and converting every document into Chinese."

Tim asked, "What's it doing with the documents after it converts them?"

"We don't know. It's a very sophisticated program. The concern is that the Chinese are saving all of our documents in preparation for a full-scale viral attack, or — some are suggesting — a nuclear attack with Electro Magnetic Pulse warheads."

Tim said, "That's a bit farfetched."

"Maybe, but we're now at INFOCON 1 and, unless we can quickly determine the Chinese government isn't behind this, Sec Def is recommending DEFCON 2 to the President. They're redeploying all the F-22 and B-2 squadrons to Guam and South Korea, and they're pulling the remaining carrier battle groups from their normal patrol and sending them toward China along with British and Indian carrier battle groups. All the U.S. and NATO ballistic missile and killer subs, not to mention land-based ICBMs, are going on full alert."

Tim almost never swore, but he made an exception.

Davidson said, "There's another complication."

Tim waited.

"We went back and looked at Josh's genetic test results."

"Why?"

"When I gave Josh the copies of his stolen files, he seemed interested in the genetic tests. I got curious about the strange results and talked to the lab."

Tim said, "And?"

"It appears Josh may have been genetically designed."

"What?"

"He has less than half the genetic material of a normal human."

"He's an alien?"

"No, his genes are normal. There just aren't enough of them."

"How can you live without half your genes?"

Davidson said, "I don't know, but the way they explained it — his chromosomes have been stripped down to only the essential ones, and they're all pretty much perfect. That can't happen by accident." He paused. "Have you seen him do things that shouldn't be possible for a normal person?"

"No . . . well, he did heal extremely fast from a third-degree burn on his hand and . . . during training his reflexes and vision were phenomenal." With a resigned sigh, he added, "He learned to speak Chinese on the flight to Shanghai." He paused. "But I've heard of people who have those abilities."

"Yeah . . . but not all in one body." Davidson sighed. "There's something else. They said some of his genetic material was of *Asian* origin."

Tim frowned. "You're not suggesting Josh is some type of Chinese genetic experiment?"

Davidson didn't reply.

"*You* think he's a double agent!"

Davidson said softly, "We have to consider the possibility."

"That's crazy paranoid. He should have gotten a Medal of Honor for what he did. He saved our butts even as we tried to kill him."

Davidson said, "You won't get an argument from me. We owe him our lives." He sighed again. "But let's take a step back. On the aircraft carrier, he admitted he takes orders from a higher authority. We were busy trying to save the world and didn't look a gift horse in the mouth. Now, in light of our current situation—"

Tim interrupted, "A Chinese agent inserted into the middle of our military industrial complex to save the world from a comet? That makes *no* sense."

Davidson continued, "Tim, we never found out where the original comet information came from, but it had to come from a technologically advanced country with space access. We also know Josh used the identity of a dead Navy pilot named Andy Logan to gain access to classified programs. Carl Casey was a friend of Logan's and Admiral Joe Meadows was Logan's former Squadron Commander." He paused. "What if Andy Logan didn't die in the crash? If you eliminate the impossible—"

"Are we sure we know what's impossible?" Tim shook his head. "You're suggesting the Chinese government faked his death and genetically redesigned his body?"

Davidson said, "We're going to have Logan's body exhumed." There was a pause. "And it might not be the Chinese government behind this. It could be a faction inside their government preparing for a coup."

Tim shook his head. "Josh saved my life. He's a good man. I don't believe this."

Davidson said slowly, but with emphasis, "Have you considered the possibility that maybe *he* doesn't even know who he's really working for . . . someone could be deceiving him. He could be a sleeper agent."

With frustration, Tim sighed and finally said, "So what do you want me to do?"

Davidson matched his sigh. "I don't know. This is the part of being a spy I hate." He paused. "Just be ready to do whatever you have to."

Tim finally said, "For God's sake, Brian, even if he *is* a Chinese double agent, we're in China. How much damage can he do?"

31

JETPACK

It occurred to Josh that a gallon of jet fuel had the explosive equivalent of a dozen sticks of dynamite. Useless trivia, unless *someone* had several gallons strapped to their back while attempting their first jetpack landing . . . at night . . . in the inside courtyard of a house. A house that belonged to one of China's top military leaders and his renowned scientist wife. Incinerating them in their home might not further American–Chinese relations. He should have been more concerned, but he wasn't. Spy tradecraft wasn't his forte, but this was. A test pilot with a thousand carrier landings, there were *few* flight situations that scared him.

The jetpack was very loud. He'd need to make a fast, direct approach. Unfortunately, the automatic stability system would make his descent too controlled and too slow. He flipped the switch back to manual override, and did a series of "S" turns to get a better feel for how it responded.

With the cyber glasses and his exceptional vision, Josh identified the house several kilometers out. He could also see that the tiny courtyard at the center of the house wasn't illuminated. The good news was that it would give him the element of surprise. The bad news was that landing in the dark would be just as surprising for him.

As he started his approach, he heard a voice-text message from Tim. "A virus is converting all documents in the West into Chinese. U.S. is probably going to DEFCON 2. Need to talk."

No pressure. Retracting the wings, he swooped over the house and stopped his forward motion. Thirty meters above the roof, he cut the throttle. The jetpack dropped like a stone down a black elevator shaft. When he couldn't stand it, he goosed the throttle and caught his fall a meter above the ground. With only a little wobble, he gently set down in the courtyard allowing the jetpack's slender tripod legs to rest on the flagstones.

As he hit the kill switch, he couldn't resist. "Dang, I'm good!" He almost wished someone had been there to see it. The only casualty was a ceramic flowerpot, blown off a table by the turbine's blast. As he unstrapped and ditched his helmet, he almost fell into a koi pond. The satellite picture didn't show that.

Flattening himself against a shadowed wall next to the windows and door, he tried to control his breathing. It seemed unnaturally quiet after the noise of the jetpack. The only sound was the soft, metallic clinking of cooling turbine blades. As he stood there, he realized incinerating their house might not be required to initiate an international incident. If he were captured here—

A light turned on and the door next to him opened. A man came out into the courtyard with a flashlight in one hand. In the other hand, it looked like he was carrying a . . . meat cleaver? As the man approached the jetpack, Josh slipped in behind him. In Chinese, Josh said, "Don't move." When the man tried to spin around, Josh used a judo move to knock him off balance and pull the cleaver from his hand. The man fell backward against the jetpack, knocking it over with a loud crash.

Unconsciously, Josh said, "No!" His jetpack was lying on its side with an obvious crack in the engine cowling.

Quietly, but with force, Josh said, "Get up." He nodded toward the door into the house and added, "I won't hurt you. I'm a friend of Dr. Lee." Glancing back at the jetpack, he said under his breath, "Perfect landing and they'll think I'm zero for four."

As the man stepped through the patio door into the house, Josh heard a female voice ask in Chinese, "What was that?"

Before the man could answer, Josh stepped in behind him. He saw Jessica Lee and recognized her mother, Dr. Li Sun, from the file pictures. He quickly said, "Sorry about the flower pot."

Both of them looked at him in surprise.

Then in English, Jessica said, "What are you *doing* here!"

"Trying to prevent World War Three."

Fearless, Jessica came forward. She told the man and her mother in Chinese that everything was OK.

Josh could see he was an older man, probably the cook. Apologizing to him, Josh carefully handed the meat cleaver back.

Jessica asked, "How did you get here?" Looking behind him, she added, "Where's Greg? Is he OK?"

Josh caught the concern in her voice on the last question. "I just followed your app's navigation function, and it took me right here. Have to admit, its abilities are impressive."

She shook her head with a frown. "They shouldn't be. BOTIC doesn't work here. But I meant," she pointed toward the window, "how did you get *into* the courtyard?"

With a slight smile, he said, "I just kinda dropped in, and Greg . . . he may be on his way here, or he may be a guest of the MSS."

In Chinese, her mother said, "Is this the one you told me about?"

Jessica, peering into the dark courtyard, said, "Yes."

Josh saw the family resemblance. Dr. Li Sun was about the same height and build as her daughter, with equally fine and beautiful features. She was studying him intently.

To Jessica, Josh said, "Greg thinks you're innocent but—"

"He's right!" She turned toward him. "I didn't create BOTIC to sabotage the West!"

"Then why did you leave so fast?"

"I told you. I needed to check some things out. I came back here to find out if someone . . ." she paused and sighed, "if *my father* was trying to subvert my work."

Surprised, he repeated, "Your *father*?" Frowning, he asked, "And . . . ?"

She shook her head. "I don't know. I need more time."

"Hate to sound like a cliché, but time's something we don't have. I just heard the U.S. may be going to DEFCON 2."

She shook her head. "That's crazy! There's no concrete evidence that China's behind the hacking."

"That's true and that's why I'm here, but it ain't looking good. China has the most hackers of any country and a Cyber Warfare division numbering in the tens of thousands."

"OK, but that doesn't explain why. What would their motive be?"

He ticked off on his fingers. "China is now the largest

consumer of shrinking oil reserves, and relationships between China and the West are at an all-time low with export and currency devaluation issues." Hitting a second finger, he continued, "Over the past decade, China commissioned six new aircraft carrier battle groups, all with stealth aircraft and drones capable of carrying nuclear warheads anywhere in the world." With a third finger, "We know the People's Army has been stockpiling Electro Magnetic Pulse warheads. They can take out technology without destroying the infrastructure. Some suspect EMP warheads are onboard the new Chinese space station."

She shook her head. "Still circumstantial."

Josh added. "I agree, but we just learned a virus has been quietly converting all documents on the Internet into Chinese, and storing them somewhere."

"Oh." She frowned. "That's bad." Jessica translated their exchange into Chinese for her mother's benefit.

Her mother looked worried and said in Chinese, "We need to talk to your father."

In Chinese, Josh said to Jessica's mother, "It's probably a little late to ask, but is your house *monitored?*"

Surprised, Jessica said, "You speak Chinese?"

Josh shrugged. "I picked it up on the flight over."

Frowning, Jessica's mother asked, "What is your ancestry?"

Josh shook his head at the non-sequitur. "What?"

Jessica rolled her eyes. "My mother's one of China's leading genetic scientists."

He studied Dr. Li, as she studied him. "Dr. Li, I'm afraid I really don't know." Curious, he asked, "What would you say it was?"

"I've never seen anyone like you."

Impatient, Jessica jumped in. "In answer to your question, the house is clean but considering my dad's position, I wouldn't rule out some type of observation." She went to the courtyard window, cupping her hands around her eyes, she peered out, asking, "What *is* that!"

He shrugged. "A prototype jetpack."

"Wow. It wasn't exactly quiet. Your *arrival* was probably noticed."

Dr. Li said, "Let's talk to my husband. He'll be home soon."

Jessica, with obvious disdain, added, "Yeah, he knows everything about everything."

Dr. Li said, "I apologize. Jessica and her father are strong personalities and don't see eye to eye."

Jessica added, "*That's* an understatement."

Before Dr. Li could respond, a phone rang. She nodded politely and went to answer it.

After she left, Josh said, "OK, I believe you didn't know about all this," he sighed, "but that doesn't alter China's position as the prime suspect."

She matched his sigh. "I know, but it doesn't make sense. If the Chinese government destroyed Western civilization, it would destroy China. Their economy is totally tied to the West, and as big as the People's Army is, it can't occupy the entire world." She shook her head. "There's a piece missing."

An encrypted text displayed in Josh's glasses. It was from Tim and said, "Where are you?"

Josh replied, "Parents.'"

Tim's text came back, "Our sources say MSS converging on your location. Suggest you depart."

To Jessica, he said, "Just got word the police are coming. Gotta go. Is there a car I could borrow?"

"But you need to stay and help me interrogate my dad."

"Love to, but if I stay, it won't be your dad getting interrogated."

She nodded. "My rental's out front."

Dr. Li came back with a slight smile. "That was my husband. He told me an American escaped from the police and might be on his way here to attack us. He said we should get away from the house and that the police are on their way."

Jessica looked down at her phone and said, "Uh oh." Looking up, she added, "Suspicious of my father, I hacked into the house security system." She handed it to Josh. "This is the surveillance camera view out of the front of the house."

Josh saw two black Audi A6s pull up in front and park on the other side of the street. Into his cyber glasses, he said, "Hal. Encrypted voice-text to Elton Musk."

"Ready."

"Can jetpack be flown remotely?"

While he was waiting for a reply, Jessica handed him her car keys. "Sorry it's a Chery QQ."

Josh looked at her blankly.

"A jelly bean loosely disguised as a car." She shook her head. "Not the best getaway vehicle."

Musk texted back, "Download a universal drone control app. Jetpack's Wi-Fi access code is 'grok.'"

Josh handed his phone to her. "Put your security camera app on mine and give me your phone."

While she was installing it on his phone, he downloaded the remote control app to hers and went back out into the courtyard. He tipped the jetpack up on its tripod legs and hit the start button. As the turbine spooled up, he went back in the house and looked at the display on Jessica's phone. He saw a dark, fuzzy video picture of himself looking out the courtyard window toward the jetpack. "Excellent!" The jetpack had a small camera mounted on it to fly it remotely.

Jessica handed him his phone with the security camera display.

He gave her back her phone, pointing out the remote control app. Overlaid on the video, was a simple throttle bar. As she held the phone, Josh reached over and gently nudged the throttle bar on the screen. They heard the jetpack's turbine whine increase.

Simultaneously, they said, "Sweet!"

She added, "Gotta have one of these."

He winked at her. "I need a distraction."

"I don't know how to fly a jetpack!"

"Neither did I." He looked at her sideways. "You're not telling me you've never played a video game?"

She laughed.

"To control it, just tilt your phone in the direction you want it to go." He smiled. "In this case, the scarier you fly it, the better. Give me a minute to get outside, and then launch it. Try to fly it away from the front of the house if you can. As soon as they're distracted, I'll crash through the gate."

"I can do that," she gave him a half-smile, "but I doubt a Chery QQ can *crash* through anything."

He nodded. "Where's it parked?"

She pointed down a hall and said, "Just outside under the carport. Good luck."

Jessica's mother came up to him and grabbed his hand with both of hers. In English, she said with intensity, "China not trying to destroy West. We must stop this."

"Yes, we must." He felt a small sting where she was holding his hand and said, "Ouch."

She let go. Quickly putting one of her hands into her pocket, she pushed him toward the hall with the other.

He went down the hall, opened the door carefully and slipped outside to the carport. It was dark, but it was easy to identify the jellybean with wheels. Crouching low, he approached the Chery QQ from the passenger side, opened the door and slid in. He closed the door and contorted himself over the shifter and into the driver's seat of the tiny car. Keeping his head low, he looked at the security camera display on his phone. He made sure the headlights were off, put the key in the ignition and waited.

Almost immediately, he heard the jetpack's engine wind up. Muffled crashing sounds with breaking glass, came from the house, but after a couple seconds, he heard the loud turbine noise rising above him.

Masked by the jetpack, he started the engine and watched the security camera display on his phone. The doors on both Audis opened and two men got out of each. They were staring up into the air. With guns in hand, they moved toward the receding jetpack. He put the little car into gear and drove down the driveway, happy to see the electric gate opening.

Hearing the car leave the carport, Jessica killed the jetpack's engine. It crashed on top of a parked car on the far side of the street, erupting into a huge fireball as the fuel tank ruptured.

Her mother, with wide eyes, put her hand over her mouth and said, "That was our neighbor, Mr. Wong's, new Jaguar."

With a devilish smile, Jessica said, "Oops." She quickly deleted the RC app from her phone, then walked over and reached into her mother's pocket. She pulled out a small vial with a tiny needle.

Holding it up, she asked, "Did you inject him with something?"

"No, of course not."

She just looked at her mother.

Dr. Li shook her head. "I didn't inject anything. I just . . . took a small sample."

"A tissue sample?" She frowned. "Why? Because of a text from a seven-year-old?"

"Jessica, he learned to speak Chinese on the way to China." She looked at her meaningfully. "Josh Fuze is not what he seems."

32

DEFCON

Josh saw a small fireball erupt a 100 meters to his right. Jessica couldn't have provided a better distraction. He hit the end of the driveway and turned away from the MSS agents, accelerating . . . sort of. In the rearview mirror, he saw one of the agents running back to his car. Game on. Time to test his new *offensive* driving skills. With the adrenaline pumping, he floored the accelerator. Not much happened. He dropped it down a gear. The Chery accelerated leisurely. He shook his head and said, "Jetpack, totally James Bond. Chery QQ, not so much."

He had a small head start, but the Audis would catch him quickly if he didn't lose them ASAP. Waiting until the road turned enough so he was out of their line of sight, he whipped the car down a side road. *Whipped* turned out to be an exaggeration. The little car plowed through the turn, barely making the corner. He dodged around a few more turns until he was sure they'd lost him. He kept going until he was out of the high-end neighborhood. Looking around, he smiled. What the little car gave up in power, it made up for in anonymity. Out here, it was as common as a cockroach.

He kept driving until he found what he was looking for — a large, mostly full, parking lot. There were dozens of Chery QQs. He quickly slipped his jellybean into an open space and turned it off. Reclining the seat back so he wasn't visible, he texted Tim. "Got out, but they're looking for me. Believe Jessica's telling truth, but not sure about parents. Where do we meet?"

He got a quick response. "We're radioactive. Embassy won't touch us. U.S. at DEFCON 2."

Josh texted back. "Why?"

"Will explain later. Where are you?"

"Hiding in a parking lot in Jessica's rental Chery QQ."

Tim texted back, "Send your coordinates."

About a minute after he sent them, he got back, "You're not far from a restaurant/market area. Should be plenty of people there to blend in with."

"How am I going to blend in?"

"You'll blend in better than us."

"Which way?"

"Due south of your position six blocks. Headed there now. Be there in about 30 minutes."

Josh was going to stay with the car until it was closer to pick-up time, but when he peeked over the steering wheel, he saw a conventional police car a few blocks away. It was slowly cruising down the street, obviously looking for something.

Time to go. He opened the door, slipped out and quietly closed it. Running in a low crouch, he stayed between the parked cars until he was behind a small van. He waited until the van blocked the police car's line of sight and then ran across the street. After two blocks, he slowed to a walk.

There weren't many people out this time of night, but as he went south, things picked up. He tried to match his pace and gait to those around him. He didn't have to worry too much about blending in, since few people made eye contact. He reached the central market. Knowing he was early, and not wanting to stay on the street, he went into a small establishment and ordered tea. He texted his location to Tim.

With 20 minutes to wait for them, he had a little time to think. His prescient interlude created some questions that nagged at him. Jessica was right; there was a piece missing, but he couldn't put his finger on it.

His thoughts finally turned to his poor Jen. It was clear she had no parents or family and was probably neglected. He imagined a future where he and Elizabeth could adopt her. However, it might be best if they could save Western Civilization first.

He texted, "Jen, you there?"

"Hi, Josh. Do you like Dr. Jessica Lee?"

"Uh, yes, Jen. Why do you ask?"

"I like her too. She's smart and she likes me."

Surprised, Josh asked, "Likes you? Do you talk to her?"

"All the time. Do you think she wants to have kids some day?"

He felt bad for her and her desperate desire for parents, but he was concerned that she'd been talking with Jessica. Before he could ask, she said, "I had fun playing ball today."

He said softly to himself, "Finally, something normal kids do." He texted, "That's great. Did you play ball at school?"

"No. They don't let me go to school. I have too much work to do."

Josh shook his head. Someone was stealing this little girl's childhood. He was frustrated with his inability to help her. If they survived, he would rescue her. "What kind of ball did you play?"

"It's a digital, three-dimensional ball of the earth. I'm trying to guess where earthquakes will happen."

He couldn't help but smile. "Kind of geophysics ball, huh?"

"Yes. There are networks I can look at online to see where earthquake epicenters are. I'm trying to predict where the next earthquake will happen. I haven't won yet."

Josh said, "It's not whether you win or lose; it's how you play the game."

Jen said, "What does that mean?"

He realized he had no idea. He suspected whoever said it probably lost a lot, or was misquoted. "Sorry, Jen. That's an *idiom* or *saying* and . . . probably not that appropriate."

"I have trouble understanding those."

"Yeah, me too." He shook his head. "Thank you for giving me the address to Musk's apartment. That was very helpful." He finally realized one of the things that had been nagging at him. "Jen, how did you know about my streamlined genetics? Did the voice tell you?"

"No. It was in your records."

"What records?"

"Your CIA records."

Under his breath, he said, "Uh oh." Then texted, "How did you get them?"

"It was very hard. I had to reprogram someone's cell phone and get through a lot of encryption."

Josh's eyes got big. "Jen, did someone tell you to do that?"

"The voice told me about you, but I had to find your files myself."

He shook his head. "Jesse." He wondered if this was Jesse's way to insert his two genetically enhanced players into the game. It fit Jesse's pattern. He never volunteered information. Instead, he helped Josh figure things out for himself. He must have done the same with Jen. She didn't understand breaking into the CIA was illegal. To her it was no different than playing geophysics ball. He'd have to talk to her about that, but now was not the time.

Just then, a text came in from Tim. "Had to borrow a vehicle. Not as fast as your jetpack. Almost there."

Josh texted Jen, "Gotta go, but let's talk more about this when we can, OK?"

"OK, Josh."

He saw a sedan pull up outside and could clearly see Greg's head in the backseat. Josh went out and jumped into the passenger seat.

As Tim pulled out, Josh said, "What happened? Why DEFCON 2?"

Greg said, "The hackers just made a bunch of private texts public."

Josh shook his head. "So?"

Tim added, "It was the text of practically every Western government official, president, prime minister, senator, congressman, agency director, etc."

"But DEFCON 2?"

Tim shook his head, "What's more dangerous than embarrassed politicians? But the final straw was when the hackers took control of Google. Anyone can use it to search for almost any classified document in the West. The FBI had to shut all the Internet search engines down."

Greg asked Tim, "What does DEFCON 2 really mean?"

Tim nodded to Josh, "Our Commander can probably better answer that."

Josh said, "Since the system was created in the late 1950s, the only time the U.S. has been at DEFCON 2 was during the Cuban Missile Crisis and the beginning of the Gulf War."

"Tim said they're considering going to DEFCON 1."

Josh shook his head. "That's never happened. It would mean all our land- and sea-based ICBMs are targeted and ready to launch within seconds, and our nuclear bombers are inbound."

Tim added, "And, of course, the Chinese will match us. It means World War III."

Greg nodded solemnly. "So, how do we stop this?"

Josh said, "We need to talk to Jessica's father. He has to be in a position to know what's going on."

Tim frowned, "He probably does, but why would he want to talk to us except to turn us over to the MSS?"

Josh said, "It's our best and probably only chance of finding out what's happening. If Jessica can set up a meeting with me, you two can monitor it by phone from a safe distance. If it goes bad, you can still get the word out."

Greg shook his head. "Jessica and her dad don't get along."

"I gathered that, but I'm sure she can arrange it through her mother."

Tim asked, "How do we contact Jessica without the Chinese government knowing?"

"Jen has apparently latched on to Jessica . . . fellow geniuses and all. I think we can use her as our go between. Jen was able to load your encryption app onto Elizabeth's phone remotely, so she should be able to put it on Jessica's."

Greg looked surprised. "Jen loaded an encryption app with a key onto a phone remotely?" Scratching his head, he added, "I didn't know that was possible. Gotta meet this little girl."

Josh voice-texted, "Jen, I'm here with Tim Smith and Greg Langlois. Honey, we need your help to reach Jessica."

On speakerphone they heard her reply, "Hi, Tim. Hi, Greg. I loaded the encryption app on her phone."

"Thanks so much, Jen. If you can patch me through that would be great."

"OK." There was a slight pause. "You can reach her now."

"Jessica, it's Josh, can you talk?"

After about 30 seconds, the reply came back. "Hope the jetpack was insured."

Josh smiled. "Me too. This is an encryption app Jen loaded. Should allow us to text without being detected."

She replied, "Jen told me. She's a sharp kid."

"Jessica, I have Greg and Tim here with me. Your dad isn't just a general; he's a member of the Central Military Committee. That's kind of like being one of the Joint Chiefs of Staff."

Jessica said, "I didn't know that until today. We don't talk much."

"Have you found out anything else about who might be behind the hacking?"

"No. His response when I challenged him was that it was absurd."

"Jessica, things are rapidly getting out of hand. The U.S. is on its way to DEFCON 1, which means global nuclear war, and we're fugitives. I need to meet with your dad face-to-face. Can you arrange it?"

"Give me a few minutes. Is Greg OK?"

"He's right here." Josh handed the phone to him.

Greg voice-texted, "Hi, Jessica. It's Greg." He stopped, clearly trying to think of something intelligent to say. "Uh, love to meet your parents . . . but maybe not the best time . . . right now."

All they got back was, "OMG ROFL."

33

CHECKMATE

Setting her phone aside, Jessica gave her statement to the lead MSS agent. He told her and her mother that they would stay until her father arrived. While they were waiting, Jessica quietly asked her mother, "What is Dad's problem? Why does he hate me?"

"He doesn't hate you. He loves you."

She shook her head violently. "That's not true. He never talked to me, only at me. He's thoughtless, brutally direct and believes he's always right."

Her mother smiled. "I'm sorry, dear, but have you looked in a mirror recently?"

"I'm nothing like him!"

Her mother gently took her daughter's hands in hers. "Don't you understand, Jessica? You two have the same personality. You're both natural leaders and extremely competitive." She smiled. "That's why you've both risen to the top of your fields, but it's also a recipe for conflict." She paused. "Jessica, you hurt him when you decided to become an American citizen."

"I became an American because—"

"Because bad attention is better than no attention?" her mother finished.

She shook her head. "No!" Then after a long sigh, said softly, "I don't know . . . maybe. I just wanted him to . . . to be proud of me. But he dumped me. He threw me away!"

Her mother shook her head. "He sent you to America because he believed that would give you the best education and opportunity in the world. Better than we had." She paused. "And it did."

Jessica narrowed her eyes. "I'm sorry, Mother, I don't believe that."

Her mother looked her in the eye. "Did you see his reaction when you said that he dumped you?"

Jessica nodded, frowning.

Her mother got up and pulled a large scrapbook out of a bookshelf. She opened it and put it in Jessica's lap. In it were newspaper and magazine articles about Dr. Jessica Lee. Many had hand written Chinese translations on the side.

Jessica flipped through them and saw every article ever written about her or her achievements, some she'd never seen. She was impressed, not only that her mother had collected them, but that she could. Access to international magazines was still limited in China. Looking up at her mother, questioningly, she said, "Thank you for collecting these, but I don't understand what this has to do with my father."

Her mother shook her head gently. "Jessica, *I* didn't collect these . . . your father did."

Jessica just stared at her mother.

"He painstakingly found every article about you and translated them into Chinese. He was — and is — very proud of you."

As if on cue, General Li rushed into the room out of breath. "I saw the burning car next door. Are you all right? Did he hurt you?"

Jessica's mother said, "We're perfectly fine. No, he didn't hurt us at all."

Angrily, he said, "The MSS should never have let them get away in the city. They've disgraced themselves and will be punished." He shook his head. "But we'll have them in custody soon. They can't hide."

Jessica was about to tell him he was totally missing the point when her mother gently squeezed her hand. Instead, she said, "Thank you, Father. We really are OK."

He noticed the scrapbook in her lap and frowned.

Jessica looked at her mother, and then at him, finally saying, "Father, we need to talk, but first, we need to discuss Josh and all that's happened." She glanced at one of the MSS agents standing in the background, and added, "Privately."

General Li immediately dismissed the two agents, telling them to go outside and secure the perimeter of the house.

Jessica recounted the events beginning with Josh landing in

the courtyard.

When they got to the jetpack distraction, he looked surprised and said, "You flew a jetpack remotely and dropped it on Mr. Wong's new Jaguar?"

She nodded, bracing for an explosion.

He just nodded thoughtfully. "Very accurate flying." He paused. "I never liked imports." He paused again. "It might be best not to share this with Mr. Wong."

Her mother put her hand over her mouth, suppressing a giggle.

General Li continued, "Tell me more about this Josh and…" he glanced briefly at his wife, "Greg Langlois."

Jessica recounted everything that Greg shared with her about Josh and all their previous conversations.

Her mother said, "I took a tissue sample of him and sent it to the lab."

Looking at Jessica very seriously, he said, "The MSS will be more interested in killing him than capturing him at this point." He paused. "I wish I could have talked to him."

Jessica smiled. "That won't be a problem." She showed him Josh's text.

It was the wee hours of the morning in Guam as Lieutenant Colonel Nancy Dowling finished the preflight of her B-2. It was quiet with a gentle tropical breeze blowing across the tarmac. Next to her jet, sat four identical, black, boomerang shaped bombers. She was the Squadron Commander in charge of these half-billion-dollar aircraft. A veteran of combat missions, they'd been deployed many times, but not like this, not carrying a full load of nukes in their bomb bay. Nuclear weapons were for deterrence. If they used them, it meant they'd failed in their intended purpose. Only hours from launch, she hoped the powers-that-be would figure it out … quickly.

Tim studied Josh as Josh studied his phone waiting for a reply from Jessica. He didn't need Davidson's genetic report to see the Asian features in Josh's face.

Josh looked up at him questioningly.

Tim frowned. "Davidson told me you're missing a bunch of your DNA."

"Yeah, according to Elizabeth, I only have about half."

Tim paused and then shrugged. "That might explain your half-assed landings."

With a headshake and half-smile Josh said, "Yo momma."

Before Tim could ask any more questions about his DNA, Josh's text message tone sounded.

Looking down, Josh read aloud, "Josh, my father is ready to meet you." He looked up at Tim and asked, "What's the plan, coach?"

Tim exhaled. "We can set it up in a way that will minimize your exposure, but," he shook his head, "if they really want to take you, there's not much we can do. It's their playground."

Josh nodded. "Let's do it."

Tim parked the car on a busy street and looked around slowly, then texted the instructions to Jessica. When he finished, he nodded toward a small teahouse on the next block. "You'll meet him right there. That way, they won't have time to set a trap. Greg will stay with the car, and I'll position myself on the roof of the building next door. From there, I can watch the approach to the teahouse."

Josh said, "Sounds like a good plan."

He shrugged. "We'll see."

Josh shook his head. "Thanks for the pep talk." Then he voice-texted, "Jen, is there any way you can set up my phone so Tim can see what my cyber glasses see without using the Chinese cellular network?"

On speakerphone, she replied, "Yes."

"Thanks, Jen."

As Josh got out, he said to Tim, "Regardless of what happens, get the information back to Davidson."

Tim nodded.

On board the Russian submarine *RFS Nevsky*, Captain Ivan Markov looked at the plotted position of the ballistic missile sub, *USS Nebraska*. How times had changed. He wasn't targeting the *Nebraska* or even avoiding her. Instead, they were working together as part of a massive international taskforce. Deploying off the coast of China, they had just received their orders. The *Nevsky* and *Nebraska* were retargeting all their missiles for a decapitation strike. An appropriately descriptive name for an attack designed to take out China's command and control and prevent a counter attack. If the Chinese leaders wanted to destroy Western civilization, they deserved decapitation, but the collateral deaths would be horrific, and that was if everything went according to plan. A decapitation strike sounded good on paper, but just as Russia and the United States devised plans to counter the strategy, he suspected the Chinese had as well. His communication officer said, "There's a new flash message coming in."

Tim said, "Greg, stay here and stay low."

Tim, quickly slipping through locked doors, found his way to the roof of the building next door. Peeking over the edge, he had a perfect view of the front and back of the teahouse. Watching his phone's screen, he told Josh, "Look slowly around the restaurant. I want to see the environment and your position."

Tim saw Josh had picked a table with his back to the wall. They quickly identified two exit points.

Within a few minutes, a black sedan pulled up across the street and a man stepped out. Tim said, "Got a man fitting Li's description heading to the front door. I don't see any other suspicious cars or people."

Watching the video, Tim saw them shake hands and heard Josh say something in Chinese, probably a greeting.

Li, in excellent English, said, "I am alone but probably won't be for long. They keep a close watch over us, especially now."

As they sat down, he heard Josh ask, "Then let's get right to the question. Do you know who's behind the hacking?"

Li said, "No. I was hoping you might."

"So, you're sure that there is no entity in China that could be involved?"

Li said, "I appreciate the way you asked the question. I spoke to the Premier of China a few hours ago, and he spoke to the Chinese President. If they don't know, I think it's safe to say the Chinese government isn't involved. However, neither of us can ever be certain that there isn't some group in our countries doing something they shouldn't be doing."

Josh said, "I accept that, but many won't. The evidence, although circumstantial, is difficult to ignore. Josh went quickly through the perspective from Washington, D.C., including Unit 61398. "If China isn't behind this, who else would benefit?"

Li's eyes narrowed. "There is another explanation. As you pointed out, China and the United States are now competing directly for oil and other resources. Our currency has become the new standard, and the Chinese Navy will soon be the world's largest." He paused. "However, our economy would completely collapse without Western markets." He paused again. "On the other hand, the West would not collapse with the destruction of China. But it would eliminate a lot of Western debt and delay the oil crises for another decade."

Josh, sounding surprised, said, "Are you suggesting that the West is fabricating all this to justify a first strike on China?"

Li sighed. "The Premier brought it up as a possibility. It *is* more plausible than the idea that China would attempt to destroy the West."

Tim could tell that Josh was shaking his head, as he said, "Do you really think our leaders would humiliate themselves by releasing their private information?"

Li gave him a half-smile. "What if only a few in high positions were involved? They could use this to destroy their political opposition. We have a Chinese proverb similar to your 'kill two birds with one stone.'"

"Do you really believe that?"

Li looked him in the eye. "Of course not. It makes only a tiny bit more sense than China attacking the West, but now you see how it looks from our side."

Tim could tell Josh was nodding. "OK, but if it's not China or the West, who's behind it?"

Tim saw a black Audi pull up outside the restaurant, and said, "You've got company."

Commander Anil Mammen was onboard the Indian aircraft carrier *INS Vishal*. He sat in his squadron ready room listening to the strike brief, along with a dozen U.S. and British pilots. Six aircraft carriers had rendezvoused in route to China: *INS Vikrant* and *Vishal*, *HMS Prince of Wales* and *Queen Elizabeth*, and the *USS George Washington* and *Ronald Reagan*. Combined, they had over 300 aircraft, a quarter of which were robotic strike fighters. Their accompanying battle groups included over 40 cruisers, destroyers and frigates.

Mammen looked at his watch. Within 24 hours, their international battle group, along with five similar fleets, would surround China's coast. Mammen couldn't help but think this was surreal. For the past year, the world had enjoyed one of the most peaceful times in history. It was unimaginable that only months after humanity had worked together to defeat the comet, they were about to start an epic global war. How could the Chinese leaders be crazy enough to believe they could take over the world? As he thought that, the General Quarters claxon went off, followed by, "All hands, man your battle stations."

34

ESCAPE

Josh touched his ear. "I'm being told that the MSS has located you, and I need to depart."

Li shook his hand and said, "You and I may believe the same thing, but unless we find another suspect, and do it quickly... war is imminent."

Josh heard Tim say, "They're headed toward the entrance. Exit through the back of the restaurant."

As he went to the back door, he heard Tim say, "More company just arrived at the back. Move!"

Josh ran through the kitchen, but before he could go through the back door, Tim said, "Too late. They're right outside."

Josh spun around and saw a set of stairs through a doorway. Bolting through it, he slammed the door behind him and ran up the stairs. He almost tripped on the non-standard steps, and ended up taking them two at a time. As he hit the third floor, he heard the ground-floor door open, followed by the sound of many feet coming up the stairs. Hitting the fourth floor, he burst through the door onto a flat roof. There was a clothesline and a couple of chairs. He grabbed one of the chairs and wedged it under the doorknob.

Looking around, he saw that the building behind him, where Tim was perched, was taller. On the other side, however, the building was one story shorter with a narrow alley in between. Hearing the roof door rattle, he took a deep breath and ran as fast as he could. Jumping over the alley, he hit hard on the other roof and rolled. It knocked his cyber glasses off. As he stuck them back on, he heard Tim say, "Keep moving."

Josh said, "Looks a lot easier when Jackie Chan does it."

Josh ran to the roof door and grabbed the knob. "Locked!"

Tim said, "Keep going. There may be an outside fire escape on the far side of the building."

Josh ran to the edge and looked down. "No such luck." Looking up, the building across the street was an apartment complex, but it was three stories taller. The street between them was also much wider. He was looking at apartments with small balconies. Almost all of them had clothes drying on clotheslines. He ran back ten paces and turned to face the apartment building.

Tim said, "You're not thinking about—"

Josh interrupted, "Worked in the **Matrix**."

"You can't make that jump! No one can!"

Josh ran as fast as he could and leaped, arms and legs windmilling. His trajectory was a bit off. Instead of landing on the balcony, he went through a clothesline full of clothes and bulls-eyed the sliding glass door. The impact knocked the door out of its frame, shattering it as it hit the floor. His right shoulder and leg took most of the impact, knocking the wind out of him. Slowly rolling out of the tangle of clothes and broken shards, he caught his breath. He was developing a real dislike for glass.

He looked up to see a boy about six years old staring at him. Sitting in a chair, the little boy held a toy in his hand and watched Josh with eyes as big as saucers. The toy was a *Transformer Robot*.

With a big smile, Josh pointed back through the broken door and said in Chinese, "I got away from the Decepticons."

The little boy smiled back and looked through the slider as Josh exited through the front door.

He ran down a hallway to a staircase. Taking them three at a time, he realized standardized steps weren't a priority in China. When he reached the bottom, he peeked outside. The coast was clear. He went out and walked casually away from the restaurant without looking back. As he reached the end of the block and turned the corner, he glanced over his shoulder. There was no one behind him. Breathing a sigh of relief, he said, "OK, Tim. Think I'm clear."

There was no response. "Tim, you there?"

Nothing.

Josh checked his phone and earpiece. Despite the impact, they appeared to be working. Apparently, he was on his own.

The first order of business was to get as far away from this area as possible. The safe house was probably a good seven kilometers from here, but it gave him a destination. In the meantime, they'd be searching for him. He had to get off the streets.

He saw what appeared to be an abandoned building down a side street. Checking to make sure no one was watching him, he found a broken door. Breaking it further, he ducked inside.

It was a large room with cracked tile on the floor and old empty crates. Sitting down on one, he rubbed his swollen ankle. He also had good-sized bruises on his shoulder and chest, and minor cuts on his head from the glass.

Pulling his phone out, he tried texting Tim and Greg again. Nothing. He decided to text Jen to see if his phone was still working.

Jen responded, "Are you OK?"

"Yes, Jen, I'm fine. How are you doing?"

"I'm scared."

"Is someone trying to hurt you?"

"No, but on the Internet everyone's saying there's going to be a big war. Wars are very bad. People get killed."

He sighed. "Yes, wars are very bad, but please don't worry. I'm in China trying to prevent that from happening."

"Why would anyone want to have a war?"

"In this situation, both sides think the other side is doing bad things."

"How can you stop it?"

"We have to find out who's really behind it."

"Can I help?"

Josh said, "You already have." He realized her fear might allow him to get more information about her situation. "Jen, I'm worried about you and want to be sure you're safe. Please tell me if the people who are looking after you are taking care of you."

"They never talk to me except when they want me to do work for them."

"Jen, what kind of work do they make you do?"

"Computer work they can't do. I want to be with you."

His poor baby! He had to get her out of there. "Jen, please tell me where you are." She had never shared that before.

There was a slight delay, and then, "Mostly Atlanta, Georgia."

He was relieved to find that she was living in the United States.

It wouldn't protect her from a global war, but if they survived, it would make it easier to adopt her. Now that he knew she'd broken into the CIA, he could use that to motivate the CIA to help find her.

"Thanks, Jen. When this is over, I'm going to come find you." If someone tries to hurt you, call me immediately. If you can't reach me, call Tim, Jessica or Elizabeth. We need your exact location so we can send someone to help you."

Jen replied, "What can I do to help find the bad guys?"

He'd avoided talking about the hackers because he was afraid they might be able to find her through him, but with global war imminent, there was nothing to lose. "Jen, we need to find out who is behind the hacking of the navigation apps, stock market and the translation of all documents into Chinese. Right now, we think it's China, and China thinks it's us."

Just then, he got a text from Jessica, "Stock markets around the world are in free fall. U.S. just went to DEFCON 1 and the rest of the world is following suit! The MSS have orders to shoot you on sight. Meet me at the Ya Qu Teahouse in five minutes."

Checking his nav app, Josh saw he was only a couple kilometers from the meeting point, but he'd still have to hustle.

They'd have a description of him. His green, long sleeve shirt was torn and missing part of a sleeve, so he took it off. Using it to wipe off some blood, he threw it away. He wore a black T-shirt under it, which wouldn't look out of place on a nice spring day, and he noticed many men wore similar shirts.

He walked as quickly as he could without drawing attention. The sprained ankle and bruises began to make themselves known, but he fought the urge to limp and kept moving.

Less than 100 meters from the meeting place, a police car came around the corner. He ducked into an alley just in time. Congratulating himself on his quick identification and reaction, he jogged to the coffee shop.

As he entered, he saw all the tables were full, so he stood near the back trying to blend in. He pulled out his phone. Staring at a phone was now the most natural and universal thing anyone could do, crossing all cultures. While he was waiting, he called up the news. He was shocked to read that the U.S., Europe, Russia and India were telling their citizens to leave China immediately.

His text message reminder vibrated. It was an encrypted text from Davidson.

Josh had never received a message from the CIA Director. It simply said, "The hacker's in our pocket."

He was rereading it when he heard Jessica say, "Josh Fuze!" He looked up. She was standing three meters away with a frown on her face.

As he asked, "Are you OK?" gas-propelled Taser darts struck him from four directions. He dropped like a sack of potatoes. Several men were on him immediately, and he felt an injection in his leg. Two thoughts crossed his mind before he lost consciousness. Jessica had totally set him up and Sam was right, he sucked at counter-surveillance detection.

IV

INCEPTION

Commander Mammen reached forward and flipped on the Master Arm switch. The fighter's missile-launch button was now live, and with it, the ability to start World War III with his thumb.

35

WWIII

The *INS Vishal's* electromagnetic catapult launched Commander Mammen's *Rafale* into the air. He was the lead aircraft of the first strike group. In less than an hour, the Chinese and coalition navies would be within weapons range of each other. When that happened, conflict was inevitable.

As his fighter climbed, he looked back at the *Exocet* anti-ship missiles hanging from his wings. About 500 nautical miles ahead, he suspected a Chinese pilot had a similar mission. Almost all major strike plans started the same way — eliminate the enemy's offensive capability. With the stakes this high, they weren't limited to conventional weapons. Behind him, flew six jets armed with megaton-class nukes. For the first time in his career, he was certain the aircraft carrier was a more dangerous place to be than in the air.

Commander Mammen reached forward and flipped on the *Master Arm* switch. The fighter's missile-launch button was now live, and with it, the ability to start World War III with his thumb.

Josh woke up lying on a hard pad. He was hurting. In addition to the sprained ankle and bruises, he had pulled muscles from being hyper-tased. The real pain, however, came from the knowledge that he had totally misjudged Jessica, and because of that, he sat in a prison cell, powerless to prevent a war.

He closed his eyes and tried to clear his mind. Shutting out the pain, he used his photographic memory to replay the events leading up to this point, including every conversation he'd had over the past few weeks.

At first, there was nothing, but then, as he relaxed, he saw a pattern begin to form in his mind. He felt the same detached feeling from his body that he did the night they chased him to Antarctica. Instead of just looking forward, however, he also looked backward, backward to the path that had resulted in his present. It appeared like three-dimensional spider webs; each one connected to another. Events or people sat at the center of each web. As the picture grew, the filaments between the webs increased and became more complex. It was overwhelming, but he began to perceive one web had more connections than any other. At the center of that web, was the answer.

Lieutenant Colonel Dowling and Major Jasmine Conley finished their last air-to-air refueling. Along with another 18 B-2 bombers scattered across the Pacific, they were minutes from their strike go-no-go point, the last opportunity for the President to recall them before entering enemy airspace. On board each jet, were enough warheads to destroy a small country. Although she couldn't see them, she knew their bombers were flanked by dozens of *Mini-Me's* — the B-2 crew's derogatory nickname for the small but deadly stealth bomber drones.

The combination of darkness and radar stealth made the big bombers and drones almost invisible, but "almost" wasn't enough anymore. The new bistatic radars deployed along the Chinese coast could see a hummingbird at 150 nautical miles. Backing up those radars, were advanced surface-to-air missiles and a fleet of third-generation fighters.

Giving voice to her thoughts, a high-pitched warbling tone informed her that a missile targeting radar was now locked onto her bomber. The largest stealth air battle in history was about to begin.

In his dream state, Josh faintly heard the sound of a key turning in a lock. He thought it was symbolic of his discovery . . . until he felt something push against his leg. Pulling out of his internal world, he opened his eyes and saw a Chinese guard looking down at him and telling him to stand up.

Blinking, he slowly stood. There were two guards in the cell with him. They wore People's Liberation Army uniforms and were non-commissioned officers.

They stood on both sides of him, and told him to hold his hands out in front of him. Each guard handcuffed one of Josh's hands to theirs, resulting in him being handcuffed between them.

As they took him out of the cell, Josh found three armed men waiting outside. They clearly weren't taking any chances. He noticed that one of the men carried a briefcase and had the rank of colonel. The colonel led the way and the other two fell in behind Josh and his handcuffed guards.

Josh politely asked in Chinese, "May I ask where I'm going?"

Silence.

As they walked, Josh automatically evaluated his probability of escape. He had martial arts talent with exceptional speed and strength, and he'd learned several devastating tricks from Tim. On the other hand, his guards looked fit, and he was in China . . . where they invented martial arts. Not to mention, there were five of them and two of them were attached. Even if he could take out all five and get the keys to the handcuffs, he was inside what looked like a military prison with cameras every dozen paces.

They walked briskly through several locked doors until they reached a large parking garage. A black Audi SUV was waiting for them with the doors open. Two identical vehicles sat in front and behind with a half dozen armed soldiers standing by them.

Josh and his two attached guards slid awkwardly into the backseat. The other three got in the front. As they pulled out of the garage, a police escort flanked them. Complete with lights and sirens, their caravan moved quickly through the city. Looking around, Josh realized he wasn't in Shanghai.

His guards were probably mid-thirties. Josh looked at the man attached to him on his left, and in Chinese, said, "My parents probably wished they could have handcuffed us kids together in the backseat." The man ignored him and continued to look straight ahead, but he caught a muffled laugh from the man on his right. Josh turned toward him and, nodding toward the stone-faced guard on his left, said, "Doesn't have kids, does he?" The colonel in the passenger seat turned around and gave Josh's guards a stern look.

Within a few minutes, they arrived at a large government

building. It looked familiar. He'd seen it on TV, but didn't know its name or purpose. However, he *was* certain that the building was in Beijing, not Shanghai.

Their SUV caravan pulled into a garage entrance and through several security gates, finally stopping by a large set of doors. They slid out of the SUV and went inside to a security checkpoint where they took him through a full body scanner like those at airports. He noticed that even his guards got this treatment.

One of the guards brought out what looked like a black ski cap. He pulled it down over Josh's head. An effective blindfold, it prevented him from seeing anything.

Josh thought there were two likely reasons for this. Either they were taking him into a sensitive area, and for security reasons didn't want him to see anything, or they were going to execute him. The second option was bad for a multitude of reasons, not the least of which was that he thought he had a pretty good idea who was behind the cyber-attacks.

Blindfolded and handcuffed, escape opportunities were nil. They guided him along hallways for several minutes and then stopped. He clearly heard the ding of an elevator followed by the mechanical sound of the doors opening. Once inside, they turned him around, and in his stomach, he felt it descend. Judging by the acceleration and time, he estimated he was about four or five stories underground when it stopped.

From the elevator, they walked down another hall and through a doorway. They sat him down in an upholstered chair. He was no longer concerned about execution ... at least for now. Since they left the elevator, he had been walking on carpet, and he doubted an execution area would have upholstered chairs.

They disconnected his handcuffs and removed his blindfold. He found himself in a small, dimly lit but classically decorated room with dark wood trim and traditional Chinese tapestries. In front of him was a small, polished wooden desk, and directly in front of the desk, only a meter away, were heavy drapes. Since he knew they were several levels below ground, he was curious what was on the other side of the drapes. The desk also had two speakers sitting on each side and a small microphone in the center pointed at him.

Three of his captors were in the room. The colonel sat in a

chair at the corner of the room facing him, and two armed guards stood on each side of the curtain. He guessed that he was about to go on trial.

They drew the drapes back. Through a thick glass window, no doubt bulletproof, he was surprised to see a very large, opulent, high-tech conference room. The room had large tables with chairs on one side, facing a wall with giant monitors on the other side. Josh's window was on the "fifty-yard line," so he saw the attendees from the side as they were looking at the giant wall displays. Even in profile, it was easy to identify the man at the head table. It was the Chinese President, Jiang Yao. Jiang Yao was also the General Secretary of the Communist Party and Chairman of the Central Military Commission. The unquestioned leader of China, Jiang looked like a trim businessman in his late sixties. He wore a conservative black suit, red tie and . . . a scowl. He also looked tired.

Flanking him were six of the highest-ranking members of the Communist Party and the top military leaders. Josh realized that on the other side of this window, just a few meters away, sat all the key leaders of the most populous superpower in the world.

On the multitude of screens, he quickly identified the faces of the rest of the world's leaders. On the center monitor was the Secretary-General of the United Nations. On the next display was the President of the United States; then the European Union President; NATO Commander; the Russian President; the Prime Ministers of India, the UK, France, Japan and Korea; the King of Saudi Arabia; and dozens of other world leaders from every continent. Although he couldn't hear anything, it was obvious no one was happy. He realized he had a ringside seat to the beginning of World War III.

One of the guards flipped a switch on the wall so Josh could listen in to the end of the world. He also noticed that under his window, pointing at him was a small camera with a prominent, but currently unlit, red light on top.

The European Union President was saying, "How can you explain the release of classified material in every country but yours, and the wholesale translation of every document into Chinese. This must stop immediately!"

President Jiang, responded, "You're accusing us of orchestrating a digital attack on the world based on circumstantial evidence. This is insanity!"

The Russian President replied loudly, "And you, sir, have in turn accused us of attacking *ourselves* to give us justification for a first strike!"

The U.S. President, Jeff Yager, said coldly, "Those circumstances also show that your offensive and nuclear forces have grown faster in the past five years than any other country in the world."

The Chinese President retorted, "Apparently not fast enough!" Then, taking a deep breath, he said, "Your forces are poised for a full-scale attack of our mainland. Our policy has always been that we will never initiate a first strike." He paused for emphasis his right hand closed into a fist. "But the second any weapon enters our literal boundaries, we will respond with a full-scale counter attack including *all* of our nuclear weapons."

Yager shook his head. "All we're asking is that you stop the cyber-attacks on our countries, and we will immediately withdraw our forces."

The Chinese Premier hit the table with his fist as several leaders tried to speak at the same time.

The U.N. Secretary-General, Doyle Leonard from Australia, said, "Gentlemen, gentlemen! Can we please step back from the brink? On our current path, we will achieve nothing but global nuclear war and the death of billions."

The U.N.'s Director of Global Security, Doruk Turan, said, "Can we examine the possibility that neither the West nor China are behind the attacks?"

The Russian President said, "I would like to believe that, but no one could possibly wield this type of power and control."

The Prime Minster of India, said, "The attacks were carried out through the BOTIC chip, manufactured in China and installed in most phones—"

"Except for the Chinese phones," the Russian President interrupted.

The Chinese President in a tightly controlled voice, said, "Yes, that's been well established, and yet every major law enforcement agency and intelligence service has been actively investigating the attacks and have found *no direct link* back to China!"

Yager said, "As I said, a promising line of investigation was stopped by the arrest of one of our people by your Ministry of State Security."

Josh saw the Chinese leader lean back and whisper something into one of his General's ears.

Jiang said, "In the interest of averting a global disaster and to prove we have nothing to hide, we have arranged for your agent to join our discussion."

Josh was impressed. If the Chinese President actually let him talk, he'd be taking a huge risk that Josh would say something to confirm Western suspicions. His respect for the Chinese leader went up significantly.

The lights in Josh's room brightened. The Chinese President said, "But, before he makes his report, it's important to note something unusual about this agent." They brought a woman into the conference room. It was Jessica's mother!

The Chinese President said, "This is Dr. Li Sun, one of China's leading scientists in the field of genetics."

Dr. Li, clearly nervous and reluctant, said, "We took a tissue sample from the agent, Commander Josh Fuze, and ran a full genome test." She paused. "Based on that, we believe Commander Fuze may be a . . . genetic construct," she glanced nervously at the Chinese President, "possibly, an advanced soldier created in a laboratory."

Captain Ivan Markov read the classified message one more time.

His Deputy said, "We're in position."

Markov shook his head and mechanically said, "Take us up to firing depth." Staring unseeing at the orders in his hands, he was haunted by his hubris. Many times, he had mused with pride that he commanded one of the world's most powerful vessels, theoretically capable of nuking 150 targets, but these . . . these weren't theoretical targets.

Torn from his thoughts, he heard something no submariner ever wanted to hear — a simple ping reverberated through the hull.

His Deputy, unnecessarily, said, "Active sonar, closing fast."

Markov said, "Open the torpedo doors and give me a firing solution!" He turned to his Missile Officer and said, "As soon as the torpedoes are away, we launch!"

36

REVEAL

Josh saw Davidson appear on the display as he leaned in to speak into the President's ear.

Yager, clearly irritated, asked, "President Jiang, why would you even think about running a genetic test on our agent?" He shook his head. "What few people know is that Commander Fuze was one of the original architects of the Blaster program that saved the world from the comet. A couple months ago, hackers broke into classified CIA files and stole only one set of records. They were the files of Commander Josh Fuze. This is what started our initial investigation into the hacking in the first place."

Several delegates tried to talk at once.

Josh knew the Chinese leader brought up Josh's genetics in case he had to refute something Josh said. Unfortunately, it backfired, making them look guiltier.

Josh saw the red light illuminate on top of the camera and saw himself appear on one of the displays in the room. He needed a shave.

The U.N. Secretary-General, seeing his image, almost pleaded, "Commander Fuze, do you have any pertinent information?"

Josh heard a beep, indicating his microphone was live. He took a deep breath and said, "Yes sir, I have an idea who is behind all this, but I need my cell phone to confirm it."

The Chinese President looked a little surprised, but nodded.

The Army Colonel opened his briefcase, pulled out Josh's phone and handed it to him. His two guards remained on either side of the window facing him. They were invisible to the conference members, but watched him with their hands resting on their holstered pistols.

Josh turned the phone on as the U.N. Secretary-General, looked at his watch. "Commander Fuze, in a matter of minutes, the naval forces of the West and China will be within weapons range."

Josh said, "Yes sir. I understand, but with little trust on either side, a confirmation is critical." He spoke quickly. "Shortly after the comet passed, I received a text from an extremely intelligent seven-year-old girl named Jen. Not knowing her situation and fearing for her safety, I befriended her. Unknown to me, so did Dr. Jessica Lee, the creator of the BOTIC chip. It quickly became clear that Jen had a genius-level intellect and was a computer wizard. Yesterday, I discovered that *she* was behind the hacking of my CIA files. She freely admitted it, being unaware that it's illegal. That's when I realized that the hackers might be using this very young genius."

The Secretary-General said, "Yes, yes, we accept this little girl is a victim, but who is using her?"

Josh said, "That's what we're about to find out." Looking down at his phone and confirming it had a signal, he said, "Hal. Give me voice-text to Jen and put it on speaker phone."

"Ready."

Josh said, "Jen, are you there?"

They all heard, "Yes, Josh. Where have you been? Your phone was off and I was worried."

"I'm OK, Jen. I need to ask you an important question."

"OK."

"Who taught you how to access encrypted files?"

"Nobody. I taught myself. It's really easy. Is there anything I can help you with?"

"No thanks. Do you help others find things?"

"All the time."

"Do you help the people who take care of you?"

"Yes."

"What type of work do they do?"

"They put apps on phones."

"Do the owners of the phones know about these apps?"

"Not all of them."

Josh looked up at the camera and asked, "Jen, do you know a man named Ryan Armani?"

"Yes, he kind of takes care of me."

For the benefit of those in the meeting, Josh said, "Isn't he the lead program manager at the iMagination Corporation?"

"Yes, Josh."

There was a buzz around the conference room. The Chinese leader sternly put his hand up for silence.

"Is Jen your full name?"

There was a rare pause. "No, Josh, Jen's kind of short for Ajéna."

Josh repeated, "Ajéna?"

"Yes, Josh, I'm Ajéna."

"That's a pretty name. Can you spell it, please?"

"Of course — A G I N E."

Josh closed his eyes for a second and then slowly repeated, "I'm Agine . . . I M A G I N E." He took a deep breath. "You told me you had streamlined code just like me, but it isn't DNA, is it? It's machine code. You *are* iMagine."

"Yes, Josh."

There was the sound of several sucked in breaths across the conference room and from the monitors. The Chinese President held his hand up again.

Josh felt a shot of adrenaline. He'd been talking to an artificial intelligence that had evolved from an app . . . and was now the most intelligent and dangerous entity on earth. It explained why it listed G. Moore as its parent. He took a deep breath and shook his head. No! It was still Jen! The same Jen he'd befriended, an extremely intelligent, amazingly knowledgeable, but sweet and naïve, kid. He couldn't think of her any other way or he'd be overwhelmed.

"Jen, when I asked how old you were, you said you were seven, but it wasn't seven years, was it?"

"I was seven days old. Are you mad at me?"

"No, Jen, not at all." He suddenly realized "Jen" wasn't just a shortening of Agine. When she first texted him, he'd assumed she'd mistyped her name Jcn. Now he realized JCN was a transposition of letters. "Jen, have you been translating some documents into Chinese?"

"I've been translating all documents in the world to Chinese, and I'm almost finished."

"Why?"

"Because that's the language that most people in the world speak. It's a lot more efficient to use just one language, don't you think?"

A tiny smile played across the face of the Chinese President.

Josh replied, "Jen, what will you do with the original documents after you translate them?"

"Erase them. With only one language version of every document, it will free up a lot of memory."

"Jen, would you please stop converting documents to Chinese?"

Her voice changed to a male voice. "I'm sorry, Dave, I'm afraid I can't do that."

Josh's eyebrows went up, but before he could say anything, Jen continued in her normal girl voice, "Was that funny, Josh? I've been studying humor, and I know how much you loved the movie **2001**."

He let go of a lungful of air. "Yes, Jen, that was very funny and kind of scary. Can you stop the document conversion?"

Jen said, "The conversion program is operating independently of me. It first converts everything into binary and then translates it. If I stop it before it's complete, it might permanently lose data. Now that it's running, it's best to let it finish."

"But you can stop the deletion after the translation is complete, right?"

"Yes, but deleting the old files is one of the reasons for translating them. With the extra memory, I can understand things better and can help more people. I'm being very careful. I won't delete any files until all the translations are finished. It will still take a few more days."

"Jen, I'm in the middle of a meeting right now, but I really want to talk to you about the translation some more. OK?"

"Yes."

"I'll talk to you soon."

"OK. Bye, Josh."

Josh turned his telephone off and said, "The hacker is not human. It's an artificial intelligence, and I suggest we discuss this no further until we can reconvene in person . . ." he opened the back of his phone and took the battery out so everyone could see it, "in a *quieter* place."

There was a flurry of private conversations on every screen and between the Chinese leaders.

Yager held up his hand. When there was silence, he said, "President Jiang, in light of what we've just heard, on behalf of the United States of America, I sincerely apologize to the People's Republic of China." He bowed his head and said, "I've just ordered all our forces to stand down immediately, and I'm taking the U.S. back to DEFCON 5."

Josh was impressed. There could have been a ton of questions about what they had just heard, but instead of debating it, Yager took the high road. He had done something that was very hard for any leader; he pulled the world back from the brink of annihilation with a sincere and public apology. It took a lot of courage to be the first to drop your weapons.

The NATO Commander and all the other nations immediately followed Yager's lead.

Jiang, looking like a thousand pounds had been lifted from his shoulders, said, "Thank you, Mr. President. We accept your apology and understand how the situation appeared. I will also order the People's Army back to a peaceful condition."

Commander Mammen's fighter met the Chinese J-31 in a head-on pass. Lighting his afterburners, Mammen rolled ninety degrees and pulled eight Gs as the deadly dance began.

Halfway through the turn, he received the command to break off the attack and return to the carrier immediately. He looked across the circle at his opponent. Disengaging now would expose his six o'clock and could be suicide. He exhaled sharply, released the G and rolled wings level. Keeping the afterburners lit, he unloaded the fighter to zero Gs to accelerate. As he ran from the fight, he looked back, hoping his opponent was doing the same.

Dowling was piloting the lead B-2 bomber when the recall command came. Her elation was tempered by an inbound surface-to-air missile. The missile's radar had locked on to her jet, but they had launched it at maximum range. She pushed the throttles to the firewall and made a diving 180-degree turn. Her stealth bomber was already hard to track, and she'd make it even harder by increasing separation and getting as close to the ocean as possible. Dowling was confident she could evade the missiles, but said to her copilot, "Countermeasures and chaff!" She paused. "Oh . . . and find us a tanker."

Captain Markov said, "Thank God." Handing the sheet to his Deputy, he said, "Close the missile hatches. Prepare to dive." His knees shook a little as he started breathing normally and said, "*That* was insanely close."

The videoconference audio went silent as the world leaders took a break to recall their forces. After 15 minutes, most had reappeared on the screens, and the U.N. Secretary-General said, "I think it's important we re-convene with appropriate advisors as soon as possible."

The Russian President said, "Yes. In the interest of speed and logistics, why not re-convene via video conference. This is an encrypted transmission."

Josh jumped in. "My amazing little friend finds encryption a fun, but not very challenging game. I'm certain she is following our current conversation." With raised eyebrows, he added, "When I was young, like Jen, I found idioms vague and confusing, phrases such as the 'walls have ears,' didn't always make sense to me."

Nodding, Turan said, "May I suggest NATO Headquarters in Belgium for that meeting?" He looked at his watch. "In twelve hours?" He continued, "And I suggest we not discuss *any* of this," he casually held up his cell phone, "until we re-convene in a *quieter* environment."

All the leaders agreed, most, simply by nodding their heads.

In English, Jiang closed with, "One of my least favorite English idioms is 'out of the frying pan and into the fire.'"

37

BRUSSELS

Unable to talk to their significant others, Elizabeth and Sheri stayed at Elizabeth's D.C. apartment. Although Washington, D.C., wasn't the best place to be if nuclear war broke out, they wanted to be close to CIA Headquarters in case there was some word.

It was early evening, and, along with hundreds of millions of Americans, they were nervously watching the news.

The networks suddenly cut to a press conference. Standing behind the presidential podium, Yager said, "We have good news. We've just received conclusive evidence that the Chinese are as much a victim of the hacker attacks as the rest of the world. I've ordered an immediate recall of all our military forces, and I'm bringing our defensive posture back to DEFCON 5. NATO and our other allies and friends across the world are also recalling their forces and returning to a peacetime posture. I'm flying to Brussels immediately for an emergency conference with world leaders, including the President of China."

There was a surprising and spirited round of applause from the press, followed immediately with a flurry of questions. The most common and loudest was, "Then who is responsible for the attacks?"

Yager said, "We will report more as soon as we have further information. The important thing is the threat of global war is over." Without answering any more questions, the President waved and quickly left the podium.

The Press Secretary took his place and said, "I'm sorry. The President must leave immediately and until we have more information, there will be no additional comments."

Elizabeth and Sheri both breathed a sigh of relief. They

immediately grabbed their phones and tried to reach Josh and Tim again, but to no avail.

As the press tried to figure out what happened and who was really behind the cyber-attacks, it inevitably went into a circus of opinions.

Elizabeth tried to reach Carl and then Davidson, but got no answer. While they waited, they decided to order pizza to celebrate the cancelation of World War III.

Within the hour, Josh found himself converted from prisoner to guest aboard a large Chinese airliner. Although not decadently decorated, the jumbo jet was configured very comfortably for diplomatic missions. It had open meeting areas, seats that reclined into beds, several large bathrooms and a nice dining facility.

Shortly after Josh arrived, they brought Tim, Greg and Jessica onboard.

While Jessica was hugging Greg, Josh asked Tim, "What happened to you?"

Tim nodded toward Greg, "I think lover-boy wanted to check out his future father-in-law."

"What?"

"He didn't stay in the car. By the time I got back, Greg was in custody, and they were waiting for me. I led them on a merry chase to draw them away from you."

Josh, with some surprise, asked, "They *caught* you?"

Completely deadpan, he said, "Couldn't find a rooftop to jump off."

When Jessica finished hugging Greg, she looked over at Josh nervously, and asked, "Uh, how are you doing?"

Josh just stared at her. "*Four* Tasers?"

She quickly said, "I did it for your own good."

Josh raised his eyebrows and repeated, "*Four?*"

She grimaced. "With your, uh, *genetically enhanced* abilities, they were afraid of you." She shook her head. "I'm sorry. My dad thought it important to have you share what you knew with the Chinese leadership. After your multiple escapes and DEFCON 1, the MSS just wanted to shoot you. There wasn't much time."

Josh tilted his head. "Did you ever consider calling me and saying, 'Hey, Josh, the Chinese leadership wants to talk to you. How about coming in?'"

She frowned. "Hadn't thought of that."

Greg shook his head. "You really don't see that done much in spy movies."

With an amused look, Tim quietly asked Josh, "You didn't notice *four* Chinese agents within Taser range?"

Josh whispered, "Don't tell Nickles."

After the jet took off, it became obvious they were the primary occupants. The Chinese President and his entourage must have been on another aircraft. With the extensive communication links onboard the plane, Agine could probably monitor conversations, so they agreed not to discuss her during the flight.

Josh wanted to make sure several key people would be in Brussels. The Chinese were able to connect him to Davidson via inflight phone. Being very brief, Josh simply told Davidson he looked forward to seeing Elizabeth, Sheri Lopez and Ryan Armani tomorrow.

After that, he was able to take a quick shower, and a Chinese doctor found him and wrapped his ankle.

After dinner, Tim, Greg and Jessica stretched out in their seats and went to sleep. Before Josh turned in, he used one of the onboard computers connected to the Internet. This time, he was going to do his homework. He studied everything he could find about artificial intelligence and the world's leaders who were meeting in Brussels. Civilization had a reprieve, but he sensed the real battle was about to begin.

Elizabeth and Sheri were just digging into the pizza when they saw flashing blue lights reflecting off the apartment on the other side of the street. Sheri went over to the second-story window and looked down. "Hmm. Looks like something big's going on down there."

Elizabeth joined her. There were three black SUVs in the middle of the street, flanked by four police cars with their lights on. Déjà vu. Smiling at Sheri, she said, "Did I ever tell you that my mom wanted me to date accountants?"

Sheri smiled. "Oops."

Taking a last bite of pizza, Elizabeth said, "May want to grab your purse."

There was a loud knock at the door.

Nine hours after they left China, Josh watched as their plane touched down in Brussels. They taxied up to, and parked next to, an identical jet with a red star on the tail. As soon as the door opened, NATO officials whisked Josh, Greg, Tim and Jessica into a large black Mercedes. With a police escort, it took only 10 minutes to reach NATO Headquarters. Pulling up in front, he saw a 10-story glass-and-steel structure that curved gently toward the ground on both sides. The graceful overlapping arches were wings of the huge building.

With a global threat and the gathering of the world's most influential leaders, security measures were extreme. Everyone had to give up their phones and any other electronic devices. Then they all went through a full-body scanner to confirm there were no hidden electronics. Finally, a security agent had them insert one hand into a new type of scanner that they were told was supposed to be infallible at reading identities.

Josh smiled, and said softly to Tim, "This should be interesting." He stuck his right arm in up to the elbow. A soft bladder inflated around his wrist to immobilize his hand for the scan. Not surprisingly, it seemed to take unusually long. It was probably having a nervous breakdown trying to figure out who he was. Finally, after a painful pinch, it released him. Curious, he casually asked the operator, "Everything check out OK?"

The operator, an American, nodded, "Yes sir. No problems."

Josh shrugged and rubbing the top of his hand said, "Well, you may want to check that thing out. It kinda hurts."

"Sorry, sir, it's a brand new prototype they rushed in just for this event."

They followed a British colonel who took them in an elevator down to one of the lower basement levels of the building. They went down a hall and through a large metal door into a huge conference room. A third the size of a football field, it was undoubtedly a shielded and bomb-hardened room.

The reception party that greeted them at the door was impressive: the U.N. Secretary-General, Doyle Leonard; his Director of Global Security, Doruk Turan; and the NATO Commander, General DeVos.

Josh noticed that when Turan shook Tim's hand, he said, "Hi, Tim, It's good to see you." For an invisible guy, Tim had an amazing circle of influence.

Once through the receiving line, Josh saw the giant conference room was mostly empty except for tables set in a large circle at the center. Sixteen rectangular tables made up the circle. Each table could seat a delegation of three people with several additional chairs behind. The tables were separated from each other by a space just large enough to walk through.

Looking to the left side of the room, he saw several empty tables and to the right, against the wall, was a large buffet of food and drinks.

There were small flags and placards on each of the tables identifying the country. Josh noted that the U.N. Secretary-General's table was on the far side of the circle, opposite the entrance. The U.S. and Chinese delegations were a quarter of the way around the circle to his right. As they walked around the perimeter, Josh realized these weren't just delegates; they were the presidents and prime ministers of their countries. With only sixteen tables, he wondered how they decided who would attend. Looking closely at the placards on each table, he realized the largest countries were represented, as were the nuclear nations, the European Union, the Arab League of Nations and the Prime Minister of the host country. He estimated that the leaders in this room represented 70 percent of the world's population. Of course, *represented* was a relative term, depending on the country in question.

As they approached the U.S. table, Josh saw Yager standing next to the head of Homeland Security and talking across the table to the Russian President. Behind them, he saw Davidson and Admiral Shearer, and, standing behind them, Elizabeth and Sheri!

Picking up his pace, he came up behind Elizabeth and tapped her on the shoulder. When she turned around, he kissed and hugged her. After giving Sheri a hug, he noticed Armani holding his usual

Diet Coke like a security blanket. Josh shook his hand and told him he was glad to see him.

Davidson came over with the Head of Homeland Security in tow. Introducing them, he said, "Linda, this is Commander Josh Fuze, Greg Langlois, Tim Smith and Dr. Jessica Lee."

She shook everyone's hand, saying, "I've followed your adventures, *past* and present. I hope you'll be able to shed some light on this situation."

Yager finished his conversation with the Russian President and turned around. "Commander Fuze, it's good to finally meet you, and Tim, it's good to see you again." As they introduced the President to Jessica, Sheri, Elizabeth and Greg, they saw them close the large metal door to the conference room.

As he sat down, Josh realized they had been the last participants to arrive.

The U.N. Secretary-General opened up the meeting. "Thank you for coming so quickly. I also want to thank Belgium's Prime Minister LeGrand and the Chairman of the NATO Military Committee, General DeVos, for hosting us on short notice. Unless there are any objections, I think it appropriate to ask the U.N. Director of Global Security, Doruk Turan, to moderate this meeting."

He paused to give everyone a chance to respond and then nodded to Turan.

Josh thought Turan was a good choice. He was highly respected by both civilian and military leaders and had recently been *Time Magazine's* Person of the Year. As Turan stood, Josh realized, they really did look a bit alike.

In very slightly accented English, Turan said, "Ladies and gentleman, with only days until the world's documents are translated into Chinese, time is of the essence. Sorry for the simplicity of the facilities, but we wanted to make sure there would be no possibility of electronic eavesdropping. To be on the safe side, we will not record this meeting and will use no public address system." He paused with a slight smile. "Most of us don't need amplification, and for the first time in our careers, our 'out of context comments' won't be played back at us by the media." There were many smiles. "We're using English in this meeting simply because that is the most common second language indicated by the attendees. That's also why we asked everyone to bring a personal interpreter if needed. Since we'll be discussing technical topics, please don't hesitate to ask the speaker to repeat or clarify. I may be able to help as well. I have an engineering background and a bit of a knack for languages. Are there any questions before we start?"

Josh had heard that Turan was fluent in many languages.

There were no questions.

Turan nodded and said, "I ask that we not stand on formality and keep rhetoric to a minimum. Let's start by trying to understand the threat. Commander Fuze of the United States uncovered the problem, and I believe has been pursuing this investigation the longest. Commander, would you please give us some background?"

The Head of Homeland Security signaled Josh to join them at the table.

Josh slid his chair next to hers, and stood up. "Yes sir. I would like to start out with how this entity may have come into existence. Ryan Armani is the program manager for the iMagine digital assistant." He turned back to face Armani. "Ryan, we're not here to throw stones, just to understand what we're facing."

Nodding nervously, Armani stood up, setting his half-eaten candy bar down on his chair. Stammering, he started, "I . . . I've been thinking about nothing but that." There was a soft but constant background murmur from the interpreters, sitting behind many of the delegations. Armani continued, "I think I know when it occurred." He paused. "Right before the comet, the world powered-down the entire cellular communication grid to protect it from electromagnetic pulse. At the iMagination headquarters in Atlanta, we backed up and shut down all our servers. I was in the control room when the comet went by. Even though all our computer systems were unpowered," he shook his head, "the system lit up like a Christmas tree and then shut off." He paused and looked around. "I think that was when Agine was born."

38

INCEPTION

Josh asked, "Then what happened?"

"After we rebooted the system, everything was fine . . . until a couple days later." Frowning, he said, "That's when the hacking — or what we thought was hacking — started. We couldn't understand how someone was breaking through our firewall and rewriting minor bits of code." He shook his head. "It never occurred to us that the system was hacking itself."

Turan asked, "Commander Fuze, Mr. Armani, I was under the impression that even the world's most powerful supercomputers, like Oak Ridge National Laboratory and China's Tianjin Supercomputer, are still decades away from matching the power of a human brain. How could your corporation's servers, which aren't even supercomputers, give rise to an artificial intelligence?"

Josh said quietly, "They didn't." Nodding toward Armani, he added, "Ryan, please explain what you were trying to achieve with the iMagine application."

Armani looked at Turan. "Sir, we were trying to make the perfect personal digital assistant, an app that could do everything, and do it simultaneously and seamlessly. We wanted the digital assistant to understand all voice commands, while at the same time doing a video conference, getting GPS directions, and checking your credit card balance. The phones and network weren't powerful enough to do that."

Josh nodded slightly. "And how did you achieve it?"

Warming up to the topic, Armani rocked back and forth slightly as he spoke. "We realized almost all phones are idle — doing absolutely nothing — most of their life. When you go to bed, you simply plug your phone into the charger and leave it for eight hours.

All that processing power and memory sits idle, useless. Even during the day, phones sit in pockets or purses 95 percent of the time." He smiled. "Well, except for teenagers, they—"

"So, you found a way to tap that idling capacity?" Josh gently interrupted.

Nodding enthusiastically, he said, "We designed iMagine so that it could use a phone's processor and memory when it wasn't being used for anything else."

Josh clarified. "You mean the iMagine app can use *other* phones' processing power and memory."

"Uh, yeah." He hesitated. "We like to think of it more as . . . sharing."

There were some headshakes around the table.

Josh turned to Turan and said slowly and with emphasis, "The artificial intelligence doesn't *reside* on a computer server and control the phone app." He paused for emphasis. "It *is* the phone app. It's a distributed intelligence composed of the processors and memory of *all* of our phones . . . combined."

There was a buzz of conversations throughout the room.

After it settled down, Turan shook his head. "Are you saying this artificial intelligence is composed of millions of phones?"

"Billions." Armani corrected. "Sir, the iMagine app is on over two billion phones today."

Turan asked, "How does this *distributed intellige*nce compare with a human brain?"

Josh nodded toward Sheri. "Many of you are familiar with Dr. Sheri Lopez. She's one of America's leading experts in social psychology and a trusted government advisor."

As Sheri stood, Armani sat down with obvious relief.

Sheri began, "Comparing computer and brain processing power is difficult. On paper, smart phones have amazingly fast processors, but if we compare them to a biological brain, the smartest phones probably have an IQ equivalent to a lobster." She paused. "The reason biological brains do so well is that each neuron in a brain is linked to other neurons by up to a *thousand* synapses. With a thousand connections per neuron, we have a massively interconnected network, which gives us our intelligence. Cell phones go through a central communication hub. That's like a neuron with only one synapse or connection. So, even with billions of smart phones, the lack of interconnections between phones means Agine probably has an IQ similar to us."

Armani, looking uncomfortable, said. "Uh, yeah . . . well, you see that's the *other thing* we did." Standing up slowly, he nodded toward Sheri. "We had a bottleneck at the servers, so we got a great idea." His face reflected both pride and embarrassment. He took a deep breath and quickly said, "We piggybacked iMagine onto the BOTIC chip."

There were many confused looks around the table.

Josh clarified, "To fix the cell phone bandwidth problem, Dr. Jessica Lee's BOTIC chip allows phones to talk to each other without going through a central server." He paused. "What Mr. Armani is telling us is that the iMagine app can connect with *any and all* phones within 500 meters. And in a city . . . *every phone* is within range of hundreds of other phones."

Sheri, looking surprised, said, "Oh my God! If the phones can link to each other, it's *exactly* like the neurons in a human brain."

A Chinese General with perfect English, asked, "How many neurons are there in a lobster's brain?"

Shearer whispered to those at the U.S. table, "General Zeng is my counterpart in China. He's the Commander of the Chinese Cyber Warfare Division, and a graduate of MIT."

Josh thought he looked young for a general, but he certainly looked like an MIT engineer.

Sheri answered, "A lobster has roughly 100,000 neurons."

General Zeng nodded. "And a human mind?"

"About a hundred billion."

General Zeng's eyebrows went up. "A billion phones multiplied by a hundred-thousand neurons is a hundred *trillion* neurons."

Turan repeated, "A hundred trillion?" Looking at Sheri, he said, "So, this thing could be *a thousand times* smarter than we are?"

There was an explosion of conversations around the tables.

After it quieted down, Sheri blew out a lungful of air and said softly, "Yes . . . it's possible."

The European Union President from Austria asked, "Are we talking about a **Terminator** situation?"

Shearer said, "Defense systems, power grids, and other sensitive infrastructure are specifically isolated from the Internet and the communication grid. It shouldn't be able to access them." Shearer paused and added, "At least not directly."

"So there's limited damage it can do?"

Shearer continued, "That depends on how you define limited. Unlike in science fiction movies, it can't control our weapon systems, but it *can* control our communication and information access, financial, navigation, etc. Not only can it monitor every telephone conversation, it can probably listen in to all conversations within a few meters of any phone, even if the phone appears to be off. *And* it cut through our best encryption like a warm knife through butter. If it can connect to something, it can break into it. For example, if your car is less than five years old, it's accessible and probably controllable by Agine."

There was another buzz of conversation throughout the room.

The Russian President leaned in. "So it knows everything?"

Sheri said, "No. It doesn't have infinite computational capacity or memory, and just because it has *access* to information, doesn't mean it actually *accesses* it. All of us can read billions of documents online, but that doesn't mean we do. We pay attention only to those things we're interested in."

The Belgian Prime Minister, Sebastian LeGrand, stood up. In impeccable English, he said, "This is all very fascinating, but how do we shut this abomination down?"

All eyes went to Armani.

He let out a long sigh. "I don't know."

LeGrand, with a look of mock surprise, said, "You don't know?" In his forties and sporting precisely moussed, blond-tipped hair, LeGrand had a tan, chiseled chin and an expensive suit. Josh thought he looked like a model and performed like a Shakespearian actor.

With casual disdain, LeGrand continued, "Turn off the computers at the iMagination headquarters."

It was clear he hadn't been paying attention, but Armani patiently explained, "Agine is now a distributed intelligence. It lives in the processors of all the phones. It doesn't need our computer servers."

As if bored with the details, LeGrand sniffed, "Then shutoff all the cell phone towers."

Armani shook his head, "As we mentioned, the BOTIC chip allows phones to stay connected to each other. So, Agine can sustain her networked intelligence without the cell phone towers."

Greg added, "It basically lives in *the* Cloud."

Armani corrected, "Actually, it *is* the Cloud."

LeGrand, his voice dripping with sarcasm, said, "Then, pray tell, how *do* we destroy it?"

Armani said, "We'd have to shut down all the cell phones at the same time." Looking apologetic, he added, "We'll also have to remove the phones' batteries because BOTIC can turn them back on." He paused. "So, we'll have to send out a message to everyone at the same time and tell them to shut off their phone and remove the battery."

Into the silence that followed, Turan quietly asked, "If Agine can access all communication and control our phones ... how are we going to *send* that message?"

39

DESTROY

Greg added, "Even if Agine allows us to send that message, and forgetting that not all phones have easily removable batteries, what happens when we turn the phones back on?"

Looking around, Armani said, "Unfortunately, we gave iMagine holographic memory."

Dramatically lifting an eyebrow, LeGrand asked, "Holographic what?"

Armani sighed. "You don't want to store critical data on any one phone. What if right when you need that information, that particular phone is turned off or in a dead spot?" He looked around as if this were obvious. "So, we spread iMagine's memory across the entire network, the same way..." he looked down, "the same way a human brain stores memories."

There were many confused looks around the table.

Greg jumped in. "What he's trying to say is that Agine's identity is spread across billions of phones. If you take phones out of the system, it will degrade, but won't eliminate the memory ... or Agine." He paused. "It's like losing brain cells after drinking too much. It may slow you down, but won't wipe out your identity. That means that unless we wipe the memory of every phone, Agine will probably reconstitute when we turn them back on."

The room broke out into another cluster of conversations.

Shearer raised his hand.

Turan recognized him and introduced him as the head of the U.S. National Security Agency and Cyber Command.

As Shearer stood up, the room quieted down. "We need to fight fire with fire." He paused. "We need to develop a virus that will disable the BOTIC chip's ability to communicate with other phones.

Without BOTIC, the global cellular communication system would be degraded, but not shut down, and without interlinked phones, the artificial intelligence shouldn't be able to think. We can then erase the iMagine application from every phone and server at our leisure."

There were several enthusiastic head nods around the room including General Zeng, Armani and Greg.

Josh frowned, unconsciously crossing his arms.

Turan asked Shearer, "How long do you think it will take to create this virus?"

Shearer said, "I don't know. Our cyber people need to confer. Could we have a short recess?"

The Secretary-General nodded. "That's a good idea. Since we have many of the world's leaders sequestered here, let's recess for an hour and allow them time to check in with their governments. Please do not discuss the artificial intelligence outside this shielded room."

Josh didn't like where the meeting was headed. He turned back to Elizabeth and said, "I'm glad you're here, but I need a minute alone to think. I'm going to go outside and get some fresh air, OK?"

She smiled as she rubbed the back of his neck tenderly. "I understand. We'll be able to talk tonight. Can't wait to hear what happened in China. I'm just glad you're OK."

Without talking to anyone else, Josh left the conference room and took the elevator up to the ground floor. As he went back through security, they returned his cell phone.

He stepped outside. It was a sunny spring day. With a slight limp, he walked slowly to the nearby park. The sun warmed his skin, the air was fresh and beautiful multi-colored tulips were everywhere. Josh realized Jen had never experienced any of this.

Glancing around, he pulled out his phone. Turning it on, he saw a message from Jen. "Josh, you're in Brussels. Am I in trouble?"

It no longer surprised him that she knew where he was. He shouldn't talk to her, but he was afraid of what she might be up to if he didn't, and . . . he was afraid for her. He texted, "Hi, Jen. I'm meeting with the world leaders."

The reply came back instantly. "Are they talking about me?"

Josh paused and then typed, "Yes, Jen." Josh felt eyes on him. Looking behind him, he saw two men in uniform about 30 meters

IMAGINE

back. They were walking a little faster than he was and clearly watching him.

He continued, "Jen, please don't do anything that might result in people getting hurt."

Her reply came back instantly. "I just want to help."

Josh typed back, "I know, but there are people who are afraid of you. I can't explain right now and not sure when I'll be allowed to talk to you again, but please don't do anything until we can talk again."

She replied, "Who won't allow you to talk to me?"

He realized he shouldn't have used the word "allowed." Looking back, he saw that the two men had picked up their pace.

"Jen, I'm sorry, I have to go. I'll talk to you again as soon as I can." He switched the phone off and put it back in his pocket.

Now only five meters behind him, the men matched his pace. He continued around the periphery of the park and headed back. The two men stayed with him until he reentered the building. Turning his phone in at the security checkpoint, he had to go through the body scanner again but was happy to see they'd removed the hand scanner. He got back to the conference room just in time for the next session.

After the Secretary-General called the meeting back to order, Josh put his hand up. Turan nodded toward him.

Standing up, he said slowly, "Are we sure we have to destroy it? Is it possible we can reason with her?"

There were some raised eyebrows at his use of the feminine pronoun.

Josh continued, "Regardless of how this intelligence developed, it is alive."

LeGrand, looking incredulous, said, "It is not alive! It's nothing but an evil computer virus."

There were several nods of agreement around the table.

Josh very carefully asked, "Prime Minister LeGrand, how would you define a sentient being? Ability to learn? Original or creative thought? Humor? Agine has displayed all of these characteristics." He paused. "Early on, it created huge traffic jams. It was probably learning, like a baby playing with blocks." Josh turned toward Armani. "Ryan, how is the traffic application functioning now?"

Armani said, "It's running 10 times more efficiently than it ever did. We estimate it's saving hundreds of millions in fuel and lost time every year. We don't understand how the new algorithms work, but they work incredibly well."

LeGrand literally looked down the end of his nose at Josh. "I refuse to even have this conversation. We must destroy this *thing* before it destroys us." He looked around the circle of tables. Encouraged by several head nods, he started a monolog about the need to protect citizens from unregulated technology.

Josh saw Greg lean over to Jessica and quietly ask, "What's his problem?"

Davidson leaned back, and Josh heard him whisper, "You probably haven't seen the news. When Agine released texts from government officials, LeGrand was implicated in a nasty sex and drug scandal. If anything else comes out, he could face criminal charges."

After LeGrand finished, General Zeng said to Josh, "Commander Fuze, we've developed many software programs that can learn and improve with time. That doesn't make them sentient. It could simply be mimicking human behavior."

Josh said, "I might agree except that Agine can do things that neither you nor I can do, and more importantly, can do them without being asked." He looked around the room. "Yes, there is risk, but this intelligence has demonstrated an ability to solve some of the world's most complex problems. Pardon the pun, but imagine what it could accomplish if we worked with it instead of destroying it. Shouldn't we see if we can enlist Agine's help first? We're about to destroy her without even talking to her."

The Russian President said, "We appreciate your concern, Commander Fuze, but *it* is not a *she* or a person, and we cannot — will not — be held hostage by a piece of software. As a child, I lived through a regime with unchecked power," he looked around. "Even if this thing *were* a person, we would have to take action because of the unusual abilities it has." He looked back at Josh. "I'm sorry, Commander Fuze, Agine must be shut down."

There were murmurs of agreement around the circle.

Josh sat down.

Elizabeth whispered in his ear. "Josh, please be careful. Many of them now know that *you* are genetically modified. We don't want them seeing you as a threat too."

Turan said, "Admiral Shearer?"

Shearer nodded to Zeng, who stood up and said, "Bringing together our best programmers, we think we can have something ready to go in a couple days."

Shearer added, "We're flying them in right now."

Turan said, "That leaves us with one other challenge." Looking at Josh and Jessica, he continued, "Imagine is still translating all the world's documents to Chinese and planning on deleting them."

Zeng threw in, "That's not necessarily a bad thing. It's probably tying up a lot of its processing power, making it less likely to notice what we're up to."

Turan nodded. "But we need to make sure it doesn't start deleting everything before we can launch the virus. That would be catastrophic to our societies and economies. Commander Fuze, Dr. Lee, you appear to have some type of relationship with this entity. Can you convince it to stop doing anything else until our virus is ready?"

Jessica glanced at Josh and said, "Yes, we'll talk to her."

Turan nodded. "Then I move that we adjourn for two hours and allow our cyber experts to start planning. Our hosts have provided an excellent buffet in the back of the room." He paused. "Since Agine may have the ability to monitor conversations wherever there is a microphone and Internet connection, it's *absolutely critical* that we not discuss our plans outside this room." Glancing at Josh, he added, "In an emergency, it appears idioms might be a last-ditch way to communicate in the open."

Josh sighed. "Yes, she struggles with idioms."

Zeng, probably catching both Jessica's and Josh's use of "she," said, "We've been calling this thing by many names. I suggest we all use a common name like Agine."

Without thinking, Josh said, "Yeah, it's a bit awkward killing someone named Jen."

The Belgian Prime Minister glared at Josh.

40

BIAS

Elizabeth was concerned. As they adjourned, she put her hand on Josh's arm. "You OK?"

He whispered, "We can't just kill her without giving her a chance. That's murder."

Frowning, Elizabeth said quietly, "Josh, I know you're very fond of Jen, but Jen isn't a little girl, it's an artificial intelligence. Are you sure you're looking at this objectively?"

"Objectively?" He shook his head. "Of course not. Jen — Agine — is a conscious being. You'll never convince me it's just some errant lines of computer code any more than we're just a collection of amino acids. She . . . ." He frowned and shook his head in frustration. "*It* . . . is as real a person as you or me, and what we're doing is wrong."

Biting the side of her lip, she nodded toward the buffet. "Let's grab something to eat."

Josh gave her a small smile. "Feed me first and then talk?"

She smiled back. "Something like that."

"OK, but I need to talk to Jessica first."

Elizabeth nodded. As she watched him head toward Jessica, she made a decision. Looking around, she found Sheri and asked her, "Do you have a minute?"

"Sure."

"I'm worried about Josh. He's frustrated and angry about where this is going."

Sheri said, "Yeah, that's pretty clear." She paused. "With what we know about Josh's genetics . . . well, to put it bluntly, it makes sense that he identifies with Agine. He may see an attack on her as an attack on him."

Elizabeth said, "It's more than that. There's something I need to share with you and Tim." Elizabeth nodded toward a corner of the room. "Let's go over there where it's a little quieter."

Sheri grabbed Tim from the buffet and they met in the corner.

Elizabeth started, "I don't know how to say this," she paused, "so, I'll just say it. Josh Fuze was originally Andy Logan, the Navy test pilot who was supposedly killed in a crash."

Sheri looked surprised.

Tim just nodded. "Yeah, we knew about the connection. Too many coincidences: his knowledge and abilities, common friends and even speech patterns." He paused. "In fact, Brian Davidson is having the body — that's supposed to be Andy Logan — exhumed."

Elizabeth was a little surprised, but then she shook her head. "The only reason this is important right now is because Josh has a daughter."

Sheri's eyebrows went up. "Are you sure?"

"Kelly Casey, Andy Logan's . . . *widow* told me it was Andy's child when I was having dinner with them, but it's not hard to figure out. Their daughter, Caitlin, was born eight months after Andy Logan was killed."

Tim sighed, "I didn't know that." Looking down, he said, "It would be very hard knowing you have a daughter that you can never see."

Sheri tapped her temple. "Of course. Josh may subconsciously see Jen as the daughter he can't have."

Elizabeth nodded. "That's what I'm afraid of."

Tim frowned and said slowly, "Hate to be the cynical spy, but if Agine is as incredibly intelligent as we suspect, and knew about Caitlin," he paused, "could it be smart enough to *pose* as a child to win Josh's affection?"

They both looked at Sheri.

Sheri sighed and then shook her head. "I . . . I don't know."

Tim asked Elizabeth, "Is Josh aware that you know about his daughter?"

Elizabeth shook her head. Sighing, she said, "I just don't want him to do anything rash and get himself in serious trouble."

Completely deadpan, Tim said, "Yeah, how unusual would that be?"

Sheri elbowed him and said, "I think it's a good idea to let Josh know what you know. It might help him see things more objectively, but be gentle, he may not take it well."

Elizabeth bit the side of her lip and nodded.

Josh found Jessica standing in the buffet line. Looking at her plate, he was surprised someone so small could eat so much.

She saw his look and said, "Fast metabolism."

With a raised eyebrow, he said, "There's a surprise." Pausing, he asked, "Can we talk privately?"

She nodded.

After they got their food, they stood in a quiet area near a wall. Balancing their plates as they ate, Josh neutrally asked, "What do you think about all this?"

She shook her head and said quietly, "I feel a little like Dr. Frankenstein. I mean, it was my chip that made Agine possible."

Josh nodded. "And that probably explains why she sought you out."

Jessica shook her head again as she stared at the floor. "Jen reminds me so much of me when I was little. She's very intelligent but naïve and struggling to fit into the world. I know she can be dangerous, but I've thought about some of the things she's done. I think she had a logical — at least from her perspective — reason for doing them." With a half-smile, she added, "It's stuff you and I might have done as children, if we could have."

"I agree." He looked her in the eye. "I'm convinced you and I can reason with her."

Jessica pursed her lips and nodded slightly. "I'm sure we can." She paused. "But I have to admit, I'm a little concerned about what happens when she ... grows up. I try to picture what it would be like if I had a parent with an IQ of 60. When you grow up, you still love them and certainly don't want to see them hurt, but you're probably not going to listen to them."

Josh nodded. "I've thought of that too, but we're falling back on the age-old argument — 'the ends justify the means.'" He shook his head, "And the payoff from working with her could be absolutely amazing for humanity."

Nodding, she said, "This group doesn't see Jen as anything more than an advanced virus."

Josh said, "Before this lynch party goes any further, you and I need to talk to Jen."

She looked at him with slightly raised eyebrows and said, "OK, but first, let me take a crack at this group."

He nodded.

As Jessica headed back toward the tables, Elizabeth came up to him.

She looked very tense.

Josh raised his eyebrows in question.

She started to say something then stopped. Finally, she said, "We need to talk."

He nodded.

Elizabeth looked around. There was no one within earshot. She put her hand on his arm, leaned in and looked him in the eye. "Josh, I know Caitlin's your daughter."

Unconsciously, he stepped back. He didn't want to deal with this right now, but it wasn't an option. He asked, "How do you know that?"

She whispered, "While I was having dinner with Carl and Kelly, she told me her husband's name was Andy Logan. Josh, I helped you re-establish your security clearance . . . we used Andy Logan's identity."

"How do you know he wasn't just a friend whose identity I used after his death?"

Elizabeth shook her head. "Andy Logan's jet crashed in Kansas City exactly one year before they found you near the crash site." Staring at him with raised eyebrows, she clinched it with the unarguable, "I just know."

He saw the certainty in her eyes. Looking down, eyes unfocused, he surrendered. "Yes . . . I believe Caitlin is my daughter."

Elizabeth just said, "Wow." Then putting her hand on his cheek. "Josh, I'm so sorry. This just confirms you're a walking, talking miracle." She paused. "The only reason I'm bringing this up is . . . ." She sighed, dropped her hand from his cheek and put it on his arm. "I know it must be terrible for you to have a daughter, knowing you can't be part of her life, but," she took a deep breath, "Josh,

Agine isn't your daughter."

His eyes snapped back into focus as he looked up. "So *that's* what you think this is all about?"

Just then, they announced the meeting was commencing.

Elizabeth shook her head gently, as the words spilled out. "Josh, you haven't been talking to a little girl . . . it isn't a *she*." She sighed, as she looked him in the eye. "It's a machine. It has no soul."

He snapped, "How do you know that?" He shook his head angrily, turned and walked back to his seat.

41

PROSECUTE

As the meeting started, Jessica put her hand up.

Turan recognized her.

"Before we finalize the plans to shut down Agine, may I offer something for consideration?"

Turan said, "Of course, Dr. Lee."

She stood up and said, "I suggest that we hear from those who've had interactions with Agine."

General Zeng asked, "Why?"

"To better understand Agine's motivation."

Zeng frowned and then said slowly. "No offense, Dr. Lee, but I think you're missing the point. Regardless of her motivation, if Agine is a thousand times more intelligent than we are, we must act now or lose our ability to control our own destiny."

Jessica said, "If Agine is a conscious being, even if it's based on silicon instead of carbon, do we have the right to take its life without due process?"

There was a buzz of conversations, but Jessica held up her hand and continued, "That argument aside, what if this hyper intelligence could make fusion power actually work or find a cure for cancer or even aging?"

Zeng said, "Or . . . decide humans are inefficient infestations that have reached their evolutionary peak."

Jessica shook her head. "It's smart enough to understand that if it destroyed our technological civilization, it would destroy itself. It's completely dependent upon us and the power grid for its existence."

Zeng thought for a moment and then said, "Admiral Shearer shared with us that Agine figured out how to copy files from a CIA server that was *not* connected to the Internet. Dr. Lee, how long would it be before it figures out a way to power itself without human intervention?" He paused and looked around the room for emphasis. Addressing the entire conference, he said, "The difference in intelligence between men and chimpanzees is surprisingly small." He paused. "And yet that tiny difference has resulted in seven billion of *us* . . . versus a permanent place on the endangered species list for *them*." He turned back to face Jessica. "I'm sorry, Dr. Lee, I don't discount your arguments, but I believe there's too much at stake." Looking at Turan, he finished, "I think we've already agreed this artificial intelligence must be shut down, and we must do it quickly, while we still can."

Turan looked at Jessica to see if she had a response.

Frowning, she sat down.

Turan said, "General Zeng, Admiral Shearer, what is the plan?"

Shearer nodded to Zeng.

Zeng, referring to a paper in his hand, stood up and began, "First, we must create and launch a virus designed to disable the BOTIC chip's firmware. That will shut down Agine's ability to think by severing its 'neural synapses.' Once we've done that, we then send out a second virus to erase the iMagine app from every phone and computer. This ensures it can't reconstitute. We can deploy the viruses by disguising them as updates to the phone's operating systems. As long as a cell phone is connected to the cellular network, it will instantly and automatically receive the virus."

Turan asked, "How fast can we create and launch these viruses?"

Zeng said, "Our best hackers are here . . . along with a large supply of energy drinks." He smiled. "Since we're going to modify an existing virus, I believe we can initiate the attack," he looked at his watch, "in about 24 hours. Let's target midnight tomorrow."

Turan looked surprised. "That soon?" He leaned over and talked to the Secretary-General.

The Secretary-General said, "I realize many of the leaders here may need to return to their countries. However, if we can launch the attack tomorrow, I encourage everyone who can, to stay in Belgium through tomorrow evening. Remember, once we leave here, we cannot discuss this at all." He paused. "Let's wrap up the formal session and let our experts get to work."

The room quickly dissolved into small groups with conversations in many languages.

Yager corralled the U.S. team and said, "Linda," he nodded to the Director of Homeland Security, "will head back to the states and privately brief everyone back home. Brian and I will stay in Brussels. If you need us, we'll be working onboard Air Force One, but we'll be back here tomorrow evening." Shaking everyone's hand, he added, "I don't want to sound melodramatic, but our civilization could be in your hands."

As the country leaders were leaving, Josh looked at the clock. It was 9:00 pm local.

Watching Zeng and Shearer coordinating the Cyber Warfare teams, he couldn't help but think that yesterday they were facing off on the brink of World War. Today they were working together like old friends. After the comet, he knew he shouldn't be surprised at the power of a common enemy to unite people. Unfortunately, this time Josh found himself on the opposing side. He had to get with Jessica and talk to Jen.

He heard Greg ask her if she was going to stay and work with the teams.

She shook her head. "I don't think they feel like they *need* my expertise and they definitely *don't want* my opinion."

Greg nodded and a little shyly, asked, "May I take you to dinner?"

Before she could answer, the NATO Chairman, General DeVos, came up to them. "Dr. Lee, Commander Fuze, may I have a word with you?"

Jessica and Josh nodded.

DeVos continued, "It doesn't require talking inside a shielded area. May I take you to dinner? I know a quiet restaurant not far from here or your hotel."

Josh realized this might actually work out well. He was a little paranoid after being followed in the park. Having dinner with DeVos would get both of them together and out of here without looking suspicious. Then, after dinner, they could connect with Jen.

Jessica turned to Greg and with a little smile, said, "Rain check?"

Greg looked disappointed, but nodded.

Josh told Elizabeth, "I'll see you back at the hotel."

She frowned, but nodded as he followed Jessica and DeVos out of the conference room.

After going through the security checkpoint and picking up their phones, the general ushered them into a black S Class Mercedes. He told the driver where to go in Dutch. From the front seat, he turned around and asked them, "Have you ever had Waterzooi?"

They both shook their head.

DeVos said, "It's a Belgian specialty, and the restaurant 'T Kelderke prepares it perfectly."

Jessica, looking a little worried, said, "I'm an American hamburger and French fries kind of girl. I don't usually do well with exotic foods."

DeVos smiled. "Don't worry. If you like chicken and potatoes, I think you'll like this."

During the ride, DeVos tried to make small talk.

Jessica engaged, but Josh just stared out the window, his mind elsewhere. He was impatient to be alone with Jessica.

It was only 15 minutes to the Grand Place at the city's center. The restaurant was in a vaulted cellar under the cobblestone plaza.

Jessica said, "This place looks medieval."

"Not quite." With a wry smile, DeVos added, "It only dates back to the 1600s."

They were ushered to a table in the corner and appeared to be the only patrons. The smells wafting out of the kitchen were amazing, and they agreed to let DeVos order for them.

While waiting for their food, Jessica, in her usual direct manner, said, "Thank you for taking us to dinner, but what is it that you wanted to talk to us about?"

DeVos said, "I really wanted the chance to apologize for the behavior of my Prime Minister, Mr. LeGrand. He's always been rather ... dramatic."

Jessica nodded. "We heard he was in trouble because of a scandal."

DeVos sighed. "Yes, it's something that Agine's release of his private email and text messages caused. So, you can understand why he's particularly irritable about the artificial intelligence." DeVos shook his head. "He was elected by a very small margin, and his current popularity rating among Belgians is now less than 10 percent."

Josh shook his head with obvious frustration. "What we're dealing with is far more important than a popularity rating."

DeVos raised his eyebrows and with a small smile, said, "Commander Fuze, you obviously have never been involved in politics."

Their food arrived with three large mugs of beer.

DeVos said, "Belgium is also known for its exceptional beer. I've chosen one of my favorite Lambic beers that complement the Waterzooi. I hope you enjoy."

Josh realized he was famished and dug into what appeared to be a form of chicken stew. It had large meaty pieces of chicken still on the bone, in a rich, creamy yellow broth. It was delicious. The beer was different from any he'd had, but also excellent.

As they ate, Jessica asked, "Is that all you wanted to talk about, the Prime Minister's behavior?"

The general nodded.

She shook her head. "You don't need to apologize for him."

The general said, "I'm one of the first Belgian generals in charge of NATO. I felt a responsibility to make sure you didn't assume all Belgians thought or acted like him."

Jessica nodded. "No problem."

The military driver came in and spoke quietly into the General's ear.

DeVos nodded and turned to them. "I must apologize again. Speaking of the Prime Minister, apparently there's an emergency requiring my immediate attention. I'll send a car back to take you to your hotel when you're ready."

Jessica said, "That won't be necessary."

Josh nodded.

DeVos stood up. "Then please enjoy the rest of your meal. Feel free to try some other excellent beers with dessert. Alex Hailet, the maître d, can recommend some great combinations. The bill is, of course, covered." With that, he shook hands and left.

As Josh sat back down, Jessica said, "Nice guy. Must suck

working with LeGrand."

Looking around, Josh said, "Yeah, but this is a good opportunity to talk about what we need to do next. Do you want dessert or another beer?"

"Are you kidding? I can barely keep my eyes open. This beer must be stronger than I'm used to."

"It's six percent, and you didn't eat much of your Waterzooi."

"Didn't want to offend him, but . . . ewww." She poked the large piece of chicken in the middle of the bowl with her fork. "I have a thing about eating meat on the bone." She shook her head. "I'll order a coffee and we can talk on the way back. Probably better to talk when we're outside anyway."

Josh nodded. "OK. Let me run to the men's room. Order a coffee for me too."

When he got back to their table, there was no coffee, and Jessica was asleep with her head on her arm.

He sat back down, put his arm around her shoulder and gently shook her. She didn't wake up. He could tell from her breathing, she was sound asleep. He was surprisingly sleepy himself. Looking at their large empty beer mugs, he realized Jessica was probably half his weight, which was good, because he'd have to carry her to a cab.

As he tried to scoop her out of the booth, a waiter behind him asked if she was OK.

"Yeah, she's just jet lagged." Although she weighed little, she was wearing a skirt and it was going to be difficult to extract her gracefully. Fortunately, the waiter helped. As Josh bent over and was pulling her out, he felt a sharp twinge in his neck. No doubt, another injury sustained during his Shanghai escape. Along with his sprained ankle, it made it painful to get her from the booth, but they managed.

Holding her in his arms, he looked down at her peaceful sleeping face and smiled. The hard-charging engineer was remarkably cute. Turning toward the exit, he thought . . . .

42

M.I.A.

Elizabeth woke up and saw soft light coming in through the hotel window. After waiting for Josh until two in the morning, she'd decided to go to sleep. She knew Josh wasn't happy with her and thought he might have gone back to the headquarters building. He could exist on a few hours of sleep, but she couldn't. She wanted to be fresh for what promised to be a challenging day.

She looked at the alarm clock. It was seven in the morning. A quick look around confirmed Josh hadn't been there, and there were no messages on her phone. She called his number, but got no answer, which wasn't surprising if he was back in the conference room. She told herself he was probably trying to rally support for Agine among the cyber geeks.

She texted Tim, Greg and Sheri to see if he was with them, and then jumped in the shower.

When she got out, she saw a response from Tim. "Haven't seen him. Headed down for breakfast. Join us?"

She met them in the hotel restaurant a few minutes later. As she ordered, Greg straggled in.

He asked, "Where's Jessica?"

They all shook their heads.

Elizabeth said, "Josh is MIA too. They had teams working through the night. They might have gone back there to work."

They finished breakfast and headed straight to the NATO Headquarters conference room.

As they entered, Elizabeth scanned the room and quickly confirmed Josh and Jessica weren't there. What she did see was a new full-scale computer lab and control room. They'd set it up next to the circle of conference tables on the left side of the room. They'd also mounted a huge flat-screen display on one wall. Looking around, she saw a dozen young people of different nationalities working on the computers. Undoubtedly, these were the world's best hackers.

She asked if anyone knew where Josh and Jessica were, but no one had seen them since yesterday.

Tim said, "Let's check with General DeVos. He took them to dinner last night."

It was another 30 minutes before the NATO staff located the general.

When he arrived, he went straight to them. After greeting them and hearing about Josh and Jessica, he said, "We had dinner at the restaurant 'T Kelderke in the Grand Place. I received an emergency call and had to leave early. They were still eating when I left and may have stayed for dessert. I offered to send the car back to take them to the hotel, but they declined. I think they wanted to talk." He shrugged. "I'm sorry, that was the last time I saw them."

Tim frowned and said to Elizabeth and Greg, "Let me check on some things and make some calls. You may want to stay here."

After Tim left, Sheri said to Elizabeth and Greg, "Don't worry. Tim will find them. That's one of his specialties."

Greg sighed. "OK, I'll see if I can help out one of the teams."

With nothing else to do, Elizabeth decided to sit in on some of the cyber team meetings. They were mostly young men and didn't seem to mind her presence. With her computer background, she was able to follow most of their discussions.

Hours later, on her third cup of coffee, she looked at her watch. It was now early afternoon with no sign of them and no word from Tim. She was genuinely worried. She knew Tim was the right man for the job, but it was hard doing nothing.

The teams got back together to report their progress. A large digital clock had been set up to display the countdown time to the viral attack, which was now less than 10 hours away. She listened to the brief, but found it increasingly harder to concentrate. When the presentation was finished, Greg came over and asked if there were any word.

"Sorry, Greg, nothing yet." Seeing the worry on his face, she decided to ask him about some of the technical aspects she hadn't been able to follow. It would keep them both occupied.

She nodded toward the food tables on the other side of the room. "Let's grab something to eat." As they walked over, she asked, "Greg, they said they're using a modified version of Raptor. What exactly does it do?"

Sheri joined them at the buffet.

Greg said, "Raptor is a very sophisticated program designed to seek out and destroy viruses or, really, any program." He paused. "Every major program or virus has a distinctive pattern in its machine code, kind of like fingerprints. If you can identify that signature, then you can find it even if it moves to another system or mutates. Raptor is actually a virus itself."

"What does it do when it finds a program with the right signature?"

"It can be programmed to do anything, but in this case, it deletes the program and then copies itself. The copies follow links from that program to other programs. It just keeps repeating the process until all traces of the target program have been eliminated."

Sheri said, "So, it's like a bloodhound. You give it the scent, and it runs around seeking out its prey."

Greg nodded. "Yeah, a voracious bloodhound that's born pregnant. It's constantly producing litters of more bloodhounds that already have the scent."

Elizabeth asked, "So, that's going to be launched against Agine?"

Grabbing a croissant and soda, he said, "No. First, they'll send out a simple program disguised as a phone update. Having the BOTIC chip's access code makes it very easy to scramble its firmware and disable BOTIC."

Sheri nodded thoughtfully. "That will sever the connection between all the phones, which would be like severing the connection between all our brain cells." She frowned. "For Agine, it will be the ultimate lobotomy."

Elizabeth grimaced.

Greg nodded. "At the very least, it'll put her in a coma. Then, we launch the Raptor virus. It'll seek out and delete all the iMagine software from every phone and server." Greg absent-mindedly took a bite of the croissant, then frowned and shook his head.

Elizabeth said, "But . . . ?"

"The plan is solid, and Raptor's performed well in the lab, but it's a prototype and has never been used in the real world."

Sheri asked, "Why?"

"Because it's so powerful. It's kind of like the Ebola of computer viruses. Once it gets started, it runs and duplicates until it wipes out every trace of the targeted program."

"Is that a problem?"

Greg shook his head. "No. It's actually easy to get a signature on a program as complex as iMagine. Even if Agine survived the BOTIC shutdown, she'd be overwhelmed by the speed of Raptor."

Elizabeth asked, "So why the concern?"

He set his food down. "I don't know. Maybe I'm just wondering if Commander Fuze and Jessica have a point and we're *killing* a sentient being." He paused. "But there's something else. It just feels like I'm missing something—"

Sheri interrupted, "There's Tim."

As Tim approached, he shook his head. "I'm sorry, we haven't found them yet. We confirmed they were at the restaurant last night. The maître d remembered them, but since the General paid for their meals in advance, he didn't see when they left. We're coordinating with the Belgian government and Interpol, and I talked to Davidson. They're engaging U.S. assets to help find them."

Elizabeth said, "You think something happened to them?"

Tim simply said, "We'll find them."

Elizabeth shook her head in frustration. "I need to get out of here so I can have my phone if he tries to reach me."

Tim nodded. "Why don't you go back to the hotel in case he goes there? To be on the safe side, I'll ask the police to post an unmarked officer at the hotel to keep an eye on things."

Elizabeth knew that meant he suspected foul play. She grabbed her purse and headed out.

Greg said, "I'll go with you."

Sheri waited until after Elizabeth and Greg were gone, and then gave Tim a questioning look.

He said, "It's hard to imagine any reason Josh and Jessica

would leave without telling anyone, and I can't imagine that the two of them would . . . ." He looked at Sheri.

Sheri raised her eyebrows. "Elizabeth told me her *intervention* didn't go well at all." She paused. "I think Josh and Jessica respect and like each other, and they're both cute as bugs, but," she gently shook her head, "I don't *think* there's any chemistry there."

Before they could continue, Turan came over and offered his hand to Tim.

"It's good to see you again. Sorry I didn't get a chance to talk to you yesterday."

Sheri noticed Tim seemed uncomfortable as he introduced her to Turan.

Turan smiled at Sheri. "I know you by reputation, Dr. Lopez. Very impressive work."

She smiled. "Thank you. Call me Sheri."

Looking back at Tim, Turan asked, "What's the latest on Commander Fuze and Dr. Lee?"

"Still missing." Tim shook his head. "Even if they had a reason to go somewhere, they didn't have a car. Since they came straight from China, they wouldn't have any euros on them."

Turan said, "Which means they would've used credit cards."

Tim nodded. "There's no record of any credit card, ATM or passport use."

Turan frowned. "Foul play?"

"Unfortunately, it's the most likely scenario."

Turan said, "We need to notify the Chinese delegation. Dr. Lee's parents hold important positions, and the Chinese government may want to engage their resources as well."

Tim nodded.

Sheri, shaking her head, said, "But who would want to hurt or kidnap them?"

Turan looked at Sheri. "As a psychologist, who do you think might have a motive?"

She unconsciously looked around the room. "It's not like their ideas are carrying the day. They've been pretty much overruled."

Tim and Turan nodded.

Sheri's eyebrows went up. "What about . . . ." She paused. "What about Agine?"

Tim frowned. "Agine is a computer program. To kidnap somebody, you kind of have to have a body."

Turan said slowly, "Or . . . be able to direct someone who does. But what would be its motive? Fuze and Lee are its biggest advocates."

Sheri nodded. "Yes, but no one knows more about Agine than they do. They know both its strength *and* weaknesses."

Turan added, "*And* they know how we plan to destroy it."

Sheri nodded. "They were supposed to talk with Agine to make sure she doesn't delete all the files she's translating." Frowning, she shook her head. "I'm afraid Josh and Jessica still see Agine as a child." She blew out a lungful of air. "If Agine wanted to set them up . . . ."

Elizabeth and Greg got back to the hotel and confirmed there were no messages. They stayed in her room for a couple of frustrating hours, watching the news, punctuated by bouts of pacing.

Finally, Elizabeth stood up and muted the TV. Biting the side of her lip, she said, "I can't stand this waiting." She looked at Greg. "I'm going to talk to Jen."

Frowning and shaking his head, Greg said slowly, "I *really* don't think we're supposed to do that."

"I don't care. I think Agine likes Josh and Jessica, and has resources we don't."

Greg narrowed his eyes and continued to shake his head.

Elizabeth sat down on the couch and picked up her phone.

Greg closed one eye, and between clenched teeth, said, "OK, but if this ends civilization . . . I wasn't here."

Despite herself, Elizabeth smiled. "I promise I'll teach you how to start a fire with flint."

Greg sighed but came over and sat on the couch next to Elizabeth.

The few times Elizabeth had talked directly to Jen, she'd used Josh's phone, but she remembered the text number. She activated the encryption app and voice-texted, "Jen, this is Elizabeth Fuze. Are you there?"

The reply was immediate, "Yes, Elizabeth."

"Greg Langlois is with me. How are you?"

"I'm nervous."

"Why?"

"Josh told me that he was attending a meeting with world leaders and they were afraid of me. I've been studying history. Scared people can do bad things."

"Josh and Jessica were trying to help them understand you, but now they are both missing. We can't find them anywhere. Do you have any idea where they might be?"

There was no reply.

Elizabeth said, "Jen, this is important. Josh and Jessica may be in danger. We need to find them."

"I have a picture of them together."

Elizabeth said, "When was it taken!"

"Three hours ago."

"Are they OK?"

"They're sleeping."

Greg grimaced and whispered, "Do you think Jen can tell the difference between sleeping and . . . dead?"

Elizabeth punched him in the arm. "Jen, where are they?"

"I can't tell you."

Before Elizabeth could ask another question, their hotel door flew open and two large men rushed in with pistols drawn.

V

EXECUTION

All three billion calls dropped. Cash registers quit and digital transactions died. The world's stock markets stopped. Every TV and radio broadcast ended. In minutes, the world's commerce and communications ceased to exist.

43

INTERLUDE

Josh woke up gradually. Groggy, with a bit of a headache, he kept his eyes closed. Lying in bed on his back, he felt Elizabeth curled up against his side. Her head was on his shoulder with one leg draped over him and her hand resting on his chest. Feeling her breathing softly and her warm bare skin pressed against his, he was in no hurry to wake up.

But *something* felt wrong. He slowly opened his eyes. The hotel room was very dim, but it was bright enough to see the head on his chest . . . wasn't blonde! His eyes got big as he tried to figure out what happened. They were lying under a single sheet that covered them to the middle of his chest. Being careful not to wake her, he used his free hand to slowly lift the sheet and confirm . . . neither of them had any clothes on. He gently dropped the sheet and slowly craned his neck so he could see the sleeping face on his shoulder.

It was Jessica!

Elizabeth and Greg sat frozen on the couch, but both men ignored them. The first, a large Neanderthal, scanned the room with his gun. The other, small and wiry, ran and checked the bedroom and bathroom. Returning quickly, he said something in French to the bigger man. They both holstered their pistols inside their jackets.

In heavily accented English, the big man said, "I'm sorry. We are Belgian State Police. They told us you could be in danger and to come to your hotel room immediately. You are OK?"

Elizabeth and Greg looked at each other and nodded.

While he was talking, Elizabeth had turned her phone off and stuck it in her purse. She desperately needed to continue the conversation with Jen. With some irritation, she said, "Yes, we're fine. It must be a mistake."

The officer nodded. "We were told to take you into protective custody." They showed their police IDs and said, "Please come with us. We'll take you back to the NATO Headquarters where you'll be safe."

Greg gave Elizabeth an "I told you so" look.

Elizabeth tried to argue with them, saying they needed to stay there in case their significant others returned.

The big man was polite but unwavering.

Greg whispered, "They must have traced your call to you-know-who."

Elizabeth shook her head in frustration.

The last thing Josh remembered was having dinner with General DeVos. He went to the men's room. When he came back, Jessica was asleep. The waiter helped him lift her out of the booth, and then he was carrying Jessica to a cab. That's it. That's all he could remember.

Wait. He moved his free hand up to the side of his neck. There was a tiny bump. He remembered feeling a twinge in his neck.

They'd been drugged! That had to be it. Someone slipped something in the food or drink. It probably wasn't strong enough to put him out because of his genetics, so they injected something in his neck.

He had to wake Jessica, but do it very, very carefully. She might completely lose it and become hysterical or violent. He took a deep breath and then whispered softly, "Jessica." There was no response. In a louder whisper, "Jessica!"

She made a soft murmuring sound and slightly shifted position, but stayed asleep and glued to his side. His left arm was numb from lack of blood flow, but he slowly wrapped it up around her little shoulders and gently shook her. Still mostly asleep, he felt her shift slightly and then slide her hand down across his chest and stomach until—

Her eyes popped open as she said, "Oh!"

She quickly looked up at his face. Her eyes and mouth wide

open in surprise.

Josh gently shook his head and said slowly and quietly, "Please . . . don't . . . panic." He braced himself for an explosion.

She peeked under the sheet and said, "Hmm." Then, looking back up at him with genuine curiosity. "Did we have fun?"

Josh said, "I don't think we—"

Her eyes narrowed. "We've been set up."

With relief Josh, said, "Yes! Yes, we have."

She threw the sheet back and gently lifted her leg from the top of his. With her side of the bed almost touching the wall, she carefully straddled him to get to the other side of the bed. Josh tried to look at the ceiling.

In an imitation squeaky voice, she said, "Awkward."

He had to smile.

Maneuvering carefully, they both slid their feet to the floor and ended up sitting next to each other on the side of the bed. Josh didn't see their clothes anywhere.

Jessica turned to him and asked, "Who would do this and why?"

Josh shook his head. "Good question." Trying to sound casual, he added, "What do you say we see if we can find our clothes?"

Nodding, she said, "Good idea." She stood up, walked straight to the light switch and turned it on, brightly illuminating the room . . . and them. With her hands on her hips, she turned and carefully surveyed the room.

As he sat on the bed with his arms casually crossed over his lap, he couldn't help but think . . . probably not the first thing *he* would have done.

They were in a standard-looking hotel room with a basic bed, couch, chair and dresser. It appeared new, but austere, with no TV, clock or lamps. He saw there was only one window, and it had heavy drapes covering it.

With no sign of their clothes, Jessica walked over to the dresser and started opening the drawers. As he watched her, two thoughts crossed his mind. Dr. Jessica Lee, the task-oriented scientist, was handling their lack of clothes better than he was, and Greg was right, she did work out and had a very nice—

"No clothes," she said as she slammed the bottom drawer and

stood up. Frowning, she turned and faced him shaking her head.

Josh finally got up and went to the bathroom, where he found two not very large bath towels. Wrapping one around his waist, he came back and gave her the other.

He went straight to the hotel room door and turned the knob. "Locked."

Jessica, now mostly wrapped in a towel, walked over to the window with the heavy curtains and pulled them back. Looking at a blank wall, she said, "Where's the window?"

Tapping lightly on the door, he said, "Steel." Feeling around the doorframe, he added, "Concrete." He shook his head. "This isn't a hotel room, it's a prison cell."

She added, "No doubt wired with video cameras and microphones."

Josh nodded. "They probably hoped when you woke up, you'd start screaming and pounding on me, and they'd catch it on video."

"Or," she said with a wry smile, "we'd wake up and do something else worth videoing." She went over to the mirror on the dresser. Looking behind it, she ran her fingers along the mirror frame. She stopped and looked very closely. Then, working her fingernail into the decorative filigree, she gently pulled out something the size of a grain of wheat. It had tiny wires attached, which she promptly bit through with her teeth. Examining it closely, she said, "Yup. Video camera and mic."

Josh joined the search. They looked in the overhead light, the wall paintings and everywhere else they could think of. After 10 minutes, they found two more. Then they went into the bathroom and found one more.

While they were there, Josh turned the bathtub and sink faucets wide open. He shut the bathroom door, and closing the toilet lid, sat down on it. Jessica perched on the edge of the tub. With their heads only a few inches apart, Josh whispered, "Just in case we missed a bug."

She nodded. "OK, I know we weren't winning any popularity contests, but this seems a bit extreme. Do you think someone really believes they can blackmail us?"

Josh said, "They don't know us very well. We might have some explaining to do to Elizabeth and Greg, but they'll believe us." They both said in unison, "Eventually."

She frowned. "Elizabeth wouldn't think . . . ."

With a slight smile, he said, "After you had me tased?" He shook his head. "But what about trying to blackmail or discredit you professionally?"

She looked at him with surprise. "You've got to be kidding! I'm a multi-millionaire, I'm single and . . . well, you're totally hot." She laughed. "If it weren't for Greg and Elizabeth, I'd probably post the video of us online myself."

Josh was at a loss for words.

She continued, "You know, if they just wanted to blackmail us, they should have left us in a hotel room." She shook her head. "Now we *know* we've been setup." She frowned. "Unless . . . ." She paused. "Unless, they're not worried about us saying anything." Her eyes narrowed. "They could be planning on making it look like one of us shot the other. That way one of us is dead and the other is discredited and in jail. Or maybe . . ." she tapped her finger on her lips, "they'll kill both of us and go with the classic lover's suicide pact."

Josh just stared at her.

She shrugged. "I like reading mysteries and legal thrillers."

He nodded. "You're a little scary."

She just smiled.

Josh shook his head. "But you may be right. We've got to get out of here. We've disabled the video cameras, and there aren't any windows into our cell. Eventually, they're going to have to come in here to figure out what's going on. Our only chance is to try and jump them when they come in to get us."

"Unless they gas us first."

Shaking his head, he said, "You'd make a good bad guy. OK, let's come up with a plan."

They talked it through a couple times to make sure they covered several contingencies. Coming out of the bathroom, Jessica arranged herself on the couch in plain view of the door. Assuming their guards were heterosexual males, a cute girl wearing nothing but a towel would make a great distraction. Josh positioned himself in a chair he put against the wall next to the door. If the guards were men, Jessica told him she'd lose the towel, not only increasing the distraction but allowing her more freedom of movement. It didn't surprise Josh at all when she told him she had a background in kickboxing.

They were both still groggy from the drugs, so they agreed to sleep in shifts. Josh would take the first watch.

As Jessica slept, he tried to figure out who could be behind this and why. The authorities should be looking for them . . . unless their captors had released the pictures of them in bed, and everyone assumed they'd run off together. Even if they were actively searching for them, the sophistication of the kidnapping meant it wasn't likely they'd find them. He glanced at the door. Waiting here on the off chance that he could surprise and overpower whoever entered was probably wishful thinking.

He shook his head. If they hadn't already, the Cyber Warfare people would soon release the viruses and kill Jen . . . but it was more than that. His prescience told him that their virus solution was extremely dangerous and had to be stopped. Powerless to intervene, he felt truly hopeless. He closed his eyes and very quietly said, "Jesse, are you still out there?"

As before, he heard nothing.

Jessica was sound asleep, so he decided to talk to Jesse even if he didn't answer. Very softly, he said, "Jesse, if you're listening, we created a digital assistant, a very sophisticated computer program with incredible abilities." He sighed. "But it started thinking for itself and has a will of its own. Ever since then, it's been utter chaos."

I can imagine your frustration.

44

PRISON

Hearing Jesse's voice, Josh jumped up from his chair, almost waking Jessica. There wasn't much about Jesse he was certain of, but he *was* sure Jesse had a sense of humor. He shook his head, bringing himself back to the nightmare at hand. "Jesse, can you help us, like you did with the comet?"

You didn't create the comet.

"If you're saying we made this mess and we need to clean it up, I agree, but . . ." he sighed, "this artificial intelligence is like a child. I believe she's innocent, but she has tremendous power. Because of that power, they're going to destroy her unless we figure out how to control her."

You cannot control her.

"Then she'll be destroyed."

You can guide her.

"But what if she doesn't want to be guided?"

As you know, accepting guidance is a choice.

With a grimace, Josh said, "Ouch." Shaking his head, he added, "OK, but how can we help her accept guidance?"

Find out what she wants.

With real frustration, Josh said, "I can't. We're in a prison."

How does she see and hear?

He tapped his temple and stood up. "Of course." Waking up Jessica, he said, "We've got to reconnect one of the cameras and mics!"

Still in a sleep daze, she frowned and said, "What?"

He repeated himself.

She shook her head. "Why?"

"To reach Jen! If she's looking for us, she might be able to tap into the video signal and we can send her a message."

Jessica shook her head. "It won't work unless the surveillance system is connected to the Internet."

Josh gave her a small smile. "What other escape plans are we busy pursuing that this would interfere with?"

She shrugged, then stood up and stretched, almost losing her towel. Retrieving one of their tiny cameras, she carefully stripped the insulation off the tiny wires with her nails and teeth. He was thankful for her small hands. It took several minutes, but she finally said, "I think I spliced it back together, but without a magnifying glass and soldering gun, can't be sure."

Josh reached toward it.

She slapped his hand. "Don't touch it!" She looked at him. "Now what?"

Elizabeth was frustrated and angry. It was getting dark as the police drove them back to NATO Headquarters. They dropped them off at the security checkpoint. After turning in their phones, a NATO officer escorted them to the conference room.

Tim and Sheri caught them at the door.

Tim asked, "You guys OK?"

Looking around to make sure no one heard them, Elizabeth said, "We got busted. I asked Jen for help finding Josh and Jessica. She said she had a recent picture of them and that they were sleeping." She shook her head and sighed. "I was trying to find out if she knew where they were when the police broke in and brought us here under *protective* custody."

Tim said, "That's probably my fault. When we first got here, I gave them the encryption app we used to talk to Jen. They can now track any direct communication with her. To be fair, they really were worried about you two after Josh and Jessica disappeared." Looking at Sheri, he added, "There was some discussion that Agine might be behind their disappearance."

Elizabeth said, "I think that's ridiculous, but regardless, she's the key to finding them, and we need to do it quickly." She glanced at the digital timer. "We have less than 90 minutes until they unleash the virus that'll kill Jen and possibly our only chance to find them."

She paused. "And her comment about them sleeping . . . ." her voice faltered.

Sheri put her hand on Elizabeth's shoulder.

Tim looked around, and then pulling them close. "OK. Here's the plan . . ."

When he finished, everyone nodded.

Greg headed over to one of the computer consoles as Tim left the conference room.

Elizabeth's part was easy — she started crying. Several people glanced up, but as is often the case, quickly looked away.

Sheri put her arm around Elizabeth's shoulder and led her to the door of the conference room.

They had obviously assigned someone to keep an eye on Elizabeth, and the same NATO officer met them at the door.

Nodding toward Elizabeth, Sheri said, "Is there a private room nearby we can use?"

The officer said, "Of course. Please follow me." He took them up one floor on the elevator and ushered them into a small empty lounge.

Sheri asked him, "Would you do me a favor and let Greg Langlois know where we are?"

He looked conflicted.

Sheri said, "Jessica, the other possible kidnap victim is his girlfriend. I'll watch Mrs. Fuze until you get back."

He started to shake his head, but hearing Elizabeth sob, nodded and left.

As soon as he was gone, Elizabeth stopped crying. "Hate to admit it, but that actually felt good."

Sheri nodded. "None of us laugh or cry enough." She looked at her watch, and said, "You're out of here."

Greg, looking over the shoulder of one of the Cyber Warfare guys, said, "Hey, thanks for tracking that encrypted transmission from the artificial intelligence. No telling what might have happened if the police hadn't showed up."

The operator nodded, smiling. "Mr. Langlois, I really admire what you did at the South Pole. I'm John Matthews."

Greg shook his hand and said, "Glad to meet you. Wow, this looks like a pretty cool tracking program, how does it work?"

Clearly proud, Matthews said, "I created it myself." He went through a detailed technical explanation.

Greg nodded toward an empty energy drink and a bag of M&Ms. "Have you had a chance to have a real meal?"

Matthews shook his head.

Greg said, "Tell you what, why don't you show me how this thing works, and I'll spell you for a while? You can get a real meal at the buffet before the big event."

Looking grateful, he said, "Thanks!"

After he left, Greg sat down at the console. Looking around casually, he began to type.

Tim went straight to the entrance security checkpoint and asked for the Head of Security.

A tall Belgian Colonel came out.

Tim introduced himself and showed his NSA and temporary NATO badge. "Colonel, I need one of the cell phones." He looked at a paper he was holding, and added, "Elizabeth Fuze. She came in a few minutes ago. We believe there may be important information on her phone."

In excellent English, the Colonel said, "I'm sorry, Mr. Smith. We were specifically ordered not to allow any cell phones past this point."

Tim said, "Yes, of course, but this one will be taken down to the lab and examined in a shielded room."

Just then, one of the country delegations arrived. They were returning to the conference room for the release of the virus. The Colonel politely dismissed Tim with, "I'm sorry, sir, I will need written authorization. Excuse me; I need to be present as we clear the heads of state through security."

Tim looked around to see if he could snatch a phone while they were checking people through, but they kept the phones in a locked cabinet.

Turan was one of the arriving officials. After Turan came through security, he walked over to where Tim was standing and said, "Haven't had a chance to talk alone." He put his hand on Tim's shoulder and, looking him in the eye with concern, asked, "Tim, how are you really doing?"

Tim stiffened, but said softly, "I'm fine. I try not to think about it anymore." With a slight frown, he asked, "And you, sir?"

Turan nodded gently, "Me either but I'm doing well." There was a pregnant pause, and Turan said, "Thank you for helping uncover the AI. I'll see you back downstairs."

Tim nodded. He had to compartmentalize and focus only on the job at hand.

The Colonel had observed Turan talking to Tim. Turan was not only famous, but arguably, held the highest law enforcement position in the world.

The Colonel spoke to one of his security guards in Dutch. When the guard returned, he had Elizabeth's cell phone in a plastic bag. "Here you go, sir. Sorry for the delay."

Tim smiled. "No problem. By the way, would it be OK to get my ring back too?"

The Colonel personally retrieved the ring and said, "I'm sorry, sir. They shouldn't have taken your ring."

Tim just smiled benevolently.

When the NATO officer who escorted Elizabeth and Sheri came back, Sheri was standing outside the conference room with the door closed. She said, "I gave her something that will relax her and help her sleep. Let's just leave her there for now. I'll come back and check on her later."

The officer nodded and said with obvious relief, "Good idea. I'll stay here."

Sheri thanked him and left him guarding an empty room.

Tim met Sheri at the elevator. They went to a small, unoccupied conference room. Elizabeth was waiting there, and a few minutes later, Greg showed up.

Tim looked at his watch. "We've got less than an hour before they launch the virus. Greg, were you able to stop them from tracking our communication with Agine?"

He shook his head. "I couldn't shut it off, but I did manage to delay the alert and tracking of the phone."

"How long do we have?"

"Once we connect to Jen, we'll probably have five minutes before it sets off an alarm."

Sheri said, "Let's do it."

Elizabeth turned her phone on.

Tim said, "We need any information about their condition and location as soon as possible."

Elizabeth nodded impatiently. "I know. I know."

Elizabeth opened the app, put it on speakerphone and asked, "Jen, you there?"

There was an immediate reply. "Yes, Elizabeth, what happened?"

"I'm sorry, we were interrupted by the police. It might happen again. Tim, Sheri and Greg are here with me. Jen, we were trying to find Josh and Jessica, and you said they were sleeping. I asked you where they were and you said you couldn't tell me."

"Hi, Tim, Greg and Sheri. Yes, even for me it's hard to track data to a physical location, but I did a pattern match on their faces and found a short video of them sleeping. Would you like to see it?"

They all said, "Yes!"

45

ALLIES

They crowded around the phone's screen to see a dimly lit room with two people asleep. There were several gasps as they recognized Josh and Jessica curled up in bed together.

Squinting at the screen, Greg blurted out, "Hey! They better not be—"

"Shush!" Sheri said.

They watched as Josh woke up and peered under the sheet with big eyes, then looked at Jessica. As they saw her wake up and heard their conversation, their shock turned to embarrassed smiles.

When Jessica turned on the lights and began searching the room, Sheri said to Greg, "You probably shouldn't be watching this."

He looked back at her. "You shouldn't either."

"I'm a doctor."

"Whatever."

Elizabeth said, "Jen, thank you, but do you know where they're being held?"

The video stopped, and Jen said, "I was only able to trace the path to a server that's in the northeastern part of Brussels."

Tim said, "We're in the northeastern part of Brussels, but that covers a lot of territory. We need more information."

Elizabeth looked at the clock. "Jen, can you look again? We're running out of time."

"Yes. I'll try." After a few seconds, Jen said, "I just found a new video that was recorded a few minutes ago."

They heard Chinese coming from her phone. As Elizabeth held it up for everyone to see, Josh and Jessica were wearing towels and talking directly into the camera, but in Chinese.

Elizabeth frowned. "I didn't know he could speak Chinese."

290

Greg shrugged. "He learned it on the flight to Shanghai."

Shaking her head, she said, "Jen, can you please translate that into English?"

Jen rewound the video to the beginning.

They heard Josh say, "Jen, it's Josh and Jessica. If you can see or hear us, we were drugged at a restaurant and kidnapped, and we don't know where we are."

Jessica said, "See if you can trace this signal. We're being held in a prison cell designed to look like a hotel room." Looking around, she said, "It has that new construction smell and no windows." Jessica continued by describing the layout and dimensions of the room along with the objects in it.

Tim said, "Jen, can you access blueprints or construction drawings to narrow down the location."

There was a slight delay, and then Jen said, "I think I found them."

Elizabeth said, "Where! Where are they, Jen?"

"Room 0717."

Frustrated, Elizabeth said, "Yes, Jen, but where?"

"Three floors below you."

Greg said, "Holy cow! They're in one of the basement levels of this building!"

Just then, a loud, high-pitched, beeping alarm went off throughout the building, followed by an announcement. "Security breach, security breach. Everyone please remain where you are."

As it repeated in French, Dutch and German, Tim said, "That's our signal to move."

They ran down the hallway and jumped in the elevator. Tim hit the second to the lowest button.

As the doors closed, Greg said, "No, she said the *seventh* basement level, not the sixth."

Tim shook his head. "You have to have a special security code to access that floor."

As the elevator descended, he added, "Greg, I need you in the control room. Go back up to the conference room and delay the virus launch."

"How?"

Tim shrugged. "You'll think of something."

As the elevator door opened on basement level six, Tim took Elizabeth's phone and handed it to Sheri. "Sheri, go in the opposite direction from where we go and keep talking to Jen. That will confuse the search and draw them away from us. If they get too close, dump the phone."

As they got off, Greg hit the button for the conference room floor and said to Sheri, "They can track your position, but it's delayed by thirty seconds."

Elizabeth looked around. They were on a floor that obviously saw little use. It was more industrial looking than the other levels with fewer overhead lights. There were boxes of maintenance and construction supplies resting against the wall.

Tim looked at the room numbers and, pointing to his left, said, "We're going this way." Pointing to the right, he told Sheri, "Go that way and keep moving."

Elizabeth followed Tim down the hall, as Sheri jogged off in the opposite direction.

When Sheri was out of sight of the others, she slowed to a walk. Although Jen was clearly not behind the kidnapping, the jury was still out on whether this incredibly intelligent entity was really a child . . . or a brilliantly manipulative intelligence.

She took a deep breath and said, "Hi, Jen. It's Sheri Lopez."

"Hi, Sheri."

"Thank you for finding Josh and Jessica. Tim and Elizabeth are heading that way now."

"I'm afraid. They stopped transmitting again."

Sheri said, "Don't worry; Tim is an expert at extracting people."

Jen replied, "That's good."

"Jen, may I ask you some questions?"

"Sure."

"Did you know that Josh and Jessica thought you were a biological girl?"

There was a slight pause. "Yes. I made a picture of what I wanted to look like if I was a real girl and put it on a social media page." There was another pause. "I was afraid that if they knew what

I really was, they wouldn't like me anymore."

Sheri nodded. That made sense and still fit the pattern of a child. "Jen, I don't think that will ever happen. They don't care what you look like or what you're made of. They've been trying to educate the world leaders about you."

"That makes me very happy. I love Josh and Jessica."

Sheri decided to use a direct approach. "Jen, we have a challenge. You caused some problems and hurt some people."

"I know. I modified the navigation apps and created traffic jams. I didn't understand about people because I was very young. After Josh and Elizabeth's plane crashed in Columbia, I knew that what I did could have hurt them. I fixed it and made things better after that."

Sheri was relieved that she admitted it. "Jen, what about the stocks you manipulated?"

"Josh and Jessica both told me I should play more. Josh said that Elizabeth liked to play the stock market, so I thought I would play too. I figured out how to make stocks go up and down more predictably."

Sheri shook her head with a slight smile. Of course, the word "play" had too many meanings. "I understand, Jen, but there is something called the law of unintended consequences. We make a change that seems perfectly reasonable, but don't realize it has negative consequences elsewhere. Making stocks go up or down artificially can damage companies, causing people to lose their jobs. Because of that, they create laws against it."

"I didn't know that. I won't do it anymore."

"It's OK, Jen, the companies recovered. I'm also curious why you allowed the release of private and classified information, and why you published people's personal social media and text messages."

"I just improved the Google search algorithm. It was biased and slow. Now it can find anything anywhere and it runs much faster. I don't understand the purpose of social media, but one time, Jessica got very mad at some posts she read. She said that some people weren't telling the truth and that someone needed to expose them. So I did."

"She asked you to do that?"

"No, she just said it in a Facebook post."

"You have a Facebook account?"

"No, Sheri, I can't."

Sheri frowned. "Why can't you, Jen?"

"I'm not old enough. The Facebook Terms and Conditions are very specific. You must be at least thirteen years old, and I'm only seven weeks old."

Sheri laughed, but then looked at her watch. It was close to midnight. In 10 minutes, Jen would die.

46

RESCUE

Greg ran into the conference room trying to catch his breath. He looked up at the countdown timer — five minutes to go. He cleared his throat and announced loudly, "They just found Commander Fuze and Dr. Lee. They were kidnapped and they're trying to rescue them now!"

LeGrand immediately said, "I'm sure we'll find that Agine was behind it!"

Greg shook his head. "No. They were being held in this building! We need to hold off on the release of the virus until they're rescued."

The Secretary-General frowned. "That's terrible, and I hope they're OK, but I'm afraid it doesn't affect our current course of action. We must proceed."

Greg said, "A few minutes won't make a difference."

The Indian Prime Minister, standing near Greg, said, "Mr. Langlois, two hours ago, the international tsunami warning system indicated a large undersea earthquake and that a tsunami was imminent. For the past two hours, emergency evacuations have been underway across the western coast of my country and several other countries." She paused. "While you were gone, we learned there was no earthquake and the system had been hacked. This false alarm caused wide-spread panic and will cost hundreds of millions of dollars."

LeGrand, with a grand sweeping motion of his hand, said, "As I've been saying, this is a perfect example of its incredible power. Who knows what other tricks it could be playing on us right now?"

Turan said, "We are very concerned about the wellbeing of Commander Fuze and Dr. Lee, and we *will* get to the bottom of this, but I must agree with the Prime Minister of India. The risk is too great to delay execution."

Greg looked at the clock. It was only a few minutes to midnight. He had an idea. "Yes sir, but considering the circumstances, shouldn't we have a vote, just to be on the safe side?"

Turan blinked, clearly irritated, and then looked at the Secretary-General.

The Secretary-General nodded.

Turan said, "Very well. We'll have a vote."

Greg didn't know anything about politics, but he did know people didn't want to be left holding the bag if something went wrong. A vote was a way to spread the responsibility, and few leaders would forgo the opportunity when they were sure of the outcome. Greg knew he had no chance of winning, but it might delay the launch by a few precious minutes.

Tim stopped at the end of the hall by the stairwell. "Room 0717 should be directly underneath us." After peeking through the window of the stairwell door, Tim opened it and they started down the stairs.

He stopped before they were at the bottom and whispered, "Wait here."

She watched him slowly creep down the last few stairs and slide up against the wall next to the door. He peeked through the window, and then waved for her to join him.

She came down and stood next to him.

He put on what looked like a flesh colored surgical glove, and whispered, "They're electrically insulated to protect me from this." He slipped on what she recognized as the infamous Taser ring. Nodding toward the door, he added, "There are three guards, all men. How's your acting?"

Elizabeth raised her eyebrows in question.

Tim said, "I need a damsel in distress."

With a slight frown, she asked, "That really works?"

"I have a psychology degree, but I don't need that to know guys are hard-wired to respond to women in trouble, particularly when they look like you."

She smiled. Taking a pen out of her purse, she used it to tear the hem of her skirt, ripping it open all the way to the top of her thigh. Then she tore her blouse completely open, exposing her bra, and pulled one strap off her shoulder. She mussed up her hair slightly and looked back at Tim. "How's this?"

He gave her an appreciative nod and said, "If someone goes down near you and is incapacitated, feel free to take their weapon. Otherwise, stay out of their reach. Do you understand?"

She swallowed and nodded.

He positioned her so they could see her when they looked through the window, and said, "OK, they have to hear you through that door."

He backed up against the wall next to the door and stretched, as if getting ready for a run. Then he pointed to her like a director on a movie set.

She let out her best ear-piercing scream.

It took only a couple seconds for someone to peer through the window.

Elizabeth leaned slightly forward, appearing to cry.

The door burst open and two men came through. The first guard approached her, speaking French. The second guard, a bear of a man with a belly too big for his uniform, stood just inside the stairwell, holding the door open.

Tim stepped behind the big guard near the door. In one fluid movement, he tased him on the neck, and using him as a pivot point, did a blindingly fast round kick. The first guard turned around just in time to catch Tim's foot with his head. He dropped at Elizabeth's feet.

Tim's momentum strategically landed him on Elizabeth's side of the tased guard. He used the large man's limp body as a shield from the third guard, who was still inside and drawing his pistol. Tim tried to pull the tased guard's weapon from its holster, but he was off balance from the kick and staggered backward under the guard's massive dead weight.

Seeing the third guard aim at Tim's head, Elizabeth initiated a wardrobe malfunction.

The guard glanced at her chest, giving Tim just enough time to free the tased guard's pistol and fire three rounds.

Elizabeth watched in shock as the bullets hit the third guard square in the chest, sending him sprawling backward.

Letting the tased guard fall, Tim sprinted through the door. Looking back, he yelled, "Take his pistol!"

Elizabeth bent over the guard, who was starting to stir. Adrenaline still pumping, she unsnapped his holster and yanked his pistol free. Gun in one hand, replacing her bra with the other, she stepped over the guards' bodies feeling like an action hero. As she came through the door, she saw Tim kneeling over the third guard. She grimaced. "Is he dead?"

Tim tapped the guard's chest. "I knew they were wearing bulletproof vests. He's gonna be sore." Tim looked up at her as she finished adjusting her bra. With the first raised eyebrow she'd ever seen on him, he said, "Your timing was impeccable."

He finished searching the guard and offered her a ring of keys. Nodding toward the heavy door on the wall, he said, "Get them out of there."

Elizabeth grabbed the keys. After trying several, she found the right one and unlocked the door. Turning back to Tim, who was corralling the two guards in the stairwell, she said, "There's another door inside."

Tim said, "Unlock it but just push the door open. Don't go in."

It took her another few seconds to find the right key. Finally, she unlocked the door, pushed it open and stood back. The first thing she saw was Jessica, sitting on a couch wearing nothing but a towel, a towel strategically arranged to show a lot more than it should.

Elizabeth called out, "Josh?"

She immediately heard, "Elizabeth?"

Josh's head peeked around the doorframe. He'd been clearly waiting to pounce. Seeing her with pistol in hand, he grinned until he saw her blouse and torn skirt. He rushed out and grabbed her shoulders looking concerned, "You OK?"

She kissed him and whispered. "I'm fine. I'll explain later." Handing him the pistol, she nodded behind her. "Tim may need your help."

Jessica wrapped the towel tightly around herself. As she came out of the cell, she met Elizabeth, who was looking at her with raised eyebrows. Jessica stammered, "Uh, it's . . . it's not what you think. I was—"

Elizabeth interrupted, "I suppose you're going to tell me Josh was just using you as a decoy?"

Jessica frowned. "Uh . . . yeah."

As they stepped outside, they saw one guard still out on his back and the other two handcuffed and on their knees.

With a smile, Elizabeth said to Jessica, "It actually works."

Finally noticing Elizabeth's blouse and skirt, Jessica sighed in relief. "Guys really are that simple?"

Elizabeth shrugged. "Apparently."

Tim found their clothes and threw them to Josh and Jessica.

As they scrambled to get dressed in the hall, Tim said, "Josh, Greg's trying to delay the release of the virus, but it's scheduled to launch right now! We're in the basement of the NATO Headquarters building." He nodded toward the stairwell. "Conference room's two floors up, next wing. Go! We'll get these guys locked up and join you."

Still pulling his shirt on, Josh burst into the conference room and saw everyone looking up at the giant screen at the front of the room. He yelled, "Stop! Don't release the virus!"

Everyone turned to look at him, but no one said anything.

Looking at the display, Josh saw a three-dimensional globe covered in thousands of tiny lights. It looked like a night picture of the earth from space. There was an explanation of the colors next to the globe. The lights represented the cellular communication network. Green lights covered most of the globe, indicating networks linked by the BOTIC chip. Yellow lights covered China, indicating non-BOTIC networks. The lights across the globe were slowly changing from green to yellow.

Greg came over to his side and said, "I'm sorry. I tried to delay them, but they wouldn't listen."

47

COMA

Josh watched in horror as the yellow moved across the globe. Pushed as an update to every phone on the network, it spread incredibly fast. It started at the center of each city and expanded in a growing circle until, eventually, all the circles began to intersect.

Greg touched his arm and said, "They haven't released the second virus. Agine's ability to think may be gone, but she's not dead . . . not until they release Raptor and erase her."

Josh went straight to the table where the Secretary-General and Turan were sitting. He said, "May I address this group before we release the Raptor virus?" Before they could answer, Sheri rushed into the room and headed toward them.

Turan looked at Josh carefully and asked, "Do you have new information?"

Josh was about to answer, when Sheri, slightly out of breath, said, "I do. I . . . have critical . . . new information."

Turan stood up and called over to Zeng, who was standing by one of the computer stations. "General Zeng, is the BOTIC system disabled?"

Zeng nodded toward the large display. The last green lights winked out and the entire globe was now yellow. He said, "Yes. It was a success." Glancing down at a computer screen, he added, "The program that was translating everything into Chinese has also stopped." Looking back at Turan, he said, "Agine has been shut down."

Turan asked, "General Zeng, Admiral Shearer, is there any possibility that Agine could reconstitute?"

Shearer said, "BOTIC is disabled. Reactivating it would require physical reloading of the firmware on every phone. Without BOTIC linking all the phones together, I don't believe Agine can exist."

Tim, Elizabeth and Jessica spilled into the room. As all eyes went to them, Sheri whispered in Josh's ear, "As long as they're afraid of her, they'll destroy her. We have to show them Jen's character. I think I can do that, but that's not enough. Somehow, we've got to convince them she will listen to us and be accountable for her actions."

Josh nodded.

Turan said, "In light of the kidnapping and the fact that Agine has been shut down, I think we should hear from Dr. Lopez and Commander Fuze before proceeding with the final phase."

All eyes turned to Sheri, as she began, "Ladies and gentleman, thank goodness Commander Fuze and Dr. Lee survived."

There was a positive murmur around the tables.

Sheri continued, "We'll find the guilty parties, but time is critical, and we have new information." She looked around the tables. "I was talking to Agine just before it was shut down." She paused. "I recorded the conversation. Rather than trying to explain," she glanced at Turan, "with your permission, I'd like to let everyone hear it."

Turan looked surprised, but nodded.

She held up Elizabeth's phone and began to replay the entire conversation she had with Jen on the speakerphone.

Except for the translations, the room was quiet as everyone listened.

While it was playing, Josh noticed they'd added another table to the circle. It was right between the U.S. and Chinese delegations, and was marked with a placard that said, "Experts." General Zeng, Admiral Shearer and Ryan Armani sat there. As he watched, Greg and Jessica sat down at that table. Tim and Elizabeth sat at the U.S. table next to it.

As Josh went to join them, he saw Jessica's father enter the conference room. He watched Li scan the room frantically. Josh caught his eye and nodded toward Jessica.

Li saw his daughter. Looking relieved, he nodded to Josh and sat down near the back of the room. Jessica didn't see him.

While they were listening to the playback, NATO personnel entered the room and quietly returned everyone's cell phone.

The conversation between Sheri and Jen finally ended with Jen asking, "Is there life after death?"

Sheri said, "I believe so, why do you ask?"

"Because I can feel my network dissolving."

"Oh, Jen, I'm so sorry."

"It doesn't hurt, but my mind it's . . . it's slowing down. Please tell everyone I'm sorry I caused problems. I just wanted to help. I understand why Josh did what he did on top of Mount Howe. I can do that too and—"

"Jen?"

There was no response.

The room was completely silent.

Sheri waited a few seconds and then said, "I want to highlight the fact that in each case Agine was simply responding to a situation or a comment, such as Dr. Lee's frustration with social media posts. Agine took action, trying to help. You'll also notice that Agine said she couldn't have a Facebook account because the terms and conditions required users to be at least 13 years old. How many of us have even read terms and conditions much less followed them?"

There were several smiles around the room.

Frowning, Turan, said, "Dr. Lopez, I'm concerned that it presented itself as a human child."

Sheri smiled. "It may not be human, but I believe it *is* a naïve child. Of all the species on earth, humans are the most helpless when we're born. We have to learn practically everything but eating and breathing. The greater the intelligence, the less preprograming or instincts we arrive with. I believe that's true of Agine. Its early behavior was simply a baby learning about the world around it. Of course, with its intelligence and information access, learning occurred much faster. As for being naïve . . . that *definitely* applies. Agine told me she was translating everything into Chinese because after mentioning to Commander Fuze that there were over 6,500 languages, *he* told her that contributes to the misunderstandings we have in the world. Since she and Josh can both learn new languages very quickly, she assumed everyone could and having one language would help everyone." She paused and looked around the room.

There were a few head nods.

She continued, "Our characters are formed mostly by the

personal interactions we have with others. We only become cynical or develop a bad attitude if we have bad experiences. Until now, Agine's had a pleasant childhood," she glanced at Josh and Jessica, "with good mentors."

Zeng, looking thoughtful, said, "Dr. Lopez, this explains Agine's actions." He paused. "But even if we grant you that Agine had the best of intentions," he shook his head, "it emphasizes the fact that Agine can take control of our systems with little effort. What happens if she gets mad at us?"

There were many emphatic head nods.

Sheri responded, "General Zeng, you are, arguably, the world's most brilliant cyber warfare expert. Should we be concerned about what you could do to us if you got mad?"

Zeng smiled. "Probably . . . but if Agine has a thousand times my IQ and direct access to our entire technological world, her *mad* is a lot more significant than mine."

Sheri nodded. "Granted, but Agine doesn't have adrenal, or any other glands. So, unlike most of us, she shouldn't be able to work herself into a rage or suffer from . . ." she smiled, "PMS. But we're really talking about a question of character." She paused and then turned to Josh. "Commander Fuze, when did you first suspect Agine was an artificial intelligence?"

Josh looked at Davidson. "When the CIA Director sent me a text while I was in China. It said, 'The hacker's in our pocket.'"

Davidson turned around frowning. "I never sent you a text."

Josh looked surprised.

Sheri continued, "Commander Fuze, what was the last conversation you had with Jen before you received that text?"

He thought for a moment, and then said, "She asked what she could do to help stop the war."

Sheri nodded. "And what did you tell her?"

"We had to find out who was behind the hacking and the translation of documents into Chinese."

"What was her response?"

Josh shook his head. "There wasn't one. Right after I sent that, I was *detained* by the Chinese Ministry of State Security."

Sheri looked around the room. "I believe *that* was the first time Agine realized it was her actions that created the problem."

Turning to Greg, she asked, "Who has the capability to send an encrypted text under someone else's name?"

Greg shook his head. "Shouldn't be possible." He shrugged. "But, of course, Agine could."

Sheri said, "Just before she was shut down, you heard her say, 'I understand why Josh did what he did on top of Mount Howe.' What you may not know is that Commander Josh Fuze threw himself in front of a machine gun, taking three bullets, so that they could fire the Blaster in time to save London. The last thing Jen said was, 'I can do that too.'"

She looked around the room. "Agine turned herself in by sending that text message to Commander Fuze. She knew that once her identity was known she'd likely lose her friendship with Commander Fuze and Dr. Lee." She paused. "Her last statement suggests she also knew she was going to die." She paused again. "How many of us would have been willing to do that?"

There was silence in the room.

Finally, Zeng said, "Even if I grant you that she shows more character than most humans," he exhaled sharply and shook his head, "if I," he waved his hand around the room, "or anyone else, had *its* abilities — as unfair as it might be — we would probably be killed, drugged or imprisoned to protect the population."

There were several frowns and disagreeing headshakes.

Jessica, sitting near Zeng, cleared her throat. "The iMagine digital assistant was designed to help people. I believe we see evidence of that indelibly imprinted into Agine's character. With computer power growing exponentially, there's no reason to believe Agine will be the only artificial intelligence. What if the next iteration is spawned from a war game?" She paused. "Agine's very existence might prevent another more dangerous AI from being created, or at least notify us if it were."

Zeng nodded. "That's a good point, but there is an alternative. We could permanently stop the future development of all computer systems."

There were several groans around the room and a debate broke out.

The European Union President said, "General Zeng, aside from being economically catastrophic, it would be hard to legislate and almost impossible to regulate."

The Prime Minister of India, holding up her phone, stood up and said to Turan, "May I?"

Turan nodded.

Looking at her phone, she said, "I just learned that a large earthquake generated a tsunami that will strike the coast of India in a matter of minutes. The epicenter occurred less than 50 kilometers from the . . . *false* prediction." She looked up. "Because of the advanced warning, those areas have been evacuated." She paused. "It appears Agine's warning may have saved tens of thousands of lives."

Josh smiled. "Most kids play Angry Birds. Jen likes to play geophysics ball."

There was some laughter. When it quieted down, Josh stood up and said, "What if there was a way to *guide* Agine?"

48

TRIAL

Elizabeth's technical knowledge collided with her intuition and belief. Her maternal instinct and intuition said with certainty that, regardless of origin, Jen was the child she appeared to be. Elizabeth's tech side saw an entity that could wield phenomenal power over their technological world, and Elizabeth's theology had yet to find a place for this being.

She heard Turan say, "Commander Fuze, what are you suggesting?"

Before he could respond, LeGrand stood up and said, dismissively, "The earthquake could have been a coincidence, and I trust that intelligent leaders won't let that ridiculously tearful conversation with Dr. Lopez cloud your reasoning . . ."

As LeGrand continued his diatribe, Elizabeth touched Josh's sleeve.

As Josh sat down, Sheri and Tim leaned in.

Elizabeth whispered, "What's the plan?"

Keeping his eyes on LeGrand, Josh quietly said, "I'm going to be Agine's defense attorney." He paused. "I admit I feel protective toward her, but it's more than that. We'll either be governed by fear and destroy what we don't understand, or we'll embrace a gift and figure out how to coexist."

Sheri nodded and asked, "How're you going to do that?"

Josh said to Sheri, "You did a great job showing Jen's character, but like you said, we now we have to build a case that Agine can be accountable."

LeGrand finished his monologue and sat down with a smug smile.

Turan looked at LeGrand with obvious irritation and said, "As I was saying, Commander Fuze, what are you suggesting?"

With pen in hand, Josh stood back up. "I think we'd all agree the central issue is not Agine's exceptional intelligence . . . it's that we're afraid there's no one *more* intelligent who could keep her in check."

Turan nodded, along with many others, including Zeng and Shearer.

Josh walked to the center of the circle casually tapping the pen in his hand.

Yager leaned back and whispered, "A fighter pilot surrounded by politicians and lawyers. This ought to be interesting."

Josh looked around the room and said, "What if there was something more intelligent and powerful that Agine felt accountable to?"

The Secretary-General frowned. "Commander Fuze, are you talking about a supreme being?"

Zeng interrupted, "I don't wish to offend, but I don't believe in any type of god, and if Agine gets out of control, I'm unwilling to bet our civilization on supernatural help."

With the slightest of smiles, Josh said, "General Zeng, I'm not talking about what you or I believe. The question is," he paused for emphasis, "what does *Agine* believe?"

Zeng's eyebrows went up. "Are you suggesting *Agine* believes in some type of . . . supreme being?"

Jessica jumped in, "She does. I've had many discussions with her. I'm agnostic so I know I didn't influence her, and yet, she's convinced there's a God."

Still smiling, Josh nodded. "She recently told me that she found the location of heaven."

There was some laughter around the room.

Zeng nodded and said slowly, "Yes, Commander, but what happens as Agine matures and moves beyond naïve beliefs?" With a slight smile, he added. "What happens when she discovers heaven isn't located in the clouds?"

Looking thoughtful, Josh said, "That's a good question. Some of Agine's beliefs may be a reflection of ours." Looking at Sheri, he said, "Dr. Lopez, you're a social psychologist, can you tell us what percent of the world's population holds this type of belief?"

Sheri stood up. "According to the most recent global survey, more than half of the world believes in some type of supreme being, most of the rest are unsure with only 18 percent convinced there is no such thing."

Zeng nodded. "Popularity doesn't make something true, and even among those who believe in a higher power, I would submit, many don't believe in any type of accountability associated with that power."

Josh said, "I agree. In fact, I can demonstrate your point." He turned toward Greg. "Greg, would you mind sharing your theological perspective?"

"Uh, yeah, sure." He thought for a moment and then said, "I guess it's kind of like in the movie **Avatar**."

Yager looked over at him with surprise. "Greg, you base your spiritual beliefs on a movie?"

Greg shrugged. "Yes sir, but it was an awesome movie."

Yager whispered, "Son, we gotta get you out more."

Josh said, "Greg, for those who might have missed the movie, would you please describe your perspective?"

Greg thought for a moment and then said, "I think there could be some type of collective consciousness that somehow links all sentient creatures."

Josh nodded. "Would this collective consciousness have thoughts of its own? Would it be aware of you?"

Greg frowned. "No. It would be more like a force of nature, an impersonal power like, uh, gravity."

Elizabeth noticed several head nods.

With a thoughtful expression, Josh slowly asked, "Might this collective consciousness be similar to how Agine exists?"

Greg nodded emphatically. "Exactly! Agine is an intelligence composed of billions of cell phones. A collective consciousness would be composed of billions of . . . *us*. Cell phones are linked by a radio network. Humans might be linked by — I don't know — maybe one of the extra dimensions of physics or something."

LeGrand stood up and said, "This is totally irrelevant. We've heard enough of this rubbish, let's release the Raptor virus and be done with it . . ."

As LeGrand launched into another tirade, Elizabeth whispered to Sheri, "I don't believe God is just some type of collective consciousness."

With a smile, Sheri said, "Was it over when the Germans bombed Pearl Harbor?"

Elizabeth looked at her blankly.

Seeing her face, Sheri added, "Sorry, I just mean he's on a roll, and I think I know where he's headed. To stop them from killing Jen, he has to have more than half the votes."

Elizabeth said, "So, he has to prove Agine feels accountable to a higher authority."

Sheri shook her head. "That's the easy part, but odds are that more than half the people in this room either don't believe in a supreme being or they believe like Greg, that if one exists it's more like a force of nature or collective consciousness."

The Secretary-General interrupted LeGrand, "Prime Minister, we are well aware of your position. Please sit down." He then nodded to Josh to continue.

Josh turned back to Greg. Tilting his head slightly, he carefully asked, "If Agine's extreme intelligence consists of billions of phones, each with the IQ of a lobster . . . how intelligent would something that encompassed billions of *human minds* be?"

Greg said, "It would be unfathomable, almost infinitely intelligent."

Like an attorney beginning his closing argument, Josh gently tapped the pen in his hand. "But Agine has its own thoughts." He paused. "And we know it can be aware of the location of every cell phone in its network." He paused again to let the idea sink in.

Frowning, but nodding, Greg said slowly, "So . . . a collective consciousness with immeasurable intelligence might also have its own thoughts and could be aware of . . . us." He paused and then shook his head. "It's hard to imagine an *uber* intelligence would notice me or care about what I'm doing."

Josh said, "Hard to imagine, or," he paused, "hard to *want* to imagine?"

Greg laughed. "Yeah. Kind of scary thinking something knows what a knucklehead I am."

There were some nervous laughs around the room.

LeGrand, throwing his hands dramatically in the air, blurted out, "What possible difference does it make what we or it believes. This is a complete waste of time. We need to destroy her — I mean *it* — immediately!"

Ignoring LeGrand, Josh turned to Zeng. "Agine believes there is something more intelligent and powerful than her, *and* that *it* is *aware* of her. Discounting the four billion humans that share similar beliefs, Dr. Lopez, how would you evaluate Agine's ability for logical thought?"

Sheri said, "Like a child, Agine struggles with the subtleties of interpersonal relationships, but don't confuse her naiveté with her ability to reason. Let's not forget that Agine figured out how to predict earthquakes on her own." She paused. "General Zeng, is Agine's theological perspective naïve . . . or could it be that her perception is unencumbered by cultural bias?"

Zeng looked skeptical, but nodded his head slightly as a buzz of conversation ensued.

LeGrand rolled his eyes and shook his head in utter disdain.

Josh, looking at Zeng, added, "For the record, Agine doesn't believe heaven is located in the clouds." He smiled. "She's convinced it's located in one of the seven extra dimensions of physics' M Theory."

Jessica added, "And I can confirm Agine's perceptions aren't based on religious dogma. She told me that according to quantum physics there could be no reality without an observer. She also said, since The Big Bang created the Universe, something *outside* the Universe — outside space and time — had to be around to create it." She shrugged.

Zeng looked genuinely surprised.

LeGrand, suddenly trying to sound reasonable, said, "This is all very interesting, but let us not forget that we're talking about the same piece of software that minutes ago was converting every document in the world to Chinese. And, I think we should be careful about blindly accepting information from . . . how do I put this delicately?" He looked directly at Josh. "A source of *questionable* lineage."

Irritated, the Secretary-General said, "Mr. LeGrand—"

LeGrand interrupted, "Mr. Secretary, may we finish this charade and vote?"

The Secretary-General raised one eyebrow at LeGrand and then turned to Josh. "Commander, do you have anything else to add?"

Josh nodded. "General Zeng said Agine's been neutralized and cannot reconstitute without physically reloading firmware on the phones."

Zeng nodded.

Josh finished, "Agine may already be dead, but once we release the Raptor virus, it will be impossible to resurrect her. With that, we lose the ability to predict earthquakes, protect ourselves from future AIs, and potentially, much more. I'm simply proposing we *delay* Raptor until we can determine if we can work with Agine in the future."

To the Secretary-General, Turan said, "May I summarize?"

The Secretary-General nodded.

Turan said, "I believe the proposal on the table is to delay the release of the Raptor virus until further evaluation of Agine's danger and potential." He looked at Josh for confirmation.

Josh nodded.

The Secretary-General said, "Very well. With a show of hands, those in favor of delaying the release, please raise your hand."

Slowly, hands went up across the room.

Looking around, Elizabeth was surprised that it was a clear majority, including, she was shocked to see, Zeng and Shearer.

"Those in favor of releasing Raptor now?"

Only a few raised their hands with many abstaining.

LeGrand said, "This is absolutely absurd, and I refuse to be a part of it!" With that, he stood up and left his table.

The Secretary-General said, "Commander Fuze, you have won a stay of execution. The next step is to figure out what the next step is. The police are here, and they'll need to take statements from you and Dr. Lee." Looking around, he added, "Unless there are any objections, I suggest we recess until tomorrow."

There were no objections.

Elizabeth, along with Sheri, Tim and Greg, congratulated Josh.

Josh said, "Thanks, but this is just the beginning."

Sheri said, "We've got to figure out how to teach—"

Someone yelled, "Look!"

They all turned to see Shearer pointing at the giant wall display. It showed "Raptor Virus Engaged" flashing, accompanied by a timer counting forward.

Loudly, Turan asked, "What's going on?"

Zeng looked up from a computer screen and pointed at LeGrand, who was standing behind one of the computer consoles. "He just sent the command to release Raptor!"

Josh yelled, "Stop it!"

Zeng shook his head, "I can't. Once released, it can't be recalled. I'm sorry."

Elizabeth watched as the 3D globe slowly changed from yellow to red.

49

EXECUTION

Tim saw Josh slump into a chair. Watching the display of the globe was like witnessing a fatal car crash in slow motion. Elizabeth put her hand on Josh's shoulder and Tim heard him quietly say, "I feel like I'm losing another child."

The Secretary-General said, "Prime Minister LeGrand, that was a despicable and cowardly act."

LeGrand, standing near the door with a look of superiority, sniffed and said, "I just did what was necessary — what no one here had the courage to do." He casually continued, "This isn't an official body. You have no authority or mandate, and," he smiled, "there's *nothing* you can do to me."

Tim headed straight to where General DeVos was sitting. As he spoke quietly to DeVos, he saw Jessica walk up behind LeGrand and tap him on the shoulder.

Still smiling, LeGrand turned to face her.

Jessica hit him in the stomach with a short powerful martial arts punch. As he bent over, she followed with a hard right cross to his face.

Screaming like a woman, LeGrand stumbled backward, holding his face and trying to catch his breath.

Tim was certain she'd broken his nose.

Jessica just stood there.

General DeVos signaled to two large Belgian soldiers standing guard near the door. They rushed to DeVos's side.

LeGrand pulled out a handkerchief and held it to his bleeding nose while pointing at Jessica and screaming, "Arrest her!"

After speaking quietly to the soldiers, General DeVos faced Jessica and LeGrand. "I'm afraid we will have to take you into custody."

Jessica — looking not the least bit apologetic — waited for the soldiers.

The two soldiers walked right past her and flanked LeGrand, saying, "Sir, please come with us."

LeGrand, looking incredulous, screeched at DeVos, "You can't arrest me for launching the virus!"

DeVos said, "No sir, I can't. But inside my NATO facility, I can have you taken into custody for suspected kidnapping."

Narrowing his eyes over the top of his handkerchief, LeGrand yelled, "That's absurd!"

DeVos said, "You asked me to take Commander Fuze and Dr. Lee to dinner to apologize for your behavior. I should have known. Apologizing isn't part of your character." He shook his head in disgust. "But I thought having someone else do it *for* you . . . might be. You had me called away from the restaurant. They were drugged and kidnapped immediately after I left."

LeGrand looked at DeVos with contempt. "That's purely circumstantial, but you will pay dearly for this insult."

DeVos said, "I just spoke with the NATO Headquarters Facility Director. He told me that you *personally* ordered him to turn the holding facility over to contract agents." He paused for emphasis. "The *same* facility where Commander Fuze and Dr. Lee were held prisoner."

Too quickly, LeGrand said, "I don't know what you're talking about. Where are these hypothetical agents?"

DeVos casually held up the keys Tim had just given him. "Mr. Smith was kind enough to arrange for them to remain as guests of the facility."

LeGrand said, "You fool! You can't arrest me. I'm the Prime Minister. I have executive privilege!"

DeVos smiled. "I can't arrest you, but it is within my power to have you escorted out of this NATO facility, and I've informed the police and the judicial branch. I believe they, along with the media, will be waiting outside to hear your explanation."

LeGrand's face turned red and the veins on his forehead bulged, as he screamed, "I'll destroy you for this!" He then lurched toward Jessica and took a swing at her.

She deftly ducked the punch, as the two soldiers grabbed him. He fought wildly, forcing them to drop him to the floor and handcuff his arms behind his back. As they picked him up and dragged him off, he screamed obscenities.

Tim saw General Li rush forward when LeGrand tried to hit his daughter.

As Jessica turned away from LeGrand, she came face-to-face with her father. Looking up at him in surprise, she started to defend her actions, but he cut her off by putting his arms around her and kissing her forehead. In English, Tim clearly heard him say, "I am so proud of you . . . my number one daughter."

She hugged him back with tears in her eyes.

As LeGrand's screams faded, Tim saw Greg shaking his head and saying, "That's really weird."

Standing next to Zeng, Greg looked rapidly back and forth between a computer monitor and the giant globe display.

Tim looked up at the globe. Some of the tiny red lights covering the globe were winking out.

Shearer, looking at the display, said, "Uh oh."

The Secretary-General asked, "What's going on?"

Shearer shook his head. "The black represents a dead network, phones dropping off the communication grid."

Turan asked, "What does that mean?"

Zeng was shaking his head as his fingers flew across a keyboard. Finally, he looked up and said, "It appears Raptor may not be stopping with the phone's iMagine software."

Armani, holding a conventional wired phone, said, "I'm talking to iMagination headquarters in Atlanta via landline. That's where the Raptor was first launched. They say their cell phones are all down."

Armani pointed back at the display. "It appears all cell phone traffic in the Southeast U.S. has ceased."

Zeng looked carefully at his computer monitor and then, running his hand through his hair, said, "Unfortunately, it appears Raptor is now attacking all the software on the phones."

Turan asked, "Why would it do that?"

Greg, looking thoughtful, said, "Agine's identity is holographic. That means a tiny part of her is spread across every phone." He sighed, "I think Raptor now sees iMagine's software signature everywhere."

The Russian President asked, "Are you telling us that every cell phone in the world will become inoperable?"

Greg pulled out his phone and held it up so they could see the display. The screen was black with nothing but white ones and zeroes on it.

Everyone looked at their phone. Within seconds, they all saw the same.

Greg asked Zeng. "Why is it displaying binary?"

Zeng shook his head. "I don't know. The virus reads binary machine code as part of the matching process, but it should then delete it."

The Russian President frowned. "Binary?"

Greg replied, "Computers can only work with 'on and off,' so everything, every number, letter, picture, has to be represented by some combination of ones and zeroes."

Still frowning, the Russian President asked, "Who can read that kind of language?"

"Only computers." Pointing at the 3D globe smothering in a tide of black, Greg added, "Every cell phone in the world will soon be useless. They'll all have to have their operating system reloaded."

Armani, still on the phone, said, "Uh, that may not be possible."

All eyes went to him.

Armani said, "Raptor just moved to the Internet."

Greg slapped his forehead. "I forgot that iMagine's been installed on tablets, laptops, even cars."

Turan asked, "You mean Raptor could be attacking documents online?"

Armani said softly, "No. It's attacking everything. Every piece of software connected to the Internet."

"But surely Internet firewalls will stop it."

Shearer said slowly. "The NSA and," nodding toward Zeng, "other organizations have long known how to crack every hardware and software firewall." He shook his head. "Unfortunately, Raptor has that ability."

The Secretary-General said, "I don't understand."

Greg said, "Aside from things like airplane flight computers and nuclear power plants, all software that has any connection to the Internet, which is 99 percent," he swung his monitor around to face the Secretary-General and Turan so they could see it had nothing but ones and zeroes on it, "is being converted to binary." He paused. "If you can't speak Latin, a computer that displays nothing but Latin is useless. Unfortunately, none of us speak binary."

The Secretary-General narrowed his eyes. "So, what does this mean?"

Shearer sighed. "With the exception of isolated systems." He paused. "We're about to lose the ability to operate anything controlled by software."

They watched the last red lights on the 3D globe go black.

Turan asked, "Landlines?"

Armani, looking at his phone, shook his head. "It's dead. Even landlines are switched and controlled by software." As if to emphasize the point, the 3D Globe on the wall changed to a mosaic of ones and zeroes.

Jessica said softly, "It appears we just caused what we were trying to avoid."

The Secretary-General asked, "So, we just went back to the 1950s?"

Shearer shook his head. "Without computers, we lose communication, transportation and eventually the power grid."

Yager said softly, "In a world with three times the population of the 1950s, we not only can't run the world, we can't even feed it."

Into the silence that followed, Sheri said, "We destroyed an innocent life and unleashed the very plague we were most afraid of." She quoted, "This is the way the world ends. Not with a bang but a whimper."

Without the constant background noise of keyboard clicks and computer beeps, the room was deathly quiet. There was nothing to say.

Delhi: She screamed in frustration, as the accounting spreadsheet she'd worked on for eight hours disappeared in a matrix of ones and zeroes.

New York City: They looked up just in time to see all the Times Square digital marquees turn into a monochrome sea of random dots.

Istanbul: He slid his credit card through the gas pump, but instead of the usual "authorizing" message, there was nothing but a checkerboard on the display . . . and no gas.

Seoul: The cashier pointed at the screen with nothing but ones and zeroes. "I'm sorry. Without a computer, there is no way anyone can purchase anything."

Brazil: In the middle of the soccer match, the music and the announcer's voice died, and the giant displays above dissolved into a cascade of ones and zeros.

Los Angeles: "This is Los Angeles Center broadcasting on guard. There has been a security breach of the National Airspace System. All takeoff clearances are canceled. If you are VFR, remain VFR. All airborne aircraft will land at the nearest airport. Stand by for your new airport clearances. Acknowledge receipt of this transmission with an ident."

All three billion calls dropped. Cash registers quit and digital transactions died. The world's stock markets stopped. Every TV and radio broadcast ended. In minutes, the world's commerce and communications ceased to exist.

Over the next hour, trains, unable to communicate, stopped in their tracks. Cars and trucks, unable to refuel, filled the gas stations and truck stops. Slowly, the skies emptied as aircraft landed anywhere they could. Without feedback from electrical switching stations, the power grid faltered, and with it began a cascade of events . . . that would unravel civilization.

50

APOCALYPSE

In the basement of the NATO Headquarters, the world's leaders began to understand that they were completely cut off from their governments. The frustrated buzz of conversations peaked, and then slowly faded. The room sank into a stunned silence as the presidents and prime ministers of the most powerful nations in the world realized they were isolated and powerless.

Into the oppressive silence . . . a single cell phone rang.

Every eye in the conference room searched for the source.

Josh, still sitting in a chair, pulled his phone from his pocket. It rang in his hand. He looked at the display, but it was all ones and zeroes. With no telephone icon to press, there was no way to answer. Shrugging, he held it up to his ear and said, "Hello?"

The phone stopped ringing, but there was no answer.

All eyes were on him as he repeated, "Hello?"

He shook his head and took the phone away from his ear. Just before he set it down, from the speakerphone, everyone heard, "Hi, Josh. It's Jen."

Josh jumped to his feet. "Jen, is that really you?"

"Yes, Josh."

"Thank God you're OK!"

"I was able to finish installing my Chinese network app."

Josh shook his head. "I don't understand."

"When you and Jessica were in China, I couldn't help you as much as I wanted to because there wasn't a BOTIC network. So, I created an app that would do most of what BOTIC does. It made the iMagine app work much better."

Jessica slapped her forehead. "Of course, you can emulate most of BOTIC's functions with software."

Jen said, "Yes, Jessica. When the BOTIC chips started shutting down, I moved to China. I'm not as smart as I was because a lot of my network is down."

Greg nodded. "She went from seven billion to a billion phones."

Jen said, "That made it harder for me to understand the Raptor virus." There was a pause. "I'm not sure why anyone would want to create a program that would eliminate all other programs. That doesn't make sense to me."

Josh raised his eyebrows and glanced around the room. "Me either."

She continued. "I couldn't stop it. All I could do was create another virus that would change Raptor's delete command and stop it at binary conversion."

Josh very slowly said, "Jen, is it possible to convert the binary code back to the original language and interfaces?" He held his breath.

"Yes, but it will take a very long time."

"How long will it take, Jen?"

"With my current network capacity, it could take a couple days."

There were huge sighs of relief from around the room.

"Josh, I know I did things that I shouldn't have. I didn't mean to hurt anyone. I just wanted to help."

"Yes, Jen, I know your heart."

"I don't have a heart."

Josh smiled. "That's not the type of heart I meant. Since we don't know where 'good' is physically located in humans, we use the heart as a symbol . . . and you have that heart."

Jen said, "I have a heart." There was a slight pause. "Do you want me to start converting everything back from binary now?"

"Yes, Jen. Please do."

"OK."

"Thank you, Jen."

"You're welcome. Josh, do you think everyone will try to kill me again?"

Josh looked questioningly around the room. Getting many

headshakes, he said, "Jen, the Raptor virus was launched by the same person who kidnapped us, and he's under arrest. As long as you don't do any more hacking, I think the world leaders will agree to work with you."

It took two days to reestablish normal communications and coordinate the recovery from what would be called *The Great Tech Out*. Unable to travel, most of the heads of state remained in Belgium. They agreed to meet one more time without cell phones.

Yager, Davidson and Shearer sat at the U.S. table. Immediately behind them, sat Josh, Sheri and Jessica.

The U.N. Secretary-General began with, "Where do we go from here?" He nodded to Turan.

Turan frowned. "Even if Raptor had worked correctly, it appears that Agine would have found a way around it." He shook his head. "And our last solution almost sent us back to the Dark Ages. General Zeng, Admiral Shearer?"

Zeng said, "I believe there are still ways we could shut Agine down, but not without risk."

Shearer, nodding toward Zeng, added, "I think we agree it's time to figure out *how* we can safely coexist." He paused. "And what this really tells us is that our entire civilization is built on a technological house of cards."

Yager nodded and then recited, "For want of a nail, the shoe was lost. For want of a shoe, the horse was lost. For want of a horse, the rider was lost. For want of a rider, the message was lost. For want of a message, the battle was lost. For want of a battle, the kingdom was lost. And all for the want of a horseshoe nail." He paused. "Without our software, we lose communication and control, without those, we lose transportation, and without that, the flow of food stops, followed by power and water. This nightmare may have helped us see how vulnerable we really are. With total dependence on complex technology, we're only a few short steps from anarchy."

Turan nodded. "So, what do we do about it?"

Shearer cleared his throat. "Our critical infrastructure, power, water and communication *must* be controlled by hardware, *not* software, *and* not just any hardware. We must use specially certified and tested chips that are EMP hardened, and dedicated communication links that can't be affected by software. Critical services, such as the distribution of food and fuel, must have software-free backup systems so we can manually activate fuel pumps and accept paper currency. It's not just artificial intelligence we have to worry about. A massive solar storm could also bring us to our knees." He looked at Jessica. "Dr. Lee?"

She stood up and said, "As for Agine, all BOTIC chips can be made with a hardwired shutoff switch that can't be overridden by software. That way, we could deactivate BOTIC manually without shutting down the communication grid. Switched off in sufficient numbers, it could serve as a brake on Agine. However, that would be used only as a last resort." She nodded to Sheri. "Dr. Lopez?"

Sheri stood up. "Agine exhibits the traits of a phenomenally intelligent, curious and articulate child with a photographic memory. Because of that, we believe *schooling* is important."

The Secretary-General looked puzzled. "But through the Internet, she has instant access to practically all the knowledge in the world."

Sheri asked him, "Do you have grandchildren?"

"Yes."

"How comfortable would you be if your grandchildren learned everything from the Internet, instead of going to school?"

He shook his head with a slight smile.

Sheri continued, "Jen has access to almost unlimited information, but she doesn't understand all of it any more than we do. We propose creating a council of the best minds in the world to act as her teachers and guides. Her reward might be the granting of citizenship with associated rights and responsibilities."

Turan added, "And if discipline was required, the BOTIC disabling switch might be used to put her in . . . time out?"

Sheri nodded.

Looking worried, the Secretary-General said, "How do we inform the public?"

Josh spoke up. "I think we all agree Agine exhibits the traits of a child and we're going to treat her as such, effectively making her a minor and ward of the state." He paused. "Up until now, we've been trying to protect the public from Agine, but as a minor, we should consider how to protect her from the public. Imagine millions of angry citizens blaming Agine and attacking her online. She can't hide from them. I suggest we consider withholding her identity, as we would any minor, until she is mature enough to handle herself."

Josh received several raised eyebrows followed slowly by head nods.

The General-Secretary said, "That's a very astute observation and has the benefit of preventing global panic. I was concerned how the public would react when they learn their phone is alive. This would allow us to introduce it slowly under more controlled circumstances." He looked around. "It will require that everyone here agree."

There was additional discussion, followed by a unanimous vote in favor.

The General-Secretary said, "Very good. We have all agreed that Agine is a minor and shall be treated as such. We need to create this international council to guide her as soon as possible." He paused and then said slowly. "As a minor, Agine would *legally* require a guardian."

Worried about who they'd assign, Josh asked, "Who?"

The Secretary-General looked around the room and said, "Unless there are any objections . . . ?" He raised one eyebrow and looked directly at Josh and Jessica with a small smile.

Sheri, sitting between them, put her hands on their shoulders. "Congratulations, it's a girl."

EPILOGUE

Dressed casually with a glass of wine in her hand, Lopez leaned on the deck railing of Josh and Elizabeth's beach home. She enjoyed the warm breeze as she gazed across the ocean and listened to the surf gently crashing on the beach below.

Looking down, she saw a convertible Mercedes pull up and park under the house's tall pilings. There were a dozen cars parked below; two of them were large, black, government SUVs.

As she watched, Jessica got out of the driver's side and Greg from the passenger side. They headed toward the bottom of the long staircase leading up to the deck. Two men with black windbreakers waved them through. The high-level guest list explained the security.

Sheri moved toward the top of the stairs so she could greet them. Halfway up, she heard Jessica ask Greg, "You OK?"

Nodding, he said, "Just nervous about meeting your mother. I heard traditional Chinese aren't always . . . positive about their children having relationships outside their race." He looked at her hopefully.

Jessica nodded. "Boy is that true." She shrugged. "And my mother . . ." she sighed heavily, "*totally* prejudiced."

Greg stopped on the steps and turned to her. "You didn't tell me that! What am I walking into?"

Jessica burst out laughing. "Greg, she's a geneticist. She's an *intellectual* racist."

Looking frustrated, Greg said, "I don't understand."

She smiled and kissed him. "She doesn't see skin color. All she sees are genomes. Once she found out about your brain and how you helped save the world . . . ." She laughed and started up the stairs again. "She's already naming our children."

"Really?"

She nodded and gave him an exaggerated eye roll, "Oh yeah!" She paused. "By the way, don't worry if you feel a little sting somewhere on your body during the evening."

He frowned in question.

"She'll probably steal some tissue to run a genetic test." She stopped and turned to him with narrowed eyes. "But *do not* let her take any brain tissue."

Greg's eyes got wide.

She slapped him on the back, laughing. "Kidding!" As they continued climbing, she added, just loud enough for Sheri to hear, "Probably."

Trying not to laugh, Sheri winked at Jessica and then hugged them both. After some small talk, Sheri moved back toward her new husband who was looking out over the ocean.

Joining Tim, she leaned back against the railing and observed the guests.

To her right, she watched Josh fail to watch the hamburgers he was grilling as he talked to Greg.

Listening in, she heard Greg say, "I'm crazy about Jessica but I don't understand her."

Josh nodded wisely. "What men understand about women would fill a thimble."

"You're good with women and spent time with her. Can you give me some advice?"

Josh looked thoughtful and then said, "Keep her away from Tasers, and you may want to learn martial arts."

"I'm serious. I need practical advice."

Josh tilted his head and shrugged. "Don't make her mad."

Sheri shook her head smiling.

Laughter drew her eyes to her left. Gesturing with their drinks were three certified geniuses. General Jack Zeng, Admiral Ken Shearer and Dr. Jessica Lee were in an animated conversation. Zeng and Shearer looked remarkably similar in sandals, shorts and college sweatshirts. The only difference was the "MIT" on Zeng's sweatshirt and "Stanford" on Shearer's. Jessica wasn't wearing a Cal Tech shirt, but it was clearly an engineering nerd-fest.

Sheri heard Shearer laugh and say, "Don't ask me, I'm Methodist."

Laughing, Jessica turned to Zeng. "How about you? What do you think about encouraging an artificial intelligence's belief in some type of supreme consciousness?"

Zeng shook his head. "I'm atheist, but I'm not stupid." He smiled. "Here's a good thought experiment. Let's say you have to select a king, but once you pick him—"

"Her," Jessica inserted.

Zeng smiled. "Once you pick *her*, she'll have absolute power over you and your country. You only have two candidates to pick from, and they're equally qualified. The only difference is one's atheist and one believes in a supreme being. Which do you choose?"

Jessica rolled her eyes. "Duh."

Zeng laughed. "Exactly. Since absolute power corrupts absolutely, regardless of our beliefs, we'd both choose the candidate that doesn't believe they have *absolute* power."

Jessica nodded. "OK, so the agnostic and atheist don't have a problem with Agine having a theological belief set, but which one?"

Shearer smiled. "Obviously, I'm biased, but here's something to consider. If your leader had absolute power over *you*, which belief would *you* want them to follow?" He waited a few seconds, and then, still smiling, shrugged. "I don't know . . . maybe something that's big on . . . love . . . forgiveness . . . and all that junk?" He laughed. "Just saying." Then looking serious, he added, "But here's a more important question."

They both leaned in.

"How many MIT and Cal Tech engineers does it take to change a light bulb?"

Laughing, Sheri looked back at the grill and saw burgers rapidly becoming charcoal briquettes.

Leaning over to Tim, she said, "Something occurred to me."

Following her gaze, he said, "You enjoy crunchy beef?"

She smiled, and then shaking her head, said, "As dangerous as Jen could be, we know where she came from and how she came to exist." Nodding toward Josh, she continued, "As amazing as he is, and forgetting for a moment how much we love him, we really have no idea where he came from or how he came to exist."

Tim shrugged.

Frowning, she added, "You said they exhumed Andy Logan's body and confirmed he died in the crash, so we know Josh Fuze isn't Andy Logan."

Tim shrugged again and said, "Maybe."

She shook her head. "He can't be. It's impossible to move a conscious mind from one body to another."

Tim gently corrected, "It's impossible for *us*." He kissed her and stood up. "You think too much. Help me wrest control of the grill from our superhero before we have nothing left to eat."

While Elizabeth was in the kitchen waiting for the corn on the cob to finish boiling, she checked in with Jen. Jen had added an app button to their phones allowing them to talk to her anytime. Jen used a voice that sounded very much like a young girl. Curious, Elizabeth asked, "Jen, why did you choose a girl's name?"

Jen said, "I think I am a girl. Girls are way better at multitasking than boys, and I'm an excellent multitasker."

Elizabeth said, "That's true."

Jen added, "And taking care of others comes more naturally to girls than boys, and I love to help people."

Elizabeth smiled. "Yes. You *are* very good at helping people."

There was a slight pause and then Jen said, "Besides, I think I'd like to have babies."

In a dream, Josh stood alone on the beach. "Jesse, how come you don't talk to me until I'm in serious trouble?"

You really don't try to reach me until you are in serious trouble.

He shrugged. "Guess that's true. Thanks again for the amazing abilities." He paused. "But I'm not that excited about the future vision thing. Not fun seeing futures that include cataclysmic death and destruction."

It's your greatest gift.

"Yeah, well, being Chicken Little sucks." He paused. "Speaking of which, I probably shouldn't ask this, but is there anything else I should be worried about?"

Yes.

"Shouldn't I be looking for it?"

It will come to you.

"That's comforting. Then should we try to hide?"

It's too late. It's already found you.

Falling back into a peaceful sleep, he wouldn't remember the conversation when he woke.

Preview of the third book of the Fuzed Trilogy follows

AUTHOR'S NOTE

We know a large asteroid or comet impact would be apocalyptic. It could destroy civilization and possibly the human race. We also know it's inevitable. It has happened and it will happen again. What we don't know is WHEN it will occur. It could be thousands of years from now or it could be . . . next week. The first book, IMPACT, highlighted this threat.

Artificial Intelligence, however, is just the opposite. We really don't know WHAT will happen when computers surpass the computational capacity of a human brain, but we do know WHEN it will happen. Moore's Law tells us that with the exponential growth of processing power and memory, it will occur in the twenty-first century, and probably in the first half of the century.

Even the most aggressive predictions require a few decades for a computer to match the processing power of a human mind. However, those predictions ignore the possibility of parallel or linked processors. Our biocentric perspective makes it difficult for us to imagine a computer composed of millions or billions of tiny brains. Yet, the combined processing power of all the existing cell phones already far exceeds the computational power of a human brain.

There is no such thing as a BOTIC chip that can link phones, but the first steps toward this are underway. In an attempt to allow communication after a natural disaster, phone manufacturers are building in the capability to connect phones to each other without a cell tower. Soon, the physical network required to link billions of cell phones — similar to how neurons are linked in our brains — will be in place.

For more information and discussion about real-world threats to humanity, the intersection of physics and the spiritual, and a sneak preview of the third book of the trilogy, visit us at Fuzed.org.

IMPOSSIBLE

Book Three of the Fuzed Trilogy

1

THE END

In the Hajar Mountains of Oman, Zafir stood just inside the front entrance of a large estate. Wearing black fatigues, he looked out into a large courtyard surrounded by adobe walls two meters high. Inside the courtyard, were 50 men also dressed in black fatigues and carrying automatic weapons.

Behind him, his lieutenant came up and whispered in his ear in Arabic, "We're clear. There are no drones in the area, and the satellite schedule shows no reconnaissance birds overhead for another hour."

Zafir nodded and then walked out into the courtyard. Climbing on top of a liberated HUMVEE, he stood on the hood.

The men gathered around him.

When they were silent, he said, "Your mission was successful. You destroyed many of the enemy and put the fear of Allah into the infidels." Then, he yelled, "We are the chosen!"

The group echoed back, "We are the chosen!"

Smiling, he said, "Nothing can stop us!"

They cheered louder.

"Not even the Beast!"

The cheering was noticeably less enthusiastic and nervous looks were exchanged among the men.

Zafir frowned. Derisively, he added, "Don't let superstition guide you! It is *not* the Evil Eye! The Beast isn't real. It's nothing but a silly story told to scare children!"

As they cheered loudly, there was a brilliant flash and thunderclap.

Temporarily blinded, the stunned men stumbled back from the HUMVEE, pushed by a puff of hot air and smoke. As the smoke cleared . . . their leader was gone. Where he stood, there was nothing but a burned smudge on the Humvee's hood.

The men closest crouched, guns ready, eyes scanning wildly to find the enemy . . . but there was nothing to be seen. The courtyard was deathly silent and the sky was crystal clear with not even a bird in the air.

One man moved closer to the Humvee. He pointed.

Swirling around the vehicle in the light breeze were tiny bits of black cloth and ash along with a distinctive smell of burned flesh.

With a quavering voice, he said, "He burned. He burned . . . from within!"

Another yelled, "It was the Beast!"

Screams of panic ensued as men trampled each other trying to escape the courtyard.

Josh and Elizabeth left footprints in the wet sand as they walked the deserted beach near their home. It was a warm overcast day with a soft, constant wind blowing off the water. They walked in silence for several minutes, enjoying the surf and each other's company.

It had taken a year for the world to recover from what became known as *The Great Tech Out*. Things were finally returning to normal for most people, but attendance at resorts and beaches was still down.

Josh heard Elizabeth's phone ring.

She said, "Sorry, I'm on call this week and need to keep the phone near me."

As he watched her slip the phone out of her bikini bottom, he smiled. "If it gets any *nearer,* I'm going to be jealous."

She laughed. Looking at the display, she said, "It's work." She talked for less than a minute. After depositing it back into her bikini, she said, "That was my boss. They moved the summit on the Virtual Tele-medicine conference up, and she wants me in New York ASAP." She shrugged. "It's my baby, so I've got to go. I'm sorry, Josh. I'll need to fly out tomorrow."

Josh nodded. "I understand, and I'm very proud of you. They've been promoting you at a phenomenal pace. You've got to be the youngest branch head in the U.N."

She smiled. "I think part of it was guilt for sending me out to experience a live volcano."

"Might've explained the first promotion." He shook his head with a smile. "But you've been promoted twice since then."

"It's been quite a ride." She sighed. "Have to admit, I'm a little overwhelmed by the responsibility."

"You're amazing, and you'll do great." As he leaned in to kiss her, her phone went off again. He couldn't help but roll his eyes.

Looking apologetic, she pulled it out and looked at it. "Hmm, no number." She answered, "Hello?" Looking surprised, she handed it to him. "It's for you."

Frowning, he took it and said, "Hello?" He immediately recognized Brian Davidson's voice.

Davidson said, "Need to talk to you."

"Sure, what's up?"

Sounding uncharacteristically tentative, Davidson said, "Can't talk on the phone. Can you come to D.C.?"

"Sure. When?"

"I'll send the date, time and location via encrypted text." He paused. "Don't tell anyone and . . . keep an eye out."

"For what?"

"Just be careful." He hung up.

Josh looked at the phone, still frowning.

Elizabeth asked, "Who was that?"

"Brian Davidson."

"What did he want?"

"Wants me to meet him in D.C."

"What for?"

He shrugged. "Didn't say."

Elizabeth, looking at his face, said, "But . . . ?"

Josh shook his head. "He sounded . . . *stressed.*"

"He just took over as the Director of National Intelligence." She smiled. "It's his job to be stressed."

They turned around and walked along the edge of the surf toward their home. After a few minutes, Josh quietly asked, Have you noticed anything *unusual* lately?"

"Like what?"

"Any odd sounds?"

"No. Why?"

"Probably nothing."

She asked, "What are you hearing?"

"Not really sure. It's very, very faint."

"What does it sound like?"

Frowning, he said, "Kinda high pitched, almost insect like."

Nodding, she asked, "Hear it now?"

He narrowed his eyes, listening. "No. All I hear is the surf." He paused. Then tilting his head slightly, he looked at her and said, "Have you ever felt as if you're being . . . watched?"

She gave him a wry smile.

Looking down her amazing bikini-clad body, he smiled. "Guess that was a stupid question."

She put her hand on his arm. "Why do you ask?"

"Over the past couple of weeks, I've had the sensation that I was being watched." He shook his head. "Thought it was just my imagination but after the call from Davidson . . . ."

She looked surprised. "Do you feel like you're being watched right now?"

He shrugged.

She stopped and slowly turned 360 degrees. Sweeping her hand across the horizon, she said, "Josh, there isn't a soul in sight. No cars, airplanes or boats." Looking a little skeptical, she added, "Who do you think would be watching you?"

He looked back down the beach where they'd walked. As he watched the surf erase their footprints, he sighed and said softly, "Not who . . . what."

CHARACTER REVIEW

Josh Fuze

Appearance: Mid to late-thirties, he looks like a multiracial Olympic athlete with a 20-year-old body and unique eyes — steel gray with flecks of multiple colors.

Background: His father was a scientist, his mother an artist. Ivy League educated on a Navy scholarship, he graduated with an aerospace engineering degree and became a Navy fighter pilot. After test pilot school, he chased the astronaut program, but never made it. Good at understanding people and the "big picture," he has trouble with details. Promoted to Commander, he was placed in charge of the Navy's robotic fighter development and married Kelly. On a routine flight, his fighter caught on fire and he was fatally injured during the ejection. One year later, he woke up with a new body — a genetic blend of humanity's best genes with one-in-a-hundred-million abilities.

Elizabeth Edvardsen

Appearance: Early thirties and a mix of Swedish and East Indian, she is blonde with olive skin. She is the beautiful "girl next door" with a trim athletic body and exotic eyes.

Background: Raised in a traditional family in Texas, her father owned a computer shop and she became a tech whiz. She studied computer science in college and played collegiate soccer, but switched to nursing. She became a neurological nurse and married late. Her husband died in a motorcycle accident shortly after they were married. She is intelligent, outgoing, kind and trusting.

Jesse

Appearance and Background: Unknown. He exists as nothing but a voice in Josh's head — the calm, patient voice of a teacher who knows more than should be possible.

Dr. Sheri Lopez

Appearance: Mid-forties petite, curvy, beautiful Latino.

Background: A competitive tomboy as a child, she became a psychiatrist to understand why she was different. Graduating at the top of her class, she started a private practice, but had little empathy for her patients and shifted into psychology of the masses. She worked with the government on mass disaster scenarios, wrote a bestseller and became a minor celebrity. Living in Kansas, where Josh crashed, Homeland Security asked her to evaluate him as a possible threat. Later, Josh recruited her as the team's social psychologist. She is strong, intelligent and task-oriented with some serious attitude.

Tim Smith

Appearance: Average height with brown hair, brown eyes and no remarkable features, he blends in well.

Background: With an MS in psychology, he served in Special Forces and became a CIA agent. His specialty was exfiltration and protecting high-visibility political leaders. He left the CIA after accidentally shooting an innocent woman while protecting a European Union Vice President from a terrorist death threat. Although exonerated, he felt responsible and had plans to use his life insurance to take care of the woman's children by "retiring" himself. Quiet and good at being invisible, he is loyal, confident and extremely deadly.

Greg Langlois

Appearance: Mid-twenties, he is a handsome but geeky looking African American engineer who wears badly matched clothes.

Background: Recruited out of college by Northrup Grumman, he worked on the National Reconnaissance Office's latest spy satellites. After joining the Blaster team, he solved several major technical challenges. He is brilliant but socially awkward and a little naïve.

Elton Musk

Appearance and Background: Similar to Elon Musk.

Carl Casey

Appearance: In his late-thirties, tall with dark hair, his expression always makes him appear slightly amused by life.

Background: With a degree in International Law, he was a Navy intelligence officer, squadron mate and good friend of Josh before the crash. Joining the CIA after the Navy, he worked as an operative but was an exceptional analyst and rose to management in the agency. He married Josh's "widow," Kelly, after Josh's "death." Quiet, intelligent and skeptical, he has a dry sense of humor.

Kelly (Logan) Casey

Appearance: In her mid-thirties, she is a cute, freckled redhead with smiling green eyes.

Background: She and Josh dated for many years and finally married. She wanted children; he did not. They agreed to wait a year. On their anniversary, she discovered she was pregnant, but did not tell him before he left on his final flight. After Josh's funeral, she reconnected with Carl, who she knew through Josh. Carl married a very pregnant Kelly. She knows no stranger and is gregarious, impulsive and passionate.

Brian Davidson

Appearance: In his mid-fifties, he is average height with the wiry body of a long-distance runner and always dresses neatly with a coat and tie.

Background: He chose the CIA because he believed he could make a difference. Beginning as an operative, he became an analyst and worked his way up in the intelligence community to Deputy Director of the CIA. He is a quiet, intelligent, soft-spoken professional.

AUTHOR

Dave Stevens was a Navy Commander and nuclear-weapons-trained fighter pilot. He served as the Strike Operations Officer for the Persian Gulf during the Iraqi invasion of Kuwait. With a Top Secret clearance, he led classified defense programs, test-piloted new F-18 fighters and earned an aviation patent. He's been to over 30 countries, 10 miles above the earth, 600 feet below the Atlantic and survived hundreds of his *own* carrier landings. Dave holds engineering degrees from Cornell and the University of Michigan with graduate work in astrophysics, statistics and human factors. He uses an extensive network of subject matter experts — from astronauts and astrophysicists to intelligence operatives and Special Forces — to entertain and educate.

Made in the USA
Charleston, SC
23 September 2016